Delicate
ESCAPE

USA TODAY BESTSELLING AUTHOR
CATHERINE
COWLES

This is a work of fiction. Names, characters, places, and incidents are either the products of the author's imagination or are used fictitiously. Any resemblance to actual persons, living or dead, businesses, companies, events, or locales is entirely coincidental.

Editor: Margo Lipschultz
Copy Editor: Chelle Olson
Proofreading: Julie Deaton and Jaime Ryter
Paperback Formatting: Stacey Blake, Champagne Book Designs
Cover Design: Hang Le
Couple Cover Photography: Wander Aguiar

This one is for me.
And for anyone who has been made to feel less than.
Silence that noise.
You are beautiful and wonderful just as you are.

Delicate
ESCAPE

Prologue

HOW MANY WAYS COULD YOU KILL SOMEONE IN YOUR MIND? Nikki and I had gotten creative over the past few months, coming up with some real gems.

"Buried alive with fire ants," I said, burrowing deeper into the overstuffed couch in her tiny apartment.

She scoffed from her spot, sprawled on the floor, wineglass precariously balanced in her hand. "Not nearly bad enough. I'm going with...eaten by piranhas, starting with his dick."

I snorted, taking a sip of my drink. "Maybe he could just choke on his lies," I muttered.

Nikki sat up in one swift move, her red hair flying around her face and wine sloshing out of the glass. At least it was white and not red. Even though she was tipsy, her eyes narrowed on me in a now familiar way. One that managed to be both fierce and gentle. She was the kind of best friend who had your back—one of the few who hadn't been swayed by Brendan's bullshit.

"You need to tell someone. Someone who can actually do

something to his ass. Or I'm going to run him over with my car," Nikki grumbled, setting her wineglass on the coffee table.

I squeezed my knees to my chest, trying to take comfort in the pressure as if I could hug myself out of my current situation. "And say what? I'm getting heavy-breathing phone calls from an unknown number?"

"Sel, he got you freaking fired. From a job you worked your ass off for."

I had. Undergrad in business. Masters in nonprofit business management. Countless hours of unpaid internships and volunteer work. All to land a job at my dream organization: The Literacy Project. But all that had gone down the tubes this morning when I found out I'd been fired.

"There's no proof," I said softly. But an ache took root in my chest. I knew Nikki was right, even though there wasn't a shred of evidence. Brendan's fingers stretched far, and his grip could be strangulating.

Nikki let out a huff of air. "You know it's him. Tossing money around and pulling strings."

I worried the corner of my lip as pressure built around me—as if I were being suffocated by the air itself. It was starting to feel like Brendan was *everywhere*. I'd thought breaking up with him would be the end of it. That I'd be free. But it had only been the beginning.

"This has to be it," I said, finally meeting her eyes. "He won. And I think that's what he's wanted all along. Maybe I can finally move on."

I just wasn't sure where that would be. Los Angeles didn't feel like home anymore. For so long, I'd loved living here. The live music scene, museums, and amazing restaurants with every type of cuisine imaginable. I'd always felt like I could melt into the sea of people and get lost in their diverse uniqueness. Now, it felt like every single pair of eyes could be watching.

"Maybe," Nikki mumbled.

I leaned over the coffee table and squeezed her hand. "Thank you for being the bestest friend a girl could have."

She just scowled at me. "I want to junk-punch him before I throw him to the piranhas."

I choked on a laugh. "Have at it."

But the laugh quickly died away. I'd only told Nikki bits and pieces of the bad stuff. If she knew it all, she really *would* be gassing up her car for a hit-and-run. But knowing that just made me love her more.

I stood, picking up my wineglass and emptying its contents. "I need to get home. It's almost time for Moose's dinner."

Nikki shook her head. "Better keep that beast fed. If you don't, he's liable to take off a toe in your sleep."

That had a genuine smile stretching my face as I carried my glass to her sink. "He'd never."

Nikki grunted as she struggled to her feet. "Keep telling yourself that. You ordered a car, right?"

I shook my head. "I switched to Fresca after my first glass."

Her mouth fell open. "You bitch. I've been getting sloshed, and you're sipping freaking Fresca?"

I chuckled as I pulled Nikki into a hug. "Sorry, babycakes."

The truth was, I never had more than a single glass of wine these days. My anxiety had already reached the red zone, and I needed all my faculties.

Nikki hugged me tighter. "Want me to come with you? I can sleep on your couch tonight."

God, she was an amazing friend. "I'll be fine. I'll probably stay up late looking at what other nonprofits might be hiring."

Nikki held on, not letting go. "You're an amazing person. Don't let his bullshit make you think anything else."

My eyes burned, tears struggling to break free. I did everything I could to beat them back. Because there were times that I'd started to wonder if I was, in fact, the person Brendan said I was. That I was manipulative, cruel, sick, and a slut.

Two years ago, I would've laughed if someone had said I'd think those things about myself. It was shocking how fast things could change. How quickly a mind could be twisted. And how long it took to undo that kind of damage.

"Love you, Niks," I whispered.

"Love you, too," she said, finally releasing me. "Text me when you get home, or call if you want someone to talk to while you're getting inside."

The burn was back, tears fighting to fall. She'd been the recipient of more than one phone call when I freaked myself out thinking I was being followed, only to realize it was an innocent bystander going about their business. She never complained.

"Thanks," I said, quickly kissing her cheek and grabbing my purse.

I headed out of her small apartment on the outskirts of Silverlake and down the sidewalk toward my car. It was still plenty bright out, but my head was on a swivel, taking stock of everyone around me. There was the typical hipster fare, a couple making out near a café, a family with two young kids running circles around the parents... Nothing out of the ordinary.

I still felt twitchy. I walked faster, moving toward my Subaru hatchback that had seen better days. She'd seen plenty of action before I bought her in college and had officially passed her prime now. But since I was out of a job, an upgrade wouldn't be happening anytime soon.

Beeping the locks, I slipped into the vehicle and winced at the tote bag full of produce on the floorboard. I hadn't planned to stay at Nikki's for as long as I had. Hopefully, the bag of farmers market finds would be all right.

Shutting the door behind me, I locked it and let out a breath. My eyes caught on my reflection in the rearview mirror. My blond hair was in disarray, and my pale green eyes had dark circles under them. But I didn't look away, not even when my eyes filled.

"You're a good person," I whispered. "You're not who he says you are."

My phone dinged, and I fished around in my purse for the

device. As I pulled it out, it chimed again, the screen lighting up. My stomach hollowed out as a text flashed on the display.

Unknown Number: *Seen this?;-)*

The text had a screenshot of an article. *Actor Brendan Boseman Donates One Million to The Literacy Project*. My hands trembled as I scanned the short piece.

Mr. Boseman, best known for his roles in box-office-gold rom-coms and superhero megahits, was captured touring the nonprofit's West Adams location here in Los Angeles. "Reading is something I've always been passionate about. And being a part of The Literacy Project's mission to give people the tools they need to succeed is an honor."

More unshed tears burned the backs of my eyes, a mixture of anger, fear, and frustration at the blatant bullshit that streamed out of his mouth. Brendan's idea of *reading* was scanning *The Hollywood Reporter* and cursing anyone who got a job *he* wanted. I couldn't read any more. It was too much.

I'd given everything to The Literacy Project: ridiculously long hours at low pay, courting countless benefactors to keep us in the black, and jumping in on tasks that had never been in my job description. And all because I believed in their mission. *And* because I loved being a part of something that changed lives. Now, it was all done. Gone.

A tear slipped down my cheek and fell onto my jeans, making the indigo strands darken as it sank in. Maybe this was what I needed—the final straw to make me leave LA and start fresh. A chance to truly be free.

It wasn't like I had anything left here other than Nikki. Everything had been slowly and deliberately stripped away. I swallowed the anger that surged, grabbing my key from the seat and sliding it into the ignition. Twisting it, I had to try three times before the engine caught.

Just one more thing I couldn't afford to fix. But I ignored it and headed for home. Even at four in the afternoon, rush hour had already begun, turning my ten-minute drive into twenty. As I pulled up in front of the rundown fourplex, the hairs on the back of my neck rose.

I glanced around the residential street, doing my now standard scan. Nothing out of the ordinary: a couple walking their fluff ball of a mutt, a young woman pushing a stroller, a couple of teens shouting as they raced their souped-up bikes down the street.

But I felt eyes on me. Familiar anxiety took root, and quick on its heels, frustration. Because I didn't know if the feeling was warranted or if I was losing it. I grabbed my phone and quickly typed out a text.

> **Me:** *Home. Going to feed Moose and make dinner. Make sure you eat something so you don't wake up with a hangover from hell.*

> **Nikki:** *Already ordered pad thai and pad see ew. Going to sop up all that alcohol.*

My mouth tried to curve as I shut off the engine, but it couldn't quite get there. I grabbed my purse and the tote bag with my farmers market goodies, then climbed out of my hatchback. As I slid my phone into my pocket, I did another quick scan before heading up the walk.

My gaze jumped at every flicker of movement around me as I moved, bracing. But I just kept going. It was the only answer. If I let myself fall, I knew I'd never get up.

My feet hurried across the cracked pavement and up the chipped concrete steps. Punching in the code to the building, I waited for the buzz and stepped inside. I quickly shut the door behind me, making sure it latched, then moved to the door marked 1B.

I unlocked the deadbolt, then the doorknob. When the door swung open, a beep sounded. A deep meow greeted me as I plugged in the alarm code.

"Hi, Moose," I said to the dark room—dark because every curtain in the place was pulled.

When I landed the tiny apartment, I'd loved it for its

windows—all that natural light. Now, all I had was the artificial kind.

I flicked on the switch as Moose wound through my legs. As soon as I threw the deadbolt, I bent to pick him up, grunting as I lifted all eighteen pounds of his Maine Coon self. He instantly began to purr, butting his head against my chin.

I cuddled him close, letting the sound and feel of his gray fur soothe me. "What do you think? Time to leave LA? Maybe we could land somewhere with a yard. I could teach you to walk on a leash."

Moose let out a warbled meow as if to say: *What the hell, lady?*

I chuckled. "Okay, pause on the leash training. How about some dinner?"

Another meow.

I grinned as I set him down, keeping the tote bag over my shoulder. My hands trembled as I moved through the space, flicking on light after light. That slight shake told the truth. Brendan really had won.

My life here was done. The only option I had was to leave— and pray he didn't feel vindictive enough to mess with my life wherever I landed.

I felt for the kitchen light and flicked it on. The counter was in complete disarray. Fruit from the bowl had spilled out, and I noticed an orange with what looked like teeth and claw marks in it. I gave Moose the side-eye. "Playing soccer again?"

He licked his paw and scrubbed it over his face.

Then, I saw the true goal of his mischief. The treat feeder with its camera had been knocked over, looking like it had been bashed around. I righted it and put the unharmed fruit back into the bowl.

"Seriously? The vet says you're already overweight."

I swore Moose glared at me. Then he let out a bellowing meow.

"Don't give me that kind of back talk or no treats after dinner." He hissed.

I had to bite my lip to keep from laughing. At least I had

Moose. No matter how bad things got, he always managed to make me laugh.

Setting my tote bag on the counter, I set to work putting away my produce, trying to dodge the swipes of Moose's paws along the way. As I tidied, I began concocting a recipe in my mind. One of my favorite challenges was coming up with something based on whatever had looked best at the farmers market.

I'd have to get more creative with my lack of salary now, but that would just make the game more challenging. We were finally in peach season, so I grabbed two. I'd also snagged some of the first mini heirloom tomatoes of the season. That, with some burrata, herbs, and balsamic, would be perfect with the crusty bread I'd bought from the local baker's stall.

My stomach rumbled as if agreeing with my plan. As I began pulling out ingredients, my phone started buzzing in my pocket. A cacophony of dings followed—every kind of alert my phone could give. Text. Email. Phone call. All at once.

My alarm system let out a warning beep—the kind that said if I didn't input the code in two minutes, it would go haywire. Then the stereo burst to life, blaring some rock song, the television following suit at a deafening level.

Moose let out an annoyed yowl. I hurried toward the alarm pad, plugging in the code as I pulled out my phone, still buzzing angrily in my pocket. The screen was filled with a laundry list of notifications, but they moved too fast for me to focus on any of them. And the dings just kept sounding.

I silenced the phone and tapped on my email. The inbox read: one thousand six hundred and fifty-three. My heart rate picked up speed. I'd had *six* unread messages this morning. That was it.

I tried to scan the subject lines, but they moved too fast as more poured in. I could only grasp a few. Warnings about my credit being compromised. Ads for penis enhancement and weight loss. And porn. So much porn. The kind that turned your stomach.

Exiting out of my inbox, I clicked on my texts. Message after message. Too many to count. There was one chain from my bank.

Did you approve this charge? $1,309.13 to Sex Toys, Inc.

Did you approve this charge? $10,237.53 to Hollywood Escorts.

Charge after charge. Each one worse than the one before. Then my blood ran cold.

Unknown Number: *This you?*

There was no link to follow. It was simply a screenshot. From a porn site. Of me.

My entire body vibrated as my ears rang. Some part of my brain computed that my alarm system was doing that warning beep thing again, but I couldn't move. All I could do was stare down at the photo.

It was me. There was no denying that. The brightly colored comforter on the bed was a dead giveaway. I was standing in the middle of my room, my top off as I reached for the button on my jeans, blond hair cascading down my bare back.

Changing. I'd been changing. The photo was a screenshot of a video. A five-minute video. Which meant this kept going.

My breaths came quicker, hiccuped half sobs tripping over each other. Another screenshot. Me. My face fully toward the camera, green eyes utterly unaware as I stripped down. Naked. Every part of me on display. On the internet.

This wasn't happening.

The alerts just kept pinging on my phone. Emails, texts, phone calls. Fraud alerts. Low balance warnings. Links to my new porn listings. All as the stereo and television blared in the background.

The tears came fast and hard, like acid tracking down my cheeks. And then a voice rang out. One I knew.

"Remember who's in charge, Selly."

My blood turned to ice as I searched for something—anything—to defend myself with. My hand landed on a stone bookend in the shape of a flower. I gripped it as I moved toward the voice.

Each step ratcheted up my heart rate, but as I moved into the kitchen, there was no one.

Then a chuckle sounded, deep and raspy, as the light on

Moose's camera and treat dispenser turned from blue to red—the color that meant it was engaged.

"You wanted to be a whore, Selly. I just made your dream a reality."

Brendan.

I moved as fast as possible, ripping the cord out of the electrical socket and smashing the camera against the wall. But it was too late. I knew it.

Because those shots from my bedroom meant there were other cameras. They could be everywhere. He could be watching me even now.

I needed to run, to get out, but I couldn't get my feet to move.

The corners of my vision darkened, and my fingers prickled. And then the darkness took me under.

Chapter One

THE FIRST TENDRILS OF SUNLIGHT STREAMED THROUGH MY kitchen window as a series of almost barking meows sounded below me.

I sent Moose a warning look. "I'm going as fast as I can."

It wasn't good enough. He leapt onto the counter—a feat, considering he now bordered on twenty pounds of beefy glory. He hauled off and smacked my arm with a paw the moment he reached me.

My eyes narrowed on him. "Seriously?"

He simply licked his paw and began washing his face.

"Don't think I believe that innocent act for one second," I huffed, mixing his wet food with some dry. When I was done, I carried the plate into his corner of the living room, where I had a place mat and a cat tree. His bell jingled as he hurried to follow.

I bent and lowered the bowl. Moose was on it in a flash, batting my hand out of the way like the vicious little monster he was—but an adorable monster.

As I straightened, my gaze caught on the pen I'd set up for the foster kittens I'd be getting in the next couple of days. The babies had a litter box, heated blankets, and a little house to retreat into. It was the perfect little nook. Something about creating it had soothed me. Making a home for them where they were safe, warm, and happy. It gave me hope.

Even though my world had been torn apart, I could put theirs back together.

Glancing at Moose, I surveyed the bowl. Already almost halfway gone. A true fiend for food. I turned and headed down the hallway, the floorboards creaking beneath my feet.

The old cabin in the Central Oregon mountains had lain vacant for years. As he aged, the previous owner had sold off his land piece by piece. When he finally passed, the house and remaining land had reverted to the state. The house had been so dilapidated that no one wanted it—no one but me.

I'd gotten it for a steal, even if the hot water only lasted four minutes, and the living room floor sloped to the right. The best part about it was that the land was state wilderness or fields used for grazing and stretched as far as I could see. The only visitors I had these days were cows and horses. Just the way I liked it.

The small log cabin was nestled in the forest, but enough of the tall pines around the house had been cleared to let in plenty of light—sunshine that allowed a garden and greenhouse to flourish. But the trees still offered enough protection to make me feel somewhat…safe.

Everything about the home was perfect, and it was only thanks to Nikki that it was even possible. She'd helped me set up a trust to purchase the property. Each month, I mailed her cash hidden in the bottom of a tin of bakery treats, which she then used to pay the small mortgage for me. No trail led back to me—nothing Brendan could trace.

Because I'd all but disappeared.

No email address. No phone number. No cable or computer. No tech of any kind. I'd closed every account and deleted every piece of my digital footprint I had control over.

But there were some I didn't. Photos and videos of me at my most vulnerable still floated around the internet, and there was nothing I could do about it.

My throat wound tight on instinct as I swallowed down the burn. There was nothing I could do. I'd tried. It would've likely taken thousands of dollars I didn't have for the lawyer fees, and I still wouldn't have gotten it all. Because bastards in the dark parts of the internet lived to hold those kinds of things hostage.

Instead, I let Selena die. She simply faded away into nothing, each piece of her erased like writing in the sand at high tide. Now, I was Thea. My blond hair had been transformed into a deep brown, and my pale green eyes were now the shade of mud thanks to contacts. No one would recognize me if they'd seen those cruel photos or the handful of shots the paparazzi had snapped of me and Brendan when we were together.

I pulled a brush through my brown locks, checking the roots. I'd need a touch-up this weekend. But I had what seemed like a lifetime of dye in the hallway linen closet. I splashed water on my face and then slathered it in lotion and sunscreen. After my shift at the bakery, I'd head to my gig at the nursery, and the sun could fry you in an hour if you weren't careful.

Checking my watch, I hurried to dress in jeans and a tee, making sure there were no new holes I'd missed. I slipped on my boots and headed back toward Moose. "You going to behave today?"

The cat meowed from his perch on the tower in front of the window.

"Who am I kidding? You're always up to no good." I made quick work of checking the locks on every window, then gave Moose one last scratch.

He did that chattering thing again as I headed for the front door, wanting me to stay put. But he'd be fine. He had cat TV—the massive picture window pointed toward the garden and the forest beyond it.

One day, I'd give him a better view. A giant picture window overlooking Castle Rock or the mountain range to the east. Maybe both.

It was the thing that had stopped me on my road trip escape

from LA to Oregon. The breathtaking beauty could freeze you to the spot—the golden statues of Castle Rock and the purplish snow-capped Monarch Mountains. Something about the vastness of it all had made my problems seem small. And the way the small town of Sparrow Falls was nestled into that vastness made me feel safe for the first time since I'd met Brendan Boseman.

I let out a breath as I stepped outside. Even though we were deep into June, the mornings were chilly in the mountains. But the hummingbirds were already out. A smile tugged at my lips as I watched while two deftly navigated the garden to the feeders I'd placed throughout. Something about the creatures and how they hovered and darted touched me. While delicate, they were warriors in their own right. Escaping enemies left and right.

I forced my gaze away, pulling my sweatshirt over my head and turning to lock the door. Some might consider the deadbolt extreme. It didn't look like a normal lock on a home, and it had taken me months to save up the sixteen-hundred-dollar price tag. But when someone lived through what I had, you did whatever it took to keep intruders from your home. A dozen of these deadbolts wouldn't be enough.

I knew it was a coping mechanism. Some tiny measure of control when so much of that very thing had been stripped from me. But it helped. The sound of the lock clicking. My keys tucked into my pocket. They were never off my person. Never anywhere someone could lift them and make copies.

Just like I placed alarms on each and every window. Not ones wired to any electronics, just those that would blare a horrendous sound if the windows were opened. You could create your own tech-free alarm system if you were creative enough. And I'd found a book at the library that helped with ideas. Motion sensor lights, window shields that allowed me to see out but prevented anyone from seeing in, and a garden that would tell me if anyone had been in its midst.

It didn't matter that I hadn't seen or heard from Brendan in al-most two years. The routine was ingrained in me now. And it did soothe. It was more than simply thinking it kept me safe. It was almost like compulsively knocking on wood. The routine kept me safer than the actual locks and sensors did.

Because even though I'd braced my first few months in Sparrow Falls, Brendan hadn't found me. And as each day passed, a little more traitorous hope filled me that he wouldn't. That he'd forgotten about me and moved on with his life.

Sliding my keys into my front pocket, I grabbed my helmet. I lived for the months when I could ride my bike into town. It might take me thirty-plus minutes, but it saved on gas, and the trip was also a meditation of sorts—with a stunning backdrop.

Today was no different. I pushed off, riding down the gravel road that would take me to the two-lane highway into town. The cool morning air stung my cheeks, but in a way that reminded me I was alive. I never took those reminders for granted.

As I reached the edge of the forest and rode into the pastureland, a cow let out a bellowing moo in greeting. "Morning, Bessie," I called back. I had no clue if it was the same cow from yesterday. They all looked identical to me. But they were freaking adorable, just the same.

Turning east toward town, I got my first peek at the breathtaking mountains, just as the sun crested their peaks. The early rays painted the forests and fields in a riot of color—the kind of creation I never would've gotten in LA. And that was a gift, too. A path I never would've expected but was grateful for all the same.

My bike hit the rumble strip, and I cursed as I righted it. I probably shouldn't let that gratitude get me killed.

I kept a closer eye on the road for the rest of my trek. It wasn't long before I reached the outskirts of town. Sparrow Falls was the kind of picturesque place you saw in movies but never thought actually existed. Many of the brick buildings flanking the main street through town dated back to the early nineteen hundreds, but they'd all been painstakingly restored. And new builds had to be thoroughly vetted to ensure they fit with the look of the place.

The community had pride in their town. You could see it in how the flower beds were meticulously maintained at each and every corner of Cascade Avenue. How there was rarely a speck of trash to be found anywhere. But the place had heart, too—the kind that freaked me out at first.

People in LA mostly minded their business. But not here. As you walked by the locals, they greeted you with a hello or a head dip. They offered to help if your hands were full and held doors open if they were in front of you.

Those simple kindnesses made it harder to stay anonymous. Threading the needle between careful and rude was a tricky balance I failed at most days. But a part of me hoped I could finally simply *be* in this new life.

I pulled my bike to a stop in front of a storefront with huge glass windows and a teal sign above them that read *The Mix Up*. The letters were perfectly imperfect in a way that represented the chaos of the woman who owned the place. But Sutton's haphazard energy was only matched by her kindness, and the combination was incredibly endearing.

Locking my bike to a lamppost, I crossed to the door of the bakery and keyed in the code to the electronic lock. It made a whirring sound and then a pop. I pulled it open, the bell overhead tinkling. Strains of country music drifted out of the kitchen, and the space was toasty warm.

"Morning!" I called.

A second later, Sutton appeared in the kitchen entryway. Her blond hair was piled on the top of her head, and she had what looked like a butter knife stuck through the bun to hold it in place. Flour dusted one cheek and speckled her hair, but I didn't miss the dark circles beneath her eyes.

I had no idea how Sutton managed to get up sometime between three and four every morning to prep the day's goods. Add on running a business and raising a seven-year-old little boy, and I was pretty sure she was superwoman.

"Morning, Thea. How's it looking out there?"

"It's going to be a beauty."

"Hopefully, that means lots of tourist dollars," she said with a grin. "I've got the bread, scones, muffins, and croissants already out.

The sweet and savory Danishes are cooling. And I'm working on the cupcakes now."

I frowned at her. "How many cups of coffee have you had today?"

Sutton's lips twitched. "Just a few."

"Mooooom?" a slurred voice called as footsteps sounded on the back stairs leading to the small apartment above the bakery.

"Right here, baby," Sutton called, moving toward the little boy's voice.

He appeared a second later, clad in pajamas covered in hockey pucks and sticks in bright colors. His light brown hair was darker than his mom's, but they had the same piercing turquoise eyes.

The moment he was within arm's reach, he launched himself at Sutton. She caught him with an oomph as he nuzzled into her, then rubbed a hand up and down his back. "Sleep good?"

"Mm-hmm," he mumbled.

Sutton bounced him in that soothing way that seemed almost second nature for most mothers. "I swear he's still half-comatose when he gets up."

I grinned. "Waking up is hard." Moving around the two of them, I tickled the little boy's side. "Morning, Luca."

"Hi, Thee Thee," he whispered.

Sutton chuckled. "I'm going to get him ready for camp. You good to handle opening?"

I nodded. "I'll get the coffee brewing and then switch to cupcake duty."

"You're a lifesaver. I'm in the middle of the cookie monster ones."

"Me want cookie," Luca mumbled against his mom's shoulder.

I laughed. "I'll see if I can finish one in time for you to take in your lunch."

Luca lifted his head, turquoise eyes colliding with mine as he gave me a sleepy smile. "You're the best, Thee Thee."

My heart squeezed. God, the kid was sweet. "You are."

Sutton gave me a thankful smile as she headed back up the stairs. He was really getting too big for her to be carrying around, but I wasn't surprised. She was one of the strongest people I knew.

I moved my way through the space. Sutton had done an amazing job bringing it back to life this past year. The walls were a pristine white, but dark, exposed beams soared overhead, and antique, shabby-chic-looking chandeliers illuminated the space. Teal banquettes lined the walls, bringing in a whimsical pop of color.

But the true stars of the show were Sutton's baked creations. While we carried a wide array of options, she specialized in cupcakes, and each one was a work of art. She had everything from butterflies to rainbows to princesses. And she had themed confections for every holiday. Even freaking Arbor Day.

I got to work brewing our standard decaf and regular in the coffee urns as I hummed along to the country song spilling out of the speakers. I'd never really been a fan of country until I started working here and ended up inundated with it, thanks to Sutton. It was probably more that I hadn't been exposed until now.

Country wasn't exactly a staple in LA, and growing up in the valley, it hadn't been much of a thing there either. Over time, I'd slowly found myself enjoying the storytelling tunes and unique guitar strains. I hummed along as I glanced at the clock. Still fifteen minutes until we had to open.

I moved into the kitchen, the music louder there, and slipped an apron over my head, then quickly washed my hands before grabbing the food dye to turn the white icing blue. A new song came on.

I grinned as I grabbed the large mixing bowl and stirred in the blue coloring, all the while singing along off-key to the lyrics about finally kissing someone new and being unbothered by whatever your ex was up to. God, I longed for that kind of freedom. To remember what it felt like to have my lips tingle from the contact, and a flutter take root in my belly with the excitement of what could be.

"Sounds like tortured cats reaching for those high notes," a deep voice said, amusement lacing his tone.

The shock of the voice, the deep rasp of it, the presence of it all, had me whirling around. The only problem with that was that the bowl of bright blue icing was still in my hands. When I stopped moving, the frosting did not.

It flew out of the bowl and landed squarely on the chest of the man standing opposite me—chest, because even though I was on the tall side, he was taller, towering over me at what had to be six three or four. A white T-shirt was pulled taut over that broad, leanly muscled chest—one now covered in blue icing.

My mouth went slack as my eyes went up, up, up to collide with now familiar amber orbs that had me sucking in a sharp breath. Eyes that were full of sparkling amusement, but somehow also seemed sharper than others I encountered.

Eyes that made my stomach flip and my pulse thrum faster. Ones that had *DANGER* in huge capital letters flashing in my mind. So, there was only one thing I could say.

"Oh, shit."

Chapter Two

Shep

G OD, SHE WAS BEAUTIFUL. STANDING THERE IN THE MIDDLE OF
the kitchen, singing the kind of off-key that made your ears
bleed. But she was so free while doing it. I should've stayed in
the doorway longer, really taken in all that was her.

Because I didn't think I'd ever gotten to see Thea this carefree or
uninhibited before. She was the type of guarded that meant a dozen
locks, triple-enforced walls, and a barbed wire fence. But I'd seen
hints of the real her over the months I'd been coming into the bakery.

Glimpses that told me the truth about the woman behind the
walls. Ones that made me want to lean in closer.

But taking her in now, I couldn't help but chuckle. Her mouth
opened and closed as she took in the bright blue frosting dripping
down the front of my shirt. When she finally managed to speak, it
was only to curse.

I laughed harder, and that only made her glare.

"It's not funny," she snapped.

"Come on, Thorn. It's a little funny."

Thea's spine straightened as if her spinal column had filled with steel. "Thorn?"

I arched a brow and reached for a towel on the counter to mop up the mess. The tee was toast. But it was a small price to pay for a chance to see Thea riled. It made her deep brown eyes burn with a heat I couldn't help but imagine lighting in other scenarios.

"Thorn. Fits your prickly personality."

She gaped at me, her mouth opening and closing yet again. "You broke into the bakery and scared the hell out of me, and *I'm* prickly?"

I just grinned at her. Riled. So much better than her usual brush-offs. "Door was open."

That had Thea's mouth snapping closed.

"I just figured you were open early. But no one answered when I called out, and I heard some horribly off-kilter singing coming from the kitchen. I had to investigate."

Thea's cheeks flamed as she set the bowl of icing on the counter. "I thought I was alone."

"I know," I said simply. That was why it had been such a gift. A single moment of Thea being truly herself.

She moved toward the doorway, carefully giving me a wide berth. "I'll get you a T-shirt to replace that one."

"You don't have to—"

"I do," she clipped, bending over to rummage through the stack of tees with different bakery logos.

I was going to hell. Because as Thea bent over, her jeans pulling tight across her heart-shaped ass, I couldn't look away.

She pulled a lavender shirt free and straightened, holding it out to me. "Here."

The tee was large enough to fit me, but the front had a bright pink cupcake with *Cupcake Cutie* written below it in a squiggly script.

Her lips twitched as she held it out. "Problem?"

I met her stare head-on. I knew a challenge when I heard it. Grabbing the neck of my T-shirt at the back, I pulled it up and over my head, then tossed it into the trash can behind the counter. "Real men wear purple."

Thea's gaze slid from my face down to my bare chest, and I didn't miss the way her pupils dilated as she swallowed hard.

I held out a hand for the shirt. "See something you like?"

Her eyes snapped back to my face. "Just wondering why the town's golden boy is stripping down in the middle of a place of business."

I shrugged and pulled the purple shirt over my head. "I don't have a problem with nudity. Do you?"

The moment the words passed my lips, Thea stiffened, her face paling slightly.

Shit. "I'm sorry," I said quickly. "I'm an ass. I was just joking around—"

She shook her head. "It's fine. Just tell me what you'd like to drink or eat, and I'll get it for you. On the house."

It obviously wasn't *fine*, and that had my gut churning. I'd clearly stepped in it. And the way I'd done so had me kicking myself over and over. It also had me worried. "You don't have to cover my breakfast," I said softly.

"I think that's my choice," Thea argued, moving around me, once again giving me a wide berth. "Black coffee, right?"

"Yeah," I muttered, crossing behind the bakery case but giving her plenty of the space she seemed to need.

"Pastry?" she asked.

As I made it to the front of the case, where I should've been all along, I scanned the contents. The thought of downing one of the sweets this early turned my stomach. But there were a few other options. "I'll take a ham and cheese croissant."

Thea nodded, her dark hair sweeping across her olive cheek. But she didn't say a word. I didn't push. I already felt like enough of an ass.

Thea snapped a lid on the coffee just as Sutton emerged from the back, Luca's hand in hers. She sent me a wide smile as she brushed some flour off her shirt. "Morning, Shep."

"Morning," I greeted, then grinned down at Luca. "Hey, buddy."

He grinned, exposing a missing incisor. "Mr. Shep! Can I help you build again?"

I chuckled. "Anytime. We can always use another good man on the job."

Luca's chest puffed up. "Mom, can you take me? Can you?"

Sutton just shook her head. "You have to go to camp first."

"But after? Pleeeeeease?" he begged.

"Maybe later this week. I thought you wanted to go to the ice rink today."

Luca looked absolutely tortured by the decision.

"The construction zone will be there, buddy. There's no rush," I assured him.

Luca let out a tiny huff, as though the weight of the world were on his shoulders. "Ice today, building tomorrow."

I held out a hand for a high five. "Good choice, my man."

Sutton sent me an exhausted smile. "Thanks."

"Anytime," I assured her.

As she hurried toward the door, a flicker of movement caught my attention, right before a different sort of guilt flooded me. I forced a smile. "Hey, Mara. How are you?"

Her return grin was so bright it had that guilt digging in deeper. "Pretty good. You?"

"Doing well. Just grabbing some breakfast," I said, glancing toward Thea as I pulled out my wallet.

Thea's gaze quickly darted away from my face. "I told you. On the house. For the whole…" She made some nonsensical gesture with her hand that had me fighting a smile. "Icing thing."

Mara looked back and forth between Thea and me. "Icing thing?"

"Just a little early morning mishap," I said, pulling two twenties out of my wallet and stuffing them into the tip jar.

"Shep," Thea chastised quietly.

I dipped my head to meet her gaze. "It's your choice whether or not to charge, but how much to tip is mine. Sorry about the assholery."

Her plump, pink lips pressed into a hard line before popping apart again. "All good."

It wasn't, though. Thea's behavior was all wrong. The kind that said she'd been hurt before. And that had anger stirring somewhere deep, with a completely unwarranted heat behind it.

I didn't know Thea. Not really. I'd been coming into the bakery since it opened months ago, taken in by her striking beauty. But she hadn't shared anything with me that let me truly get to know her.

All I'd gotten were minuscule snippets. Brief moments when she let her guard down. Usually, when she was teasing Luca or laughing with Sutton.

And I hadn't learned much more from my sister, who worked with Thea at the local nursery. The most I could pull out of Rhodes was that she thought Thea was running from something. The question was…what?

"Shep," Mara said, bringing my attention back to her.

More guilt sparked at the flicker of annoyance I felt at being forced away from Thea. I really was an ass.

Mara smiled tentatively. "Do you want to stick around? We could have breakfast together. I've got an hour before my shift starts at the hardware store."

Hell. Mara and I had ended months ago. We'd dated for about six weeks before I realized we just weren't a match. It wasn't that she wasn't a good person. She was. But that only made ending things harder. Telling someone you thought you were better as friends never went over well.

And now, it was like Mara thought she could convince me otherwise. She was never overly pushy about it, but there was a steady, uncomfortable pressure. She'd find a way to ask me to spend time with her every couple of weeks. I was running out of ideas for gentle letdowns.

I cleared my throat. "Meeting Anson at a new site."

Mara's expression fell, and my guilt dug in deeper. "Okay. Maybe another time."

I tried to hide my wince as I avoided her suggestion. "Have a good day."

I glanced over my shoulder as I started toward the door. "Stay away from the blue frosting for a while, Thorn."

Thea instantly scowled at me, but the heat was back behind those dark eyes. Something a hell of a lot better than the flicker of fear I'd seen earlier.

I felt a tug to find out what had caused it and wipe it from the Earth. But that was wasted energy. Because I'd probably fail her, too.

Chapter Three

Thea

THE BAKERY BUZZED WITH THE HUM OF THE BREAKFAST CROWD. This and the lunch rush were usually my favorite parts of the day. They were busy enough that I lost myself in the steady pace of taking orders and delivering food. I didn't have time to think about anything but the next task.

But not today.

Today, all I could think about was Shepard Colson. The way his eyes twinkled when he teased. How the early morning sun had caught on his hair, making those hints of auburn beneath the deep brown flare to life. And the expanse of muscle he'd exposed as he pulled his ruined T-shirt over his head.

"Earth to Thea."

I jolted at Sutton's teasing voice. "Sorry, what?"

She pressed her lips together to keep from smiling. "Walter has an order up."

The cook in his mid-seventies gave me a wave and a wink.

"Sorry," I mumbled again.

"It's almost like something has you off your game," Sutton sing-songed. "Or maybe it's some*one*."

I couldn't help the slight stiffening of my muscles—the tension that wove through them like strands of steel wool. "I just didn't get enough sleep last night," I muttered, grabbing the two plates Walter had waiting.

I dashed around Sutton and moved straight to the table with a couple from out of town. "Here you go. Did you need anything else?"

The woman beamed up at me. "I think we're good. This looks amazing."

I did my best to answer her smile with one of my own but was only marginally successful. "Just flag me down if you change your mind."

By the time I rounded the counter again, Sutton had finished ringing up her customer and turned to face me. "He likes you."

That tension pulled tighter. "Who?" I played dumb, moving to the bakery case to adjust our stock.

"Thea," Sutton said, leaning against the back counter laden with completed orders.

"Hmmm?" I kept straightening the pastries until they would've passed a drill sergeant's inspection.

Sutton didn't say anything. It was the ultimate mom move—waiting me out until I was forced to straighten and look her way. But when I did, it was to find nothing but gentleness and a hint of worry on her face.

That was worse. I didn't want Sutton looking deeper. I knew she already saw more than I should've allowed. But that happened when you started letting people in. She and Rhodes had both seen the cracks in my façade.

"He's a good man," Sutton said softly. "Did you know he helped me with a few things around here for nothing just because he saw me struggling with the reno on my own?"

My stomach twisted. I hadn't known that, but I wasn't surprised. Rhodes had shared more than a few stories about the ways her brother went above and beyond for the people he cared about. But I didn't want to know. Not when I already felt the buzz of attraction. That hum was dangerous, potentially lethal. Which meant one thing: I needed to stay far away.

"I'm not interested in dating," I told Sutton. "Not Shep or anyone else."

She sighed. "I get it. I really do. I know what it's like to get burned. It makes you hesitant to put your hand anywhere near the stove again."

Understatement of the century. "I'm good, Sutton. Really. It's just not something I'm looking for." And I *was* good. Having Brendan destroy so much only made me value what I had now all the more. Moose, my home, my garden, even the tendrils of friendship I'd found with Sutton and Rhodes. I didn't need more.

Sutton's lips pressed together as if she were holding back something she desperately wanted to say. Then she gave in to the temptation. "I just don't want you to miss out on something amazing because you're scared. Men like Shep are one in a million."

I studied her for a moment, something that felt a whole lot like jealousy flaring to life. "Do you like him?"

Sutton's eyes flared. "No! Not like that. He's a friend. That's it. But I've seen the way he watches you."

I stiffened again, and Sutton saw it.

"Not in a creepy way. Like he'd give anything to simply have you look his way."

I bit the inside of my cheek. I knew I had to give Sutton something, or she'd never let this go. And I desperately needed her to set it down. "I just can't." I let my eyes bore into hers, imploring. "It's not in the cards for me."

Because even if a man were the best person on the planet, my mind would play tricks on me. Wonder when he'd turn. I'd constantly be looking for the ulterior motive beneath the kindness. And always asking how he might eventually destroy me.

That wouldn't be fair to anyone. And it wasn't something I wanted to live through either. Not again.

Sutton's expression fell, but she reached out and squeezed my hand. "Okay. But I'm always here. Whatever you need."

I nodded. "Thank you."

"Can you take the counter? I think my cake has cooled enough for me to frost."

"Of course." Guilt surged at the rush of relief I felt at her distance. But I needed some time to shore up my defenses. They had gotten perilously thin.

As Sutton disappeared into the kitchen, she and Walter started singing along to an old Tim McGraw ballad. I wiped down the counters and the bakery case, scouring every speck and spot and trying to think about anything but the fact that I was lonely. There was no way for me *not* to be when no one in Sparrow Falls knew who I truly was.

The sound of footsteps had me straightening and tossing the rag into the sink. I forced a smile, greeting the regular. "Morning, Raina."

She gave me the same hesitant smile she always did, her light brown hair sweeping her face as if shielding her from the world. "Morning."

"Nutella muffin and an Earl Grey tea?" I asked.

Raina nodded, her hair shifting to reveal more of her hazel eyes. Her makeup was subdued, but she clearly had an expert hand in applying it. Still, I could see the hint of a bruise beneath the concealer, right across her cheekbone.

A burn lit in my throat. It wasn't the first time I'd seen something like this: a bruise on her arm peeking out from under her sleeve, a scattering of discoloration on her wrist as she paid. But I'd never seen anything on her face until today.

Raina handed me a ten-dollar bill. "Keep the change."

"Thank you," I said, trying to keep my voice steady as I hit buttons on the cash register. A buzz flared in my ears, and my mind raced. Maybe I was seeing zebras when the truth was horses.

I didn't know the first thing about Raina, other than the fact that she was about my age, quiet, and ordered the same thing every day. Maybe she was into kickboxing or had taken a softball to the cheek. Or…it could be something darker.

Possibilities swirled as I picked up a muffin with the tongs and slipped it into a bag. It only took a matter of seconds to prepare her tea after that. Turning to face her, I pasted a bright expression on my face. "Here you go."

Raina answered with that same tentative smile. "Thank you."

I tried to read beneath her words and see if there was some silent cry for help, but I couldn't read anything as she took her breakfast and headed for the door. There was nothing but the calm, quiet exterior I saw most mornings.

But I knew what it was like to paint a picture for the outside world that was so opposite of what you actually felt. I'd been so good at it that I sometimes believed the lies. Until it all came crashing down.

Only Brendan's weapons hadn't been fists. They'd been words and manipulations. He'd left no bruises. And the scars burned into me weren't anything the eye could see.

Which only made me feel crazy, just like he'd said I was.

And it was all a reminder of why I needed to stay far away from Shep Colson—or any man like him. Because if something seemed too good to be true, it usually was. And even if it wasn't, I'd be too scared to reach for it anyway.

Chapter Four

Shep

THE HOUSE WAS A COMPLETE GUT JOB. BUT THAT ONLY HAD THE phantom buzz of energy lighting beneath my skin. My fingers itched to put pencil to paper and begin sketching out what could be.

That was always the high. Transforming something that people saw as trash into treasure. And while I loved using every form of tech imaginable to bring that to fruition, I always had to start with old-school pencil and paper.

Something about the way the graphite scratched across the page opened my mind to possibilities. And this place was nothing but. It was a bigger undertaking than anything I'd done for myself by a factor of ten. But that only heightened the buzz.

I stared up at the enormous farmhouse that must date back to the 1920s, at least, close to when this part of the state was settled. The siding was a weather-beaten gray that had probably once been white. It needed a new roof, for sure. But the bones? They were steady.

I wanted to knock out half a dozen walls. Put in windows. But that would all come with time—that and more than a little sweat equity.

But owning a construction company came with perks. Discounts on materials and access to workers were two of them.

My phone dinged, and I looked down, shaking my head. My siblings were ridiculous. It didn't matter that only two of us were related by blood or that we'd each joined the family anywhere from birth to age sixteen. Our bond and shit-talking game were strong.

The group chat the seven of us shared was constantly being renamed, each person trying to one-up one another or give someone a hard time. Today, it read: *Group name changed to Hans Brolo.*

> **Cope:** *Proof of life check. I haven't heard from you assholes in over forty-eight hours.*

Texts and video calls were all Cope had for keeping tabs on us now that he was back in Seattle, finishing out his requirements after the end of his NHL season. So, I didn't blame him for the request. And the chat had been quieter lately. There'd been more side check-ins after Rhodes was kidnapped, tortured, and almost killed by a man I'd hired and worked alongside for years.

The now familiar burn of guilt returned, acid spreading through my chest and eating through muscle and marrow. I hadn't seen Silas's sickness or twisted cruelty, and my sister had almost lost her life because of it.

> **Kye:** *Dude, maybe stay away from the life-or-death jokes for a while.*
>
> **Fallon:** *Sensitivity chip, Copeland.*
>
> **Kye:** *Shit. If Fal full-named you, you're fucked. Duck and cover.*

Fallon and Kyler always had each other's backs in a way that made me wonder if they could communicate without even speaking. When Kye came to live with us at sixteen, he hadn't wanted to talk to anyone. But, somehow, Fallon always seemed to reach him.

A photo appeared in the chat—Rhodes holding up a pitchfork

and standing in front of a brown pile of something, her other arm in a cast.

> **Rhodes**: *Nobody will dare cross me today.*
>
> **Kye:** *Yeah, because you're standing in a pile of shit.*
>
> **Rhodes:** *Whatever works.*
>
> **Cope:** *Sorry, Rho. I was an insensitive ass.*
>
> **Rhodes:** *I thought we were past the tiptoeing-around-me stage. I like jokes better.*

It had been almost a month since her ordeal, and while she didn't want us worrying, I knew the truth. She still carried the scars of what happened—and more than just the skin-deep ones.

I was thankful she'd found comfort in my best friend, Anson—words I'd never thought would pass through my brain. Still, somehow, my broody friend was a match for my sunshiny sister. And it worked.

Knowing that Cope and Rho would play the back-and-forth guilt game for hours, I went with the one tool of distraction I had. I snapped a picture of the house in front of me and hit send.

> **Me**: *Put in an offer. What do you think?*
>
> **Cope:** *That your ass is going to get haunted the moment you try to step inside.*
>
> **Kye:** *Or murdered. That definitely looks like it's home to some lumberjack ax murderer.*

The house was in the middle of nowhere. Desolate. Set on over five hundred acres and nestled between national forest land on one side and a ten-thousand-acre cattle ranch on the other.

But that isolation called to me more now than it ever had before. I needed a place where I could simply be without the pressure of all the things expected of me. Or the weight of all the people I'd let down at different points in my life.

I wasn't an idiot. I knew the heaviness of that weight began at birth. But what did I expect when I'd been abandoned at no more than a few weeks old? Left in one of those safe-haven boxes at a fire station one town over, with no clue as to who I was or where I'd come from.

I was lucky as all hell that the Colson family had adopted me. They were the only family I'd ever known. But I couldn't help but wonder what had made someone leave me in that box. And what was it about me that made me so damn unwanted?

Another ding sounded, bringing me out of my spiral.

Cope: *Now who's making death jokes?*

I sighed, flipping the chat to *mute*. My eldest brother, Trace, and my youngest sister, Arden, had already pulled that move. Their replies to the group were few and far between. Arden's mostly suggested that we had no lives. And Trace's were to keep us in line—county sheriff, through and through.

But I didn't blame them. Cope and Kye would go in circles for hours. And right now, I had work to do. With one last glance at the house, I headed for my truck. Beeping the locks, I climbed inside and started it up.

The clock read three-thirty. I had plenty of time to stop by the nursery before heading home to dive into rehab plans. I dropped my phone into the cupholder and headed in that direction.

It took me a good fifteen minutes before the rustic sign for *Bloom & Berry* appeared. The nursery was my one-stop shop for all things landscaping and also the work home to my unofficial expert. I pulled into a spot on the outskirts of the gravel lot and went in search of Rhodes.

The photo she'd sent gave me a clue as to her location. I wandered around the greenhouses and through the central courtyard, complete with a tiny café. But it wasn't until I smelled the hint of manure that I found her.

Rhodes had her dark hair threaded through the back of a baseball hat in a makeshift ponytail. With each strike of her pitchfork into the massive pile of compost and animal dung, the tail swung. I winced as she one-handedly turned over the manure mixture.

"Should you be doing that?" I asked as I adjusted my ballcap to shield my eyes from the sun.

Rhodes straightened, turned to face me, then leaned on her pitchfork. "I know you keep tabs on me via Anson, so that means I know that *you* know that Dr. Avery cleared me for physical activity. This cast won't hold me back." She lifted her arm, waving the plaster-covered limb to punctuate the point.

"Probably wouldn't hurt to take it easy your first full week back," I suggested.

Annoyance flickered in her hazel eyes. "I have been stuck behind that damn cash register for days. What I need is sunshine and to feel useful again."

I sighed. "Sorry, Rho-Rho," I muttered.

"Not you, too." She groaned.

My lips twitched. "What can I say? Cope's rubbing off on me."

"Cope needs a hobby," Rhodes grumbled. "Something other than checking up on me."

"Being a ridiculously overpaid professional hockey player isn't enough?"

"Clearly not." She shifted, tipping her head back to better study my face. "So, new house already?"

I tried not to shift, knowing it would give away my unease. But I couldn't stop myself. "The place on Juniper Lane is done. It was time."

Rhodes just shook her head. "Don't you ever want to actually *enjoy* the places you painstakingly rehab?"

I didn't. The longest I'd lasted in a place after it was done was two months. And that had been torture. Everything was too pristine. Too perfect. I craved mess and chaos, and putting it all back together again, making it better than ever before.

"Is it a crime to love what you do?" I asked, unable to disguise the hint of defensiveness in my tone.

Rhodes was quiet for a moment, her assessing stare penetrating. "Of course, not. But I can't help but wonder what exactly you're running from."

"Maybe I'm not running *from* anything. Maybe I'm running

toward it." That's what I'd always told myself. That I was chasing the buzz of creation. Rebuilding.

"Maybe." Rhodes leaned the pitchfork against her wheelbarrow. "You doing okay with everything?"

By *everything*, she meant the fact that *Dateline* had run a full-episode exposé on Silas Arnett and his decades-long reign of terror last night. I swallowed the bile churning. "Shouldn't I be asking you that?"

Rhodes shrugged. "We could ask each other. Since we both care, and we've been through some shit."

I hadn't been through anything. Not compared to Rhodes. I didn't deserve the check-ins and worry. But she did. Not only had she lost her entire family at thirteen, but the bastard had come back to finish the job. And he'd gotten close to her through me.

"I'm good. How are *you*?" That was what I really wanted to know. No, it was what I *needed* to know. Because maybe if I was sure Rhodes truly was all right, I could release some of the guilt that was eating me alive.

"Well, if I actually believed that lie about you being good, I would be good, as well. But since I don't, I'm annoyed."

A chuckle slipped free unbidden, and I wrapped an arm around Rhodes, giving her a noogie through her hat.

She twisted, batting at me with her good arm. "Stop it!" She turned, pinching my side, *hard*.

"Shit, Rho," I grumbled, releasing her and rubbing my abused skin.

It was then that she really took me in. "What are you wearing?"

I glanced down, suddenly remembering I was still in the *Cupcake Cutie* shirt from earlier. I'd gotten shit all morning from my crew. "Had a little incident at the bakery."

Rhodes arched a brow. "Incident, huh?"

"Minor spill, that's all."

"Did Thea dump a cup of coffee over your head?"

I scowled at my sister. "You sound like you'd be proud of her if she did."

One corner of her mouth kicked up. "I like that she keeps you on your toes. You're too used to women falling at your feet."

My scowl only deepened. "They don't fall at my feet."

Rhodes scoffed. "You've got that whole golden-boy thing. They love you a little too much. You need someone who isn't putty in your hands."

I didn't feel very golden, especially not this past month.

"Oh, crud," Rhodes said, glancing at her watch. "I forgot I was supposed to grab the newest kitten fosters for her."

"For Thea?" I asked. God, I was pathetic. Desperate for the tiniest clue about the woman.

Rhodes nodded. "She's officially on Nancy's Wags & Whiskers roster now."

Rhodes and our grandma, Lolli, had been involved with the animal rescue for years, but I hadn't known that Thea had gotten plugged in. Somehow, it didn't surprise me, and the knowledge had me opening my mouth before I could stop myself.

"I can drop them off at her place."

A knowing smile spread across Rhodes' face, but she didn't give me a hard time. "You sure?"

"I'm done for the day."

"All right. I'm texting you Thea's address, and you have Nancy's."

I'd done more than a few errands for the rescue, mostly hauling donations of food, toys, and blankets for Lolli. She could get the most tight-fisted business to open their coffers for the cause.

"Sounds good."

Rhodes paused for a moment, seeming to mull something over. "You're a really good brother. You know that, right?"

Her words sliced, each one like the painful press of a blade. "Rho."

"You are. What happened wasn't your fault any more than it was mine or Anson's."

The burn came back, deeper this time. "I should've seen it."

"No one did. And if you keep carrying around that misplaced guilt, it will drown you."

I heard the fear in Rho's voice, which only made the guilt worse. So, I did the only thing I could. I pulled her in for another hug. "Love you, Rho-Rho. Even though you currently smell like horse shit."

She laughed, just like I hoped she would. That sound, plus knowing that she was still alive and breathing, and that Silas hadn't won, would have to be good enough for now.

Chapter Five

Thea

THE LATE-AFTERNOON SUN BLAZED DOWN, AND I LET IT SOAK into my skin as I walked across the back of my property. The view of the never-ending forest never got old. My footsteps slowed as I really took in everything around me.

The hint of pine in the air was just a little different than every other pine tree scent—something unique to Sparrow Falls. Like the crystal-blue sky with its cotton candy clouds drifting by, and the epic vastness of the surrounding wilderness that made me feel so small.

It didn't matter that I felt a little lonely at times, where I wished someone could truly know me. I was lucky as hell to be here and have this place.

An ache took root in my chest as I wished Nikki could see it. I'd sent a couple of Polaroids with my money one month, but photos didn't do this place justice.

I tipped my face up to the sky, letting the sun bake my skin for a moment longer. This was enough. I had my garden, my books, Moose. I was safe. Reaching for more was just greedy.

Sighing, I headed for the greenhouse. When I lived in LA, I'd been a frequent shopper at the many farmers markets in and around my neighborhood. I loved inventing recipes from my finds there, but I'd had no idea what actually went into creating all that amazing produce.

I did now.

The corners of my mouth tipped up as the old greenhouse came into view. When I moved in, I was instantly taken with the space. The bottom fourth of each wall was constructed out of rich, aged wood. Above that was pure glass.

A few of the panes had been cracked or smashed, but with a little research and elbow grease, I'd replaced each one. Learning how to keep plants alive had been a harder endeavor. I'd read books and articles at the library and done a series of trial-and-error experiments. But almost two years later, I had it down.

I adjusted the large wicker basket on my arm and opened the door with my other hand. The moment I stepped inside, thicker air hit me, the kind that kept all the plants happy. I set the basket on the bench in the middle of the space.

Something about tending to the fruits and veggies soothed me. Creating something positive, nurturing it, and helping it grow had healed something in me. The same way fostering tiny kittens did. It was as if caring for them knitted something back together in me.

I got to work watering, weeding, and pruning. As I did, I surveyed what I needed to harvest. Leeks, summer squash, the first tiny strawberries. The avocado tree I'd planted was now pushing against the glass at the top of the greenhouse. I'd have to do something about that soon. And I knew the corn I'd planted just outside had a few ears ready to go.

My mind was already whirling with what to make. Summer squash and corn salad with roasted leeks for flavor. Maybe something with the strawberries for dessert. Sutton would have a better idea about that than I would. Even though I'd been working with her for months, I still hadn't mastered that art.

I moved quickly through the space, picking what I'd need for the evening's meal. I stopped at a catnip plant in the corner and grinned. Breaking off a sprig, I stuck it into my basket and headed for the door.

Heading across the back of the property, I climbed the steps of the back deck that had clearly been added later in the small cabin's life. I'd eat out here tonight. I didn't have a table, but I could easily eat on the chaise lounge. And I'd bring Moose out on his leash so he could get some outside time.

I tugged my keys out of my pocket and unlocked the specialty deadbolt on the back door. As I stepped inside, Moose greeted me with a warbled meow. I grinned and moved to scratch behind his ears. His little nose was already twitching.

"Give me a second, and I'll bring you your drug of choice."

He answered with the chattering protest that always made me laugh. I hurried into the kitchen, dumped my basket, and plucked out the catnip. My gaze caught on the clock, and I cursed. Rhodes would be here at any moment.

I quickly crossed to Moose with the catnip sprig. He dropped to his back paws like a meerkat, his front paws hooking around my hand and jerking it to his mouth.

"Jeez, watch it. You're going to take off my finger if you're not careful."

But he was already gnawing on the leaves, clearly in heaven. I grinned as I crossed to the kittens' pen to double-check everything. At six weeks, they wouldn't be able to climb the pen's walls, but it likely wouldn't be long before that changed. Kittens were more than a little resourceful.

Moose let out a baleful meow.

I straightened and sent him a pointed look. "The kittens won't steal your catnip, so chill."

Glancing at the pen again, I frowned. I needed a little more litter in the litter box. I moved toward the small half bath off the living room that also served as my kitten storage area. Opening the cabinet beneath the sink, I tugged the litter free and froze.

Dread settled low in my gut as I took in the water under the sink. I quickly pulled everything out, only to find more water. Not pools of it, but like everything had been doused in it over time. My hand skimmed over the pipe as I studied it. I didn't see a leak, but that didn't mean one wasn't there.

I stood, looked around, and caught a slight shimmer on the linoleum floor next to the sink. I crouched low. That was damp, too.

Shit. Shit. Shit.

I needed to turn off the water to the house. I probably needed to call a plumber. Just the thought of someone being in my house—anyone at all, but especially a stranger—had pressure building in my chest. My rib cage tightened around my lungs, making it hard to take a full breath.

"One thing at a time," I whispered.

Maybe I could figure it out myself. There had to be a library book on finding a leak. I might be able to get there before it closed.

But first, I had to shut off the water to the house so it didn't get worse. That was the last thing I needed.

Striding out of the bathroom, I rounded the corner to the front door. The guest bath was along an exterior wall, at least, so I hoped the damage was minimal. I scanned my front yard, looking for anything that would denote some sort of shutoff.

I'd never owned a home until this one. My life in LA had consisted of one apartment after another. Even growing up, I'd never had a typical home with a yard. It wasn't something my parents could afford.

Finally, my eyes locked on a small cover in the ground. I hurried toward it and pulled it up, then reached for the rusted shutoff valve that looked older than the house itself—if that were possible.

I tried to twist it, but the thing didn't want to move. Pressure built behind my eyes. "Come on," I muttered, putting more force behind my movements. With a grunted oath, it finally shifted. But not in a good way.

One moment, I was crouched over the opening. The next, water was shooting into my face. It soaked me in seconds, taking out my hair, my tank, and everything else in its path.

I stumbled back, panic searing me. Then I realized the shutoff valve was still in my hand. It had come clean off.

Crouching low, I tried to come at it from an angle so as not to get doused again, but I was still getting soaked as the pipe screamed in protest.

Shit. Shit. Shit.

I didn't have the first clue what to do. How to stop it. How to fix it. Nothing.

A door slammed, making me jerk to my feet and whirl around.

Shep stood there, a look of pure confusion and amusement on his face. "What the hell happened to you?"

Chapter Six

Shep

THE ABSOLUTELY HORRIFIED LOOK ON THEA'S FACE HAD ME
fighting a laugh. She was soaked from head to toe, as if she'd
decided to take a dip in all her clothes. Her mahogany hair was
in complete disarray like some small animal had burrowed in and
made a nest.

Her mouth opened, closed, then opened again. "The water shutoff," she said, gesturing at the geyser behind her.

Hell.

I'd been so taken in by the woman that I hadn't even noticed the
geyser behind her. I strode across the front yard that Thea had clearly
put a lot of work into. She definitely had an eye for landscaping. The
blend of flowers and native plants fit perfectly with their surroundings.

I crouched low, coming at the shutoff from the side so I wouldn't
get drenched. Thea bent at my side, offering me a rusted piece of
metal. "It broke off."

Jesus. That thing was older than dirt. No wonder it had snapped
right off in her hand.

"Give me a sec," I said, pushing to my feet and striding back to my truck. The kittens were safely tucked in their carrier with the AC pumping, so they'd be fine for as long as I needed to get things shut down. Leaning over the bed, I opened the lid of my crossover toolbox and rummaged around until I found the wrench I needed.

I grabbed it and jogged back toward Thea and the geyser. She stood there, drenched and staring at the stream. I didn't blame her. No one wanted a river in their front yard—or to drain their well's reserves.

Crouching again, I got to work trying to close off the water at the root. The damn thing was rusted in place, and I cursed as I put my full weight into it, dousing my shoulder in the process. After a few more tries, the water flow started to slow and then stopped altogether.

I heaved a sigh as I straightened. Thea was right there. Probably the closest she'd ever been. Her scent wrapped around me, grabbing hold and burying itself deep—something floral with a hint of coconut. She stared at the water valve as if it were some sort of snake before her head jerked up, her deep brown eyes locking with mine.

It was only then that I fully realized just how close we were—close enough that I could see every wrinkle in the wet clothes clinging to her and how they hugged every lean, sinewy curve. Everything about her was alluring grace, the kind that pulled you in and held you captive.

Thea's gaze dropped to my mouth for one beat, two. Then something snapped her out of the moment. She stepped back, hands gripped in front of her. "What are you doing here?"

It wasn't snapped out or angry, but there was an underlying suspicion to her words that had the hairs on my arms raising.

"Rho got caught up at work and asked me to bring the kittens from Nancy."

"Oh." Thea's mouth made a perfect circular shape as she said it—a shape I wanted to trace with my tongue. *Fuck.*

A little of the tension eased from her shoulders. "Thank you. I mean for the kittens and the water. I wasn't sure what to do."

"No problem." I held my hand out, motioning for what was in hers.

Thea's focus shot to the valve she still clutched in a death grip. She dropped it into my palm, and I studied it carefully.

"This is completely corroded." My gaze flicked to what I could see of the pipe heading toward her house. "Wouldn't be surprised if your pipes have damage, too."

Thea's fingers wove together, gripping tightly as if it were the only thing keeping her together. "I think there's a leak in my half bath," she said quietly.

Shit. That wasn't a good sign. Leaks could do untold damage before you even knew they were there. "Why don't you let me take a peek, and I—?"

"No." She snapped the word, and it cracked like a whip.

My brows rose at the ferocity in the single syllable. "It's no problem." I gestured to the side of my truck that read *Colson Construction.* "I do this for a living."

She quickly shook her head. "I don't want you in my house."

Annoyance and maybe a little anger flared. I was trying to help her. I— That thought cut off as I saw it, the slight tremble racking Thea's muscles. She was gripping her hands together to try to hide the shaking, but she was fucking terrified. Of me?

I took two huge steps back, giving her plenty of space. A sick wave of guilt swept through me, and fast on its heels was something I could only identify as grief. Someone had hurt Thea. There was no question in my mind about that. They'd hurt her so badly that she wouldn't even risk me coming into her home to help her.

"Okay," I said, making my voice as soft as possible. "We won't do anything you don't want to do. You're in charge."

Thea stared at me for a long moment, her eyes glistening in the late-afternoon sunlight. She licked her lips, her hands still clutched in a vise grip. "Could you tell me how to fix it?"

God, that slayed me. I knew Thea had been in Sparrow Falls for nearly two years. She'd worked odd jobs until landing with Sutton at The Mix Up and getting her part-time gig at Bloom. She was polite to everyone but had an unmistakable do-not-get-close vibe. Which meant she was doing everything alone. Had no one to help her. No one to take some of the burden.

I tried to choose my words carefully. "Maybe. Plumbing is tricky and is something you really need to make sure is done right."

Her lower lip trembled, and she pressed her mouth into a thin line to stop it.

Jesus. "Could I look at the siding? Just the outside?" I hurried to say.

Thea's gaze moved from me and traced the route the pipe would likely take to the house. She stared at it for a moment, and I could see that the structure was her haven. The only place she probably felt safe.

"Okay."

The word was barely above a whisper, but I was so damn attuned to Thea I heard it as though she'd yelled it.

"Okay," I echoed. "Gonna get a shovel from my truck."

I moved before she could stop me, crossing to my vehicle and grabbing the shovel from the bed. When I turned, it was to find Thea watching me like a hawk. I just let her. Whatever she needed to feel safe.

My gut churned, that sick feeling spreading as I wondered what the hell had happened to her. It battled with the anger taking root. Fury at whoever had put that fear in her.

I tried to shove the rage down. The last thing Thea needed was to see that. So, I focused on the task at hand, telling her everything I planned to do and waiting for approval at every step.

"Gonna dig a hole where I think the pipe connects with the house to see if I can find any evidence of a leak."

Thea licked her lips again, pink tongue darting across them in a nervous gesture. But she nodded.

It didn't take me long to find it, but I saw water pooling before I even got there. Not a ton of it, but enough. It didn't take much moisture to damage a home.

I glanced up at Thea as I knelt by the hole. Her entire body was strung tight, her typically olive skin an unnatural shade of white. "Where's the bathroom?"

"Right there. On the other side of this wall."

I sighed, turning my head to survey the corroded pipe. "I can't know for sure without getting inside, but it looks like this has been slowly leaking for a long time. I don't see the leak here, so I'm not sure where it originated from."

Thea's knuckles bleached white as she gripped her fingers tighter.

God, she was the last person I wanted to deliver bad news to. It was like kicking a puppy. "You gotta be careful with leaks. They can lead to rot, mold. Both. It doesn't have to be me, but you need to get someone who knows what they're doing inside to look at it."

Maybe something about me specifically triggered Thea. While the thought stung, it would be better than knowing she wouldn't let anyone help.

Her eyes shone brighter as she struggled to get words out. "I can't."

That struggle, the way Thea battled back tears, sliced deep. "You're killing me, Thorn. Let me help."

Her whole body shuddered. "I-I'm sorry. I just…I can't."

Chapter Seven

Thea

MY EYES BURNED AS I BLINKED AT THE KITCHEN COUNTER IN the early morning light. It was as if my eyelids were made of sandpaper and acid. Not a winning combination.

Moose batted my leg with his paw, letting out a warbled meow.

"You already had breakfast," I mumbled as I mixed the kittens' gruel. "This is for the babies."

Moose hissed in response.

"Such a drama king."

He was also probably pissed about all the tossing and turning I'd done last night. Between struggling to get to sleep and nightmares where Brendan stood over my bed screaming at me about all my failings, I'd barely cobbled together three hours of shut-eye.

It wouldn't be the first time. When I first left LA, I'd struggled to sleep at all. I'd braced for Brendan to break down the door of any motel I was at, and once I landed in Sparrow Falls, I'd been sure he'd find me eventually.

Between that and worrying that any person who looked at me

for longer than a beat had seen me naked on the internet, I'd been a basket case. The first night I managed a full night's rest, I'd cried the next morning in sheer relief. And struggling with sleep again sent me catapulting right back to that place.

It didn't help that I was struggling with a healthy dose of guilt on top of it. I'd seen the hurt in Shep's eyes when I wouldn't let him into my house. And his understanding and empathy only made things worse.

Shoving down the image, I carried the two plates to the kitten pen. The four babies were an adorable distraction. They were currently sleeping in a pile, but the moment the scent of food hit their noses, the squeaky meows began.

I lifted them out of the little house two at a time. I put the two tabbies at one plate and set the black with white paws and the gray with a white chest at the other. The little gray girl was smaller, definitely the runt. I stood and watched them for a few minutes, making sure the gray got her share so she'd put on some weight.

Moose put his front paws on the top of the pen to stare down at them, then looked up at me with complete disdain.

My lips twitched. "Don't worry. I'm taking them with me to work."

I had one of those little trailers for my bike designed to hold kids, but I hooked a carrier inside. Thankfully, my boss at Bloom was used to having animals of all sorts in his office or behind the counter. Duncan was a good sport and even fed the kittens for Rhodes and me if things got busy.

It didn't take the babies long to finish their breakfast, and since they were so little, loading them into the carrier was easy. If it had been Moose, I'd be bleeding.

The ride to Bloom was longer than the trip to the bakery, but it was another beautiful day. I loved getting to the nursery before it opened. The sparrows, hummingbirds, and butterflies were out in droves in the quiet.

I heard a door slam as I pulled my bike to a stop near the main building. Rhodes grinned as she walked toward me. "You brought the babies?"

I nodded. "They're so stinking cute."

"Gimme!" she demanded.

I laughed as I unhooked the carrier and held it out to Rhodes.

She bent, peeking through the front door and running her finger across the bars. "Hi, babes," she cooed.

The kittens meowed, and one tried to nip her finger. She chuckled as she pulled her hand back. "The gray one looks underweight."

"Yeah, I think I might add an extra formula dose for her if she'll take it."

"Probably a good idea," Rhodes agreed, straightening and pulling out her keys. She stilled, taking in my face. "You okay?"

I tried to fight the stiffening in my muscles. "Just didn't get a great night's sleep."

She sent me an empathetic smile. "Kittens keep you up?"

I opened my mouth to agree but couldn't do it. Lying to Rhodes' face just felt *wrong*. I gave my head a little shake. "I've got a leak at the house. It's a shit show."

"Damn," she muttered, slipping her key into the lock and then gesturing me inside. "Did you call a plumber yet? Shep could probably help. He's great with that stuff."

My stomach twisted as Shep's face filled my mind. The way those amber eyes had looked at me with such careful gentleness. How the sun caught the auburn undertones in his rich brown hair. The almost pleading tone in his voice for me to let him help.

I swallowed down the guilt. "He was actually there when it exploded. He shut off the main valve for me. I'm gonna head to the library after work to do some research on how to fix it." I just prayed it was something I could tackle on my own.

Rhodes' footsteps faltered in the hallway to Duncan's office. Then she stopped altogether and turned to face me. "You're going to try to fix it…yourself?"

My spine straightened, a little defensiveness seeping in. "I've figured out everything else that needs fixing."

"And that's amazing. But, Thea, this is serious. There was a leak at the Victorian, and it took weeks of restoration to fix." Rhodes knew all about the ups and downs of renovation since she had Shep and his crew bringing her family's historic home back to life. But having people in her space wasn't a trigger for Rhodes.

When I didn't say anything, she kept pushing. "If mold starts to grow because it wasn't properly dealt with, you could make yourself really sick. Moose, too."

She'd gone for the kill shot. I might be willing to risk myself, but not my cat. That overwhelmed feeling settled back over me, a panicky, trapped sensation.

Rhodes' gaze roamed over my face. "Shep'll help. I promise."

I shook my head quickly. "No." The last thing I wanted was for him to do me any more favors. And being in close proximity to him wasn't something I could risk. "He's done enough. I'll look up some other local companies."

Rhodes frowned at me. "There's really only one other construction and restoration company in town, and their work isn't as good as Shep's. Plus, the owners are jerks of epic proportions."

No one's work was as good as Shep's. I'd seen the *Colson Construction* sign in front of new builds and restoration projects alike. They all had one thing in common: They were absolutely gorgeous.

The styles were endless. Everything from modern to Craftsman, but always blending the old with the new flawlessly and effortlessly in a way that made it one cohesive vision. But I'd looked up the price tags of his creations, and they'd never even be in the ballpark of possibility for me.

"I don't need fancy, Rho. I just need functional."

Her lips pressed together. "Thea—"

"I'll be fine. I promise."

Pulling to a stop in front of the brick building at the north end of town, I swung a leg over my bike and climbed off. It was one of the places in town with a quaint storefront below and a couple of offices above. The shop on the ground level was one I'd ogled countless times as it housed shabby-chic furniture with a rustic edge.

But I wasn't there to browse. Today, I needed my lunch hour to see what Castle Rock Construction would charge to look at my leak. I'd spent the entire ride over, convincing myself it would be okay. I could watch whoever they sent like a hawk. If I employed a company instead of accepting a favor from a friend's brother, things would go faster.

And, most importantly, I wouldn't have to be so close to Shep. I wouldn't have to see the gentle pity on his face. Feel the pull of attraction. I wouldn't have to worry that he saw far too much.

For all those reasons, I could do this. My heart hammered as I looked down at myself and winced. I quickly tried to brush off the dirt streaked across my *Bloom & Berry* tee. I also had some on my khaki shorts, but at least that blended.

When I got most of it off, I looked up at the glass-fronted doors. A list of companies was painted in a delicate serif font on the front. My gaze zeroed in on the construction company, and I swallowed hard.

I could do this.

I repeated that to myself over and over as I opened the door and headed inside. Logically, I knew the chances of some other douchebag trying to plant cameras in my house were slim to none, but my brain just couldn't convince my body of that.

Whenever I thought about having someone over—even someone I trusted like Sutton or Rhodes—my hands got clammy, and my heart raced. Then everything came flooding back. The intimate images of me strewn across the internet. How a photo of me had been listed on an escort site with my phone number alongside it for *booking*. And I just couldn't do it.

But now, I didn't have a choice. I reminded myself of that as I climbed the stairs to a landing. There were four different doors and a few couches set up in case people needed to wait. I walked past an accountant's office, then a law firm, before reaching Castle Rock Construction.

My hand hovered just over the door handle. In one swift move, I pushed down before I could talk myself out of it.

As I stepped inside, a woman behind the desk looked up, a hint of surprise in her eyes—an emotion I was sure was echoed in mine.

"Raina."

She gave me a tentative smile. "Hi, Thea."

"I didn't know you worked here."

She nodded. "Yeah, it's my—"

"Hey, sweetcheeks, can you get me—?" The man's voice cut off as he stepped out of an office, gaze roaming over me. "You didn't say we had a client."

I didn't miss the reproach in his tone. It wasn't loud—most people would've missed it—but I was used to watching for the warnings of what was to come. I was familiar with walking on eggshells and constantly looking for any signs of unhappiness from my partner. So, I heard it loud and clear.

Raina did, too. Her face paled. "I'm sorry, Russ. She just walked through the door."

I forced a smile, even though my skin felt too tight, and the urge to bolt was strong. "I was just saying hi to Raina since I know her from the bakery."

Russ seemed to mull that over. "Never understood why my wife needs to go there when we got hot water here."

His wife. I struggled not to look at Raina, especially the bruise I knew hid beneath her concealer. Instead, I pushed my smile wider. "Guess you've never had one of our pastries, then."

His gaze lowered from my face to my chest. "Might just have to remedy that."

Gross.

"So," he continued, "what can we do for you today?"

The idea of having this man in my house turned my stomach, but if he was in the office, chances were, he wasn't one of the laborers. Sucking in a breath, I forced myself to push on. "I discovered a leak at my house. I'm not sure where it's coming from, but the floor in the guest bathroom is affected. And the main pipe leading to the house. I wanted to see what you guys would charge to take a look."

Russ let out a low whistle. "Leaks do a lot of damage. Won't know what we're dealing with till we get out there. Typically, a consult is two fifty, but…" His gaze roamed over me. "Might be willing to give you a discount, seeing as you're a friend of Raina's."

The man didn't hide the way his eyes lingered on my bare legs. The urge to cross them or find a piece of furniture to stand behind was strong. This time, I couldn't help but glance at Raina. It was only for a split second, but I saw that her eyes were downcast, her cheeks burning.

"And since you're a friend, I'll come out and do the consult myself." His barrel chest puffed up. "Not many get one of the owners coming out."

My gaze snapped back to him. That would be a hell-freaking-no for me. My tongue felt heavy in my mouth, suddenly thick as if I were having an allergic reaction. I swallowed, trying to get my words out while keeping my voice steady. "Thank you so much. I have a couple of other people to talk to, but I'll let you know."

Russ's eyes narrowed. "Who else you talkin' to?"

What was this, the gang warfare of construction?

"Clear Choice Plumbing and, um, Colson Construction." I wasn't sure why I stumbled over Shep's company's name or why I'd shared it at all. I guessed I was desperate for a backup.

The lines of strain deepened around Russ's mouth. "Clear Choice does good work, but they'd only be able to help with the leak, not the restoration."

I made a humming noise, not agreeing or disagreeing.

"And you should only use Colson if you want to get taken for a ride. They'll upcharge you on every little thing. It's a miracle they haven't been taken to court for fraud. Plus, the owner's a prick."

I stiffened at that. Shep was a lot of things. Pushy. Interfering.

Too charming for his own good. But the last thing I could see him doing was taking advantage of anyone. Rhodes had told me that he donated his and his crew's time to the local Habitat for Humanity organization each month. Meaning he ate his crew's salaries for those days just to help other people.

"I don't happen to share your opinion on that, but I appreciate you letting me know your thoughts. I'll be in touch if I think we're a fit for the job. Thanks for the information." I turned to Raina and waited until she met my eyes. "Hope to see you tomorrow."

She nodded quickly but did it glancing at her husband as if for approval. "You have a good day."

I dashed for the door before good ole Russ could stop me. And I kept right on going, getting on my bike and taking off back to Bloom. I made the trek in record time, a mixture of anxiety, anger, and annoyance fueling my muscles.

I was more certain than ever that Raina was in a bad situation. At best, her husband was an asshole. At worst? She was living a nightmare.

That thought turned my stomach as I swung off my bike.

Rhodes strode across the lot, carrying two massive, purple coneflower plants. "Where'd you go?"

A scowl rose to my lips without me even meaning to make the move. "Castle Rock Construction. You were right. The owner's a jerk."

Concern swept over Rhodes' face. "Which douche canoe did you get, Bob or Russ?"

"Russ," I grumbled.

"Let me guess. He hit on you while telling you he'd charge a million dollars to fix your problem."

"I should've listened to you."

Rhodes set the plants in the new display she was clearly in the middle of creating. "Normally, I would relish that sort of admission. But I'm sorry you had to deal with his assholery on an already crappy day."

I sighed. "What's his deal? I know Raina from the bakery…"

My words trailed off as I saw something pass over Rhodes' face. "What?" I pressed.

She shook her head. "I don't know for sure. All I *do* know is that Trace has been out to their house a few times. Calls from neighbors about yelling."

The sick feeling in my stomach intensified. Trace was Rhodes' eldest brother, who also happened to be the sheriff of our county. "She ever report Russ for anything?" I asked.

Rhodes shook her head. "Not once. The only thing Trace has ever been able to get him on is drunk and disorderly."

"I don't have a good feeling," I said quietly.

Rhodes reached out and squeezed my arm, her expression full of empathy. "Me either. But I also know you can't make someone ask for help."

God, did I know that. Nikki had gotten a bad feeling about my relationship with Brendan. She'd asked careful, gentle questions. And I'd lied like my life depended on it. It wasn't until after he'd ruined me that I told her most of it. But even then, I hadn't been able to tell her everything.

My vision went hazy, a mixture of the past and present colliding. "I wish there was something we could do."

"You're a good human, Thea."

Rhodes came back into focus in front of me, and I shook my head. "I'm a mess."

She grinned. "All the best people are."

Maybe she was right.

Rhodes drummed her fingers on her thigh. "So, can I ask Shep to help you?"

My stomach bottomed out at the hope in her eyes. "I don't know, Rho. It feels like taking advantage, and—"

Her hand snaked out, taking mine quickly and squeezing my fingers. "I think he needs this."

I frowned at her in confusion. "Needs to fix my leak?"

"Needs to feel like he's helping you." Rhodes dropped my hand and ran hers through her dark locks. "Not *you*. Someone. Anyone."

There was a slight desperation to Rhodes' words, which put me on edge. "Is everything okay?"

She shook her head and looked out over the nursery, but her eyes weren't truly focused. "He blames himself for what happened to me."

Something lit along my sternum, a twitchy sensation that made me want to shift in place. Rhodes had been through hell on Earth at the hands of a serial killer, and while we didn't talk about it, I knew she carried scars—both physical and emotional.

"Why would he blame himself for something a monster did?" I asked, pitching my voice low.

Rhodes scrubbed a hand over her face as if the fatigue from all that had happened was just now hitting her. "Because he hired Silas. Worked with him for years. Shep thinks it's his fault Silas had access to me."

The twitchy feeling inside me twisted into an ache. For Shep. It fit. The way he seemed to take on everything around him...of course, he would take this on, too. I swallowed hard, thinking about my blindness to a different monster. "We can't always see a person's capacity for evil. But that doesn't make us culpable. It just means we see the good in those around us."

I'd lost some of that along the way. Now, I looked for the darkness and not the light. And I'd hurt Shep by doing so. His face flashed in my mind, his stubbled, angular jaw and wounded, amber eyes.

As I blinked the picture away, I found Rhodes staring at me. There was curiosity in her gaze and a hint of worry, but she didn't open her mouth to push.

"You can ask him to help me," I said.

Rhodes' entire face lit up. "Thank you. Seriously. I really think he needs this."

"I'll pay him, though," I stressed. "I know there'll be no arguing with him cutting me a deal, but he's not working for free."

Rhodes chuckled. "You already know him too well."

And how was that? A handful of conversations that were only seconds long. Watching him from afar. Hearing Rhodes' stories.

Yet I knew the walls I'd built to keep everyone out, the ones that kept me safe, would have to be reinforced three times over with him. Not because Shep would set out to do me harm but because I sensed he had the power to slip right through my barriers.

Chapter Eight

Shep

I SLAMMED MY TRUCK'S DOOR AND STEPPED OUT INTO THE GARAGE just as the door slid closed. Twisting my neck, I felt the telltale pop and release of tension. Not enough. We were juggling more jobs than we should, and adding a personal project to the slate meant we were past our limits. But I couldn't resist the old farmhouse; it was too much of a hidden gem.

Lifting my phone, I used the app to unlock the door to my house. Most people wouldn't add a lock to the door between the garage and the home, but I wasn't most people.

I'd grown up in a house that had taken in kids from the roughest of circumstances. I knew that bad things could find you wherever you lived and thus prepared accordingly. I just used tech to do it.

The moment the door opened, a soft beeping sounded. As I plugged in the alarm code, I heard the AC kick on. Summers in Sparrow Falls had a large swing. The nights could get down to the forties, but the days could reach one hundred. I left the thermostat at seventy-eight while I was gone, but the moment my electronic locks turned, it was programmed to drop to seventy-four.

Lights flicked on automatically as I walked through the modern Craftsman. It had more room than I needed, with four bedrooms and five baths, but that just meant a higher resale value when it went on the market next week. As I opened the fridge, my phone dinged with an incoming text.

> **Mara:** *You didn't tell me the Juniper Lane house was getting featured in* The Tribune. *This is amazing! We should celebrate!*

I frowned at my screen. If you read between the lines, the text was equal parts quiet accusation, congratulations, and gentle suggestion for us to spend time together. It had annoyance sweeping through me. And fast on its heels…guilt.

As I stared at the device, the screen shifted—an incoming video call. Relief swept through me at having an excuse not to answer Mara's text. I hit accept, and Cope's face filled the screen, his penthouse apartment in downtown Seattle as the backdrop.

"Dude," he clipped. "Are you avoiding me?"

I grabbed a beer from the fridge and let the door shut as I straightened. "Some of us actually work for a living, dipshit."

"It might be offseason, but my ass was in the gym at six this morning."

Opening one of my drawers, I fumbled for a bottle opener. "Do you want a gold star? I could make you a little chart. I was up at five-thirty and just got home. What have you been doing all afternoon?"

Cope scowled into the camera in answer.

I barked out a laugh. "Sitting on your ass playing Xbox?"

His silence was my answer.

"That's what I thought. Now, what's so important that you called me"—I checked the count on my notifications—"eight times? Or were you just bored?" I knew it hadn't been an emergency. If anything was truly urgent, Cope would've followed the call with a text saying he needed to talk. But my younger brother had been hovering lately, sending me into avoidance mode.

Cope shifted on his couch. "I wanted to hear about your haunted house."

"It's not haunted."

Cope arched a brow. "That shit needs to be exorcised before you start work. I'd call a priest ASAP. Maybe get some holy water. I bet you can order it on Amazon these days."

My lips twitched. "I think I'll be good."

"You gonna stay in the Craftsman while you rehab?"

I shook my head. "Jennie's putting it on the market next week."

Cope let out a low whistle. "Where are you gonna stay?"

"Not sure yet. Probably a rental." Given how busy things had been, I hadn't had time to look for one, but I could put Jennie on the case.

"Stay at my place. There's plenty of room, and I won't be home for a few weeks."

I took a long pull from my beer, letting the cool liquid wash away the day. "You know me. I need my own space."

While Cope's house on its large pond outside of town was massive, he'd be interfering the moment he got back. And with our youngest sister, Arden, living in a guesthouse on the property, it was a little too much family togetherness for me.

It wasn't that I didn't love them or want to spend time with them. It was that I needed to know I had space and time to let everything go. To not have to be...*on.*

Cope frowned. The expression looked foreign on his face. "You always did like your weird little alone time."

I snorted. Cope and Fallon were the Colsons' biological children, along with Jacob, before he passed. So, we'd been together since the two of them were born. Cope knew all about my need to retreat. When we were growing up, I'd go to the treehouse or the creek— anywhere I could just breathe.

"Maybe I'm into meditation or just wanted to get away from your nosy ass." At four years younger than my thirty-four, Cope had been my constant tagalong.

"Hey, you asked me for playoff tickets. Now who's the tagalong?"

I grinned. "Fair enough. But what can I say? It's always a joy to watch you get your ass kicked."

Cope glared at me through the phone. "When I get home, you and I are hitting that new rink. I'll show you an ass-kicking."

There'd be no contest. Cope would wipe the ice with me. He was a beast. As easygoing as he was off the ice, he turned into another person when his skates hit it. It made me wonder what my brother was keeping so bottled up.

"Fair enough." I glanced at my watch. "I gotta go. I need to stop at Arden's before I run to family dinner."

"Okay, but quick. How are you doing?"

My gut twisted at how Cope's voice lost all its humor, and serious concern filled it. "I'm good. Why wouldn't I be?"

He sent me a pointed look. "Don't pull the bull with me. I know you better than that."

My back teeth ground together. "Rho's good. She's healing. Anson says the nightmares are better, too. So, if she's good? I'm good."

Cope was quiet for a long moment, taking me in. That study called me a liar, but he didn't push. This time. "Okay. You need to talk shit out, just call."

"Sure." I wouldn't. I'd bury it. Or I'd take it out on whatever house I was working on. But that was how I dealt. My dad had understood that. When I was growing up, he was the one who'd realized I needed to do something with my hands to work through whatever I was dealing with.

He'd put me to work fixing fences on the ranch, then helping him build a new shed or fix up the barn. Through him, I'd discovered my love for both creating something from nothing and bringing back things that had been neglected and forgotten. We'd lost him years ago, but I still felt the ache of missing him every time I started something new.

"Tell everyone hey for me," Cope said, breaking into my thoughts.

"Will do."

"Later, Bob the Builder," Cope clipped, hitting end on the call before I could say anything back.

I just shook my head and went in search of a hot shower. It wasn't long before I was clean, changed, and headed toward Cope's place. As I pulled up to the gate and rolled down my window, I heard the whir of a camera moving. The lens zeroed in on my face as I plugged in the code.

Security was necessary for Cope, thanks to his hockey-star status. We didn't get a lot of lookie-loos out this far, but there was the occasional superfan. And if security wasn't in place, they'd drive right up to his front door.

But the safety measures shielded Arden, too. Not that she couldn't take care of her own damn self.

The moment the gates opened, I eased off the brake. You couldn't see any of the structures on the property from here, just a paved road flanked by aspen trees. It curved for a handful of minutes, crossing over a creek I knew fed into the large pond the main house butted up against. Finally, the road opened to show the majestic landscape.

The house itself was a blend of deep, reddish wood, stone, and glass. You couldn't see in the massive windows, but I knew from being in on the design that you could damn well see out. One side faced Castle Rock with its golden faces, and the other had a floor-to-ceiling view of the Monarch Mountains with the pond right below them. I had no idea how Cope could leave it empty for most of the year.

I kept driving past the main house and over another bridge to a smaller guest cottage. The architecture mirrored the main structure, but this one had a massive workshop behind it—because Arden needed huge for her projects. That and a barn in the distance that housed her two beloved horses.

I pulled in next to a pickup that made me scowl. She'd had the same one since high school. Now, it was rusted in spots, and the bed was scratched to hell from her carting around materials and finished masterpieces. She needed something new. And given how much she got paid for her art, she could damn well afford it.

Turning off the engine, I slid out of my truck and headed for her workshop door. There was no question where she would be, even if the strains of hard rock hadn't given her away. Sometimes, I wondered if Arden ever went back to her house or if she just slept on the couch in here for a couple of hours at a time.

I reached out and tested the doorknob. Unlocked. My scowl deepened as I opened the door to deafening sounds I wasn't sure could be classified as music.

I took one step, and an enormous Cane Corso stepped into my path. At least the mastiff was something because Arden wasn't the slightest bit aware of my presence.

"*Beruhigen*," I told the dog, and his quivering muscles relaxed at the German command. I reached out and scratched behind his ears. "How's it hanging, Brutus?"

He leaned into me, relishing the affection.

The music flicked off a second later, but Arden didn't turn around from the drafting desk, her hand still flying across a giant sheet of paper. "What's up, Shep?"

My lips twitched. At least she hadn't turned off the security system alerts. "I'm here to get you for dinner."

"Can't. In the middle of something."

I glanced at the giant heap of metal in the center of the room. It didn't look like anything discernible yet, but it would. My gaze returned to her as I moved in that direction. "You're always in the middle of something. But if you don't show tonight, both Mom and Lolli will come over here. And you know Mom will start cleaning, organizing, and asking why there's no food in your fridge."

Arden's head flew up, sending her hair flying as piercing, gray-violet eyes locked with mine. "I went two weeks ago."

"Three," I informed her.

She cursed, dropping her pencil to the table's little ledge.

I couldn't help but chuckle. "It's family dinner, not torture."

"Yeah, yeah," Arden muttered as she ran a hand through her hair, revealing gray smudges along the side of her pinky finger and palm. "I was in a flow."

"When aren't you in a flow?" I challenged.

She stuck out her tongue at me but pushed off the stool. "All right. Just let me grab my gym bag. I'm supposed to spar with Kye later."

Arden crossed the room to the worn leather couch with smudged paint in different places. A black gym bag lay on one side. I knew it was stuffed full of her jiu-jitsu gear. As she hoisted it over her shoulder, Brutus looked up at me balefully.

"We gonna take the beast?" I asked.

Arden nodded. "*Komm*," she called to Brutus, and he let out a happy bark.

She couldn't take him everywhere, but I knew she was always more comfortable when she could. But I would be, too, given that Brutus had come to Arden after two years of highly intensive training.

She sent me an annoyed look. "Let's go."

I couldn't help but chuckle. "So demanding."

Arden just rolled her eyes and headed for my truck, helping Brutus jump into the back seat. She was quiet like usual as we drove, staring out the window at the passing landscape. I knew she was likely pulling inspiration for some new creation. But when Arden finally spoke, I realized I'd been wrong.

"Are you doing okay?" she asked, her raspy voice dipping lower.

Hell. If Arden was worried about me, I needed to do a better job of burying that shit.

"Yeah. I'm good. Just itching to get started on the new restoration project." None of that was a lie. I was okay. Living, breathing. I didn't carry the scars Rhodes did.

Arden turned toward me, her gray-violet eyes piercing. "I know what it's like to live with monsters. Ones you can recognize, and ones you can't. It changes you."

Everything in me spiraled in a vicious squeeze. I did not want her to go back to that time, even in some misguided attempt to help me. "Arden—"

"None of it was your fault," she said, cutting me off.

I snapped my mouth closed.

Arden turned back to the window. "One day, you'll believe that. But if you need a reminder, I'm always here."

I tried to swallow the burn in my throat, but I couldn't get it to move. Grace. That was the gift she was giving me. I just wasn't sure I deserved it.

Chapter Nine

Thea

"**Y**OU ARE A LIFESAVER," SUTTON SAID AS SHE SHIFTED A massive bag of flour over to the other side of the storeroom. I grinned as she swiped a hand over her face, leaving streaks of flour in her wake. She was constantly covered in the stuff. "It's no problem, really. You know I like the extra hours."

It was more than *liking* them, it was *needing* them. My credit had been thoroughly trashed during the whole Brendan ordeal. The only way I'd been able to secure a mortgage was because Nikki had assumed a figurehead role at the trust that purchased the property.

I'd had to freeze my credit so no new cards could be opened or purchases made in my name. The only money I had was what Sutton and Duncan were—thankfully—willing to pay me in cash. Every time I hid it in the tin beneath a wobbly floorboard in my closet, I felt like one of those deranged conspiracy theorists who didn't believe in banks or the government.

But I guessed I could see where they were coming from more

these days. Anything tech-related was fallible—a risk I couldn't afford to take.

So, I scrimped, saved, and hid it all away.

Sutton shifted to face me. "Everything's okay, right? I can probably extend your shifts if you need—"

I shook my head, cutting her off. Sutton was struggling with a small business and her son. She didn't need me on her conscience, too. "I'm good. I have the nursery now, and Dunc said he's keeping me on year-round."

Sutton's whole face brightened as she pulled me in for a hug. "That's amazing! I'm so happy for you. I know you love working there."

"I am a little more knowledgeable about plants than baking."

Sutton laughed as she released me. "You're good at the bread. And you're an expert taster. That's more important here. You can guide customers to their perfect treat."

I grinned back at her. "This is *very* true. And that pumpkin spice latte cupcake you're testing for fall?" I made an exaggerated fainting motion. "Perfection."

Sutton did a jump in the air, letting out a squeal like a little kid. "I loved it, too. I'll try it on the menu as soon as we hit September. Should get us in the fall mood."

"People will love it. Especially when you pair it with that drink." I knew the high school girls who came in regularly would be all over it.

"I hope you're right. I've got some watermelon ones I'm trying tomorrow, too. They're super cute. The cake is green, and the frosting's pink with mini chocolate chips for the seeds."

I frowned at her. "I'm not sure how I feel about green cake."

Sutton chuckled. "Luca wanted me to make zombie cupcakes with the batter."

"I bet he did." I marked off the second bag of flour on our inventory sheet and moved the sack to the other side of the room. "How was skating today?"

Sutton sighed as she grabbed the third bag. "He's definitely got the bug. Of course, he had to pick the most expensive sport imaginable to fall in love with."

"Hey, at least it wasn't horseback riding or Formula 1," I offered.

"True. But I wish he would've fallen in love with drawing or ballet. I can't say I'm thrilled with my kid wanting to smash into other kids on a freezing-cold ice rink."

"Fair enough. They must keep the full contact to a minimum at this age, right?" I asked.

"They don't have a team yet, so I'm not sure. I think they're still looking for a coach. But in the meantime, they've all been playing hockey superstar during open-skating time. I just brace the whole time, but at least he's happy."

The wistfulness in Sutton's voice had me turning toward her. She never spoke about her ex, and I'd never seen any sign of him. All I knew was that she'd moved to Sparrow Falls to start over. It seemed this was the place for that.

I squeezed her arm. "You're a good mom."

The corner of her mouth kicked up. "You sure about that? My kid is sitting in the store right now eating cupcakes and playing games on his tablet."

"Everyone deserves a treat at the end of the day."

"That is true." Sutton straightened. "And you do, too. Because I think we're done." She dusted the flour off her hands. "Let me give you some of our leftovers from the day."

"Not too much," I warned. "You always forget I only have one stomach."

"You need to eat more," Sutton said, heading out of the storeroom and down the hall to the main bakery.

Luca looked up as we walked in. He had blue icing from a Cookie Monster cupcake smeared across his face as he grinned. "The kittens are snoring."

I glanced at the carrier, seeing the pile of fluff inside. They were definitely getting used to people, between coming with me to the nursery and being here. "They always love a nap after they eat."

"Can I name one of them Zombie?" Luca asked hopefully.

I couldn't help but laugh. "I'm not sure the name Zombie will help a kitten get adopted."

Luca frowned. "Okay, what about The Reaper? That's what they call my favorite hockey player."

"See why I'm concerned?" Sutton asked as she handed me a bakery box. "What kind of sport gives people that sort of name?"

"The awesome kind," Luca said with a blue-stained grin.

Sutton just shook her head and grabbed the kitten carrier. "Let me help you get loaded up."

"Thanks," I said, ruffling Luca's hair. "Don't kill too many zombies."

"Can't promise that," he called, looking back at his game.

Sutton and I headed out into the evening air, still warm from the scorcher of a day. The sun hung low over the horizon, but plenty of light was left in the sky for me to make it home safely. As we approached my bike, I squinted. Something about it looked off. As we got closer, I saw what it was. Both my tires were flat.

A prickle of unease slid through me as I crouched by the back tire, running my fingers over it. A long, angry slash went straight through the rubber, and the front one had a mirroring slice.

My unease twisted into panic as I scanned the streets. I saw no one but a handful of people outside The Soda Pop—the diner a few blocks down. Other than a couple of restaurants, Sparrow Falls closed up early.

The tiny hairs on the tops of my arms rose. Someone had done this purposefully. Had taken a blade to my tires and then gone on about their night. Or were they watching right now?

Sweat broke out down my spine as panic dug in. Was it Brendan? My mind spun with all the precautions I'd taken. The trust. Never changing my driver's license from my California one. Nikki owning my car. The post office box two towns over, under the trust's name. I'd been so careful.

"Oh, my God," Sutton clipped. "Those damn teenagers."

My gaze snapped to her. "Teenagers?"

She glared at my bike. "A few of them have been causing all sorts of trouble. Trace brought them in for spray-painting the back of The Pop last week, but a few other store owners have said they didn't get the message. The boys are still vandalizing whatever they can get their hands on."

Sutton squeezed my arm. "I'm so sorry. I can give you a ride home and get you new tires."

Troublemaking teenagers. Random vandalism. That was all it was. I repeated it over and over. But I wasn't sure I believed it.

Chapter Ten

Shep

THE MOMENT THE SPRAWLING RANCH CAME INTO VIEW, A familiar feeling spread through me. A warm ache. Gratitude that this was where I'd ended up when it could've been so much worse.

The sprawling fields with grazing cattle and a dozen or so horses spread out around the white farmhouse with its wraparound porch. Mom had managed to keep it running with the help of an expert team of ranch hands, even after Dad had passed. But none of us kids had ever gotten the bug to take over the operation.

I pulled between Anson's dark truck and Fallon's car. Kye's blacked-out truck with its intricate detailing sat on the other side of Fallon's vehicle—always together, even in parking. Trace's SUV sat closer to the barn, and I knew his daughter, Keely, had likely made him come over early so she could go riding.

Shutting off the engine, I grabbed Arden's bag.

"I can get it," she said.

"So can I," I shot back.

She stuck her tongue out at me. "Always the white knight."

I didn't feel like one much these days. I felt like a murky gray one at best. As we walked up the steps, I could already hear the voices inside: Keely's squeals of delight, Rhodes' uninhibited laughter, Lolli yelling at someone.

I reached for the doorknob, testing it. Of course, it was open. I scowled down at it but opened the door.

The moment we walked inside, Keely jumped up. "Uncle Shep! Auntie Arden!" She raced toward us, leaping into the air with all her six-year-old strength. I caught her and hauled her into my arms. She immediately leaned toward Arden. "I rode Smoky, and we went so fast! I wanted to keep going all the way to the mountains, but Dad said we had to come back."

Arden smiled, reaching out to ruffle Keely's hair as Brutus sat dutifully at her side. "Maybe we can do a camping trip before you go back to school."

Keely's eyes went wide with delight, and she twisted in my arms, squirming to get down. She raced back to Trace. "Can we, Daddy? Can we?"

He grinned down at her. "Sure. Weekend after next?"

I knew it burned that Trace didn't always have his girl. His divorce hadn't been ugly, but it wasn't easy either. And it killed him every time he lost Keely for a week.

"Yes! Yes! Yes!" Keely shouted, dancing around the room.

Mom chuckled as she crossed to me and Arden. "So happy you made it." She reached up onto her tiptoes to kiss my cheek. Nora Colson wasn't a tall woman, but the fierceness in her tiny frame was unparalleled.

She pulled Arden into a hug, rocking her back and forth. "I've missed you."

Arden was a bit awkward with the affection but hugged Mom back anyway. "Sorry, Nora. Been in the art haze."

Everyone handled the name thing differently. I'd never known Nora as anything but *Mom*. But I'd also come into her care as an infant. While Trace had come to live with us at twelve, he had also quickly adopted the term. Rhodes, Arden, and Kye had all gone for *Nora*. Mom never minded. She loved all of us the same.

"Finally," Lolli huffed from her spot by the massive picture window. "I've been waiting for you to get here so I can unveil my latest piece."

She stood, billowy dress swaying, and the dozens of necklaces looped around her neck tinkling against one another. Everyone looked her way. Fallon and Kye peered from their spots on the couch. Rhodes glanced up from where she was curled in Anson's lap in an armchair. Trace looked on in a worried way.

Lolli quickly crossed to something leaning against the far wall, a towel covering it. She tugged off the covering and held it up for all of us to see. The canvas was covered in countless glittering gemstones—Lolli's latest hobby. But she couldn't simply do the normal paint-by-numbers sort of deal. She had to do her own thing—her own always inappropriate thing.

Kye started coughing, trying to cover his laugh.

Fallon gaped at the artwork, cheeks flaming red. "Is that? Are they naked? On horseback?"

"Pretty sure they're having sex on horseback, Fal," Kye said, lips twitching.

I couldn't look away from Lolli's *art*. The two people on the horse appeared human but had massive wings and definitely looked... joined.

"Don't say the s-word," Keely said matter-of-factly. "It makes Dad's face get red."

"Jesus," Trace muttered, scrubbing a hand over said face. "Let's pray my kid doesn't talk about this at horseback-riding camp."

Lolli's gaze snapped to him. "If any camp has something against talking openly and honestly about sex, send them to me."

Rhodes choked on a laugh. "I can just imagine that conversation, Lolli."

She let out a huff. "Repression will kill you. You'll die of a stroke or a heart attack. Life is for the living."

"Preach it," Kye agreed.

Fallon sent him a look I couldn't quite read. Concern or annoyance, maybe?

Kye definitely lived life to the fullest. After he'd come to live with us at sixteen, he'd gotten in more trouble than any other foster Nora had taken care of. There were late-night police station visits and countless meetings with the principal. But he'd settled, finding different ways to let out whatever haunted him.

Training in mixed martial arts. Racing bikes. And his art. It was probably thanks to Lolli that he'd found his love for drawing, but I was sure no one had expected him to ink that art on his skin and others'. And now, folks came from all over the world to have him work on them.

"So," Lolli said, glancing around the room, "who wants it for their house?"

Silence reigned around us. I swore I could hear crickets chirping. But I already had a half-naked elf man behind my office door. I couldn't do this, too.

"You prudes," Lolli grumbled.

Kye grinned. "I'll take it for the shop. My piercer's into all that fairy shit. She'll love it."

Mom glared at Kye. "Language, please."

Kye's lips twitched. "Sorry, Nora."

She just shook her head. "I should've grounded you more in high school."

Rhodes slid from Anson's lap and crossed to me. He watched her as she went, never taking his eyes off her. All careful watchfulness, making sure she was okay. Safe.

"Do you have a minute?" Rhodes asked.

My muscles wound tight, bracing, but I nodded. "Sure."

She motioned me back toward the entryway. The fact that she felt the conversation needed privacy only sent more tension threading through me. But still, I followed.

Rhodes glanced toward the living room as if to make sure no one was listening.

"Are you okay?" I asked, a whole new set of worries taking root.

"Me? I'm fine," she said quickly. "I wanted to talk to you about Thea."

The tension was back but for an entirely different reason. Thea's face had played in my mind all day at the jobsite. Her true terror at having me in her space. Her stubborn resolve to handle the problem on her own. I did everything I could to keep my voice even, almost disinterested. "What about her?"

"She said you helped her with a leak at her house."

I nodded. "As much as she'd let me."

Rhodes worried the corner of her lip. "She went to Castle Rock Construction yesterday."

I couldn't help the curse. The owner, Bob, was old school. Slightly sexist and definitely oblivious. But his son? Russ was a piece of work and always had been.

We'd been in the same year at school, and he treated everyone like dirt. But he'd hated me particularly. Loved calling me *Box Baby* in elementary and hadn't much grown out of that.

"Tell me she didn't hire them." Castle Rock did shoddy work at best, and they'd overcharge for what they *did* manage to execute.

"Thankfully, no," Rhodes said. "I might've convinced Thea to let you help her."

A hum lit my muscles, phantom energy that buzzed. "You sure about that? She wouldn't even let me inside her house to check out the issue."

Pain flashed across Rhodes' face, and I wanted to kick myself. Still, she pushed on. "I don't know what happened to her, but I know she's running from something. Dunc pays her in cash. And she doesn't have a phone or an email address."

Everything in me went on alert. "No phone or email?" I didn't know a soul without both.

Rhodes shook her head. "I think she needs someone who will go at her pace. Do whatever it takes to make her feel comfortable."

A million possibilities played in my mind, but none were good. All of them made a sick feeling take root in my gut.

"Shep?" Rhodes prodded.

"Sorry," I mumbled, pulling myself out of my spiraling thoughts.

"Will you help her?"

I swallowed through the tightness in my throat. "Of course."

But my offer of that assistance and Thea taking it were two different things. And I didn't see her letting me in anytime soon. Something about that burned. Scalded in a way I was desperate to heal. But Thea would have to take the first step. And I wasn't sure she ever would.

Chapter Eleven

Thea

A LOUD BANG SOUNDED, AND I JUMPED, ALMOST BUNGLING THE frosting I was coloring a light shade of pink.

Walter glanced at me from the wash station, concern written all over his face. "Sorry about that. You all right?"

All he'd done was set a pot in the sink—something he'd done countless times before. But today, it had almost made me give myself a frosting facial.

It didn't matter that Sutton had told me all about the vandalizing teens on the car ride home and said the tire prank was right in line with the other things they'd done. I was on edge. My gaze jumped from one thing to the next. I analyzed every person who came into the bakery, searching for anything that might mean danger.

I couldn't turn it off. Couldn't get my body to simply relax. My muscles felt more like cement than sinew.

Still, I forced a smile for the man who treated me like a granddaughter. "I'm good. I didn't sleep the best last night. I'm a little out of it."

All of that was true. I'd just left out the *reasons* for it all.

The lines around Walter's eyes deepened as he squinted, trying to read me. "Make sure you take some of our Sleepytime tea home. That always does the trick for me. Maybe put a pinch of bourbon in it."

My lips twitched as I moved to cover the icing and set it at Sutton's decorating station. "I'm pretty sure it's the bourbon sending you to sleep land."

Walter grinned and headed back to the stove. "A little bit of the good stuff never hurt anybody."

It had been so long since I'd had a drink. Even though I'd been in Sparrow Falls for almost two years without any trouble, I still didn't consume anything that might dull my reaction time. I couldn't afford to.

My drug of choice was reading. The books I picked up from the secondhand store for a nickel, or the ones I checked out from the library, thanks to Sutton's library card. The subject matter varied widely: murder mysteries, tales from other planets, and my favorite, epic romances. But I had one rule. There had to be a happy ending. There was enough hardship in the real world. I needed hope in my stories.

So, when I couldn't sleep last night, I'd picked up a book about a grumpy, single-dad cowboy who was falling for his nanny despite his heroic efforts not to. It had kept me company until three in the morning, when I finally drifted off.

I patted Walter's shoulder as I moved through the kitchen toward the register. "We all deserve more than a little of the good stuff."

He grinned at me. "Damn straight, girlie."

I chuckled as I headed behind the counter. With a quick survey, I found that Sutton was drowning. She was moving from table to table, clearing and wiping, but two other people were in line at the register.

I stepped up and smiled at a woman standing there—the same one who'd been talking with Shep the day I'd dumped icing on him. "Hi, Mara. What'll it be?"

She smiled, the action full of warmth. Everything about her fit that persona. With golden-blond hair and cornflower blue eyes, she was beautiful. And her delicate features and petite form created the kind of figure that made men want to protect her.

Just looking at her made me feel anything *but* that. With my long, gangly limbs and dingy clothes, I felt like a shabby giant next to her.

"I'll take a caramel latte with an extra shot, please. And a slice of lemon poppyseed bread."

I nodded, selecting the items on the tablet screen. "That'll be nine fifty."

Mara pulled out a credit card and held it to the reader. "Thank you."

"Of course." I hurried to fill her order, but as I did, I caught sight of a newcomer in the bakery. Rhodes' wild, dark hair was piled in a knot on the top of her head, and she was dressed in her Bloom T-shirt and shorts. The moment she saw me, her face brightened, and she waved.

I couldn't help the frisson of nerves I felt as she moved to get in line. I knew she'd planned to talk to Shep and ask him to take pity on me and help with the leak. Part of me hoped he'd said no. Then, I wouldn't have to wrestle with the beast that was my anxiety about having someone in my space.

The other part of me, the smarter bit, prayed he'd agreed. This morning, I'd had to stop at a campground for a shower. And I was currently flushing my toilets with buckets of water I'd filled in the greenhouse. I needed to find that leak and stat.

Sutton hurried behind the counter, shaking me out of my spiraling thoughts. She squeezed my arm as she passed. "I'll do drinks. What'd she order?"

"Caramel latte, extra shot."

"Got it."

I hurried to hand Mara her slice of poppyseed bread. "There you go. Your drink will be up in just a second."

I felt her gaze on me, probing. Not in a rude way, but curious. It made sense with the tail end of the fight she'd caught between Shep and me, but I didn't like the intense focus. So, I ignored it.

"Thank you," Mara said. Even her voice was musical and delicate.

I headed back to the register and took the order of a man who looked like he'd been hiking all morning. The fact that he ordered half the menu was more proof of that. Once he was settled, I looked at Rhodes.

She grinned at me. "Just gets busier and busier."

I nodded, thankful no one was behind her, and I didn't have to rush. "Tourist season is still in full swing."

"True enough." Rhodes glanced toward the bakery case. "Cherry Coke cupcakes. I gotta try one of those."

One corner of my mouth kicked up. "I have to say, I was skeptical when Sutton whipped up that recipe, but they're amazing."

Rhodes pulled a small card wallet from her pocket. "I have no doubt. Sutton has a mad genius brain when it comes to baking."

"I heard that," Sutton called from the coffee machine.

Rhodes laughed. "I'll never understand how you do it."

"One-track mind," Sutton answered. "Always thinking about sugar."

"And we're damn thankful for that," Rhodes shot back, then turned to me as she paid, a grin pulling at her lips. "Shep said he's happy to help with your project."

Relief and panic swept through me in equal measure. "Okay," I said, my voice tight as if my throat was strangling the word.

Rhodes saw the strain and reached across the counter, laying her hand over mine. "He'll have it fixed in no time, and then you won't have to stress anymore. You get off at three, right?"

I nodded quickly. I'd had to take my car today since my bike was still without tires. "I need to grab one thing on my way home, so I'm there any time after four."

"I'll let him know," Rhodes said, releasing my hand.

The fact that I didn't have a phone to text him with just made me feel like more of a freak. I did have one of those pay-as-you-go deals shoved into my nightstand, just in case I needed the fire department or the police. But it was one I'd bought with cash at a gas station just before I got to the Oregon state line.

I hadn't powered the thing up since moving to Sparrow Falls. So, who knew if it even still worked. And the fact that it was a flip phone meant sending a text would take a half hour.

"Thank you," I whispered.

Something prickled on the back of my neck, a telltale sign that someone was watching.

I did a quick scan of the room, and my eyes landed back on Mara. She was staring again as if trying to put pieces together.

Shit.

The last thing I needed was someone digging into me. When I moved here, I'd begun going by my middle name, hoping that would give me a modicum of protection. But it wasn't like I had some elaborate fake identity to protect me. If anyone had my first name and did a quick Google search, they'd find everything—including the photos that showed it all.

Bile swirled in my stomach as the heat of shame rose to my cheeks. But I shoved it all down. I hadn't broken yet, and I wouldn't start today.

Instead, I got Rhodes her cupcake and added a second to the box. "One for Anson. On me."

Rhodes grinned. "If you're not careful, the two of you are going to become besties."

I snorted at that. Rhodes' boyfriend was as surly as they came, but the way he melted around her was a sight to behold. "I don't think there's any risk of that. His communication skills are limited to grunts and scowls."

Rhodes burst out laughing. "Come on, he's getting better at using his words."

That was true enough. Because she'd changed him. Healed something in him that had brought him back to life. And that was the most precious gift.

I handed her the bakery box just as Sutton offered Mara her latte. Rhodes grinned at me. "Thanks, Thea." She gave the woman next to her a little wave. "Good to see you, Mara." And then she bowed toward Sutton. "Thank you, supreme queen of all baked goods."

Sutton burst out laughing. "I love her."

"Me, too," I echoed as Mara followed Rhodes to the door.

Sutton turned to face me. "So, you're actually going to let Shep help you?"

"Eavesdrop much?" I muttered.

Sutton just grinned. "Gotta get my info somehow."

I knew she was joking, but I still couldn't stop a little prickle of guilt from surfacing. She'd been so good to me, and all I'd given her were lies and half-truths.

All amusement fled Sutton's face. "Hey, what's wrong?"

I shook my head. "Nothing."

She sent a stern look my way. "You look like someone just stabbed you. That's not *nothing*."

I swallowed hard, trying to loosen my tightening throat. "I just… I'm not good with people in my space."

Sutton's brows pulled together. "And Shep will have to be in your house to fix the leak and the damage it caused."

I nodded. It wasn't the whole truth, but it was more than I'd ever given her before.

Sutton leaned against the bakery case. "Do you know how Shep started helping me with the reno on this place?"

I shook my head.

"He was walking by and saw me trying to lug a section of banquette on my own. He didn't even pause. Just came right up and said, 'I've got the other end.'" Sutton smiled. "When we got the first one in, he asked where the rest of them were. I was in so far over my head that I didn't even argue. When we were done, he asked me to walk him through my plans. So, I did."

Sutton chuckled, shaking her head at the memory. "He didn't tell me I was out of my mind to try to handle it on my own. He just said, 'Might help to have two sets of hands for some of this. I can give you my Saturdays this month and have my guys help place the beams when they're delivered.'"

She turned to me then, and I saw her eyes shining with unshed tears. "Just like that. Never asked for anything in return. Helped every weekend for a month. A few nights, too. Sent over a paint sprayer so I could do the walls ten times faster. He's a good man, Thea."

"I know," I whispered, my throat in a vise grip. "But I thought another man was good once. He turned out to be anything but. Now, I can't get myself to trust, no matter how much I want to."

Sutton's eyes flashed, and her hand snaked out to take mine. She held it so tightly I lost all circulation. "I know how that is, Thea. I know what it's like to think life is one thing and for all of that to change in a split second."

My heart hammered against my ribs because there was a fire in Sutton's gaze—flames of anger and hurt.

"But we can't let one bad experience sour the rest of our lives. We can't let the bad win. Make us stop living. If we lock ourselves down, we don't just keep out the bad. We keep out the good, too."

My eyes burned, the pain of her words striking deep. Because I knew she was right. I'd locked my fortress up tight. It meant I was safe, but it also meant I was alone.

I paced my front yard. Back and forth, and back again. It was a miracle I hadn't dug a trench in the graveled dirt with my boots.

I'd done everything I could think to do over the past hour and a half. After stopping to buy a new set of bike tires that put a hole in my reserves, I'd come home, settled the kittens, and played with Moose. Then I'd refilled my hummingbird feeders, but the deft escape artists hadn't enchanted me like they usually did. So, I'd headed to the greenhouse to water my plants and pull weeds. After that, I'd moved to weed pulling and watering in the flower beds around the house. My gardens were in pristine condition, but I still had more nervous energy than I knew what to do with.

The sound of an engine had my head snapping up. The road leading to my house had plenty of tree cover, but that also meant I couldn't see who was coming until they were close. But the gravel meant I heard them.

Finally, a silver truck came into view as it rounded the final turn. The way the sun hit the metallic paint made it seem more perfect. Somehow, the vehicle was impeccably clean, despite the fact that I knew Shep drove dirt roads on the regular. Shiny and perfect, just like the man himself.

I glanced down at myself. I was wearing Carhartt overalls with dirt on the knees and smudges across the stomach. The tank top I had on beneath had seen better days, too. I tried to tell myself that my messy state was for the best, but a part of me wished I'd opted for the one pair of nice jeans I had and at least a clean shirt.

A door shut, making my head snap up to see Shep striding toward me. He wore dark jeans that hugged his hips and revealed muscular thighs as he walked. His white tee strained across a defined chest that was all lean muscle. The ballcap he wore read *Colson Construction* and hid his amber eyes from view, but I felt them on me.

I swallowed hard as he came to a stop a few feet from me. "Hi," I squeaked.

"Hey, Thorn," he said, his voice rough.

I let out a breath, trying to calm my racing heart. "Thanks for, um, coming back."

"It's no problem. Water still off?"

I nodded.

He frowned. "Have you been staying somewhere else?"

I shook my head. Apparently, I'd lost the ability to form words. Even though Shep was feet away, his scent teased my nose. He smelled like sawdust, cedar, and a hint of sweat. The combination was somehow the best thing I'd ever smelled.

But Shep wasn't nearly as happy. His mouth twisted into a scowl. "You've been staying in a house with no water?"

I tried swallowing again, hoping it would clear my throat. "I've still got water in the greenhouse. I've been bringing it over to the house."

A muscle ticked along Shep's jaw. "We're gonna get this fixed so you can have water in your goddamned house again."

The ferocity behind his words had me taking a step back. It was instinct, and I couldn't have stopped it if I tried. But my action made Shep freeze. Even though I couldn't see his eyes, I saw pain streaking across his face. He, too, took a step back.

"I'm sorry," he said softly. "Not mad at you. Mad at the fact that you've got no water in your house. No one should live that way."

My tongue stuck to the roof of my mouth, but I managed to get my vocal cords to work. "It's really okay. It's like camping."

Shep's mouth looked like it was trying to smile but couldn't quite get there. "I guess that's one way to look at it." His hands moved as he took off his ballcap and flipped it around so I could finally see those beautiful amber eyes. "You think you're ready for me to go inside and have a look at the bathroom?"

The moment he spoke, I lost the awe I felt at seeing those gorgeous eyes. Because panic was setting in. Memories pounded against the carefully constructed walls in my mind. The aftermath of letting someone into my home before. The voice that echoed in my head. *"You ruin everything."*

Shep's jaw clenched, and then he forced it to release. "Okay, no inside today. There's plenty I can do out here. I'll dig around the waterline and see if I can figure out what we're dealing with. We'll just take it one step at a time. You're in charge."

A burn lit behind my eyes, fiercer this time, and I couldn't stop the tears from welling. "Why are you putting up with me?" I asked, my voice little more than a hoarse whisper.

Shep's eyes locked with mine. "Because everything about you screams that you've been fighting alone for too damn long, Thorn. You need someone to help carry the weight for a little while. I might not be able to fix everything, but I can help carry the load."

Chapter Twelve

Shep

I WANTED TO BREAK SOMETHING. NO, I WANTED TO BREAK someone. And that someone was whoever had put this level of fear in Thea. Only it wasn't just fear. It was terror.

She blinked up at me, trying desperately to clear away the tears. "Alone is the only place that's safe."

Her words scored me, leaving scars in their wake. "Alone isn't a place. It's a state of being. And no one can stay that way forever. Every person on this planet needs others. Needs to share their burdens with someone."

I felt a pull from somewhere deep. A demand that *I* be that someone.

Thea stared at me for a long moment, her deep brown eyes searching. That was the thing about Thea. She watched in a way others didn't. Withstood the quiet to give herself time to truly see. I'd seen her do it countless times at the bakery, taking time with an older woman who came in each day because she was lonely without any family around. Crouching in front of the bakery case with a little kid, helping her decide between all the amazing cupcakes.

But now, she was taking that time with me. Her intelligent gaze burrowing deep, silently assessing before she gave me anything. And when she finally *did* speak, I wasn't surprised the words packed a punch.

"Do you share your burdens, Shepard?" Her voice wasn't loud or soft, but it hit hard just the same.

I usually hated anyone using my full name. Too long. Too formal. Too many connotations of guiding sheep in the olden days.

But Thea saying it? It was like a stroke to the senses. Her tongue wrapped around each syllable like it was a precious thing.

My throat worked as I swallowed. "I've got a family that rivals a football team, who helps me whenever I need it."

A hint of amusement danced in Thea's eyes. "And how often do you let them do that?"

I snapped my mouth closed. I couldn't remember the last time one of my siblings had helped me with something instead of the other way around. It wasn't that they were selfish and didn't offer; it was that I didn't let them help. Or, more often, I didn't let them know I needed help.

Her perfectly plump lips twitched. "That's what I thought."

"Trust me," I said, "they are all up in my business. Nosy as all hell."

Thea's face softened, and I felt a little more of her anxiety melt away. "I'm glad you have that."

An ache took root in my chest because I knew Thea didn't. At least, not as far as I could see. "You have siblings?"

I wanted to kick myself because she stiffened the moment the question was out of my mouth.

"No siblings."

I nodded, wanting to know more but knowing she'd just retreat if I pressed. "They're a blessing and a curse."

Her smile was back. "I bet."

I opened my mouth to ask something more innocuous, just because I liked hearing the sound of her voice, when I heard a beep.

Thea pulled something from her pocket, silencing the sound. I realized it was an old-school digital watch. I hadn't seen one in decades.

She brushed the hair out of her face. "I need to feed the kittens." She glanced between me and the front yard. "Do you need anything? Or—"

"I'm good," I assured her. "Got everything I need in my truck. If I have any questions, I'll knock."

She slid the watch back into her overalls' pocket—overalls that in no way should've been sexy but somehow were. The way the front dipped down, exposing just a hint of cleavage from her tank top. Or how the sides were low enough that I knew I could run a hand along her waist down to her hip or…go even farther.

Jesus. I needed to get a grip.

Thea looked up at me. "Thank you. For doing this. For being… patient."

Tiny fractures opened in my chest. "We've got all the time in the world."

We didn't. Not really. The longer it took for me to get into the house, the greater the chances that mold and rot could take root and spread. But I wouldn't rush her. If it happened, I'd rip out every affected beam and replace it. No matter how long it took.

Her tongue darted out, sweeping across her lower lip. "Thank you," she said again and then hurried into the house.

I watched until she'd disappeared behind the front door. I heard the lock latch. Not just a deadbolt, but a chain, too, if I wasn't mistaken. And as I studied the industrial deadbolt on the piece of wood, I knew I wasn't.

A muscle twitched in my cheek. What the hell was she hiding from?

Chapter Thirteen

Thea

WHAT THE HELL WAS I DOING? BEING MONUMENTALLY STUPID, that was what.

Moose leapt onto the stool at the counter and slapped my arm with his paw as if to punctuate the point.

"I know I'm an idiot," I told him. "I don't need you telling me, too."

He let out one of his warbled meows in answer.

I tossed him a piece of turkey. I wasn't above bribing him so he wouldn't give me grief.

I fed the kittens and took time to cuddle each one. Then I cleaned up after them. They were tiny, but they left chaos in their wake.

After that, I cleaned the kitchen. You could probably perform surgery on the countertops now. When I was finished, I peeked out the front window and regretted it the moment the curtains parted.

At some point over the hour I'd been scouring my house, Shep had lost his shirt. The white tee was draped over the side of his truck instead of on his body like it should've been. *Holy biceps, Batman.*

A flush of heat swept through me at the sight of him working: muscles bunching and flexing as he drove his shovel into the dirt, then heaved it into a pile, a faint sheen of sweat making all that muscle glisten under the sinking sun.

I quickly let the curtains fall closed, but it didn't matter. The image would be burned into my mind for eternity.

I needed another task to busy my hands, so I went with meal prep. I told myself it was simple courtesy but knew I was a liar. I wanted more time to bask in Shep's glow and kindness. Because something about him made me feel alive again for the first time in two years.

So, now here I was, trying to come up with the best sandwich possible. I took an idea from The Mix Up menu and twisted it. Two slices of the olive bread I'd made from scratch, garlic aioli, smoked turkey, the sharpest cheddar I could find, and arugula. Then finished it with some caramelized onions.

I sliced the sandwiches in two, put them on plates, and then pulled out the bag of homemade potato chips I'd stress-baked last night. The cracked pepper I'd layered on them and the salt gave them a kick that would pair well with the sandwich.

A paw slapped my arm again.

I glanced at Moose, giving him a warning look. "Don't be rude. You've had more than enough."

He barked at me. Because, of course, I'd found the only cat on the planet that barked. Well, it was more of a chirped bark, but still. Absolutely ridiculous.

I sighed. "You want to come with me?"

Moose meowed in answer.

"Okay, go get your harness."

Maybe Moose could be the distraction I needed while coming face-to-face with Shep again. A second later, Moose raced back into the kitchen, a harness between his teeth. I bent and quickly put it on him, then grabbed two of the reusable glass bottles I'd filled with lemonade, putting them in the pouch of my overalls.

Looping the leash around my wrist, I got the plates and headed for the door. It was a juggling act to open said door without Moose taking off my hand, but I finally succeeded. As I stepped outside, I knew there wasn't much daylight left.

I felt Shep's eyes before I saw them. The warmth of his stare felt different than when anyone else looked at me. Other people were a prickle on my skin, but not Shep. He was a low, smoky heat.

I forced my legs to move and close the distance between us as I searched for the source of that heat. Shep's amber eyes were locked on me, his expression unreadable but still warm. His gaze tracked over my face and down, then stilled for a moment on the drinks and the food. It froze altogether when he got to Moose.

"What the hell is that thing?"

It was just what I needed. A laugh burst out of me. "His name is Moose."

"It should be Beast," Shep said, still staring.

Moose hissed in response, and Shep's brows flew up.

"Seriously?"

I grinned at him. "Moose can be a little touchy and senses if someone's talking about him."

Shep's gaze returned to my face, shining that smoky heat there. "Whatcha got there?"

I suddenly felt a little uneasy. Embarrassed that I'd made the man a meal without even asking if he was hungry.

Shep seemed to sense my discomfort. "Thorn?"

My focus snapped back to him. "Thought you might be hungry."

The smile that stretched across his face was like a straight shot of the sun. Pure light and warmth. It wrapped around me, digging in and illuminating places that had been dark for so long.

"You thought right." He glanced at his truck. "Let me grab my shirt."

Shep didn't wait for my answer; he simply jogged toward his vehicle and tee. But I couldn't help but keep watching how his muscles bowed and flexed in the golden sunlight.

A paw slapped my leg, and I looked down at Moose. "There's no harm in *looking*."

My cat just meowed.

"Here, let me take the plates. I feel like you need two hands for the beast," Shep offered, his lips twitching.

"Sure," I said, my voice going a bit soft.

"Where's a good place to eat?" he asked.

I hadn't thought that far ahead. Now, I was kicking myself. I knew having him inside would mean me fighting panic the whole time, but the only furniture on my back deck was a single chaise lounge.

"Thorn," Shep said quietly, "we're not going inside, so take that off the table. I'm covered in dirt, so I'm happy to sit right here. But I want us to go wherever you're comfortable."

His words hurt. They were so unbelievably kind and understanding. So many emotions warred within me: embarrassment, gratitude, relief.

"The back deck," I croaked. "We can sit on the steps."

Shep's smile was back. The sunlit glow cast out the shadows that swirled in my mind.

"That's perfect." He was already moving—not quickly but leading us to where we needed to go.

The newer deck had wide steps that gave us a makeshift table and chairs. Shep waited for me to sit and then sat several feet away.

I worried the inside of my cheek before speaking. "I'm not scared of you. Not like that."

It was stupid of me to share the information. To even give him that piece. Because it would only lead to more questions. Things I couldn't or wouldn't answer. But I couldn't stand the idea of Shep thinking I was frightened of *him*.

Shep's eyes flashed, and then one corner of his mouth kicked up. "Maybe I'm scared of the beast."

Moose let out a deep meow as if saying, *"Damn straight."*

"That's fair. He is slightly terrifying," I admitted.

But Shep scooted closer—near enough that our plates almost touched. He was quiet for a moment before he finally spoke. "I'd like to get to know you. I think it would help both of us, but I don't want to ask you anything that makes you uncomfortable. Think you can give me some guidelines?"

My throat twisted, making it hard to breathe, let alone speak. I admired his forthrightness and lack of beating around the bush. "Let's keep the questions to the present."

Shep's gaze roamed over my face, silently probing for the reason why, but he didn't ask. Instead, he did as I requested. "Favorite flower in your garden."

The tension bled out of me. "The peonies." I gestured to the plants that had grown with a fervor I could've only hoped for. Everything was shades of pink and peach. Endless beauty.

"They're pretty damn spectacular."

Warmth spread through me at the praise. "And they bring the hummingbirds."

Shep's focus moved back to me as he took in my statement. "You've got lots of feeders, too."

I nodded. "There's something about them. It's more than their beauty. They're tiny but fierce. And they're deft escape artists."

He was silent for a long moment, and I knew I'd given too much away. But it was as if Shep understood that, too. His gaze trailed away from me and over my garden. "You definitely have the touch when it comes to plants."

Relief swept through me, and I forced my fists to loosen. "I didn't at first. I've had a lot of stuff die on me. But I got the hang of it about six months into the trial and error."

"You learn way more by doing than you ever could from books or classes."

I studied Shep for a moment. "Is that how you learned the contractor stuff?"

He nodded, leaning back on an elbow. "Mostly. I went to college for business and took some design and architecture classes. Worked on a local crew part time for all four years of school. But I learned all the core skills from my dad."

I couldn't imagine a father who took the time to teach an intricate skill like building. Mine had barely been around. And when he was, it had mostly consisted of screaming fights with my mom that then resulted in the cops being called to our small North Hollywood apartment.

But I hadn't heard Rhodes mention a foster father, so I wondered what had happened to him. "It has to be pretty special that you share that."

Shep nodded, taking a sip of the lemonade. "He knew I needed to be actively doing something to work through a problem, so he gave me the skills to do that. Sometimes, we'd end up talking about the issue. Other times, just doing the work helped me puzzle through it on my own. But even now, I sometimes hear his voice when I'm working."

My fingers closed tightly around my bottle. "Did he pass?"

Shep's throat worked as he swallowed. "Car accident when I was seventeen. Fallon and Cope survived, but Dad and my brother, Jacob, didn't make it."

Everything in me constricted, weaving into intricate knots. I couldn't imagine losing both a father and a brother in a single moment. It made what I'd been through pale in comparison.

"I'm sorry," I said quietly. Those two words were so incredibly lacking, but they were all I had.

Shep's amber eyes locked with mine. "Thank you."

I had to break the connection. It was too intense. Shep was letting me see too much, making me want to lay all my secrets at his feet. My focus dropped to my plate, and I toyed with a chip.

Shep shifted, and out of the corner of my eye, I saw him take a bite of his sandwich. The groan that left his lips had my whole body waking up and standing at attention. The sound washed over me in a wave of vibration, and my gaze had no choice but to snap to his face. His lips.

"Holy hell, Thorn. This is the best thing I've ever tasted. And we've got some amazing cooks in my family."

Heat hit my cheeks, not with embarrassment this time but pleasure. It had been so long since I'd prepared something for someone else. I used to do it weekly for Nikki, and I'd had epic dinner parties with friends crowded into my apartment—before those friends were all turned.

I shoved that thought down and focused on the good of here and now. Zeroed in on how much Shep loved my creation. "I love coming up with recipes for things. It's a fun little challenge. I take whatever I have on hand, in the greenhouse, and go all mad scientist."

Shep turned as I inclined my head toward the building. He let out a low whistle. "That's quite the setup."

"I've always loved getting produce from local farmers markets, but here in Sparrow Falls is the first time I've tried to grow more than a basil plant on my own."

Shep opened the sandwich, analyzing the contents. "You grow the arugula?"

I nodded. "And the garlic for the aioli. And the onions."

Shep just shook his head. "My mom has a garden where she grows a few veggies, but this puts hers to shame. She'd love to see this."

My grip on the lemonade bottle tightened. Having Shep here was stressful enough. Another person I didn't know at all? It'd likely send me over the edge.

"Thorn," Shep said. My gaze jumped to him. "That wasn't me inviting her over for cocktails and caviar. It was just me saying that she'd love it and that I appreciate all you've put into this because I've seen her work on this sort of thing on a much smaller scale."

My gaze dropped to Moose as he rolled on his back in the grass, attacking the blades. "Sorry."

"There's not a damn thing you need to be sorry for. This is your place. You make the rules."

That burn was back, the pressure of tears gathering behind my eyes. Of frustration and embarrassment. I didn't want to be like this. Yet I didn't know how to stop.

Shep's hand covered mine. The contact was gentle, yet it rocked me. The only two people who had touched me in any way over the past two years were Sutton and Rhodes. This was entirely different.

I could feel the calluses on Shep's palm skating across the smoother skin of my hand. His heat seeped in there. It was that same sort of sunlight but from touch alone. My head jerked up, and I found nothing but empathy and kindness in his eyes.

"We all do what we have to do to make it through. I'm never going to judge you for what you need to feel safe."

As I stared into those amber eyes, I knew Shep was telling the truth. But for the first time in two years, I wished I didn't need to have all the safety precautions and walls to keep people out. Because as risky as it was, I wanted to let Shep in.

Chapter Fourteen

Shep

ANSON LOOKED UP AT THE OLD FARMHOUSE AND LET OUT A whistle. "You really went for it with this one."

"It's not as bad as Rho's Victorian," I defended.

He shook his head as he started walking around the side of the house. "Maybe not, but it's bigger, and we've only got the two of us working on it for the most part."

It would've gone a lot faster if I could've put a full crew on it, but we had too many other projects, and being the owner of Colson Construction meant I had to make choices that were the best for the company as a whole. I couldn't delay someone else's job because I wanted more workers on mine, especially when one of those undertakings was my sister's.

The best I could do was to steal Anson. And that was a lot. Because my friend did damn good work, and his attention to detail was unparalleled. It had to be the profiler in him. His time working for the FBI and burrowing into deranged minds had left him attuned to even the slightest things. It came in handy on construction sites.

"Bigger just means I'll be able to flip it for more of a profit." But the moment the words were out of my mouth, I wasn't sure they were true. Something about the ole girl called to me. And the quiet beauty of the landscape around us put me at ease.

"True," Anson said as he studied the house. "You get an official offer on your Craftsman?"

I nodded. "Above asking. We close next week, and Jennie got them to hold move-in for two weeks. Should give me enough time to find a place."

"Good luck with that," Anson muttered. "Tourist season is in full swing, and it keeps lasting longer and longer."

That was true and definitely a concern. I scrubbed a hand over my face. "If I'm not careful, I'll end up living with Cope's nosy ass."

Anson chuckled. "The good thing about that is you know he'll only be home for a few weeks at most."

Cope never stayed long. He always said it was due to work commitments, but I wondered if it was more. "He's too pushy to live with for even two weeks."

Anson was quiet for a moment before turning to me. "They're worried about you."

I stiffened. "I'm not the person they should be worried about."

He shrugged. "Maybe, maybe not, but it doesn't change that they are. Because they *care*."

"You know," I mumbled, "I think I liked it better when you refused to talk to anyone."

Anson barked out a laugh. That action alone showed how much had changed over the past few months. How much Rhodes had changed him. "You're the one who always wanted to talk about my *feelings*. How's it feel to have the tables turned?"

"Feels like shit. Thanks," I muttered.

My phone dinged, and I glanced down at the screen.

> **Mara:** *I got two tickets to the Design Fest in Roxbury next weekend. Want to come with?*

I frowned at the device. While Mara knew plenty about

construction thanks to her job at the hardware store, she found all my architectural design talk boring. She'd gritted her way through it because she wanted to make me happy, but she did a bad job of pretending.

"Why do you look like someone just dropped rotting trash on your phone screen?" Anson asked.

I sighed, flipping the device around to him. "Mara."

He shook his head. "Were you clear with her that things were done?"

I scowled at my friend. "Of course, I was."

Anson held up both hands. "I'm just saying that sometimes you aren't clear *enough* because you don't want to hurt someone's feelings. It's better to cause pain in the present to prevent agony in the future."

"Who are you? The Yoda of Sparrow Falls?" I snapped. "I told her that my feelings for her didn't run deeper than friendship and that we should leave it there."

Anson nodded. "That's pretty clear. But it looks like she might need you to hammer that point home if she's still asking you this sort of thing."

I glared down at the phone but knew he was right. Mara and I had broken up in early spring, and she was still trying to maneuver opportunities for us to spend time together, even when I ignored previous messages. My fingers flew across the screen.

> **Me:** *I appreciate the offer, but I think it's best if we don't spend any one-on-one time together. I don't want to give you the wrong impression. I think you're amazing, but I don't see a future for us.*

The moment I hit send, those three little dots appeared. Then they disappeared. Then they reappeared.

> **Mara:** *Stings that you feel that way. Especially after everything we shared. But I'll back off.*

I winced.

"Ooof," Anson muttered as he peered over my shoulder.

I gave him a shove. "Nosy much?"

"Hey, you showed me the first one."

That was true enough, but I didn't want to think about Mara or her guilt trips. "Come on, I want to show you the back. I'm thinking swimming pool."

Anson let out another low whistle. "Going full five stars with this place."

"I think it fits." I didn't always go with full luxury. I let the houses and property set the tone for the reno. I had never been one of those builders who put a McMansion on a quarter-acre lot. But this property? It fit. There was a way to blend the luxury into the land.

"Damn," Anson said as we rounded the corner of the house, and the backyard and surrounding property came into view. "If Rho and I weren't moving into the Victorian, I'd be making you an offer on this place."

I stiffened at Anson's words because I wasn't sure I wanted to give up this house. "At least you share my vision. I'm thinking pool here." And taking in Thea's incredible landscaping yesterday had given me ideas. "Natural rockscape all around, and no perfect shapes, so it feels more like a pond than a pool."

"That'll look great. You could do a water feature that reads like a small waterfall."

I could see it as Anson spoke. Something that made you think of a brook spilling over into a lagoon. "I like it."

He turned back to me. "And how the hell are you going to have time for all of this? Rho said you took on a project at Thea's, too."

I forced my muscles to stay relaxed at the mention of her name—even though she'd crossed my mind more times than I could count. Her ridiculous overalls and that cat the size of a lion. Her incredible meal and guarded kindness.

"Hoping that doesn't take too long," I lied.

Anson snorted. "Sure, you are. Got a chance to win over the one woman who's shot you down in the past decade. You're hoping that job lasts till Christmas."

The chuckle slipped out unbidden. "All right, I'm enjoying having a chance to get to know her."

He studied me for a long moment. "And what have you found out?"

It didn't surprise me that Anson was curious. He couldn't turn off the profiler's urge to analyze all the pieces of a person. Especially if they were mysterious in any way.

I mulled over the words I wanted to say, trying to figure out if talking about Thea was a betrayal. But I knew Anson was a vault, and I also knew that Rho had likely already talked to him about much of this. "She's been hurt. I know that much for certain."

Anson's face hardened to stone. He'd seen a lot of horrible things during his time with the FBI, but he especially hated anyone who harmed women.

"I'm not sure how, but the idea of having me in her house totally tweaked her. So far, I've only been able to do work outside."

Anson mulled over my words, sifting through them in his mind. "No matter what ways she's been hurt, she'll need control now. You have to let her lead. If she draws a boundary, do not cross it."

I nodded. "I haven't pushed. But I'm not sure how I can get her to trust me."

Anson's gaze locked with mine. "Time and letting her see the vulnerable parts of you. Then maybe she'll be brave enough to show you the same in her."

My truck bumped along the gravel road to Thea's house. I couldn't help but wonder if the road was privately owned or county jurisdiction. It desperately needed to be regraded. I added that to a mental list of things to look into.

As I rounded the bend, I saw a flash of dark brown hair. Thea straightened, her hand tightening around the hose she held in her hand as she watered the front yard. I knew she'd had to drag it all the way from the greenhouse to get any water.

A flicker of annoyance mixed with the frustration swirling inside me. I needed to find the source of Thea's leak so we could get the water turned back on in her house.

She watched as I approached, but when she confirmed it was me behind the wheel, I saw a little of the tension leave her muscles. That tiny easing felt like I'd won the goddamn lotto.

As I pulled into the makeshift lot in front of her house, I saw Moose bounding after a bug in the grass. I couldn't help but shake my head. I was sure if someone studied the creature, they'd find he was some sort of mutant crossbreed and not a cat at all.

Throwing my truck into park, I shut off the engine and grabbed the bag and drink holder next to me. I'd cursed myself for not asking what Thea liked to eat yesterday, but thanks to the turkey sandwiches, I at least knew she wasn't a vegetarian.

Sliding out of the truck, I headed in her direction. "Garden's looking good. Well, minus the trench I put in it."

Those plump lips twitched. "Dirt going back in place is way easier than moving it out."

"True enough." I lifted the bag in my hand. "How do you feel about takeout from The Pop?"

Something flashed in Thea's deep brown eyes. Pleasure, I realized. Then, a hesitant smile tipped the corners of her mouth. "They make the best onion rings around. I've tried to replicate them at home, but they're always seriously lacking."

"Well, I'm happy to report that I've got onion rings in this bag."

Her hesitant smile turned into a full grin. "Let me just get this water shut off."

I was about to say I'd do it for her, but Thea was already jogging in the direction of the greenhouse. So, I just made my way to the back deck where we'd eaten yesterday. As I approached, Moose eyed me warily. It was then that I saw he had a harness on, which was connected to a leash, which was clipped to a stake in the ground.

"Doesn't trust you to roam freely, huh?"

Moose hissed in my direction.

"Hey, I'm not the one who put you in a harness, pal."

Moose plunked his ass on the ground and began licking his paw and washing his face. What a weird mutant beast cat.

I set down the drinks and bag groaning with food, and removed everything so Thea could have first pick. Since I hadn't known what she liked, I'd gone with options. There was a club sandwich, a cheeseburger, a Rueben, and a cheesesteak. Then there were the sides. Regular fries, onion rings, sweet potato fries, and tater tots.

"Is there any food left at The Pop?" Thea asked, surveying my spread.

I straightened, shoving my hands into my pockets. "Wasn't sure what you liked."

"So, you bought the entire menu?"

I chuckled. "Not even close."

A piece of Thea's hair slipped from the braid it was in as she took it all in, then she lifted her eyes to me. "You didn't have to do all of this."

"I wanted to. It won't be nearly as good as your creations, but I didn't get the cooking gene like some of my siblings did." I watched as her focus returned to the food, a sort of longing on her face. "You've got first pick. I like it all."

She studied the boxes carefully and then bent, selecting the cheeseburger. I made a mental note of that.

"There are chocolate, vanilla, and strawberry milkshakes. And Cokes," I added.

Thea lowered herself to the deck step and reached for the chocolate shake. Then her eyes came to me. "Thank you. I don't get takeout very much, so this is a treat."

My gut twisted as I sat because I had a feeling money was the reason she didn't get takeout all that often. And I instantly knew I'd be bringing her meals from as many places around here as I could. I reached out and took the cheesesteak, resting it on my lap. "You're welcome."

Thea took a bite of the burger, and her eyes fell closed. She didn't make a single sound, but her expression said it all. Pure pleasure coasted across her face. And I couldn't help but think about that look in other sorts of circumstances.

Hell.

I cleared my throat, trying to shake myself out of anything resembling those thoughts. "So," I said, trying to distract myself, "what are your food likes and dislikes? Give me the heavy hitters."

Thea smiled as she reached for her shake. "Likes: cheeseburgers, anything Italian, falafel, and Indian samosas."

My brows lifted. "Falafel, huh? I'm not sure we have that around here."

She laughed then, the sound hitting me square in the chest. "Sparrow Falls is sadly lacking in both Mediterranean and Indian food, but there's actually a really good Indian spot in Roxbury."

"I didn't know that."

"Definitely worth a stop if you have to head that way."

Roxbury was a bigger town about thirty minutes from here. Occasionally, I'd head out that way if a project required specialty fixtures. "What about dislikes?"

Thea drummed her long, slender fingers against her cup. "Shellfish and melon. I think they're both a consistency thing."

"Fair enough."

She was quiet for just a moment before asking, "What about you?"

It was pathetic how happy I was about her asking me a single question. "Likes: steak, my mom's sausage and egg casserole, and Rho's peanut butter poke cake. Dislikes: parsnips, carrot cake, and beets."

Thea's lips twitched. "What did root vegetables ever do to you?"

"Maybe they were meant to stay in the ground."

She chuckled at that, and the sound made me feel like I'd won another damn prize. "Fair enough. I'll have to get that peanut butter poke cake recipe from Rho. That sounds good."

"It's amazing."

We kept eating, letting a comfortable silence settle around us. Every now and then, we'd ask each other an easy question, nothing that took a lot of thought or had any chance of stirring up demons.

But it was still the best non-date I'd had in years. The simple ease of it was nice.

When we were done, I pushed the remaining boxes toward her. "Why don't you keep the leftovers? They'll just go bad in my truck."

"I can put them in my fridge, but you should take them home. Especially if you don't like to cook."

I tried to think about the best approach to get her to keep them. There wasn't much I could do to fix whatever was going on in Thea's life, but I could do this. "How about we split it? Neither of us will be able to eat it all."

Thea arched a brow at me. "And whose fault is that, Mr. Buys-the-whole-menu?"

I grinned. "Impulse control issues." I quickly bagged up the remaining food and handed it to her. "Here. I'm going to get back to the trench. I should be able to survey the whole waterline tonight."

Thea twisted the bag around her fingers, tightening it with each revolution, but she didn't move toward the house.

A heaviness settled back in my gut. "There's no rush, Thorn. I don't set foot inside that house until you're ready for me to be there."

Her brown eyes cut to me. "Why are you being so nice?"

There was suspicion there, and I knew that if I didn't tell her the truth now—and all of it—I'd lose any shot with Thea. For friendship or more. She needed to know that I wouldn't hide things from her. Wouldn't lie. So, I gave it to her.

"I like you. Even when you were prickly as all hell, I admired it. There's something real about you. An honesty you don't see a lot these days. And there's kindness. You might try to hide it beneath those thorns you love so much, but I've seen it. And, somehow, it's more potent since you're not using it for show. You'd rather have no one see you extending a hand to someone else. That's why."

"Oh." Thea's mouth formed the shape, along with the word.

I stood, taking my Coke with me. "And you're damn nice to look at, so that doesn't hurt either."

With those parting words, I walked away.

Chapter Fifteen

Thea

I HUMMED TO MYSELF AS I GRIPPED THE KITTENS' CARRIER WITH one hand and balanced the box of bakery treats on the other— goodies left over from today that would make for the perfect dessert. Shep and I had fallen into a routine of sorts over the past week and a half.

He would show up at my place around four, once I was back from the bakery or nursery, and always with some sort of meal in tow. We'd eat on the back deck, and Shep would ask questions that stayed firmly in the here and now. He was careful never to push, letting me share whatever I was comfortable with. Then he'd get to work.

And I'd just happen to wander by a window to catch him without his shirt on after an hour or so. *Total* coincidence.

I jerked out of my lusty haze and narrowly avoided colliding with a barrel-chested body in front of me. "Sorry," I mumbled.

"Careful, darlin'. You could get hurt if you don't watch where you're going." The smarmy tone of Russ's voice made a shiver skate down my spine. I hadn't seen him since I'd made that visit to Castle

Rock Construction, and I hadn't seen Raina either. There were times she wouldn't come into The Mix Up for days on end, but she never went longer than a week. I didn't want to think about what her absence could mean.

"Long day," I said, scooting to my left to move around him.

But Russ moved with me, taking the bakery box from my hand. "Here, let me carry that to your bike."

"That's okay. I've got—"

"I insist," he cut me off.

The pulse point in my neck thrummed. I didn't want this man anywhere near me. But I also didn't want to make things worse than they already were. We were on a public street in broad daylight. Tourists were poking in and out of shops, and locals enjoyed the beginning tendrils of summer. I was fine.

I started toward my bike where I'd locked it just at the edge of the building, not thanking Russ for the so-called help I didn't want.

"So," he began, his tone falsely light, "who'd you find to fix your leak and water damage?"

"Shepard Colson's working on it."

I felt Russ's footsteps falter more than I saw it. "Must have money to burn, then."

My back teeth ground together. "He's doing me a favor. I'm friends with his sister." The truth was, Shep had only let me cover the cost of materials so far, and I knew he was giving me his contractor's discount on those. But I was determined to find a way to repay him.

Russ scoffed. "Box Baby probably just wants to fuck you."

I whipped around to face him. "Excuse me?"

Russ's chest puffed up like a ridiculous impression of a baboon. "You heard me. Don't be an idiot. He's trying to get in your pants. But be careful. Box Baby leaves a trail of broken hearts in his wake. Just ask around. He acts like the town golden boy, but the bastard's anything but."

There was so much to unpack in that tirade that I didn't know where to start, but one thing stuck. "Box Baby?"

Russ's eyes lit with cruel pleasure. "Haven't heard the story?

Shep got left in one of those haven boxes at the fire station. Even his own ma didn't want him."

The urge to slap the man in front of me was so strong I had to bite the inside of my cheek to keep from stooping to his level. Instead, I jerked the bakery box out of his hold with my free hand. "Get the hell away from me. You *wish* you could be half the man Shep is. But you never will be. Because you're a sleazy, rude, *mean* person. And my guess is, you're worse than that."

Russ's brows lifted in shocked surprise for a moment, and then he sneered at me. "Already fuckin' him, I see. Good luck when he tosses you away like the trash you clearly are."

As Russ stalked down the street, the trembling set in. He was nothing more than a bully, but I knew bullies could do unconscionable things when they set their minds to it.

"It's okay," I whispered to the kittens, who'd begun meowing at the sounds of our raised voices. "We're okay."

My hands shook as I lifted their carrier into the trailer at the back of my bike. It took three tries to fasten them into place, then I placed the bakery box in front of them so it wouldn't get jostled. But as I threw a leg over my bike, I froze.

How had Russ known I rode a bike?

The thirty-minute ride home should've calmed my nerves, but I was glancing over my shoulder every two seconds, looking to see if anyone followed. It was possible that Russ had simply seen me riding around town. That was the most likely scenario. I'd had this bike for almost as long as I'd lived here. Still, his cruelty and knowledge of my habits had set me on edge.

It reminded me too much of Brendan. Someone who had extricated every possible detail about me under the guise of getting to know me, or in the name of intimacy, and then used the information as a weapon. To aim at the places he knew would inflict the most damage.

My body shuddered as I rode down the gravel drive, swerving

to avoid potholes. Catching sight of my house and the silver truck parked in front of it had a burn building behind my eyes. Because I knew I was so close to safety.

I did everything I could to force down the tears. I thought about the flowers I planned to add to the front garden after Shep filled in the trench. I thought about what I might harvest from the greenhouse and give to Shep to pass on to his mom. I thought about how Moose loved playing in the yard and watching Shep as he worked.

All of it helped. Just not enough.

I pulled to a stop in front of my walkway. Shep was already striding toward me, a huge grin on his face. "I had to go to Roxbury today, so I got Indian. I'm not sure this will be my new favorite, but I got a bunch of things to try. And I made sure samosas were on the list. You might have to reheat stuff, but—" His eyes locked on my face, and all the pleasure drained from his. "What's wrong? What happened?"

Of course, Shep could see right through me, no matter how much happy imagery I ran through in my head. "Nothing. I'm fine."

"Bull," he growled. "You're shaking like a leaf."

I shoved my hands behind my back as if that would hide the truth.

"Thorn," he whispered. "What happened? Please."

It was the *please* that did it. The beseeching tone with a hint of desperate need. The burn was back, and I desperately tried to blink it away. "It's stupid."

Shep moved then, slowly coming into my space but giving me all the time in the world to show him I didn't want him there. But I didn't move away, didn't step back. His hand came up, and he brushed strands of hair out of my face. "It's not stupid. Not if it's affecting you like this."

My heart hammered against my ribs. I wanted so badly to just tell Shep everything. But I couldn't. There was too much shame wrapped up in it all. But I still wanted to give him something. A tiny piece that could possibly help him understand.

"I had a run-in with Russ Wheeler."

Shep's hand tightened in my hair, and a low, rumbling noise that sounded a lot like a growl emanated from him. "What. Did. He. Do?"

"He didn't touch me," I hurried to say. "He was just...a jerk, I guess. Crass, cruel. It wasn't him, not really. It's just...he reminded me of someone. Someone I don't ever want to remember."

Pain sliced through Shep's eyes. "Fuck." Then he pulled me to him and hugged me.

It wasn't that I hadn't been hugged in the past two years. Sutton and Rhodes both gave me the occasional squeeze, but it was nothing like this. Shep's arms engulfed me as he crushed me to his broad chest. I felt all that strong muscle surrounding me, could feel the beat of his heart against my cheek, and all as the scent of sawdust and cedar swallowed me whole.

A lump formed in my throat as Shep held me, not showing any signs of letting go. Slowly, my arms went around him, and I held on. I let Shep take a little of the weight I'd been carrying around for so long.

"He gutted you," Shep gritted out as his hands sifted through my hair. "Cut you right to the quick because that's the kind of man he is. And it makes me want to show him true pain."

My hands fisted in Shep's white tee. "I yelled at him."

Shep pulled back a fraction, one brow arching. "Letting those thorns fly?"

My lips twitched. "He said some stuff about you. Got my hackles up."

Shep's fingers stilled in my hair. "What'd he say?"

My mouth went suddenly dry. "It's not important," I mumbled. I was an idiot.

"Thorn," he said, tugging gently on my hair to bring my focus back to him.

I sighed. "Something about you being abandoned as a baby. In a not-very-nice way."

"Called me Box Baby?"

There was an emptiness in Shep's voice that set me on edge. "Yes," I whispered.

"Was a thing in elementary school. Russ just never grew out of it," he muttered.

My gaze lifted to Shep's. "I'm sorry. It's cruel."

He shrugged. "It's life. And it's not like it's untrue. I ended up with an amazing family in the end."

But something said Shep wasn't giving me the full story. He wasn't sharing just how much this all hurt him. But I didn't blame him. We all had tender spots we weren't ready to show the world.

"What else did he say?" Shep pressed.

My gaze shifted to the side.

"Thorn…"

"He said you were only helping me because you want to fuck me."

To my surprise, Shep burst out laughing. It was a thing of beauty. Because, this close, I not only heard every note, but I also felt them. Each vibration hit me right in the chest.

Shep grinned down at me. "I'm not gonna lie and say I wouldn't love my hands on your body, but I'm helping you because I can, and you need it. Makes me feel…worthwhile. And *I* need that."

A riot of emotions stormed through me. Panic, desire, worry. I shoved down the first two and forced my eyes to Shep's. I lifted a hand and pressed it to his cheek. The stubble pricked my palm, sending a pleasant shiver through me.

"You're worthy, Shepard Colson. You don't have to fix anything to be that. You don't have to dig a million trenches or replace feet of corroded piping. You're worthy just for who you are."

Those amber eyes flashed with specks of gold as he stared down at me. "Thea," he croaked.

I let my hand drop as I stepped out of his hold, knowing if I stood there a moment longer, I'd do something I couldn't take back. Something I knew I wasn't quite ready for, even if I wanted to be. But I could give him something else.

"Why don't you come inside? I'll reheat the takeout, and you can help me feed the kittens."

Shep's eyes flashed again. "You sure? I don't have to—"

"I trust you, Shep. Come inside."

He didn't move for a long moment, just stayed in place, waiting to see if I would change my mind. That patience and kindness had a little piece of me starting to fall. I shoved that knowledge down and moved back toward my bike.

That spurred Shep into action, a gentleman through and through. He handed me the box of bakery treats and then unhooked the kittens, lifting them from the carrier. As they meowed, he ran his finger across the front of the cage as if to soothe them.

As nervous as I was, that action soothed me, too. The simple kindness of it.

But still, my heart hammered against my ribs as I approached my front door. I slid my free hand into my pocket and tugged out my keys. My hand trembled as I found the right one. It took two tries to get it into the lock, and the sound of the deadbolt turning resembled a gunshot or cannon, some sort of deafening blow that only my ears could hear.

My hand stilled on the knob for the count of one, two, three. There was no turning back from this, but a growing piece of me yearned for the existence-altering move. To begin to let people in. To let *Shep* in.

I twisted the knob and opened the door. After stepping inside, I motioned for Shep to pass. "The kittens have a pen in the living room just down the hall."

Shep walked past me, his movements slow and methodical, giving me all the time in the world to let me correct his course if he crossed into any space I didn't want him in. That, too, was a gift. I shut the door behind me and locked the supersized deadbolt the same way I had a million times before. The only difference was that someone was on the inside with me.

My body vibrated with a mixture of nerves and anticipation as I moved down the hallway. I set the bakery box in the kitchen where Shep had deposited the bags of Indian food and followed the sounds of the soft meows coming from the living room. I came to a stop in the threshold, watching as Shep gently placed each ball of fluff in their pen—so careful and tender. It swept away a little more of the nerves.

As Shep placed the little gray female in the pen, he stood and turned to face me. He didn't move, simply studied me, a silent check-in. "How do you feel?"

I stared at him for a long moment and then told him the truth. "Good." Tears pressed against the backs of my eyes. "I wasn't sure I'd ever be able to take this step."

A mixture of emotions played behind Shep's amber gaze, but one settled in. "So damn proud of you, Thorn. How about we celebrate with some Indian food?"

"That sounds perfect." And it was.

Chapter Sixteen

Shep

"**O**KAY," ANSON SAID, LOWERING THE PRY BAR IN HIS GLOVED hands. "What's with all the fuckin' whistling?"

I stopped mid-movement, the sheet of drywall halfway to the wheelbarrow. "I'm whistling?"

"Dude, you've gone through all of The Rolling Stones' greatest hits. And let me tell you, they're not going to be asking you to join the band."

I sent a scowl his way before tossing the drywall into the container. "Apologies for being in a good mood. Not all of us can master the brood quite like you can."

Anson chuckled. "It takes studying and dedication."

I chucked a tiny piece of drywall at him.

Anson just laughed harder as he dodged it. "I'm glad you're happy. I'm just curious as to *why*."

I moved to the sheet of drywall he'd just removed, lifting it into the wheelbarrow. "Thea invited me inside for dinner."

The moment the words were out of my mouth, I felt like an idiot.

Since when did a woman inviting me into her house for dinner have me whistling a merry tune? But I shouldn't have doubted that Anson would get it. He knew what carrying trauma with you meant. How it could keep someone from living fully.

He grinned at me like some sort of deranged doll. "That's huge. How was it?"

"Good." It had been so much more than that. "She was nervous, but it never stopped her. Finally got a look at the guest bath, too."

"How bad?"

"Gut job." It would take weeks to pull out the rotted boards and make sure there wasn't any mold, then more to replace everything.

"That blows."

"Big time. But I was able to replace the damaged pipes, so at least she has running water again."

"I bet that whole house needs to be replumbed," Anson muttered.

I didn't even want to think about that. I hated the idea of Thea living in a house that needed more work than she could possibly tackle. But we'd just have to take things one step at a time. And for now, she was okay.

"Trace texted me," Anson went on as he loosened another sheet of drywall.

I grabbed it right before it fell. "You two besties now?"

"You know spending a lot of time with law enforcement is never gonna be my thing."

That was the understatement of the century. "You gonna tell me what he wanted or just hint at it?"

Anson moved to the next panel. "Wants me to work up a profile on Russ Wheeler."

I stiffened. I'd called Trace on my way home from Thea's last night. I didn't like Russ being anywhere in Thea's orbit, but the fact that he'd cornered her outside of work had me struggling not to take action myself.

"He freaked Thea out," I said, my hands tightening on another sheet of drywall.

"Trace told me. He also said that he has suspicions that Russ has been abusing his wife."

I dropped the sheet into the wheelbarrow. "Yeah. He's had a number of callouts there. He's tried talking to Raina alone and sent female officers to talk to her, but she won't press charges or talk about it. Trace has tried everything he can think of."

Anson turned to face me. "She's been conditioned not to speak. Likely isolated from anyone she's had any close ties with. He is all she has, so even if he's hurting her, she won't risk losing that."

Just thinking about someone living that way turned my stomach, let alone someone I'd known for most of my life. Raina had been a couple of years behind me in school, so I didn't know her as well as I—unfortunately—knew Russ. I didn't know who her friends were. All I knew was that her parents now lived out of state.

"Is Trace asking you how to approach?"

Anson nodded. "That and how to catch Russ in his own trap."

"Come up with any genius ideas?"

"Not yet, but I'm still working on it," Anson said.

I pulled off a work glove and wiped at my brow. "Figure out some way to keep him away from Thea while you're at it, would you?"

"You're worried about her."

It wasn't a question, but I answered it anyway. "I'm not sure what all she's been through, but it wasn't good. She doesn't need Russ's bullshit on top of it."

"You really care about her."

Something shifted inside me. It wasn't painful, but it wasn't altogether comfortable either. "Yeah. I do."

That deranged grin was back as Anson slapped me on the shoulder. "Come on. It's time for lunch. Let's go see your girl."

I liked the sound of that a little too much.

Chapter Seventeen

Thea

THE FAINT TWANG OF A COUNTRY SONG WAFTED THROUGH THE air as I moved from one table to the next, checking on refills and bussing the empties. The lunch rush was in full effect, and I wasn't exactly on my A-game.

Sleep hadn't been my friend last night. I shouldn't have been surprised when a nightmare had found me around three in the morning. There'd been too many triggers the day before.

I recounted something I'd read in a book about post-traumatic stress disorder. *Facts over feelings.* Feelings were always justified, but we had to put them into the framework of facts.

I was scared. The run-in with Russ had brought up a whole boatload of trauma I hadn't yet laid to rest. But the facts were that I was safe, Brendan had no idea where I was, and Russ was nothing but a cruel bully.

So, I focused on the good. On the here and now. I moved toward a table of tourists, their heads bent over a guidebook. "Can I get you any refills?"

The man looked up and smiled. "Sorry, we were in the throes of a hiking debate."

"Not a problem," I assured them.

The woman held up her coffee cup. "I wouldn't mind another."

"Decaf or regular?"

"Regular, please."

"Coming right up."

"Actually." The man stopped me. "We're trying to decide between the hike at Castle Rock and this one with a waterfall. Have you done either?"

I leaned over the guidebook, surveying each of them. "I've done both. But I actually recommend the hike at Broken Ridge Pass. It has four different waterfalls, and you get great views of Castle Rock. It's about five or so miles."

The woman grinned at me. "That sounds amazing. Thank you so much."

The guy just shook his head. "This is why you always ask the locals."

"Happy to help," I said as warmth spread through me. Because I was a local. And for the first time, I really felt like I was building a home in Sparrow Falls.

I moved through the crowd, grabbing a few empties and making a mental reminder to get the woman's coffee. I stopped at another table and forced a smile to my lips. I felt like an ass because Mara had never been anything but nice to me, but knowing that she and Shep had history had a green-eyed jealousy monster poking up its head inside me.

"Hey, Mara. Can I get you anything else?"

Her head snapped up from the magazine she was reading, a hand flying to her chest as a laugh bubbled out of her. "Sorry. I was in another world."

My smile came a little more genuinely this time. "I think that's the theme of the day."

Mara grinned back. "Fridays. Always a struggle bus."

"So true. Can I get you anything else?"

She shook her head. "I need to get back to work, but thanks. This was just the Friday pick-me-up I needed."

"Glad to hear it. Have a great weekend."

"You, too," Mara said as I moved to the next table.

Finishing my rounds, I headed behind the counter and filled the tourist woman's mug.

Sutton moved in next to me, pitching her voice low. "You doing okay? You can take off early if you need to."

I thought I'd hidden my lack of sleep decently well, but apparently, I hadn't. "How bad are my dark circles?"

One corner of Sutton's mouth kicked up. "You might need some of my super concealer if you were hoping to hide them."

I snorted. "At least we're in it together."

She squeezed my arm. "Everything okay?"

I turned toward her. "It really is." And that wasn't a lie. I'd let someone into my house last night. Not just anyone, either. A man. One who had a heat I hadn't felt in years stirring inside me. And I hadn't panicked or kicked him out. I might've been a little awkward, but Shep had to be used to that by now.

Sutton kept her gaze on my face for a moment, then it was like sunshine blasted out of her. "Something happened with you and Shep!" she squealed.

I clamped a hand over her mouth. "Shhh!" My face flamed because half the bakery had likely heard her yell. "Nothing happened. We just had dinner."

"So, a date?" My hand muffled Sutton's question.

I dropped my arm, my cheeks still hot. "No. I mean, I don't know. He's just been bringing food every day he works at my place."

Sutton's eyes began to glisten. "He brings you dinner every night?"

"Please, do not start crying. You know I can't handle tears."

She sniffed, waving a hand in front of her face. "Okay, okay. I'm just happy for you. You deserve this."

"Nothing's happened, Sutton." I did not need her runaway

romantic heart on this train. She'd have us married in her mind before the day was over.

Her smile only widened. "Maybe not yet, but it will."

I just shook my head, quickly washing my hands before grabbing the mug of coffee. "I need to get this to a table."

"It's the truth!" Sutton yelled after me.

I only hurried away faster, dropping the coffee with the tourists and scanning the rest of the restaurant. Mara had left, so I moved to her table to clear it. I grabbed her plate, balancing a now-empty cup on top of it, and then moved to grab the magazine she'd left behind.

The moment my gaze connected with the glossy cover, I froze. Ice slid over me, making my skin turn clammy. My heart thumped as if someone were squeezing it in a brutal grip.

A face stared up at me, one with a perfectly straight smile and shining blue eyes. I'd seen them shine at me like that. But it was nothing but a lie.

I jerked my gaze away from the photo to the headline. The words had all the blood draining from my head.

America's Favorite Superhero Heads to Oregon to Film a Western.

Chapter Eighteen

Shep

MY PHONE DINGED JUST AS ANSON AND I CLIMBED OUT OF MY truck. Sliding my phone out of my pocket, I took in the screen. *Group name changed to This Could've Been an Email.*

> **Cope:** *Shep, you get your house exorcised yet?*

I chuckled as I typed out a reply.

> **Me:** *No, but no ghostly sightings either.*

> **Fallon:** *How would you know? You haven't been there after dark.*

> **Me:** *You an expert in all things haunted now?*

> **Rhodes:** *She has watched* Supernatural *at least three times.*

> **Fallon:** *More like five. You're all going to want me on your side when you have an angry apparition.*

I shook my head as I switched the device to silent and shoved it back into my pocket. A couple of tourists held the door to The Mix Up open as Anson and I headed inside. We were met by some incredible scents that had my mouth watering the moment we stepped inside. But not even my stomach could distract me from my single-minded focus.

My gaze swept the space, landing on mahogany hair. Thea wore it down today, the thick strands curling around her shoulders. I was already moving toward her as if she had some sort of invisible pull. But as I approached, I realized she was frozen in place, staring down at something on the table.

"Hey," I greeted her.

My voice wasn't loud, but Thea still jolted, her gaze snapping to me. "Shep."

I searched Thea's face. Her skin had gone pale, and I saw a slight tremor in her hands. I couldn't help but move in closer. "Are you okay?"

She forced a smile. "Of course. Why wouldn't I be?"

"You were standing there frozen. You're pale." Anger stirred somewhere deep. "Did Russ come in here? Did he bother you again?"

Thea quickly shook her head. "No, nothing like that. I just didn't sleep well last night. I zoned out."

An invisible fist ground against my sternum. She hadn't slept well because Russ had triggered her. Just knowing that had my back molars grinding together. "Maybe you should call it a day early. Go home and rest."

The smile that came to Thea's lips was more genuine this time. "You sound like Sutton."

"Sutton is clearly a genius you should listen to."

Thea chuckled. "I'll take it under advisement." Her free hand came out then, landing on my forearm. "I'm okay, really. But thanks for checking on me."

That touch scalded in the best way, marking me. I'd never take any contact she initiated for granted. Any time she reached for me. And that heat, right along with the knowledge that she was growing comfortable with me, that she *trusted* me, felt like a goddamn precious gift. Something I wouldn't trade for all the money in the world.

Thea's words echoed in my head. *You're worthy.* She made me feel that way. Maybe for the first time ever.

Her hand slipped away, and I instantly missed it. I missed more than just the heat. I missed the connection. The buzz of energy that lit between us.

Thea's gaze moved behind me. "Hey, Anson. How are you?"

"Good. You?"

"Doing good. You guys here for lunch?" she asked.

I nodded. "Wouldn't mind one of those spinach and artichoke grilled cheeses."

Thea grinned, her deep brown eyes sparkling. "One of my favorites. Come on, I'll get your order."

She moved through the tables of people, rounding the bakery case and meeting us on the other side of the counter. Sutton looked up from where she was pulling together a box of bakery treats. "Hey, boys. How are you?"

"About to be better," I said with a smile.

Sutton laughed. "Love being able to make someone's day."

Thea tapped the tablet and looked up. Her face was still pale, but she managed a smile. "One fancy grilled cheese. What about you, Anson?"

I glanced at my friend and found him studying her. I knew it wasn't in any sexual way. He was trying to put the pieces that were Thea together. But still, a flicker of jealousy took root that was so foreign it shocked the shit out of me. Jealousy wasn't an emotion I was used to.

"I'll do the chicken salad sandwich and an Arnold Palmer," Anson said, his voice completely even.

"You want a drink?" Thea asked me.

"I'll do a lemonade. You've given me a taste for them."

Pink rose to Thea's cheeks, giving her face a healthy glow again. "You want that for here or to go?"

I glanced at my watch. As much as I would've loved to stay and watch her work, I knew Anson and I had minimal hours today.

Especially if I wanted to start demo work at Thea's later this afternoon. "Better make it to go."

"You've got it. I'll throw in some cookies. On the house." Thea was already moving through the space to gather things.

"Wouldn't hate a monster cookie," Anson called.

Thea's lips twitched. "Glad to know your weakness."

No one was behind us, so I watched as Thea gave Walter, the cook, our order and then gathered the drinks and cookies. She and Sutton moved in a tandem dance that spoke of a routine they'd mastered over the past several months, but my gaze never strayed from Thea for more than a handful of seconds.

"Jesus, you're a goner," Anson muttered.

My eyes shot to him. "Like you're one to talk. My sister has your nuts in a vise grip."

Anson chuckled. "Exactly where I like them to be."

I made a face. "Sick. I do not need to know about your guys' sex life."

"You're the one who brought it up."

"I did not. God, I'm about to eat."

Anson's grin only widened. "Fine. She know how you feel about her?"

I shifted uncomfortably. "She knows I think she's beautiful. But I also haven't crossed that line. I don't want to push things. Especially when…"

Anson pitched his voice low. "When you don't know what she's been through."

I nodded. I had no idea what Thea had battled, only that it wasn't good. The last thing in the world I wanted to do was bring up bad memories for her.

Anson clapped me on the shoulder. "She's lucky to have you in her corner."

I was sure there was someone better for Thea. Someone who deserved her more. But I was too damn selfish to step aside and let her find him. And I'd do everything I could to be the man she needed.

"Here you go," Thea said, rounding the counter. "I threw in a couple of monsters, a brownie, a snickerdoodle, and a lemon bar."

"Sugar coma, here we come," I said, shaking my head with a smile.

She handed me the bag, and I didn't miss the slight tremble in her arm. My gaze locked on it as our fingers brushed.

"I'm sure you'll burn it off working this afternoon," she said with a smile.

Concern dug deep at the fear she was expertly hiding. "Thanks," I said, my voice taking on a gritty tone.

Thea's eyes dropped to my mouth as if searching for the source of the sound. She swallowed hard, her focus moving back to my eyes. "Sure." She was silent for a count of two. "See you tonight?"

The hopeful lilt to the words sent relief coursing through me. Whatever had happened, it wasn't enough for Thea to send me away. "I'll be there."

"I'm making dinner this time," she said, her voice taking on a stern teacher tone.

"But I—"

Thea shook her head. "My greenhouse is going to explode if we don't eat some of the produce."

"All right," I acquiesced. "But I'm on cleanup duty."

"Fair. See you tonight."

God, I wanted to touch her. Wanted to kiss her right there in the middle of the bakery, no matter how much it would get the local tongues wagging. But I held myself back. "Tonight."

"See you later, Anson."

"See you, Thea," he answered before tugging me by the back of my tee. "Come on, before you start drooling."

I shoved him as we headed out of the bakery. "You're a prick."

"That's not a new revelation," Anson said, moving toward his truck and beeping the locks.

I climbed inside, setting the food on the floorboard in front of me.

As Anson stepped up, he handed me a magazine. "This is what she was staring at. The cover. Might be nothing. Could be a clue."

I looked down at the glossy paper. It was a tabloid. The same kind Mara was obsessed with. I scanned the various headlines, trying to figure out what could've triggered a fear response in Thea.

There was a celebrity divorce, a cheating scandal, a wedding, and then the cover piece about some guy I recognized from countless movies and TV shows. "The cheating scandal, maybe?"

"I dunno," Anson muttered, starting the engine. "Cheating doesn't really seem like the thing to make all the blood drain from your head."

And it had. Thea had been unnaturally pale when we walked up.

I studied the magazine harder, trying to put the pieces together. But I didn't have the skills Anson did in analyzing the human brain. "Maybe it's something one of the *people* featured reminds her of."

"Could be. Google them. Read off what you find."

I pulled out my phone and moved around the cover clockwise, starting with the reality TV couple. He'd been cheating on her with her best friend. I read the different headlines I found on both of them.

Anson made a humming noise. "Maybe, but I'm not seeing it."

Then, I moved to the main headline. The one featuring the movie star involved in one charity project after another. Only articles listing his many accolades came up when I searched his name. So unlike the reality couple I'd looked at.

But then my gaze caught on an article. *Brokenhearted Brendan.*

Something about it made me click the link. *Romance has come to an end for Brendan Boseman and his longtime girlfriend, Selena Stewart. While the couple was notoriously private, we loved the little bits we got of this Cinderella story. But word on the street is that Cinderella had a wandering eye and broke our poor Brendan's heart.*

Everything around me went hazy as my gaze zeroed in on the photo. If I hadn't made a habit of memorizing everything about Thea's face, I never would've recognized her. Her hair was blond in the picture of the two of them, hands linked. And her eyes were green. But even though the photo had been taken at a distance, I could see the dull, almost lifeless look in them. But the slope of her nose was the same. As was the tiny freckle just below her eye.

"Pull over," I croaked.

"What?" Anson's gaze jerked in my direction.

"Pull over."

He guided his truck to the side of the road, and I handed him my phone.

"It's her." I hardly registered my own voice.

Anson studied the image for a long moment, then turned to me. "She's running."

I'd known as much. There'd been no way she wasn't. But now I knew from whom. One of the most famous people on the planet.

Chapter Nineteen

Thea

I MOVED THROUGH THE GREENHOUSE, LETTING MY FINGERS TRAIL over the plants. I had so much pride in the little haven I'd created in here. It had given me the sense of accomplishment I'd so desperately needed. Doing something worthwhile when someone had picked me apart for so many years, making me feel like a failure in every possible way, was a balm.

A lump took root in my throat, growing with each plant I passed. The home I'd built here was the perfect retreat, somewhere I finally felt safe. But I should've known that Brendan would steal this from me, too. Because my escape had always been tenuous at best and so delicate a strong breeze could send it crashing down.

On my break, I'd borrowed the computer in Sutton's office to google the production Brendan was a part of. He was less than an hour away and had been for three weeks while filming some period piece about the pioneer days. People were already saying it was his chance at an Oscar and screaming about how it was finally his time.

My stomach roiled as I fought back tears. It was the worst twist of fate to hear people celebrating the person who'd been your tormentor. Calling the one they praised generous and good when they were the one who'd berated you over and over again. Pelted you with every failing and accused you of twisted actions that had taken root in their mind.

I shuddered, even though the temperature was in the low nineties. Sinking to the ground, I let the plants surround me and hugged my knees to my chest, needing the pressure, as though if I kept them there, my heart wouldn't shatter into a million pieces.

There were times I still heard Brendan's voice in my head. The vicious taunts and cruel accusations.

"You're really going to eat that? So, your ex got you skinny, and I get the fat version?"

"I saw the way you were looking at him. He's your type, isn't he? You were hoping he'd take you into that back hallway and fuck you, weren't you?"

"Such a fucking whore. I wish I'd known the truth about you when we met. But it's too late now. You ruined my fucking life."

And the sounds that accompanied them all. A glass shattering against the wall. A scream that was more animal than human, right in my face. A table slamming into a marble floor after being upended.

A single tear fell, darkening the caramel color of my overalls where it landed. I watched the wetness spread, infecting the threads around it, just like Brendan's words had poisoned my brain.

But they were always followed by sweet nothings. Apologies. Promises.

"Selly. I'm so sorry. You know I'm a mess. I don't deserve you. I should let you go, but I don't know what I'd do without you. I don't think I'd survive."

A fresh wave of nausea ripped through me as Brendan's face played in my mind. The anguish, the sorrow. Or had it all been an act?

I didn't know. Because being with him had been like slowly losing my mind. It had taken months for me to get my footing again. Over a year to truly see how messed-up our relationship was.

But there were times, in the shadows of night, when a tiny piece of me would start to doubt. Was I all the things he said? Or even some of them? My mind would twist itself into knots, trying to figure out what things were the truth and which were lies. *Did* my eyes linger too long on the waiter as I thanked him for my meal? *Was* I too interested in what Brendan's friend was telling us about his work with anti-malaria initiatives in Africa?

My fingers dug into my legs, nails cutting in, even through the canvas of my overalls. "You're a good person."

I whispered the words into the air around me. "You're not perfect. But you try to be kind. You try to do right. You're not evil."

I repeated the assurances until my heart calmed and my breaths came more evenly. But I was exhausted. Tired to the bone from fighting the ghost that never seemed to leave me be. And I wondered if it ever would.

The sound of tires on gravel filtered through the open greenhouse door. I didn't move for a second. Wasn't sure I could. I didn't think I had it in me to face Shep tonight. His goodness and light felt like everything that was just out of reach for me. Maybe something I didn't even deserve.

I forced myself to my feet and started outside. As I walked toward the drive, I imagined painting on the layers of my mask. Pleasant, calm, easygoing. Nothing amiss. Everything just as it always was.

Shep slid out of his truck, the silver gleaming in the late-afternoon sun. Everything about it was so perfectly clean…like always. So opposed to the dirty, twisted things that lived inside me.

He smiled at me, his easy grin stretching across his face as he walked. Each step made his white tee stretch taut across his chest. "Hey, Thorn."

I forced a smile. "Hi. I'm running a bit behind today. I still need to make the food. I'll probably just give you yours and then head back to my desk. I told Duncan I'd work on a design project for him, and I want to get a jump on that. It's a really good opportunity—"

"Thea." Shep's hand curved around mine. So warm and strong and *good*. "What's going on?"

I tugged free, my eyes burning. I couldn't handle feeling all that was Shep. All that would never be mine because my mind would twist whatever we shared. I'd ruin it. And maybe even him.

"Nothing. I just have a lot on my plate. Let me know if you need anything. I'll be in the kitchen." I started toward the house. Shep would do whatever he had to do. Maybe he would realize that I was a raving bitch and leave. That would probably be for the best.

"Is this about Brendan Boseman?"

I stopped dead. Blood roared in my ears as my pulse thrummed. I turned slowly around. "What did you say?"

Hurt swirled in Shep's amber eyes. "I know, Thea."

And then my whole world came crashing down.

Chapter Twenty

Shep

I WATCHED AS THE BLOOD DRAINED FROM THEA'S FACE. I HATED myself for being the cause of it, but I wasn't about to let her shove me away. Close the door on something I *knew* had been a miracle for us both.

But just as quickly as she'd paled, color returned to her face and then some. Thea's cheeks bloomed red, and her eyes flashed. "Did you look into me? What? Get your ex-FBI pal to check my finger-prints or something?"

"No." I did everything I could to keep my voice calm and even. "I saw you looking at the magazine. Noticed it tweaked you. I wanted to know why."

"Did you ever consider that it was none of your business?" she shouted.

"I care about you, Thea."

Tears sprang to her eyes then, making the brown glisten. "You can't."

"Too late," I said, taking a step toward her.

Thea took two steps back, shaking her head viciously. "You can't care. You can't look. You can't."

"What happens if I care? What happens if I look?"

She stared at me for a long moment, tears tracking down her face. "You'll hate me."

Everything in me stilled. It was as if my heart stopped beating right before it shattered. I couldn't keep myself from moving then. I ate up the space between us in four long strides.

My hand slid along her jaw to cup her face. "There isn't a thing you could tell me that would change the way I see you. The only thing it'll change is knowing just how strong you are to have made it through it all."

A sob tore free of Thea's throat, and I couldn't hold myself back. I wrapped my arms around her, cocooning her as more sobs racked her body. I never would've thought that such vicious movements could come from such a delicate form. But I shouldn't have been surprised. Thea was iron forged in flame. Stronger than anyone could've known.

I held on to her as she cried, each sob shredding my chest. But I took them all, knowing she had to let it free.

"Y-you don't know. You won't want anything to do with me."

I lifted her into my arms, striding around the house and up the deck to where the chaise lounge was. I lowered us to it, keeping her cradled against me as I did. "Try me," I whispered against her neck.

She shook her head but burrowed into me. "I don't want you to look at me any differently."

I slid one hand up and down her back as the other stroked her hair. "Did you murder someone in cold blood?"

"No," she whispered.

"You steal from the elderly?" I asked.

"No."

"Hurt a puppy?"

"Of course, not." Thea's voice was barely a rasp as she spoke.

"Then I'm not going to see you differently."

She pulled back then, her eyes searching mine. "You don't know that."

"*You* don't know. Not unless you try." My fingers wove through hers. "You said you trusted me."

"I trust you more than anyone, other than my best friend, Nikki."

That was something, Thea speaking the name of someone I'd never heard her mention before. Giving me a little piece of her past.

"Thank you," I whispered. Thea stared back at me, still not moving to speak. "Did he hurt you?"

Just having to say the words aloud was almost more than I could take. If she said yes, I wasn't sure I could stop myself from hunting Brendan down and showing him what pain truly meant, consequences be damned.

"He never hit me. Never laid a hand on me in anger. There were no bruises, no broken bones, no proof."

My brows drew together. "No proof?"

Thea pushed up fully, tugging her hand from mine and shoving her hair out of her face. I thought she might be getting ready to bolt, but instead, she pulled her knees to her chest and hugged them tightly.

"I used to work for a nonprofit. The Literacy Project. I loved it, helping people fall in love with reading and gain the skills they needed to get good jobs."

It fit. Thea was a helper. Whether it was kittens without homes, a little girl who couldn't decide what cupcake flavor she wanted, or an elderly woman who needed a friend. And when she let me in last night, I'd seen the books piled high everywhere. Everything from a book on growing mushrooms to gothic thrillers and more romances than I could count.

"That's where I met Brendan." Thea's knuckles bleached white as she gripped her legs. "He was coming in to read a children's book to some of our kids. He was so charming and kind. When he asked me out to coffee afterward, I was shocked but flattered."

My gut churned, knowing this story didn't continue down a happy road.

"I should've heard alarm bells with how fast he moved. Coffee turned into him taking me to dinner, then showing up with breakfast at my apartment the next day. He wanted all my time. He'd even joke about being annoyed that I had to work, but I thought it was sweet."

Thea swallowed hard. "It wasn't long before we were spending every night together. If I wanted to go out with Nikki and our other girlfriends, he'd pout. She saw it before I did. Saw how it would go bad."

"And how did it go bad?" I hardly recognized my voice when I spoke, it was so devoid of emotion.

"I guess I'd call it paranoia. But some part of me still wonders if I caused it."

"What kind of paranoia?"

Thea rolled her lips, pressing them together hard. "He got really fixated on my past."

My skin started to prickle, and a sick feeling took root somewhere deep. "Your past how?"

"The guys I'd dated, anyone I had the slightest bit of intimacy with." She scoffed. "It wasn't like there were many to speak of. I worked my way through college and grad school. I didn't have a lot of time for dating and parties. But he wanted to know everything."

I was quiet for a moment as I listened. Playing the numbers game with a partner was dicey on a good day, but this sounded like more.

Thea took a deep breath. "He started pushing to know details. He wanted me to make a list. Every person I'd ever kissed. Anyone who'd seen other parts of my body. How many guys I'd had oral sex with. How many I'd slept with."

She rocked her knees back and forth as if trying to soothe herself. "I thought if I just told him, he'd know I had nothing to hide. But it wasn't enough."

My fingers wrapped around the sides of the chaise as I struggled to keep my breathing even.

"He wanted to know where. Who. He wanted a full list of names. *Details.* Wanted a promise that I wouldn't speak to any of those people ever again."

I bit the inside of my cheek hard. "No one has the right to that information, Thea. Not a single fucking soul."

Her eyes collided with mine. "I don't know. He said he needed to know what could come back on him because so many eyes were on him. And then he said if I didn't tell him, I was trying to hide things. Manipulate him. But once I did…"

"He what?"

Thea's body shuddered, and it took everything in me not to pull her back into my arms. "He started drinking more heavily. Taking pills. He'd wake me up in the middle of the night, screaming at me. Demanding to know where I'd done what with whom. He looked up photos of an ex's house and started pointing out rooms. Asking if I'd fucked him here or there."

"Thea," I croaked.

Tears slid down her cheeks, but she made no move to wipe them away. I wasn't sure she even realized she was crying again. "He started demanding to know where I was at all times. If I went to the gym, he'd call before and after. Ask if any guys talked to me. If I wanted to go to Nikki's, he'd ask why. What were we doing that he couldn't go, too? Was I lying to him about us going out? What was I wearing?"

Her fingers dug harder into her legs. "And when he was on set, it was worse. I thought maybe distance would help. But I was so wrong. If I went to dinner with Nikki, he'd accuse me of not prioritizing our relationship because he might want to call during that time. He didn't even want me to go to a fundraiser for the nonprofit I worked for."

Every breath I took felt like it was covered in flames. The rage swirling deep inside me coiled like a snake, striking out at every new piece of information.

"So, I just slowly stopped. Everything. It was like I simply faded away. I went to work, came home, and braced for him to call. Sometimes, it was normal, so run-of-the-mill I wondered if I'd imagined everything else."

Thea let out a shuddering breath. "But more, he'd call in the middle of the night. Screaming, raving mad. I stopped sleeping because even when he wasn't waking me up, I was bracing for him to. And never, not once, did I consider just not picking up the phone."

My gut twisted at how small her voice sounded.

"But the other calls were worse somehow. The ones where he was kind, praising. I soaked all that up." Her tears came faster. "It's so embarrassing. I lived for those crumbs."

"Because he trained you to," I said quietly.

Thea's dark brown gaze cut to me as if just realizing I was there.

"That's the cycle. The good and then the slap." I'd learned my share about abuse growing up with a family that fostered. I'd seen some of the worst of the worst. Saw how the mental scars—not the physical—took the most time to heal.

Tears dropped from Thea's chin to the legs of her overalls. "He never hit me."

"If you think that it wasn't abuse because he never laid hands on you, you're dead wrong. He isolated you, cut you off from your support system. He deprived you of sleep, berated you. And I'm sure there's more you aren't telling me."

Her gaze shifted to the side. *Fuck.* It had gotten worse.

"You don't have to share it all." As much as I needed to know everything, I wouldn't be the monster she'd been with before. I'd let Thea share when she was ready. "But if you want to, I'm here. And I'll always be here."

"I stayed way too long," Thea whispered. "Even now, I can't explain it. It's like I slowly lost my mind. I was so exhausted and panicked that I couldn't make smart decisions."

I reached out, my fingers linking with hers. "But you're not there now."

She shook her head. "No, I'm not."

"You're hiding from him."

It wasn't a question, but Thea answered it anyway. "Nikki helped me. Her brother's an accountant. We set up a trust I could hide behind. That's what purchased this house. What pays my mortgage and car insurance. Everything else I pay in cash. I don't have a phone, a computer, nothing that's traceable."

"There are ways you can have those things. Ways to protect—"

"No." Thea's voice slapped across the space between us. "You don't know him. He has connections everywhere. People bending over backward just dying to do his bidding. And he's got a thing for computers and tech. Taught himself how to hack into people's emails, their whole systems."

A weight settled in my stomach. I knew someone else who'd been good at computers. Silas. The psychopath who'd targeted Rhodes and Anson. *Fuck.* I needed to get Anson's read on this. See what he thought we should do to protect Thea.

"Okay," I assured her, squeezing her fingers. "No tech."

A little of the tension running through Thea eased.

"You haven't heard from him since you moved here?" I asked.

She shook her head. "No. Not once. But that article, the one that freaked me out, said he's filming about an hour from here."

My back molars ground together. Too damn close. But it was also far too much of a temptation. Because it wouldn't take much to find out exactly where he was and pay a visit to the bastard.

"He's not going to find you. And even if he does, you have people around you. You're stronger, and you know the truth."

Thea hiccuped a breath. "You don't know everything he can do. All he can ruin."

I saw it then. The true fear in her eyes. She was terrified of him.

"He won't. I promise."

Thea didn't answer, and I knew it was because she didn't believe my words. I'd prove them to her. But for now, she'd had enough. Her skin was pale, her eyes rimmed in red.

"Will you go someplace with me?" I asked.

Her brows pulled together, skepticism sweeping across her face. "Where?"

Of course, she needed all the facts. "It'll be more fun if you don't know."

Thea mulled it over for a moment.

"Trust me?" I asked. It was the ultimate question. She'd given me that trust last night, but things were different now.

Her gaze locked with mine, and she sucked in a breath. "I trust you."

That was the best goddamn gift in the world.

Chapter Twenty-One

Thea

I STARED OUT SHEP'S TRUCK WINDOW AT THE FIELDS STRETCHING out around us. Ones that led to forests and then mountains. The way the grasses moved in the breeze was soothing.

I let myself be swept away as Shep drove. He didn't push or ask questions. He didn't speak at all. He simply let me be, seeming to understand that I needed the quiet to recover. My head pulsed with a low-grade headache, and my eyes burned so badly I'd had to take out my contacts.

But it didn't matter. Shep knew who I was now. There was no need to hide. I saw better without them anyway. They weren't bad to wear, but they occasionally distorted my vision. Now, I could see everything clearly.

The majestic beauty of Castle Rock and the Monarch Mountains. The way the land dipped and rolled, leading up to them both. I'd never get tired of looking at it all. So different from the gridlock of LA.

Shep flipped on his blinker, even though no one else was on the road as far as the eye could see. It made my lips twitch. A rule-fol-lower. A good guy through and through.

We stayed on the gravel road for about five minutes before com-ing to what looked like a brand-new gate. Shep rolled down his win-dow and punched a code into a keypad. A second later, the gate swung open.

The moment it did, I caught sight of something in the distance. The house looked as if it had taken a beating by wind, rain, and snow. Even this far away, I saw the sort of grayish brown that spoke of stand-ing through trial after trial.

The color fit. It made the house almost melt into the golden grasses around it. Especially since there wasn't another structure for as far as I could see.

"What is this place?" I asked, my voice sounding rusty like I was sure the hinges on every door of this house were.

"It's mine. My latest project."

I forced my gaze away from the home and back to Shep. "You bought it?"

He nodded. "Closed a couple of weeks ago. Been starting rehab with Anson, but it might take us a decade."

"You're flipping it?"

"That's the plan. Though I think it's gonna be hard to say good-bye to this one. She's got a pull."

My focus moved back to the house. She sure did. There was a majesty to her that mirrored the breathtaking landscape. And the closer we got, the more I was entranced. "How old?"

"Around the time the area was settled. Mid to late 1800s."

"Wow." It was more sound than word. So much history. How special to be a part of that.

The moment Shep put his truck in park, I was out of the vehicle and moving to get a better look at the place. I edged closer. Not able to help myself, I put a palm directly on the siding. It was rough, the wood almost peeling in places. And I could see now that it had been white at one point in time.

"Gonna have to redo all this siding," Shep said, moving in next to me.

"The color suits her."

I felt his gaze dip to me. "I think you're right. Makes it feel like the house just sprouted from the earth itself."

I nodded, trailing my fingers over the wood planks. "Like she belongs."

We were quiet for a moment, and then Shep asked, "You want to go inside?"

The corners of my mouth pulled up in a hint of a smile. "What do you think?"

He chuckled. "I was hoping that would be the answer."

Shep led me across mangled landscape and to the broken front steps. There was a combination lock affixed to the door that he quickly sorted, then he glanced over his shoulder. "Brace. She looks a little rough in her current state."

He shouldn't have warned me because the moment I stepped inside, I was awestruck. Even beneath the dust and peeling wallpaper, I saw the beauty in her bones. The rich woodwork, the ornate staircase, the high ceilings.

But there was a closed-in feeling. A formality that came with lots of rooms for countless purposes the rich likely had back then.

"I see the doubt in your face, but listen to my plan." Shep was already moving deeper into the house before I could argue. "We're knocking out all these walls." He tapped on one where some drywall had already been taken down. "Look what's on the other side."

I followed him through a set of open double doors to a large, formal living room with endless windows.

"We're taking these old windows out and putting in new, energy-efficient ones. This whole back wall will be glass, like you're living on top of that field back there. Then this wall goes down, too, because the kitchen is on the other side. Then you suddenly have an open-concept kitchen and living room, and all you see when you walk in the door is nature."

I could see the picture Shep painted with his words. And it was breathtaking. "You're melding the old with the new."

He nodded, a smile on his face like a kid at Christmas. "I'm keeping all the old woodwork. Upstairs, we're knocking out a few walls to expand some of the smaller rooms. There were thirteen bedrooms."

My eyes went wide.

Shep chuckled. "I know. What would anyone do with thirteen bedrooms nowadays?"

"Have a lot of kids?"

He grinned. "That's one way to deal with it. But I'd prefer fewer, more spacious rooms. And I'll probably take some of them out to expand the bathrooms and build out some closets. They weren't much for closets in the 1800s."

I made a humming noise. I didn't give a damn about closets, but bathrooms were another thing altogether. "You need a bathtub in front of a massive window with this view."

I always knew when Shep's eyes were on me. I could feel the smoky heat of the contact. But this time, that connection burned a bit hotter.

"Bath girl, huh?"

I moved to the window. "Nothing feels better after a long day. But a tub with this view?" I let out a low whistle. "I'd never get out."

"Good to know," Shep said, his voice going a bit husky around the edges.

I turned to face him and got caught in the hold of his gaze. I'd been right about the heat. I swore I could see golden flames flickering in those amber depths. But Shep didn't move. Didn't approach. He just watched me, letting that beautiful burn skate over my skin.

"Thanks for bringing me here."

The heat in his gaze melted into gentleness. "Had a feeling you might like it. I also thought you might want to help me break some shit after a day like today."

That startled a laugh out of me. "Break some shit?"

Shep nodded. "What do you say, Thorn? Want to help me tear down this wall so we can build something better?"

A memory flashed in my mind. One of Shep and me on my back deck, him telling me about how his dad had taught him to process his feelings. Through hands-on work. He was trying to give me the same thing.

"I could smash some walls."

A grin spread across Shep's face. "Let's do some damage."

He crossed to an organized pile of tools and various construction gear. Rummaging through some things, he came back with a pair of goggles similar to what I'd worn in high school chemistry class. He pulled them over my head, settling them in place, his hands stilling.

I sucked in a breath as I took Shep in, all that strength and tenderness. Then his hands were gone, pulling his own goggles into place. He handed me a sledgehammer. "Aim this at anything along this wall." He gestured to a wide expanse of exposed beams and drywall. "We've already cleared any pipes and electrical."

Standing there for a long moment, I took it all in. Force and violence had never been things I'd been comfortable with, especially after my time with Brendan. But I also knew I needed to let some of the ugliness bubbling inside me out—release it before it swallowed me whole.

I moved before I could stop myself, swinging my sledgehammer with all the force I could muster. It landed with a vicious thwack against a two-by-four. The board cracked and splintered.

Power surged inside me as the anger and fear I'd shoved down for so long spilled out through my limbs. I hit the wood again, over and over, until I brought the beam down altogether. I moved on to the next and the next until my arms ached, and my breathing became ragged.

Slowly, I came back to myself and turned to seek out Shep.

He beamed at me. "How do you feel?"

I took a mental survey, and shock settled into me. "I feel amazing."

But it was so much more than that. It was Shep being there for me. Listening without judging. Trying to understand and help.

If I wasn't careful, I could fall for a man like Shepard Colson. I just wasn't sure if he'd do the same with me. Not if he knew everything.

Chapter Twenty-Two

Shep

THE MOMENT I STEPPED OUT OF THE EARLY MORNING SUNLIGHT and into the old farmhouse, I was greeted by Anson's amused voice. "Did you down a dozen 5-hour Energy shots and work all night?"

I understood the question. Thea and I had made more progress in a few hours last night than Anson and I had made the two days prior. Partially because I could move quicker now that I knew where the plumbing and electrical wires were. And partly because Thea had taken to demo like a natural.

A grin tugged at my lips as a memory slid through me. Thea, hair tied up in a bun, huge goggles and mask on, covered in drywall dust, and yelling something completely nonsensical as she slammed the sledgehammer into a wall.

"Dude, are you okay? Are you having a stroke?" Anson snapped his fingers in front of my face.

I shoved his hand out of my way. "You should be happy there's this much progress."

"I am, but I figured something shitty happened that sent you angry-demoing. But you're all smiley. Something I haven't seen you be in months."

Since before Rhodes was taken. That was what he didn't say.

I scrubbed a hand over my stubbled cheek. "I brought Thea here last night. She needed to let off some steam. A few hours later, no more wall."

Anson was quiet for a long moment. "You asked her about Brendan Boseman."

Just hearing his name out loud had that fiery snake of rage flaring back to life. "Yeah, I asked her."

Anson simply waited. That was one of his gifts. He knew the power behind silence.

But I was also used to it. Had gotten accustomed to his broody ass since he'd come to work for me a few years ago. So, I met his stare and pulled out my wallet. Pawing through it, I tugged a one-dollar bill free and handed it to him.

"Not going to do a striptease for you because you flashed me a single."

I flipped him off. "I want to hire you."

"Uh, Shep, I already work for you. Have for years now."

I shook my head. "Your shrink half. That means whatever is said between us is held in confidence, right?"

Anson stiffened, instantly on alert. "I'm not a psychologist anymore, and I never really practiced beyond school."

"Doesn't mean you aren't still bound by the same privilege."

His eyes narrowed. "Well, even if my license hadn't lapsed, that confidentiality only stays in place as long I don't think someone is a danger to themselves or others."

"You don't have to worry about that." Unless Brendan fucking Boseman was his patient.

Anson was quiet for a long moment, and then he lifted the bill, making a show of shoving it into his pocket. "All right, confidentiality in place. But you know you could've just asked for that."

Sure, I could've. But Rhodes was friends with Thea. She cared about her, and Anson knew it. He'd likely be tempted to share tidbits if I didn't make certain he understood how important it was for him not to betray this confidence.

"Thea was with Brendan for years," I began.

"Abuser?" Anson asked, not missing a trick.

"Yes. But not in the way you think." Then I unloaded. I tried to keep things as vague as possible, knowing that Thea wouldn't want me to share all of it. But I was desperate and didn't have the first clue how worried I should be or what precautions we needed to take. And I knew Anson would have those answers.

The longer I talked, the more thunderous his expression grew. He began pacing, his fingers tapping out a beat on his thigh. When I finally stopped, he stilled and turned back to me.

"What do you think?"

"I think this is seriously fucked, and I'd like to remove Brendan's balls from his body."

"Gee, thanks for your professional opinion, Dr. Hunt."

He sighed and squeezed the back of his neck. "I can't diagnose someone without seeing or treating them."

"But?" I asked, sensing there was more.

"Sounds like he has a lot of the markers of someone with a personality disorder. Huge swings in how they view others, going from idealizing to devaluing, especially in romantic relationships. They sometimes exhibit reckless behavior like the drinking and drug abuse Thea mentioned."

"What does that mean for Thea now?" I asked, my voice tight.

Anson shook his head. "Maybe nothing. People live with these disorders every day. There are plenty of treatment options. But the fact that she felt she had to completely disappear after ending the relationship? That concerns me. Suggests there's more."

I knew there was more. Without a shadow of a doubt. "I can't push to find out what that more is."

"No, you absolutely cannot. She can only tell you what she's willing to. But given Brendan's behavior, there's a level of obsession."

"Meaning?" I pressed.

Anson's eyes locked with mine. "The target for his obsession was removed from his orbit. If he hasn't found a new one to replace her, he's been stewing for years."

Nothing about that sounded good. "And if he finds out where she is?"

"If Brendan realizes her location now, things could potentially become violent, even though they weren't in the past."

"How do we help her?" I could barely get the words out.

"I'm not sure there's much we can do other than help her heal," Anson said quietly. "Her opening up to you is a massive step. The fact that she's let Sutton and Rhodes in to a certain degree is another good sign. She needs to move back into life, but at her own pace. All you can do is encourage that."

The tightness in my throat made it hard to swallow, let alone speak, but I finally managed to get words out. "I won't let him hurt her."

Anson's eyes met mine. "We don't always have that control. But we can do our best to help her stay safe."

The hell we didn't. I'd already failed one person I cared about. I wasn't about to do the same with Thea.

Chapter Twenty-Three

Thea

"**D**O YOU THINK THE TOURIST CRUSH WILL EVER BE BEHIND us?" Sutton asked, leaning against the back counter.

"It'll keep on coming through summer. And then we'll have one more surge with Labor Day," I said as I wiped down the counter around the register. "People love getting in one last hurrah."

She twisted her neck to the side, cracking it. "I should be grateful, but I'm exhausted and ready for a break."

I turned to study my friend. She'd been pushing so hard to make this dream a reality for the past few months. "You need to take on some more help. You're doing too much. You need an actual eight-hour stretch of sleep."

"Mmm. Eight hours. What's that like?" Sutton asked dreamily.

"I'm serious. You're going to burn yourself out or get sick."

"I know, I know. I just don't want to take on someone else when we'll be heading into our quieter months before long."

"What about taking on a baker so you don't have to get up at three in the morning?" I pressed.

She shook her head. "The baking's the best part. When it's just me and the quiet. It's like the whole world drops away."

"I'm glad you love it, but maybe you could love it only a couple of days a week?"

Sutton laughed. "Eventually. But for now, it needs to be me."

I nodded, even though I didn't like it. But the truth was, I didn't know what Sutton's financial situation was like. I'd gotten the sense that things were tight and she went without so Luca could have everything he wanted and needed. But the bakery was doing amazingly well, so hopefully that would change soon.

"Sooooo," she began, running a towel through her fingers. "How is having Shep help out at your house?"

Just the sound of his name had my entire body waking up. That alone should've been one giant red flag. But I couldn't seem to get myself to go there.

I swallowed, trying to clear the dryness in my throat. "It's... good."

Sutton raised a brow in question, no words with it. The ultimate mom move.

"I think we're...friends."

She sighed, disappointment lacing her tone. "Thea, one does not remain *friends* with a man who looks like that."

It was my turn to arch a brow at her. "You did."

Sutton shook her head. "That's different. I'm closed for business."

I'd never pushed to know more about Sutton. Why she moved to Sparrow Falls or if Luca had a father in his life. I hadn't pushed because I didn't want Sutton to do the same with me. And maybe that made me a crappy friend. But I was breaking all my rules lately, so what was one more?

"Why? You're smart, funny, and ridiculously gorgeous. I know more than a couple of guys have asked you out."

Shadows passed over Sutton's eyes. "I had a relationship turn. Someone who became a person I couldn't even recognize. It'll take a while before I'm ready to dip my toe back in that pool."

I studied her for a long moment before pulling on all the bravery I could. "I know what that's like. Makes you feel crazy."

Empathy swept through Sutton's expression. "Makes you look back on every moment you shared with new eyes. And everything becomes a lie or a stab of grief."

"I'm sorry," I said quietly.

Sutton straightened. "I'm not. It changed me, but I like who I am now more. I found my strength. I stand on my own two feet. Take care of myself and my son. That feels damn good."

A smile tugged at my lips. She was right. I'd never be *glad* I went through what I did, but it made me realize what was important. And it made me a more empathetic person, someone sensitive to others' struggles.

"You are a bakery badass and a supermom," I said.

Sutton grinned back at me. "Yes, I am. Does that make you my trusty sidekick?"

I choked on a laugh. "At least give me a cool cape."

"Deal," she agreed.

The bell over the door jingled, and I turned, scanning the mostly empty bakery until my gaze landed on a familiar face. I couldn't help but look for any signs of bruising. There were none. On her arms either.

I smiled warmly. "Hi, Raina. It's good to see you."

Her lips tipped tentatively. "You, too."

"What are you after today?" Normally, she came in during the morning rush, but it had been weeks.

"Can I get a chicken salad and an egg salad sandwich to go, please?"

"Of course." I punched the order into the tablet and read her the total.

"I'll tell Walter," Sutton said, slipping into the kitchen.

"How have you been?" I asked Raina as she tapped her credit card to the reader.

Her gaze jerked up, surprise there. We didn't chitchat a lot. She'd always been shy, and I wasn't exactly a chatterbox. But today, I was being brave. Sutton had reminded me of all the ways my ordeal had changed me for the better, and I wasn't going to let those gifts go to waste. And no matter what was going on with Russ, Raina needed a friend.

She swallowed as she carefully put the card back into her wallet. "Good. Pretty busy." Her eyes flicked to me. "I'm sorry about that day in the office. Sometimes Russ…he just…he isn't real patient. And he doesn't like Shep all that much."

I wanted to scoff but swallowed it down. Russ was more than impatient, and his dislike of Shep seemed to border on hatred. But I didn't share any of that. Instead, I chose my words carefully. "It's hard sometimes when a partner's behavior is extreme. We can feel like it's our fault. But I promise you, it's not."

Raina's eyes widened again. Her mouth opened and closed, and she repeated the action a few times but never actually got any words out.

"I've been there," I whispered. "If you ever need someone to talk to or a safe place to go, I'm always here."

Unshed tears glistened in Raina's eyes. "I—"

"Raina," a voice snapped from the doorway. "What the hell's takin' so long?"

"I, uh," she mumbled.

Sutton appeared then, bag in hand but a scowl on her face. "I've got your order right here, Mr. Wheeler. Tossed in a couple of cookies on the house."

He just sneered. "Told ya we should've gone to The Pop. Service here has always been crap."

Raina took the bag and ducked her head. "Sorry," she whispered so only I could hear, and then she took off for the front of the shop.

I stared at the door for a long moment after it had closed behind them.

"I think I hate that man, and I don't like to use that word," Sutton said behind me.

"You and me both," I muttered.

But more than anything, I wanted Raina free of him.

Chapter Twenty-Four

Shep

MY PHONE RANG THROUGH THE SPEAKERS ON MY TRUCK AS I turned onto the dirt road leading to Thea's house. A twitchy feeling had settled in my muscles around mid-morning and hadn't left since. I wanted to see Thea and hated that I had no way to check on her during the day because she didn't have a damn phone. All because of the bastard who'd terrorized her.

I forced those thoughts down and glanced at my dash. The screen said *Trace Calling*. Given that it was only three-thirty, I knew he was on duty. My brother took his job seriously. It was more than a job to him. It was a calling. Something he'd *needed* to do given what he'd grown up in. So, he didn't usually call to chitchat during his workdays.

Tapping the button on my steering wheel, I answered. "Everything okay?"

"Everything's fine," he said quickly. "Didn't mean to tweak you."

My gut twisted. A few months ago, Trace would've given me shit for worrying just because he called. But now, he was walking on eggshells like the rest of my family. Worried because they knew the Silas thing had twisted me up and I wasn't handling it well.

"I'm fine," I gritted out. "You just don't usually call for tea and gossip in the middle of the day."

"Fuck off," Trace muttered.

That had a little of the tension easing. It was normal. "What's up?"

"Wanted you to know that I tried to have another conversation with Raina Wheeler."

I was an ass for not thinking about her or Russ since Thea's revelation a couple of days ago. My mind had been so fixated on Brendan that I'd let Russ's assholery fade into the background. But it wasn't in the background for Raina. She lived with it every single day.

"How'd it go?" I asked.

"About the usual. She shut me down and said I needed to leave because Russ could be back at any second and wouldn't like me there."

My grip on the wheel tightened. "I hate watching her fade away. When we were in school, she was so full of life. Funny, too. Now, it's like she's scared to move."

Trace was quiet for a long moment. "It's killing me that there's nothing I can do. No proof. No other charges I can bring him in on."

It had to dredge up bad memories for Trace. The way he'd been forced to live for so long. The volatile environment he'd had to survive.

"Called Fallon," he went on. "She's going to try to have a word. She's got a lot of resources she can connect Raina with."

Fallon was a social worker in Mercer County. She worked in the Child Protective Services department, but the overall office wasn't very big, so she had plenty of contacts who could help Raina.

"That's a good idea. Plus, if anyone can reach Raina, it's Fal."

Fallon had a tenderness about her. She was an empath through and through, taking on the pain of the world and not looking away. She did whatever she could to heal it.

"That's what I was thinking, too," Trace agreed. "It's my last hope. I'm out of ideas."

"You've done everything you can. More than most would do."

Trace sighed across the line. "Doesn't feel like it."

"You have," I pressed.

"I guess." He paused. "How are things with you? Rho said you're making good progress at Thea's."

I stiffened at his words. Normally, it wouldn't have fazed me that Rho and Trace were talking about me. With a brood as big as ours, we kept each other apprised of the basic goings-on in our fellow siblings' lives. But I knew this was more. This was Trace checking in.

I tried not to let the annoyance at that settle in. "Yeah. Leak was pretty bad. Working on clearing out her bathroom."

"How are you feeling about…everything?"

Trace went for it. I guessed it was better than beating around the bush. But that annoyance just burned brighter. "I'm fine. It wasn't me who was kidnapped and almost killed."

Trace sucked in an audible breath on the other side of the line.

I was an asshole. There was no way around it. "I'm sorry," I muttered.

"We're just worried about you. You took it hard, finding out it was Silas."

"Wouldn't you?" I snapped.

"Yeah, I would," Trace said. "Which is why I'm checking on your ornery ass. So don't bite my head off. Tell me how you actually are."

I let out a long breath. "I'm dealing. Spending time with Thea? It's been helping."

It was as honest as I could be. More truthful than I should've been. But there was no way around it. Thea had a calming effect, and it eased me more than anything else had the past few months. But more than that, helping her gave me a purpose I needed.

"Wanna meet this girl. You bringing her to dinner anytime soon?"

An image of Thea at the Colson family table filled my head. She'd fit. But it would also likely overwhelm her. "Not sure on that. She's a little shy."

Trace chuckled. "What? You don't want to expose her to the chaos that is the Colsons just yet?"

I grinned out the windshield as Thea's house came into view. "Don't want to scare her off."

Trace let out a low whistle. "You like her."

"I do." It was as simple as that, yet so much more.

"Well, I want to meet her whenever you're ready."

"Noted. I gotta go."

"All right. Take care of yourself, Shep."

"You, too. Tell my niece I love her."

I heard the smile in Trace's voice when he said, "She wants you to go riding with her and Arden next weekend."

"I'll see what I can do about that."

We hung up just as I pulled up in front of Thea's house. She was out front watering her garden in those damn overalls, her cat trying to attack the water as she went. The sight was beyond ridiculous, but it was somehow transfixing.

The way her hair was piled up in a bun, exposing her long, slender neck—one I wanted to trace with my tongue. How the sun hit the apples of her cheeks, making them glow. She was made for this, being in her garden and at one with the sun and nature around her.

I turned off my engine and slid out of my truck, grabbing a bag on the way. Thea's now green gaze came to me. Something about that, how she no longer hid from me—not even the shade of her eyes— hit something deep in my chest.

A smile tilted her lips up. "Hi."

"How was your day? How are you feeling?"

"Good," she said. "Relieved. I think telling you released some of the pressure that was building. That and knocking down those walls."

"I'm glad," I said, moving closer.

Moose leapt into the air, doing some sort of flip as he tried to attack the spray of water.

I shook my head. "What is wrong with that mutant cat?"

Thea scowled at me. "Nothing's *wrong* with him. And he's not a mutant."

"What'd that water ever do to him?"

Thea chuckled. "Could be here to do grave bodily harm to us all."

Moose batted at the stream but seemed to know I was talking about him because he turned to look at me and hissed.

"Moose," Thea chastised him.

The cat let out some sort of mangled meow.

I rifled through the bag and pulled out a small treat pouch. The moment I shook it, Moose bounded toward me and sat like a dog would.

My gaze shot to Thea. "You teach him that?"

She stifled a laugh. "No. But those are his favorite. He's not above bribery."

I opened the bag and bent to give him a couple. The moment my hand got close, Moose's front paws latched around it, and he yanked it toward his face.

"Jesus," I mumbled as he snatched the treats from me. "I could lose a finger."

Thea just grinned. "I'm not going to say that's not possible because it definitely is."

I moved closer to her, so close I could feel her heat. The urge to kiss Thea was so strong I had to bite the inside of my cheek to keep myself in check. Those green eyes peered up at me as she leaned closer.

One arm went around her, pulling her into me. "You really doing okay?"

As Thea stared up at me, she didn't hold anything back. I saw the war of emotions in her eyes. "I didn't sleep that great."

"Fuck," I whispered.

"It's okay."

"It's not." And I hated that she'd been struggling to find that rest alone. I wanted to be there to soothe her back into dreamland. Or tire us both out so we had no choice but to pass out. The latter sounded a hell of a lot better.

Her gaze softened on me. "Even though I didn't sleep, it was a good day. I feel…better. Braver."

Thea's words hit me like beautiful blows. "I'm glad."

"Me, too."

I bent then, unable to stop myself. My lips brushed her temple, featherlight. But the feel of her skin against mine scalded in the best way. "You're one of the strongest people I know," I whispered.

As I pulled back, our eyes locked. It would be so easy to dip my head and take that mouth. Thea's lips parted, and her head tipped back. Silent permission. Those plump, berry lips. I wanted to know what they tasted like. What they— My phone rang.

The sound was so jarring, Thea jerked in my arms. I cursed as I let her go, pulling the device out of my pocket. Jennie's name flashed on the screen. "My realtor," I said before answering. "Hey, Jennie."

"Shep," she greeted, not wasting any time before getting into it. "I'm not having any luck on a rental that meets your specifications. Best I can do is early September."

I let out another curse.

"Can you stay at Cope's place for a couple of months? Or Nora's?"

That was the thing about small towns. Jennie knew my whole family and had helped most of us with our real estate purchases. "Yeah. I'll figure it out. Go ahead and get the lease worked up for the September place."

"Will do. Let me know if you need anything else."

"Thanks, Jennie."

"Anytime."

I hung up to find Thea studying me. "What's wrong?"

I shoved my phone back into my pocket. "Nothing, really. I just need a rental while I work on the new house. She can't find me one until early September."

Thea studied me for a long moment. "It's more."

That was the thing with Thea. She always saw more. I'd sensed it while watching her from afar. But truly getting to know her, I saw it firsthand. She had a radar for wounds and scars, anything that might be amiss.

"It means staying with my mom or brother for a couple of months. They've been...hovering since Rho was taken. I didn't handle it well when I found out it was Silas."

If Thea had been willing to give me her hard truths, the least I could do was give her mine. Even if it made me look weak.

Thea's expression didn't fall in pity like I expected. She simply switched off the water and moved into my space. "You blame yourself."

Acid crept up the back of my throat. "I worked with him for almost a decade."

"And an FBI profiler who'd been trained for that long worked with Silas for years and didn't see it."

My mouth snapped closed.

"Shep," Thea said, her voice going soft as she laid a hand on my chest. "People fool us. We think they're one thing when they're really another. It doesn't say anything about *us*; it says something about *them*."

I knew what those words had cost Thea. How deeply she understood that torment. "I hate what Silas did to Rho. What he did to Anson. And it's because of me that he had the access to inflict that damage."

"And you think he wouldn't have found another way?" Thea challenged. "He was a freaking psychopath."

I let out a harsh breath. "I know. I just… It messes with me."

"Understandably. And it doesn't help when it feels like the people around you are watching you like a hawk, trying to see if you're going to break."

"No. It doesn't," I admitted.

Thea was quiet for a moment, her hand still on my chest, eyes searching mine. Then she finally spoke two words that shocked the hell out of me. "Stay here."

Chapter Twenty-Five

Thea

WHAT THE HELL WAS I DOING? APPARENTLY, I HAD NO control over my vocal cords because they just spat out words like *stay here*. That was a horrible, no good, very bad idea.

I'd be on edge the whole time. Or worse, I'd throw myself at Shep.

Because watching him walk around in those white tees that hinted at the planes of muscle I'd stalked through my window as he worked in my yard would be more than I could take. And what if he wore them with gray sweatpants around the house? Good God, I'd be powerless.

Shep stared down at me, those amber eyes searching. "Thorn. You only let me in your house for the first time a few days ago. Not sure you're ready for that."

God, he was such a good guy. Which was why I took a deep breath and said, "I'm sure."

He kept watching me for a moment.

"Really," I pressed. "It'll be nice to be able to pay you back for a fraction of what you've been doing for me."

That was apparently the wrong thing to say because Shep scowled. "You don't *owe me* anything."

I pinned him with a stare of my own. "I know you're charging me about one-tenth what you should be."

I'd gone to the hardware store on my break from Bloom the other day and perused the aisles. The prices were a heck of a lot higher than what Shep had said. Way more than a discount could make up for.

His gaze shifted to the side, and I knew I was right.

"Let me do this for you. I've got a guest room with your name on it. We'll have to share the bathroom, and I know it's not as fancy as you're used to, but—"

Shep's eyes shot back to me, cutting off my words. "If you think there's anywhere I'd rather be than here, you're dead wrong."

My breath hitched at the fire in his eyes, a mixture of annoyance and something else that had warmth stirring low. Shep had parts of me I hadn't been sure still existed coming back to life. Parts I only remembered when I was reading an especially good romance—one that reminded me there were still happily ever afters out there, even if they were just in the pages of a book.

"Is that a yes?"

He grinned. "It's a hell yes."

A laugh bubbled out of me. "Okay, then."

My hand started to slip from his chest, but Shep caught it, pressing it against his pec. "Thea, I don't want you to feel uncomfortable. So, you set the rules. I'll follow them. Whatever you need."

Such a good guy. Too good for me to reach for, but I was doing it anyway.

"You don't make me feel uncomfortable. You make me want... more."

Those amber eyes flashed gold. "More."

I nodded.

"I like more." Shep's fingers curled around mine. "Thank you, Thea."

"You're welcome."

He squeezed my hand. "Now, how about I take you to dinner?"

"Dinner?" I squeaked.

"Nothing fancy," Shep assured me. "What about The Pop? The food's a hell of a lot better hot off the grill."

I'd never eaten at The Pop. I'd gotten takeout or stared at the adorable interior through the windows, but I'd never actually sat in one of the red booths. I'd never wanted to risk people making small talk or getting curious about me. But I was done with that. If I wanted more, I had to reach for it. Which meant I could only say one thing.

"Okay."

Shep pulled his truck into a parking spot in front of the fifties-era diner with a neon-accented teal and red sign that read *The Soda Pop*. It wasn't packed since it was still early, but it wasn't empty either. I rubbed my suddenly damp palms on my jeans.

They were the nicest pair I had. I'd asked Shep to wait while I got cleaned up. He'd said I could go just like I was, but I wasn't about to do that. So, after I got Moose and the kittens situated, I'd done the best I could in twenty minutes.

Dark jeans and a white, cap-sleeve blouse with little lace accents. I'd even slicked on a little eye shadow, mascara, and some lip gloss. And yet again, I'd decided to leave the contacts behind. Because I wanted to be brave. Wanted to be *me*. When I stepped outside, Shep had done a head-to-toe scan and said, "If this is what you do with twenty minutes, I'm in trouble."

My stomach had done a series of acrobatics befitting a Cirque du Soleil show at that. But now I wondered why I thought I was so damn brave. What if someone recognized me as Brendan's ex, or worse, from one of those *sites*? Bile surged, but I swallowed it down.

A hand slipped around mine, fingers weaving. The action was so simple but grounding, making us stronger together than either of us was apart. "If this is too much, I can call in a to-go order and we can take it on a picnic somewhere quiet."

My gaze moved from the diner to Shep. There was so much understanding in his face. "I want to go inside. I've always wanted to eat here. They have those little jukeboxes on the tables."

A grin pulled at Shep's mouth. "I think I've even got a few nickels to put in a song request or two." He studied me for a second. "Here's the deal. If it gets to be too much at any point, just say you need to go. I'll get the check, and we'll be gone. We're going for more but not at the risk of pain."

There was pain right then. But it was the beautiful kind. The kind that came from a man giving you the sort of understanding you didn't ever think you'd get. "Sometimes, it's worth it. Because what's on the other side is that much sweeter for what you've gone through."

Shep's thumb swept back and forth across my hand. "Love the way you see the world." He gave my hand one more squeeze and then let go. "Stay there."

My brows pulled together as Shep hopped out of the truck and rounded the front. Then he opened my door and smiled.

That flipping sensation was back in my belly. "Such a gentleman."

Shep's hand closed around mine again the second my feet were on the pavement. "Sometimes," he whispered in my ear.

A shiver skated over my skin, the kind that held all sorts of promise. *Get ahold of yourself.*

If I couldn't even make it inside a diner without jumping the man, how would I handle living with him?

As if reading my mind, Shep's grin only widened as he led me toward The Pop.

"It's not nice to gloat," I snapped.

He barked out a laugh. "I like knowing I affect you."

I gave him my best glare, and Shep only laughed harder.

Just as he was about to reach for the door handle, it opened. Shep took a step back to let the person out.

Mara.

Her blue eyes brightened as she caught sight of him, but that brightness dulled the instant she took in our joined hands. "Shep," she croaked. "Thea. Good to see you."

I didn't miss the wince on Shep's face. "You, too," he said. "Takeout?"

Mara forced a smile. "Movie night with the girls. I'm on food duty."

"That'll be fun," Shep said.

"Yeah." Mara's gaze slid to me and then back to Shep. "You guys have a good night."

"You, too," I mumbled.

Then she was gone, as fast as her feet could take her.

I looked up at Shep. "I feel like I just stabbed her."

He shook his head quickly. "She and I haven't been together for a really long time, and it never got serious."

"She wanted it to." It wasn't a question. I'd seen the longing in Mara's eyes, both when she and Shep happened to be at the bakery at the same time and now.

"Maybe," Shep said honestly. "But I didn't feel that way about her. It wasn't…more."

My breath hitched at that. But I understood.

He squeezed my hand. "Don't let that run-in ruin our night. We need to eat our weight in fried food and milkshakes."

Shep was right. This was supposed to be a good time. The first step toward normal. Toward a *life*. "That sounds perfect to me."

He led us inside and toward an empty booth. I slid across the red leather, taking in the fifties charm as a woman in an era-appropriate pink dress with red accents approached. "Shepard Colson, as I live and breathe. I was starting to worry you'd forgotten all about us."

"I'd never, Miss Sally."

The woman with gray threaded through her hair laughed as she turned to me. "This one's too charming for his own good."

I couldn't help but answer her smile with one of my own. "And cocky, too."

Another laugh burst out of her. "I like you. Thea, right? You usually come in for takeout, though. Partial to the onion rings."

My body stiffened, but I breathed through it. This was normal. Small-town life. "Thought it was time to really get the full experience."

"Love that," Sally said. "You kids know what you want to drink?"

"I'll take an Arnold Palmer," Shep said. "What about you?"

"Diet Coke? I need time with the milkshake list."

Sally grinned. "I'm partial to the birthday cake one. Sounds weird, tastes delicious."

"I'll keep that in mind."

Sally slid two menus onto our table. "Take your time. I'll be back with your drinks."

Shep didn't look at the menu. His eyes stayed right on me. "Good?"

I nodded. "She's nice."

"She's friends with my mom, so I know I'll be getting a call from her, asking all about this."

I tugged on the corner of my lip with my teeth. "Is that a bad thing?"

"Only that my mom will have eighty-two million questions, and I wouldn't be surprised if she stops by the bakery."

More deep breaths. Small-town life. Family that gave a damn. They were good things. I just had to reframe them in my mind. "If she does that, at least I can win her over with baked goods."

Shep barked out a laugh. "Not a bad plan, actually." He inclined his head toward the menu. "What are you thinking?"

I started to look down at the options, but something caught my eye across the way. The person stood down the street a little ways and wore a hoodie pulled up so you couldn't see their face, but I swore they were staring right at me.

"Thea?"

My gaze jerked back to Shep. "Sorry, what?"

"Are you okay?" He turned to see what I'd been looking at, but when I followed his line of sight, no one was there.

"Fine. I just thought I saw…" I shook my head and took a deep breath. "Jumping at shadows."

Shep reached across the table and linked his fingers with mine. "Might be that way until you get used to this sort of thing."

I nodded, looking over his shoulder. That was always the problem. I never knew when my mind was playing tricks on me and when it was right and telling me to run.

Chapter Twenty-Six

Shep

MY PHONE DINGED JUST AS I PULLED TO A STOP IN FRONT OF Thea's house. Glancing down at the screen, I saw that one of my siblings had changed the name of the chat to *Please Return to Sender.* I grinned as I shook my head.

> **Cope:** *Shep, what in the actual fuck? You're moving in with a WOMAN? These are the things you inform your brother about.*

A few days had passed since Thea invited me to stay. I'd wanted to give her time to back out or change her mind, but she hadn't. So, here I was, with all my essential belongings in the back of my truck and everything else in storage.

> **Me:** *Chill. Not that kind of moving in.*

But that wasn't exactly right either. I wasn't sure what Thea and I were. Not only friends but not more than that either. We were in some sort of in-between. But I'd take that over anything else any day of the week.

> **Kye:** *Why do I find it hard to believe that you're moving into a*

random broken-down house in the middle of nowhere but have zero interest in the woman who lives there?

Me: *Her house isn't broken down. And even if it was, it'd be a hell of a lot better than living with you.*

Kye: *You built my house, asshole.*

I chuckled to myself, and my fingers flew over the keyboard.

Me: *Your house, I love. It's you residing in it that's the problem.*

Rhodes: *Children, play nice.*

Cope: *You all suck. You never keep me in the loop.*

Fallon: *Then maybe you should come home once in a blue moon. I swear I'm going to forget what you even look like.*

Kye: *Just find one of those billboards a few towns over. What are you selling now? Boner pills or tube socks?*

I flicked the chat on mute. They'd go on like this for hours. But I knew it was only a matter of time before I got cornered at a family dinner and was forced to explain my relationship with Thea. Only I didn't have the words to describe it. The only thing I knew was that I felt good when I was around her. And that was a welcome reprieve.

The front door opened as I turned off the engine and slid out of my truck. When Thea stepped out, the sun hit her, and I sucked in a sharp breath. That was the kind of beauty Thea had. The type that sucked the air right out of your lungs.

It was clear she'd been working in the garden or greenhouse. She wore jean shorts that were frayed at the edges, the loose threads hanging down. I wanted to trace each and every one. Wanted to know what that smooth, olive skin would feel like beneath my fingertips.

Thea's tank top revealed sun-kissed shoulders and then dipped down in the front to tease with more skin there. Her body was all long, lean curves that I'd give anything to memorize.

What the hell had I been thinking? Living in close proximity to a woman who haunted my every waking thought and my dreams, too?

I would end up doing something monumentally stupid. Something she wasn't ready for.

Thea sent me a hesitant smile. "Hi."

It was the uncertainty I saw that had me giving in. My legs ate up the space between us before I had a chance to tell them to stop. It didn't take me long to reach her, and the moment I was in her vicinity, I caught the scent of flowers and coconut. That scent could bring me to my knees.

"You okay?" I asked, my voice going gritty.

Her head tipped back, green eyes on display. "A little nervous."

I loved the honesty. It was precious. Because I knew it cost her something to give it to me. I reached out and twined our fingers. "You can change your mind. I can stay at Cope's house—"

Thea shook her head, sending tendrils of dark hair spilling out of her bun. "I want you to stay. Sometimes nervous is good. It means I'm leaning into the unknown."

I traced the back of her hand with my thumb. "You make the rules, remember?"

"I know. But I don't think I have any. Other than no wiring my house for internet."

I chuckled. "As much as I would like to run a high-speed fiber-optic cable through here, I will refrain. I have my phone. I can hotspot any internet I need."

Thea let out a breath. "Okay."

"So, we're doing this?"

She nodded. "We are. Come on in. I'll show you the guest room."

The moment we stepped inside, Moose greeted us and let out a mangled meow. I crouched low to scratch him behind the ears. "Hey, buddy."

He butted my hand with his head. After a moment, I straightened, and he slapped my leg repeatedly in answer.

"Moose," Thea chastised. "That's not nice."

He let out what sounded almost like a bark and then took off.

Thea sent me an apologetic smile. "I'm sorry. He gets demanding with food and affection. But honestly, that's a good sign. It means he likes you."

I arched a brow at her. "What would he do if he *didn't* like me?"

"You don't want to know."

A chuckle slipped free, and I didn't miss the way Thea's gaze dropped to my mouth. It was as if she was tracing it with her eyes and memorizing the sound.

I cleared my throat. "So, where am I bunking?"

Thea jolted. "Right. This way."

She led me down a familiar hallway and past the bathroom I was restoring. "You've seen the kitchen and the living room." Tiny meows sounded from the living area, and I could see the kittens tussling in their play area.

"The main bathroom is here." Thea gestured to a small bathroom with one of those tub-shower combos and a single sink.

My fingers itched to design a remodel for her. There was so much more she could do with the space.

"My bedroom is there." Thea pointed to an open door just down from the bathroom.

I only caught tiny snatches of color: a soft green comforter with pale purple accents, a photo of a field hanging over her bed—one mere feet from the other open door in the hallway.

"And this is you."

I stepped inside the bedroom. It was small but cozy. There was a quilt over the bed that looked warm, and an older dresser opposite the bed. But the two windows looked out over Thea's incredible garden, almost making you feel one with the space.

"I know it's not much—"

"It's perfect," I said, turning back to her. "I'm going to get spoiled waking up to that garden every day."

Pink hit the apples of Thea's cheeks. "I'm glad you like it."

"Love it," I corrected.

"Love it," she echoed.

We stood there for a long moment, the air charging around us.

Thea's tongue flicked out, wetting her bottom lip. "Do you need help getting your stuff in?"

I wanted to follow that track of wetness with my tongue. *Hell.* Not even five minutes in, and I couldn't keep my head straight.

I swallowed down the urge. "I've got it. I'll just unpack and then dig in on the guest bath if that's cool with you?"

Thea's head bobbed up and down. "Of course. I'm just doing a harvest in the greenhouse. I thought your mom might want some of my extras."

The offer hit me right in the damn rib cage. "She'd love that."

Thea grinned. "Basket of goodies, coming right up."

She turned and headed out of the room. I couldn't stop my gaze from dropping to her heart-shaped ass as she went. My fingers twitched at my sides, itching to reach out.

Cold showers. I'd be taking lots of cold showers.

Chapter Twenty-Seven

Thea

MY RAG MOVED ACROSS THE BAKERY TABLE IN CIRCLES AS I looked for any sign of crumbs or spills, but my mind was a million miles away. It was on Shep. His tall, muscular form moving through my house. The way his muscles bunched and flexed as he worked on the bathroom. How his tees rode up when he stretched while drinking his coffee in the morning, exposing a hint of one of those V things.

Three days.

Shep had been living with me for three days, and I was about to combust. He, on the other hand, seemed perfectly fine. I'd caught his gaze lingering on my legs or lips a time or two, but he hadn't made a single move.

I'd thought with our pseudo-date at The Pop, things were moving in that direction, but all of a sudden, it was like he was back to treating me like spun glass. It wasn't that I didn't appreciate his carefulness—because I did. It meant he cared. I was just ready for…more.

"Pretty sure you're taking the varnish off that table at this point."

I jerked up at the sound of Sutton's voice.

She laughed. "What is going on in that head of yours?"

I couldn't help the flush that rose to my cheeks. "Sorry. Distracted, I guess."

Thankfully, there were only two patrons in the bakery at the moment, and I was pretty sure they were both tourists—no one to remember my embarrassment.

Sutton grinned. "I know that kind of distraction. How is your new roomie?"

My cheeks just got hotter.

"That good, huh? Let me live vicariously."

"It's not like that," I hissed under my breath.

Sutton's brows lifted. "I thought you were rectifying that situation."

"He's not—I'm not sure if he's interested in me like that. Sometimes, I think he is. But others…"

"Trust me, honey. That man is interested with a capital I."

My stomach twisted. "I'm not so sure. He hasn't even kissed me."

"Do you want him to?" Sutton asked, cutting right to the point.

"Yes," I answered. It was as simple as that. Only I wanted him to do a hell of a lot more than kiss me.

Sutton straightened, her hands going to her hips. "This is the twenty-first century. Women run billion-dollar companies, the government, heck, they fly to the freaking moon. We sure as hell can make the first move."

I took an instinctive step back, shaking my head. What if Shep rejected me? What if I messed it up and made things awkward for the next couple of months he was living with me?

"Thea," Sutton said. "He likes you. But he probably instinctively knows you've been through some hard stuff and doesn't want to rush you."

"He knows," I whispered.

Sutton's face softened. "You told him?"

I nodded.

"I love that you felt comfortable sharing that with him. Shep is one of those miraculous good ones. That means he's going to take it slow."

"So slow I'm about to crawl out of my skin," I grumbled.

Sutton burst out laughing, then pitched her voice low. "Honey, that's what a vibrator is for. Take the edge off."

"I'm pretty sure I'd have to buy a jumbo pack of batteries."

Sutton only laughed harder, and it was infectious, bringing me under, as well.

"You two look like you're up to no good. I want in."

I turned at the voice that sounded like it smoked five packs a day. Lolli, Shep's grandmother, stood just inside the door, clutching a wrapped package in one hand and a purse in the other—a bag that looked like a bejeweled version of a pot leaf.

It fit. Lolli Reynolds was a character and a half with her hippie dresses and necklaces that weighed half her weight. But she was also the apple of our cook, Walter's, eye.

"Hi, Lolli," I greeted.

She beamed at me. "My darlings. How are you both?"

"Good," Sutton said, moving to give her a hug. "You?"

"Fabulous. I'm planning a trip to Peru. Going to do one of those ayahuasca journeys. Open my mind."

My brows about hit my hairline. "Isn't that the drug that makes you hallucinate?"

Lolli made a tsking noise. "Psychedelics are the future. You should join me. I can sense you need some energetic opening."

"I think I'm good with those pathways staying closed," I muttered.

She just shook her head and handed me the package in her hand. "I won't even punish you for being a buzzkill. This is for you."

"Me?"

Lolli nodded. "A thank-you for letting Shep stay with you for a couple of months. I know he didn't want to stay with us because Nora hovers. Or maybe"—she waggled her eyebrows—"he was hoping this living arrangement might have other perks."

Sutton put her arm around Lolli's shoulders. "My thoughts exactly."

My face flamed.

"There's nothing to be embarrassed about, dear. Sex is a very natural thing," Lolli said.

Dear God, someone kill me now.

"Did someone say sex?" Walter asked as he made his way out of the kitchen, a gleam in his eye.

I was going to crawl under the table.

"Not to you, you old coot," Lolli shot back.

"You say that now," Walter challenged, "but you don't know my moves."

"Walter!" Sutton chastised, laughter filling her voice.

"Let me take you out," Walter pressed.

Lolli just shook her head, her countless necklaces jangling. "You can't pin a woman like me down."

"I don't know, you might like the kind of pinning I do."

"Jesus," a new voice muttered. One I'd memorized. Shep made a face as he looked between Lolli and Walter. "Someone find one of those *Men in Black* mind wipe things and erase the last sixty seconds from my memory."

"Now, Shep," Lolli warned. "Like I told Thea, sex is perfectly natural—"

"Please, make it stop," I muttered.

Sutton just burst out laughing.

"You are not helping," I growled at her.

Walter clapped Shep on the shoulder. "Don't worry. My intentions are good. I'd marry your grandma tomorrow if she'd let me."

"Never going to happen," Lolli snapped.

"Why don't I open this," I said, cutting in before anyone could start talking about moves and pinning or anything else.

Lolli clapped her hands like a little kid. "Yes. Please."

I started ripping the brown butcher paper.

Shep strode forward. "Lolli, tell me you didn't."

My hands stilled as Lolli waved Shep off. "Oh, hush. Don't ruin the surprise."

"Surprise?" I was suddenly *very* wary.

"Don't listen to my stick-in-the-mud grandson. I came up with this one just for you. I know how partial you are to your greenhouse goodies," Lolli said.

That had a little of the tension easing out of me. How bad could it be if it had to do with my greenhouse?

Shep pinched the bridge of his nose. "I'm sorry for what's about to happen."

I ripped the paper off, letting it fall to the floor, and took in the canvas covered in countless glittering gemstones. It was one of those diamond art painting things. The image Lolli had created was a field of different gourds. But as I stared at it longer, my jaw dropped.

Sutton clamped a hand over her mouth to try to hold in her laughter. "Penis pumpkins," she choked out.

My face was on fire. The canvas was covered in dick gourds of every size, shape, and color, but all distinctly phallic.

Shep pinned Lolli with a glare. "Why can't you be a normal grandmother and knit sweaters or something?"

Lolli drummed her fingers across her lips. "I could come up with an interesting snowball pattern…"

"For fuck's sake," Shep muttered.

A laugh bubbled out of me and quickly spiraled into a sound I had zero control over. A snort broke free, and I slapped a hand over my mouth.

Shep's eyes were on me, and I saw such warmth in them, tenderness even.

"See?" Lolli challenged. "She likes it. But that isn't the only reason I came in."

"You came in to accept my marriage proposal," Walter cut in.

Lolli just rolled her eyes. "Nora and I would love for you to come to dinner—"

"Lolli," Shep warned. "Don't push her."

"I'm not pushing," Lolli snapped back.

My laughter quickly died away. A huge dinner would be a lot for me, but I wanted to get to know Shep's family. Though maybe he didn't feel the same.

Shep's gaze cut to me the moment I stopped laughing. It shouldn't have surprised me that he read my expression. He was so damn good at it.

In three long strides, he was in front of me. "Don't think I don't want you there, Thorn. I want you wherever I can get you. Why do you think I've been coming to the bakery every day for months? I don't even like sweets."

My mouth dropped open, and Sutton made a strangled sound.

"Now that's a little better," Lolli mumbled.

Shep shot her a warning look. "I think you've caused enough chaos for one day."

"It's not even noon," Lolli argued.

Shep turned back to me. "See you at home." And with a wink, he was gone.

Chapter Twenty-Eight

Thea

I SHIFTED ON THE CHAISE, THE LATE-AFTERNOON SUN BEATING down on me. I was trying to focus on my book. It should've had me flipping the pages at a fevered pace because the Highlander hero had just realized that he'd fallen for his wife by arranged marriage, even though she was from an enemy clan. Things were about to get explosive.

Instead, I was replaying Shep's words over and over in my head. *"Don't think I don't want you there, Thorn. I want you wherever I can get you. Why do you think I've been coming to the bakery every day for months? I don't even like sweets."*

He didn't even like sweets? Shep had been in The Mix Up almost every day since we'd opened our doors. But now that I really thought about it, he rarely got anything with sugar.

I adjusted myself on the chaise. I couldn't get comfortable. Felt like I was crawling out of my skin. I refocused on the page, but the words blurred together.

I was in such a distracted state that I didn't even hear the footsteps on the deck until the book was being tugged out of my hands. I shot up to find Shep scanning the pages, a smile stretching across his face. "Not much of a reader, but I can see that I've been missing out."

Ice slid through my veins as memories slammed into me. Brendan's voice twisted and cruel. *This is what you spend your time doing while I'm not around? Reading this trash? But I guess what else would a slut read?*

All of a sudden, hands were cupping my cheeks. "Thea, look at me."

I blinked rapidly, bringing Shep's face into focus. It was only then that I realized I was shaking.

"That's it. You're okay." His amber eyes searched mine. "I'm so sorry. I didn't mean to scare you."

"Y-you didn't."

Shep's gaze remained gentle, but his silence challenged my statement.

My tongue felt heavy in my mouth, thick, like I couldn't get the words out around it. "He hated that I read those books."

"Fuck," Shep muttered.

"I know you're not him. You're not anything like him. I just— it's like my body remembers it all and braces."

Shep's thumbs skated across my cheeks. "PTSD."

I worried my bottom lip. I'd figured out that much, trying to research why I was still so scared all the time, even though I was safe. "It's like my body's betraying me all over again."

"No," Shep said, shaking his head. "Your body's protecting you. It's trying to look out for you. It's just going to take time for it to realize that you're okay. That no one's going to hurt you."

Tears burned the backs of my eyes. "It makes me feel like a freak."

Anger flashed in Shep's eyes. "That's the last thing you are." His thumb skated lower, to my pulse point. "You're strong. So fucking brave. And you're not letting him win."

The tears wanted to break free so badly. "Sometimes, it feels like he already has."

"No," Shep clipped. "He hasn't. Look at the beautiful life you've built for yourself here. And it's only getting more beautiful."

I took a deep breath, letting it out slowly. "You don't know everything."

I couldn't look at him. Not when I was about to tell him what I had to.

The rough pad of Shep's thumb swept along the skin of my neck. "I know there's more. But I also know there's no way it could change the way I feel about you."

Tears filled my eyes. He was wrong. There was no way it couldn't. And losing the promise of those words would kill me. But it was better now than later. Just rip off the Band-Aid.

"I'm not just protective about my identity because I'm scared Brendan will find me," I said softly.

Shep's thumb kept stroking. "Okay."

The feel of his hands on me was too much. Too good. All the things I was going to lose.

I pulled back, breaking the connection. Walking to the end of the deck, I stared out at the fields that led to forests I knew disappeared into mountains. I wanted to be like that landscape, moving and evolving. Ever-changing so no one could ever catch me.

I felt Shep at my back more than I heard him. But he didn't touch me, seeming to sense that I needed some space.

"I told you Brendan was good at tech. I just didn't realize how good until it was too late."

Shep didn't say anything, just waited.

"A few months after we broke up, I got fired. There was an accusation that I'd broken the nonprofit's morality clause. But the same day, an anonymous number sent me an article about Brendan donating a million dollars to The Literacy Project."

"He got you fired," Shep growled.

I nodded at the field, not looking back. "I was almost relieved because I thought that would be it. It was over. He'd done his worst. He'd already alienated me from all my friends, other than Nikki. I didn't have anything left but work and her. I thought it was my chance to leave and start over. To finally be free."

"But it wasn't over?"

"No," I whispered. "After I got home that night, it was like my whole apartment went haywire. My TV and stereo turned on full blast, my alarm went off. Then my cell phone started alerting. So many notifications it nearly short-circuited the device."

I gripped my hands in front of me, squeezing my fingers tightly. "There were alerts for fraud from my bank. Astronomical purchases for escorts and sex toys. Lingerie. Calls and texts from strangers wanting to set up *dates* because my photo and phone number had been put up on an escort site."

"What the fuck?" Shep gritted out.

I didn't want to have to tell him the last part. The unshed tears swimming in my eyes spilled over and tracked down my cheeks. "Then there were the emails. So many porn sites, thanking me for signing up as a performer. They all had pictures of me. Videos. Because he'd put cameras in my apartment. Ones I never knew were there."

My voice shook as I kept going. "I tried to get it all down at first. Did everything I could to remove it. Some agreed, others refused, saying I'd signed a contract. But there are so many more that I couldn't even find a way to get ahold of because they're in the dark parts of the internet. Places you *never* want to go."

My breath hitched as I tried to keep the sobs down. "So, I just gave up. I never know if the next tourist who walks through the bakery door has seen every last inch of me. I don't know if someone will recognize me and tell everyone what a whore they think I am. So, he won. I'm just trying to pick up the pieces."

Shep was quiet for a long time. All I could hear was his ragged breaths behind me. When he finally spoke, his words shook with fury. "I am going to fucking kill him."

Chapter Twenty-Nine

Shep

I COULDN'T MOVE, COULD BARELY BREATHE. THE TENSION AND rage radiating through me strangled each inhale and exhale.

What kind of monster did that? It might not have been a physical assault, but in some ways, it was so much worse. Photos and videos of Thea at her most vulnerable. For anyone to see.

She turned then as if the ferocity in my voice had startled her. And when I got my first look at her face, it nearly brought me to my knees. It was more than the tears tracking down her cheeks. It was the genuine surprise at my anger.

That only made the fury burn brighter, flames wrapping around my throat, scorching the tissue there. Thea hadn't thought I'd be angry at Brendan. She'd…what? Thought I'd be mad at her? See her differently?

"Thea," I croaked.

"It's okay," she whispered. "I get it if you need to walk away."

I moved then, unable to hold myself back. I closed the distance between us in two long strides and pulled her into my arms. I could feel the wetness on her cheeks sink into my tee. Felt how her body trembled.

"The last thing in the world I want to do is walk away."

"Shep." Thea's voice shook.

"This would never make me see you differently. Other than discovering you're even stronger than I knew."

She let out a hiccuped sob.

"None of this is your fault. Not one thing." I held her tighter to me as if I could soak up all the pain. All the ways she'd been hurt.

"Most of the time, I know that. But then my mind gets twisted. It's like I still hear his voice in my head on repeat. And sometimes, I believe it."

I slid my hand along Thea's jaw, tipping her head back so those green eyes connected with mine. "You hear that voice? You come to me. I'll tell you the truth." My thumb swept back and forth across skin as smooth as silk. "Kind. Brave. Strong. Funny. So damn smart."

"Shepard." My name was barely audible on her lips.

"Will take a fucking penis diamond painting from my grandma so you don't hurt her feelings."

That had a small laugh bubbling out of her. "I hung it in the greenhouse. Above my potting table."

I shook my head. "Of course, you did. Lolli will love that." Any hints of amusement in my tone died. "This is why you haven't wanted people in your house. Because he put cameras in without your knowledge."

Thea nodded slowly. "I can't help but imagine someone else doing the same. Even if I know the chances are one in a million."

Hell. And she'd let me in after all that. Let me stay with her. It was even more of a gift now.

Thea went quiet for a long moment. "It's more than just living with the fact that those photos are out there. My head...it's a messed-up place."

My thumb stilled. "Your brain is trying to grab hold of the truth." And Brendan fucking Boseman had traumatized her so much that she couldn't see it clearly.

"Hasn't anyone ever told a lie about you, but they're so convincing, you start to believe it yourself?"

My pulse thrummed in my neck, the beat so heavy I could feel each squeeze. I had one of those lies. One that still lived in the recesses of my mind. That I was worthless. But it was tinged with the truth. That I'd been given up, abandoned. Unwanted.

"Yes," I said, the single syllable more sound than an actual word.

Thea's expression softened as her hand pressed against my chest. "I don't want to bring you into that. You're so…good. Everything I shouldn't reach for. But I can't seem to make myself walk away. It's so selfish. I shouldn't—"

I couldn't let her keep going, couldn't let those doubts be given voice. So, I stole them right from the air. I closed the tiny distance between us, and my mouth met Thea's. I took those lies and snuffed them out.

The moment my lips touched hers, Thea's hand fisted in my tee. She pulled me impossibly closer, and her taste burned into me. Strawberries and mint tea. It was the only thing I wanted to taste for the rest of time.

Thea moaned, her lips parting. My tongue stroked. God, the feel of her mouth. Warm, wet heat. But so fucking soft. Delicate. Just like my Thorn. The strength outside hid the truth beneath: that she was nothing but sweet, soft feeling.

Thea pressed herself harder against me, seeking, searching. The added pressure and contact, the promise of all that was her, had my dick hardening against my jeans.

She moved then, hauling herself up and climbing me like I was a goddamn tree. She wrapped her legs around me as I took her mouth. Heat and need spread between us, fueling each other.

A bird called overhead, loud and close, the sound so intense and abrupt that it had Thea's head snapping back and her mouth tearing from mine. I watched the realization come over her in phases. Shock, then horror.

Thea released her legs from my waist and dropped to the ground, her fingers flying to her lips. "Oh, God. I'm so sorry. I don't know—"

"Pretty sure I'm the one who kissed you," I said gently.

Thea shook her head rapidly. "But I—I *mauled* you."

My brow arched. "If that's mauling, sign me up."

"It's not funny. I climbed you like some sort of spider monkey. I attacked your mouth."

I couldn't help it, I laughed. "And I hope you do it again."

"Shep," she snapped.

I moved then, sliding into Thea's space. "Thorn." I hooked a finger through the belt loop on her shorts and tugged her closer, searching those hypnotic eyes. Her *real* eyes. "He shamed you about sex?"

Her gaze dipped down and to the side.

Bingo. What a prick.

My thumb skated across the front pocket of her shorts. "You wanting me? I'm only going to feel one way about that. Lucky as hell. And grateful. Okay, so that's two things."

Those pale green eyes came back to me. "You don't think it's... weird?"

"Hell, no," I clipped. "Just like I fucking loved whatever book it was you were reading. I mean, I don't know that I'm down for kilt role-play, but the rest? Hot."

Thea's lips twitched slightly. "I bet you'd look good in a kilt."

I barked out a laugh. "There is a lot I would do for you. But wearing a kilt is not one of those things."

"They make for easy access..."

Jesus. My dick was getting hard again. I pulled Thea into my arms, brushing the hair back from her face. "You wanna try this with me?"

Thea's breath hitched, but she nodded.

Relief swept through me. "Good. Because I want that. I want *you*. But I also think it's probably best if we take things slow." I didn't miss the disappointment on her face, and I liked that, too. "You've been through a lot. It's going to take time to erase the lies in your head, but we'll tackle them one by one."

"Sometimes, I just want to be normal. I don't want to be all twisted up inside. Even though I got away, I still don't feel free."

I'd never felt the urge to commit murder before, but it thrummed through me now—a demanding need to end the person who'd done this to Thea. But even that wouldn't be good enough. How did you come up with the appropriate punishment for a person who'd poisoned someone else's mind and made them live in fear? I wasn't sure there was anything strong enough.

"We're going to get you there." I bent and brushed my lips across hers. "You're not alone in this."

Thea's eyes shone with unshed tears, making the green sparkle in the late-afternoon light. "I've felt alone for a really long time."

I bent, pressing my face into her neck. "I know. But you aren't alone anymore."

"Shep," she whispered.

The sound of tires on gravel had my head snapping up. "You expecting anyone?"

Thea shook her head, her face paling.

"Stay here," I growled.

Half of me hoped it was Brendan fucking Boseman. I'd end him before he could blink.

Chapter Thirty

Thea

"**S**HEP, WAIT," I HISSED. BUT HE DIDN'T. AND THE WAY HE stalked around the side of my house said that whoever was on the other side would not be happy to see him.

I sucked in a breath as I followed after him, not letting it out until I heard Rhodes' voice. I quickly wiped my face, making sure it was free of tears.

"Why are you scowling at me? You're like Mr. Anti-Color over there."

"Mr. Anti-Color?" Shep parroted, annoyance clear in his tone.

I rounded the house just in time to see Rhodes gesture at her boyfriend. "You know. Averse to anything but black and shades of gray. Communicates mostly in grunts and scowls."

"Reckless," Anson growled, moving into her space. But there was amusement in the nickname, too.

Rhodes sent him an exasperated look. "Is any of that a lie?"

He pulled her into his arms and nipped her bottom lip. "Behave or there will be consequences."

Rhodes' eyes hooded. "What if I *want* those consequences?"

Shep made a gagging noise. "Please, God, make it stop. And what are you two doing here? Have you not heard of a phone?"

Rhodes stuck her tongue out at him. "We're coming to kidnap you. Dinner and a band at The Sagebrush. No arguments. We need a little fun around here." Rhodes' gaze shot to me, and I saw a pleading look there. "Don't say no. Kye and Fallon are coming, too."

A flicker of unease slid through me. Reading it, Shep crossed to me and slid an arm around my shoulders. "We have plans here."

I pressed a hand to his stomach, feeling the taut muscles there. "It's okay. We can go."

Shep's gaze swept down to me. "We don't have to."

"I *want* to."

He studied me for a long moment, trying to discern if that was the truth. But it was. It was time. Time to start *living*. Because I hadn't fought this hard for freedom, only to squander it and let Brendan continue to hold me prisoner.

I turned back to Rhodes and found her eyes locked on my hand on Shep's abs. "I just need fifteen to get ready. Do you want to come in? You could feed the kittens for me while I get cleaned up."

Rhodes' gaze jerked to my face, and she grinned like I'd just told her she'd won the lottery. "Love this. Everything about it."

"Is that why you're smiling like some feral pageant queen right now?" Anson asked, looking genuinely terrified.

"Shut up," Rhodes snapped, smacking his stomach. "My brother's happy. My friend's happy. I'm happy."

Anson sent Shep a concerned look. "Think you could tone it down? I'm worried her brain might explode from all the happy."

Rhodes whirled on him, pinching his side. As they bickered playfully, Shep turned to me. "Are you sure about this? They can hang on the back deck, or we can meet them at the bar."

I shook my head. "I'm done hiding. Not that I won't be careful, but I'm not making my life small to do it."

Shep's amber eyes burned as he dipped his head, his lips hovering just above mine. "Then let's go live that life."

Music blared from the speakers on stage as the band dropped into a cover of *Free Fallin'*. The dance floor was crowded, and the bar was packed. Usually, this sort of gathering would send me over the edge. But I felt perfectly safe as Shep slid an arm around my shoulders. And I felt like *me*.

I used to love going to concerts with Nikki at The Echo, the Silverlake Lounge, or The Greek. I wasn't a true music connoisseur like she was, but I enjoyed all kinds and the energy of a good crowd. It was just one of the many things I'd lost—one I was taking back.

Just like my eye color. I'd panicked for a moment when I remembered that I had my colored contacts out and then decided I was keeping it that way. I hated wearing the things. They made my eyes scratchy and were annoying to keep up with.

When I came out dressed in my nicest sundress paired with a worn-in pair of pale pink cowboy boots and hair curled in loose waves, Rhodes had grinned at me. "Love seeing your eyes."

Shep had just stared, his gaze heating as it roamed over me. I swore I could feel it as if he were tracing me with his fingertips. And he'd looked just as good to me, with his hair still damp from a shower and dressed in a fresh white tee, dark jeans, and boots.

And now, I felt the soft cotton of that tee as he bent to my ear. "You want a drink?"

Having a cocktail might be stretching my limits a little too far for one night. "Club soda and lime?"

Shep nodded. "Coming right up."

"I snagged a table," Fallon called as she motioned us over.

It was the first time I'd met Rhodes' foster sister and best friend, but I felt like I already knew her from all the times Rho had talked about her as we worked. She was on the quieter side at first, but as dinner went on, I saw the empathetic kindness Rhodes had described.

"Score," Rhodes said, grabbing my hand and tugging me toward the larger cocktail table surrounded by stools.

I slid onto one next to Fallon. "Did you get a drink?"

She smiled at me. "Kye's grabbing me one. It's like he doesn't trust me not to get kidnapped by a biker from here to the bar."

My lips twitched. I had noticed that the burly-looking man with more tattoos than I could count was especially protective of Fallon. Their relationship was different somehow. Like he was attuned to her every move.

"Did you get one?" Fallon asked. "I can text Kye to grab you one."

"Shep's getting me something."

The smile on Fallon's face turned soft. "You make him happy."

It was such a simple statement, but it had warmth spreading through me. Unfortunately, fresh on its heels came nerves. "It's new," I mumbled.

She reached over and gave my hand a quick squeeze. "Doesn't take a lifetime to see a change in someone. Sometimes, it just takes one honest moment to reach them."

A burn lit along my throat. "He's changing me. Making me braver. Helping me reach for things I was scared to reach for before."

Fallon's eyes shone in the light of the bar. "I love that."

A tattooed hand slid a very pink drink in front of Fallon. "I can't believe you made me order a peach crush."

Fallon choked on a laugh. "He insists on ordering my drinks? I'm going to make them as girlie as humanly possible."

"You're the worst," Kye grumbled.

"You mean the *best*," she shot back.

I felt Shep before I saw him. Some part of me recognized his heat. It had its own unique signature. His strong, tanned arm wrapped around me and deposited my club soda, then he bent, whispering in my ear, "You good?"

I nodded. "This band is pretty great."

Shep chuckled. "Doubting our ability to have good music in the sticks?"

I grinned up at him. "*Doubt* might be too strong a word."

The first strains of *You Shook Me All Night Long* came through the speakers, and Rhodes was instantly off her stool. "Come on, we have to dance!"

I couldn't help but laugh. "Big AC/DC fan?"

"It's a classic," she argued.

"She's lying. She just loves to dance," Anson grumbled.

Rhodes rolled her eyes at her boyfriend. "I already know *he* won't dance with me." She turned to me and grabbed my hand with her uninjured one. "Pleeeease?"

"Rhodes," Shep warned.

But I was already off my stool and taking Fallon's hand. "Let's do this."

Rhodes let out a little squeal as she tugged us toward the dance floor. And for the first time in *years*, I let go. I didn't think about Brendan, the pictures, or the millions of doubts racing through my head on a typical day. I felt…free.

We danced to rock songs and country tunes; even a pop song slipped in here and there. Before long, I was hauling my hair into a pile on the top of my head because it was sticking to my neck.

A guy slid in behind Fallon, wrapping an arm around her waist. She startled, quickly extricating herself from the guy's hold and waving him off. He sent her a slightly intoxicated but apologetic smile and began backing away.

But it wasn't quite fast enough. Because Kye shoved through the crowd, glowering at the guy who had paled to the shade of a vampire. Fallon tugged on Kye's black tee with some sort of design printed on the back. It wasn't long before the two of them were in an all-out argument, and the drunk dude was escaping into the crowd.

Rhodes rolled her eyes. "They'll yell at each other for a while. Want to get a drink?"

"Fallon's okay?"

"Oh, yeah," Rho said quickly. "She just gets annoyed when Kye gets overprotective."

I couldn't help but glance over my shoulder at the two of them. Kye towered over the petite woman. But as shy as Fallon seemed in certain circumstances, she showed no fear with the mountain man, jabbing a finger into his chest. *Interesting.*

"What do you want?" Rhodes yelled.

"Just water."

As she leaned over the bar to order, a hand curled around my arm, giving me a tug. I nearly fell back on my ass but righted myself, only to come face-to-face with one of the last people I wanted to see.

Russ Wheeler.

His eyes were glassy as they tracked down my body, stilling at my cleavage. "Thea. You clean up real nice."

I had the urge to cross my arms. I tried to pull free of Russ's grasp, but he only gripped me harder, his hold so tight I let out a squeak of pain.

Russ's eyes lit at the sound, and he licked his lips. "Putting on quite a show out there. But why don't we take this party somewhere private-like?"

My stomach roiled, and I yanked hard on my arm again. "Let me go."

"Don't play those games with me. You're begging for it. Come on, baby. I'll make you feel good."

The nausea intensified. "I said, let go," I snapped, shoving at Russ's chest with my free hand.

"Stop being such a cocktease. You were shaking your ass out there like a little slut. Wanted every man in this place to watch you. Now you're playing all innocent?" he snarled.

Russ made to grab for my waist but halted as I felt a wall of fury at my back.

"Get. Your. Hands. Off. Her," Shep snarled.

Russ sneered at him. "She yours? You really need to take a stronger hand with her. Whoring herself out all over that dance floor."

One second, Russ was standing there. The next, Shep's fist

connected with his nose in a sickening crunch I heard even over the music.

Russ crumpled to the floor in a wailing heap. "What the fuck?" he cried, but his voice sounded funny. Like he suddenly had a cold.

"Don't ever speak to her again. You even think of looking in her direction, and I'll do a hell of a lot worse than break your nose."

Russ was on his feet again. "You think you can threaten me, Box Baby? You're nothing but a bastard—"

Shep lunged.

Chapter Thirty-One

Shep

ARED HAZE SLIPPED OVER MY VISION AS I MOVED TO DECK THE bastard in front of me. But someone grabbed my shirt from behind just as Kye stepped between us, giving Russ a strong shove.

"Get the fuck out of here, Wheeler," Kye growled. "Shep held back. You know I won't."

"His whore started it," Russ whined.

Thea's face paled at his words, and the red haze came back. I charged.

"Hell," Anson cursed. "A little help?"

Kye turned, his eyes flaring slightly as he pushed me back. "Don't. He's not worth it."

But I couldn't stop. Thea had been hurt too much already. I wasn't about to let it happen again.

"Jesus," Anson muttered as he tried to hold me. "Have you been taking steroids or something?"

A soft hand pressed against my cheek. "Shepard."

Thea's voice was far from loud, but I still heard her above all the noise—the smoky lilt to it, the way it curled around me like an embrace.

Unshed tears shone in her eyes. "Please, don't."

All the fight went out of me, and Anson and Kye felt it, releasing me but keeping watch. I moved into Thea, my hands skimming over her. "Are you okay? Are you hurt?"

Russ was shouting in the background as a bouncer dragged him toward the door.

"I'm fine. It just took me by surprise. That's all."

She wasn't fine. I could feel the tremor in her muscles. I pulled her into me. "Come on. Let's get out of here."

"Oh, God. Thea," Rhodes said, moving toward us. "I'm so sorry. I didn't see him. I was talking to the bartender, and then someone yelled—"

"She's okay," Anson said, tugging her gently toward him. "But I think we should head out."

Fallon sent me a worried look. "Want me to call Trace? Thea should file a report. That was assault."

Thea's head snapped up. "No! No cops. I just…I just want to go home."

Fuck.

She didn't want the cops because she didn't want a paper trail.

I struggled to keep my breathing under control as I tucked her under my arm. "No cops." I sent Fallon a warning look. She wanted to believe that she could help, that laws and regulations could, but that wasn't always true.

"Come on," Kye said gruffly, wrapping an arm around Fallon's shoulders. "I'll take you home. I'll even get you a milkshake on the way."

Since coming to live with us at sixteen, she was the only person he was openly affectionate with. Maybe because her tender empathy had snuck under his walls. But, sometimes, I swore they could communicate without speaking. Like now, as Fallon stared up at him with challenge in her eyes. Then something shifted, and she simply nodded.

I let out a breath. Fallon could be a crusader and would march right up to the sheriff's office and file a report herself if she was determined enough.

Pulling Thea tighter against me, I guided us toward the exit. Just before we reached the door, a worried-looking Mara stepped into our path. "Jesus, Shep. Are you okay?"

"Fine." But my voice was tight, giving away the lie. My knuckles throbbed, and I could feel torn flesh there. I must've clipped Russ's teeth on my punch's follow-through.

"Do you need to go to the hospital? Get an X-ray?" Mara pressed.

"I'm good, Mara. Just need to get home."

Mara's gaze flicked to Thea for the briefest moment, and then she swallowed. "Right. Of course."

I didn't have it in me to feel guilty. The anger still pulsed through me, along with the need to get Thea out of there and know she was safe.

Anson held the door, and we stepped outside into the cooler night air. Just as we made it onto the street, the bouncer appeared. John shook his head. A beefy guy a few years younger than me, he'd been born and raised in Sparrow Falls.

"I'm sorry about him," John muttered, glancing at Thea. "Ma'am, I can call the sheriff's department if you'd like to press charges. But know he's been eighty-sixed. He won't be allowed back."

Thea gave him a shaky smile. "Thank you. I'm okay. Really."

"All right. But next time you come in, drinks are on us. We don't stand for that sort of thing here."

Thea relaxed into me. "I appreciate that. Thanks for being on it."

John nodded, clapping me on the shoulder before heading back inside.

"I'll be on it with a junk-punch," Rhodes muttered as she moved down the block to where we'd parked.

Anson shook his head as he followed her. "Am I going to have to bail her out of jail tomorrow?"

"The chances are good," Fallon singsonged.

"It'd be worth it," Rhodes grumbled.

We all slowed as we made it to our vehicles.

Rhodes studied Thea for a long minute. "You want us to come back with you? I could make you some tea and—"

Anson wrapped an arm around her shoulders, squeezing. "Shep's got her, Reckless."

Rhodes still waited for Thea's answer.

"I'm okay, really. Getting past freaked and on to pissed."

Fallon gave Thea a gentle smile. "Pissed is better."

Thea's lips twitched. "Agreed."

Kye sent me a questioning look. "You good? Need backup?"

I knew what he meant. He'd drop Fallon and go with me to send Russ a stronger warning if I thought he needed it. That was brotherhood right there. Even as risky as it would be with Kye's history, he'd do it. Because he always had my back.

"No, not tonight," I said, suddenly bone-tired, my hand aching.

Kye jerked his chin in my direction. "Just say the word."

I nodded at him and Fallon.

"Text in the morning and let me know if you're up for work or not. I've got things I can do on my own if you need to give that hand a rest," Anson said.

"Thanks, man."

He and Rhodes climbed into his truck as I guided Thea toward mine. I let go of her to open the door. She was quiet as she climbed up, not moving as I rounded the hood and got behind the wheel.

"Should you be driving?" Thea asked quietly.

"I've only had two beers between dinner and the bar."

She turned then, fingers ghosting over my already swelling knuckles. "I meant your hand."

I flexed it on instinct and winced as pain flared and I saw the blood smeared across my knuckles.

"I'm so sorry."

My gaze cut to her. "This isn't your fault."

"I know." There was a certainty in Thea's words that eased the anger pulsing through me. She brushed her fingers across the back of my hand. "But I'm still sorry."

"I'll pop some ibuprofen and be fine tomorrow."

Thea nodded but didn't look totally convinced as I started the engine and headed for her place. Both of us were quiet on the way home, lost in our spiraling thoughts. The moment I parked in front of Thea's house, she was out of the vehicle and waiting for me.

"Come on. I need to get some ice on your hand."

"You don't have to do that," I argued.

Thea's head tipped back, strands of hair falling out of her haphazard bun. "You're always taking care of everyone in your orbit. How about you let me take care of you for once?"

I stared down at Thea. She always saw more than the average person. "Okay."

"Good." She took my uninjured hand and tugged me toward the house. As we approached, she pulled her keys from her purse and unlocked the industrial deadbolt. With each catch of metal against metal, I was reminded just how much Thea had given me by letting me into her space. Her haven. Her *escape*.

The moment we stepped inside, Moose greeted us with mangled meows. He padded down the hallway, surprisingly light on his paws for how massive he was. He wove through Thea's legs as she walked, squawking at her.

"I swear he's yelling at you," I mumbled as we moved toward the kitchen.

"Oh, he definitely is. He's not used to me leaving him at night." She inclined her head toward the small kitchen table. "Sit."

There was an authority to her tone that had my lips twitching slightly. "Yes, ma'am."

Thea just shook her head and crossed to the refrigerator. I watched her pull out a few things, not focusing on the items but on how her sundress swished around her as she moved.

"Are you okay?" Countless others had asked tonight, but I needed to give voice to the question myself, hoping for an honest answer.

Thea stilled and then turned to face me. She leaned against the counter, letting out a long breath. "At first, I was scared. Then, I felt guilty."

I sat forward and opened my mouth to tell Thea she didn't have a thing to feel guilty about.

But she held up a hand to stop me. "Then I realized guilt was just one more lie. One more piece of poison in my brain. Wearing a sundress and dancing with friends doesn't make what he did okay. Russ is an asshole with a warped sense of reality."

She lifted a ginger ale and a bottle of pills from the counter with one hand, and an ice pack and towel with the other. "I'm not sorry you punched him. Sometimes, that's the only kind of consequence that someone like him can actually understand." Thea lifted my un-injured hand and poured three ibuprofen into my palm. "But I hate that you got hurt."

She dabbed some hydrogen peroxide on a cotton swab and gently cleaned my torn skin. The moment it was sanitized, she dabbed on some ointment I didn't really need, then stepped back, slowly wrapping the ice pack in the towel and laying it over my abused knuckles.

I looked up at Thea, gazing into those pale green eyes. "You aren't mad at me?"

She moved closer, stepping between my legs and running her fingers through my hair. "You made him let me go. Why would I be mad about that?"

"I made a scene." And *that*, I did regret. Thea didn't need more eyes on her, more attention, not when she was trying to stay under the radar.

"*He* was already making a scene."

"Stole ten years off my life when I saw his hands on you. What I would've been capable of in that moment? It scared the hell out of me."

Thea's brow furrowed, tiny lines digging in as her fingers dropped to my neck. "I'm okay."

My free hand cupped the back of Thea's thigh, just needing to feel her, to assure myself that was true. My fingers skated across her skin, feeling the smooth heat. They teased the hem of her dress, lifting the fabric there as my thumb traced circles on her flesh.

"Shep," she whispered, her voice dipping low.

"This helps. Just feeling you here. It's telling my brain you really are all right."

Thea moved in even closer, her legs pressed against the insides of my thighs, her chest close. So tempting. She lifted a hand to my face, her fingers stroking my scruff. "Maybe I need that, too."

Fuck.

"Thea," I croaked. "Not a good idea tonight."

There was a flicker of hurt in those green eyes.

I squeezed the back of her thigh. "Not because I don't want to. Trust me, I fucking want to. My head just isn't right."

The heat was back then, that green sparking and turning deeper. I saw something warring there as Thea gazed down at me. Then she bent, her lips ghosting over mine. "Goodnight, Shep."

Fucking hell.

Thea released me and stepped back, her eyes holding mine. "Tell me it costs you not to go there."

The way my balls were aching, it definitely fucking cost me. "More than you'll ever know."

Her mouth curved. "Good."

Chapter Thirty-Two

Thea

MY EYES FELT LIKE A TINY ELF HAD TAKEN SANDPAPER TO THEM overnight. Sleep had not been my friend. I'd tossed and turned for hours, replaying the night's events. I'd thought the encounter with Russ would haunt me. But that wasn't it.

It was the feel of Shep's callused fingers on my leg. The heat of him. I couldn't help but wonder how it would feel if he slid those fingers just a bit higher.

Hell.

I threw my covers off. I didn't care that it was only five-thirty. If I didn't move, I would lose my ever-loving mind.

Moose let out a disgruntled meow. He was not one for early mornings. Rolling over onto his side, he put his paw over his eyes.

"Must be nice," I muttered. Moose never had any trouble sleeping.

I moved to my tiny closet and pulled my pajama top over my head, tossing it into the hamper before doing the same with my bottoms. I grabbed my towel from a hook and wrapped it around me. When I reached my door, I paused.

Listening carefully, I didn't hear anything—no signs of another soul stirring, not even the kittens. It was too early, even for them.

I opened the door to the dark hallway. The only glow was from the slight warming outside the kitchen window. The sun wasn't up yet, but a sliver would likely appear in the next thirty minutes or so. At least I'd have light to tackle my chores.

Padding down the hall barefoot, I stilled next to Shep's door. Closed. I gripped the top of my towel harder because my fingers so badly wanted to reach for that doorknob. Wanted to twist and dare to step inside.

Instead, I moved toward the bathroom. Sighing, I opened the door. And came face-to-face with a wall of Shep.

I let out a strangled squeak as I took him in. I'd gotten a snapshot before. A peek at the wall of muscle, but I'd never had a view like this. This close, I could see every dip and ridge. The dusting of hair across his chest. The way those defined pecs dipped into rippled abs. I swore there were way more than six.

And then that V. I nearly swallowed my tongue at the sight of the muscle that disappeared into a low-slung towel.

Holy hell.

"Morning, Thorn," Shep said, his voice husky.

My gaze shot to his face. "I-I-I'm so sorry. I didn't know you were up. I mean, I didn't know you were in here. I'll just go—"

"You're fine." His amber eyes danced with amusement.

"It's not funny," I hissed. "I could've walked in on you in the shower."

"You would've gotten an epic concert then."

Annoyance flamed brighter. At his casualness and the fact that he wasn't nearly as affected as I was. "Haven't you heard of locking the door?"

Shep moved into my space. The heat still clinging to his skin from the shower wafted off him in waves. It was a heady, thick heat. A drugging one. He was without the usual sawdust scent that clung to him, but the cedar was still there, even stronger now. It had to be his bodywash or shampoo.

I had the sudden urge to sniff every bottle that resided in my shower. Use every single one so I could carry Shep with me all day. I was officially losing it.

Shep leaned even closer, reaching behind me and twisting the knob. "Lock's broken. I could fix that for you, but I'd be sad to miss out on future surprise visits."

I sucked in a breath. He was close. So close it felt like the tiniest breeze would send us colliding into each other.

Shep's gaze dropped to my mouth, then lower, taking all of me in. I watched in fascination as those amber eyes heated. But then they froze—not on the swell of my breasts or my exposed legs, but on my arm.

The heat in Shep's eyes vanished in a blink. Suddenly, they were ice-cold. "He. Hurt. You."

I jolted in surprise, glancing down at myself and following his line of sight. There, on my arm, was a distinctive handprint bruise. You could see the outline of four fingers as clear as day.

Shit.

I'd always bruised easily, but this was something else. I knew Russ had grabbed me hard. I just hadn't thought it would be this bad.

My focus shifted back to Shep. His chest rose and fell in ragged pants, his hands clenching and flexing around nothing but air as he struggled for control. I moved into him then, not caring that we wore nothing but towels or that this level of anger should've sent me running for the hills.

All I cared about in that moment was easing the fury running through Shep, the pain. I lifted a hand and pressed it to his face. "It's nothing. I'm totally fine."

"You're not *fine*," he ground out. "You've got fucking *marks* on your body."

"Marks that will fade in a matter of days. I've always been an easy bruiser."

Shep's eyes finally came to me. The coldness was gone, but hot anger had taken its place. "I should've done more than break his nose."

I slid my hand down to the back of his neck, squeezing. "No, you shouldn't have. And I'm pretty sure he'll be staying far away from me for the foreseeable future."

Shep lifted his hand, his gaze moving to my arm. With feather-light fingers, he traced the bruises. "This never should've happened."

"No, it shouldn't have. But bad things happen. That's life. I'm lucky that I had five people at my back last night. Five people who took care of the problem and made sure I was okay. But most of all, I'm lucky I had *you*."

Shep's breaths came short and quick. "Thorn." His eyes were back on my mouth.

God, I wanted to taste him. To lose myself in all the goodness that was Shep.

He leaned in. So close.

A bellowed meow broke out behind me. It startled me, and I nearly tripped over my feet as Moose moved between us, yelling at us both. I swore he sounded like a disappointed parent.

"Sorry," I mumbled. "Once he's up, he demands food."

One corner of Shep's mouth kicked up. "I'll get it. You take a shower."

"You sure?"

He nodded and made a move to slip past me. But then he stilled. He bent his head and brushed his lips across the bruised skin. "I'd do anything to take this away."

My breath hitched, coming in quick pants now. Shep straightened, moving past me and into the hallway, Moose on his heels, meowing away. But I stayed frozen to the spot, the place Shep's lips had touched still burning.

I pulled the frittata from the oven and slid it onto the stovetop. It looked amazing. But it should. I'd gone all out. Because I'd needed a distraction. After a very cold shower, I'd dealt with the kittens and then took care of the greenhouse.

But I'd still been twitchy, feeling like I might crawl out of my own skin. So, I'd decided to make a fancy frittata for breakfast. Plus, I had the heirloom tomatoes of the season. I'd paired them with mozzarella, parmesan, fresh basil, and arugula, then added some caramelized onions.

Stepping back, I was impressed with myself. All we needed was some toast from the fresh sourdough I'd made the other day, and this would be perfect.

Footsteps sounded behind me, but I didn't turn around. I couldn't. Just thinking of seeing Shep had my face flaming. I could still feel his lips on my skin. Like an echo of a burn that would mark me forever.

"Please, tell me whatever just came out of that oven is something you're sharing with me."

Shep's words had a little of the tension and anxiety bleeding out of me. Taking a deep breath, I turned. "How do you feel about a frittata?"

He grinned at me. "Sounds fancy."

"We are *very* fancy over here. Heirloom tomatoes, two kinds of cheese, greens, caramelized onions."

Shep just shook his head. "If you're not careful, you're going to have a hard time kicking me out in a couple of months."

I stilled at that. He'd only been here a few days, and already, I didn't want him to leave. I liked having the company. And more than that, I loved having *Shep* here. It was as if his light cast a warm glow that had been missing.

Shoving that down, I crossed to him. "How's your hand?"

"It's fine." Shep flexed his fingers in a testing motion, but I didn't miss his slight wince.

I grabbed his hand gently, lifting it for perusal. The skin along his knuckles was torn, and the joints were swollen and already turning black and blue. "Shep."

"It's fine." He lifted my chin, his thumb ghosting along the swell of my bottom lip. "A price I'd pay a million times over."

I opened my mouth to say something, anything, but a knock on the door cut off my words.

Shep stiffened. "You expecting someone?"

I shook my head. As a fresh wave of nerves built, I quashed them. Nobody who wished me harm would knock on my door. Taking a deep breath, I moved to go answer it, but Shep stopped me.

"I've got it. It's probably Rho checking on you."

But the fact that Shep didn't want me to answer told me he wasn't entirely sure of that. It also told me he cared. Shep wanted to stand between me and anything that might hurt me. The knowledge lit a war of emotions within me.

Gratitude that he cared. Relief that I wasn't alone in this. And fear. Because Shep couldn't protect me from everything. And I knew he would carry that weight with him.

"Trace," Shep greeted, surprise in his tone. "Everything okay?"

"Yes and no," a deep voice answered.

I'd seen Shep and Rhodes' eldest brother around town before, but I'd always tried to steer clear. I hadn't had the best experiences with law enforcement back in LA. At best, they'd been overextended, not having time for my problems that didn't exactly fit into the regular crime report box. At worst, they'd been both skeptical and judgmental, making it seem like I'd brought all of it on myself.

"Can I come in, or are you going to make me stay out here freezing my ass off?" Trace pressed.

While it was summer, the early mornings in the mountains were always cold.

Shep turned to me, not letting his brother in, a silent question in his eyes.

I laced my fingers in front of me, squeezing hard and trying to ground myself. "He can come in."

Things would look far worse if I refused him entry. And Trace would just have more questions. He might start digging and looking into me.

Shep didn't move for a moment as if giving me a chance to change my mind.

"It's okay," I whispered.

He sighed, annoyance clinging to the sound. "Come on in. But beware of the cat. He'll try to take your hand off if you have food."

Moose let out his chattering meow from somewhere in the living room.

"Noted," Trace said, stepping inside. His gaze moved over the entryway, then down the hallway to me. It stilled. It wasn't harsh or cold, but it was assessing. Something about the way those deep green eyes moved told me they took in more than the average person. And that knowledge had me swallowing hard.

"Morning, Thea. I'm sorry to disrupt you this early," Trace said, trying to keep his expression gentle.

"Where's my apology?" Shep asked, smacking his brother's arm as he moved toward me.

"The little brother who used to think it was funny to throw water balloons at me while I was sleeping does not get an apology for an early visit."

That had my lips twitching and a little of the tension bleeding out of me. "Water balloons, huh?"

Shep sent me a sheepish smile. "You should've heard him curse. Trace got pretty creative."

I chuckled. "I would, too."

Shep moved to my side as Trace approached, giving me silent support.

Trace extended a hand. "It's nice to finally meet you officially. Rho has had only the best things to say about you."

I took his offered palm and shook, noticing just how handsome the local sheriff was. Dark hair with just a hint of salt and pepper at his temples made his green eyes stand out all the more. As did the scar that bisected his eyebrow.

"Rho is just glad she doesn't have to do the heavy lifting on her own anymore," I said, trying to keep a smile in place.

Trace grinned. "That is definitely true."

No one said anything for a moment, and I couldn't help but feel like we were all waiting for a bomb to drop.

"I just pulled a frittata out of the oven. Want to join us for breakfast?" My voice had a thread of tightness to it, but at least I'd made the offer.

Trace arched a brow. "Frittata, huh? No wonder Shep wanted to stay with you instead of Cope."

Shep grinned at that. "I'm not an idiot."

"Most of the time," Trace shot back, then turned to me. "I'd love to join you."

At least I had a task. I hurried to cut slices and plate them while Shep got juice and coffee.

"That's a pretty impressive greenhouse you've got," Trace said, inclining his head to the kitchen window.

"My favorite hobby," I said as I slid a plate in front of him.

Trace eyed the creation. "You sure it's not cooking? This looks incredible."

"That's high praise from Trace. He's a pretty incredible chef himself," Shep said as he pulled out my chair.

I glanced at Trace, curiosity piqued.

He sent me an easy smile. "I didn't come by it naturally. Had to learn from the ground up. But I developed a love of it over the years. There's something about the process of creating something new."

Something about the gruff sheriff liking to spend time in the kitchen relaxed me even more. "It's meditative," I said softly.

Trace nodded. "That's a good word for it. And if I win over my six-year-old, I feel like I've won a prize."

I laughed at that. "Picky eater?"

"The pickiest," Trace said with a groan.

We were quiet for a moment, all of us taking time to eat a few bites. It was Shep who finally spoke. "You gonna tell us what you're here for or what?"

Trace sat back in his chair, wiping his mouth with a napkin. "Russ Wheeler came in at about six this morning, wanting to make a report about an assault."

The few bites of food I'd taken turned to lead in my stomach.

Shep's spine snapped straight. "You've gotta be fucking kidding me. He grabbed Thea. He—"

Trace held up a hand. "I know. I've already talked to John and the bartender who was on at The Sagebrush last night. They told me what happened. I'll get corroborating statements from patrons. This won't go anywhere."

Shep ground his jaw. "He could press civil charges."

"He could," Trace agreed. "But those won't go anywhere either."

But a court case would be costly and public. My name would be out there, easy to search, to find. My stomach roiled. But it was more than that. It could do the same to Shep just by association. My presence could mess with Shep's life and livelihood.

"I'm so sorry," I whispered, the three words barely audible.

Shep turned to me instantly, his body almost cocooning me. "This is not on you. Don't you dare take it on your shoulders."

"If I hadn't—"

"No," he snapped. "This is on Russ. And honestly, it probably has more to do with me. He has always hated me. Never knew why."

"Jealousy," Trace said. "You know his home life wasn't great growing up. His dad is just as much of an asshole as he is. Hard on him. He knew you had it good with the Colsons. And let's be honest, Shep, you've always excelled at things he struggled with."

Shep let out a long breath. "There's just something bad in him."

I didn't disagree. Russ Wheeler didn't have any redeeming qualities that I could see. But Trace wasn't so quick to go there.

"You know bad is rarely born that way. It's made. Through trauma, abuse, hardship. But once it takes root, it's hard to dig out. I keep hoping that I'll be able to stick something on Russ and wake him up." Trace's gaze cut to me, and I stiffened.

"I-I can't. I'm sorry. I just…I can't press charges."

I knew that was what Trace wanted. But I couldn't give it to him. For many reasons.

Trace sighed, lifting his mug of coffee to his lips.

"Don't guilt her," Shep growled.

Trace held up a hand, waving his brother off. "I'm not. I just…I want to put him away for a spell. Want to give Raina a chance to know what life can be like without being under his thumb."

My gut twisted, Raina's glittering eyes flashing in my mind. "I want to help her," I whispered.

Shep took my hand, squeezing. "I know you do. But we'll find a way. Fallon's going to talk to her."

"Really?" After a taste of Fallon's kind and empathetic energy, I knew if anyone had a chance of reaching Raina, it was her.

Trace nodded. "She's been trying to figure out an approach where she'll have some time with Raina without Raina worrying Russ will show up."

I mulled that over for a moment or two. "Maybe you could call him in for a follow-up to his report. Have Fallon ready to go then. You could text her whenever Russ is leaving the station."

Trace's brows lifted slightly. "Good idea. You work secret missions before?"

My mouth wanted to smile, but it couldn't quite get there. Between Russ making trouble for Shep and what Raina might be facing at home, it was all too much. "We have to help her," I said quietly.

Shadows passed over Trace's eyes. "I know. We're going to do everything we can."

Shep leaned in, brushing his lips over my temple. "We'll get a hand out to her. She just has to take it."

But when you'd been that beaten down, moving in any direction was the most terrifying thing in the world. Even if it was your only hope of freedom.

Chapter Thirty-Three

Shep

SLAMMING MY TRUCK'S DOOR, I HEADED TOWARD THE OLD farmhouse. It was the last place I wanted to be. Usually, when life got twisted, working on a new project was exactly what I wanted. What I craved. But not now.

All I wanted was to be with Thea, make sure she was okay, and that her demons weren't getting to her. I knew Trace needed to talk to both of us, but I'd wanted to deck him for laying all that on Thea's shoulders.

I'd tried to get her to take the day off. Between last night and this morning, she needed a break. Some time to recover.

Of course, Thea had refused, instead heading into Bloom to work the early shift with Rhodes. So, here I was. Maybe I could take out some of my anger and frustration in demo.

I strode past Anson's truck toward the property's front door, but just as I reached it, my phone buzzed in my pocket. Sliding it out, I grimaced as I took in the screen.

Mara: *How is your hand? Do you need anything? I could bring you and Anson lunch at the new property.*

With as small as Sparrow Falls was, and the fact that Mara worked at the hardware store, I shouldn't have been surprised she'd heard about my new project. But her text felt a touch intrusive. Normally, I'd never just ignore her—or anyone—but I didn't have the energy to deal with it today. So, I locked my phone and shoved it back into my pocket.

Opening the front door, I headed toward the demolition sounds. As I hit the halfway-open living space, Anson halted in mid-swing with his sledgehammer. He lowered it and pushed the goggles into his dark blond hair. "Wasn't sure you were going to make it. How's the hand?"

I lifted it and flexed my fingers. Pain flared to life, but nothing that meant broken bones. My knuckles were bruised, but the tears in my flesh were already scabbing over thanks to Thea's first-aid skills. "Not too bad."

Anson simply arched a brow at that.

"Really. I didn't break anything."

"Good," he grunted. "How's Thea?"

That was a far more complicated question. As I mulled over how to answer it, I tugged my wallet from my back pocket. Opening it, I pulled out another one-dollar bill and handed it to Anson.

He glared at me. "Seriously?"

I shrugged. "Are we in session, Doc?"

Anson set the sledgehammer down, resting it against some framing, then gestured for me to get on with it.

"Do you still have relationships with any of the hackers who advised your team at the Behavioral Analysis Unit?"

Anson's eyes flared comically. He was typically a master of masking his reactions to things, but this was clearly the last thing he'd expected me to say. "You know I basically cut ties with everyone."

He had. Because Anson hadn't been able to live with the fallout from an especially horrible case. One that had found him even after he left. Silas. And here I was, the asshole bringing it all up again.

"Do you think you could *get* in touch with one of them? Someone who knows their way around the dark web?" I asked. I wouldn't have asked if it was for me. I was asking for Thea. Because what she'd told me yesterday had stuck with me and played round and round in my head, only compounded by the shit Russ had pulled.

Anson studied me for a long moment. "I've got one. A guy who used to be a black hat. Now, he's more of a crusader."

"A black hat? What? Like some kind of wizard?"

Anson shook his head, his lips twitching. "Black hat means someone who hacks with malicious or criminal intent. A white hat hacks to help you find weaknesses in a system."

"So, this guy? He's a white hat now?"

Anson made a humming noise. "More of a gray hat, if that's a thing. He still hacks with malicious intent, but that malice is just directed at those who do wrong."

"That's exactly what I need." A trickle of hope bled into me. I might not be able to put Russ in a jail cell or wipe Brendan Boseman from the Earth, but maybe I could fix a little of the wrong that had been done to Thea.

"What the hell's going on, Shep?"

I shoved my wallet back into my pocket. "Confidentiality."

"I know," Anson growled, offended by my constant reminders.

"Boseman put cameras in Thea's house without her knowledge. When they broke up, he uploaded compromising photos and videos of her on every porn site he could find. She's never been able to get them off."

My voice didn't sound like mine as I spoke. It was completely detached. So opposite from the fury pulsing inside me.

"You're fucking kidding me," Anson snarled.

"I wish I were." I scrubbed a hand through my hair, tugging on the strands. "He's messed with her in every way imaginable. Got her fired from a job she loved. Fucked with her credit. Tore apart her life. And no one could catch him. She's scared that if he finds her, it'll happen all over again."

Anson's jaw worked back and forth. "I'll call Dex now. If I tell him what happened, he'll be all over this. Might just bury Boseman for fun, too."

I wouldn't be opposed to that. Just disappointed that I wouldn't be the one to do it.

Anson looked at me for a long moment before speaking again. "What you told me was already bad, Shep. But this? This is a whole other level of fixation. Obsession."

"I know."

The words cut as they rose in my throat, leaving jagged tears behind. Because we both knew what could happen when obsession turned. There would be blood in its wake.

Chapter Thirty-Four

Thea

MY GAZE MOVED FROM THE PAN ON THE STOVE WHERE POPCORN snapped and popped to the window above the sink. The moon was full, casting my garden in a beautiful glow. It was normally one of my favorite sights. Magical. But tonight, the soothing quality didn't hit.

I shook the pot on the stove as the final few kernels popped and then removed it from the heat. The scents of butter and salt teased my nose, but it did nothing to ease the low-grade annoyance humming through me. But the moment the annoyance swelled, guilt quickly followed.

Ever since the night at the bar, Shep had treated me as if I were fragile, made of the most delicate glass. At first, it had made me feel cared for. But three days later? The frustration was building. There had been no more kisses that set my blood on fire or words of promise whispered against my skin.

Shep was affectionate, sure, but all his actions were distinctly chaste. A kiss to the temple or hair. Fingers locking with mine. A hand dancing along my spine. But nothing more.

I sighed as I poured the popcorn into a bowl and put the pan in the sink to soak. Maybe that night had changed things for us. Just one more thing my past had stolen from me.

"You have a DVD player," Shep said, staring at the device as I moved from the kitchen to the living room.

His words were a statement, not a question, but I still looked up at him as I set the bowl of popcorn on the coffee table. The kittens played happily in their little pen, and Moose was on his cat tower, looking out into the night.

"It'd be hard to watch DVDs without a DVD player."

Shep looked down at the copy of *Rocky* with a mixture of awe and utter confusion. "Who has DVDs anymore?"

A laugh bubbled out of me. "Someone who doesn't have internet at their house."

Shep shook his head as he put the disc into the machine and shut the little drawer. "When I've got internet at the new house, I will be introducing you to every incredible streaming show, starting with *Yellowstone*." He crossed to the couch, lowering himself to the cushions as if he'd done it a hundred times before.

I took the other side of the couch, pulling the cozy blanket over me. Having Shep here meant I was comfortable enough to leave a few windows open, letting the cool night air in. But it was more than that. Shep made me feel…safe. Something I hadn't felt in years. Something that was beautiful.

"I've got all the classics," I argued, pointing at my small bookcase of DVDs. I picked them up in five-dollar bins and at Goodwill, constantly adding to my collection.

Shep grabbed my socked foot, digging his fingers into the arch. "I do admire your love of the *Rocky* franchise."

I had to bite back a moan as he hit an especially tender spot. "Who doesn't like *Rocky*?"

Shep chuckled. "I used to watch it with my brothers growing

up, but none of my sisters liked it all that much. Arden would probably like it now, though."

My brows pulled together in question.

"She got into jiu-jitsu when she was a teenager," Shep explained. "Trains with Kye now. Rocky would be her kind of guy."

"That's impressive." I'd always meant to take some sort of self-defense class but had never made it happen.

Shep's fingers stilled on my foot. "The gym Kye trains at has beginner classes and a women's self-defense seminar once a month."

"Your mind-reading abilities are starting to get a little freaky, Shepard."

Something shifted in his expression—softness *and* heat. "Never liked my full name. Not until I heard it on your lips."

My mouth went dry as I shifted in place. "Oh."

One corner of his mouth kicked up. "Yeah."

"Your name is beautiful," I told him honestly.

"Beautiful, huh?" Amusement laced his words.

I stuck my tongue out at him. "I think you'll survive the word *beautiful* being used to describe something about you. Your masculinity is safe."

Mischief sparked in Shep's amber eyes. "Such a smart-ass."

And then he surged forward. He went for my sides, fingers tickling. I shrieked with laughter and contorted my body, trying to escape Shep's attack. But he showed no mercy.

"Shep!" I squealed.

"Tell me again how beautiful my name is."

I snagged a pillow from behind me and whacked Shep with it.

"You've done it now," he growled.

Shep grabbed my hands and pinned them above my head, hovering over me. "Uncle?"

The laughter died on my lips. He was close. So close I swore I could taste him on the air swirling between us. The heat from his body wafted off him and bled into me as his strong form hovered over mine.

But I wanted it to do more than hover. I wanted to know what it felt like to have Shep pressed against me. To know the force of all that muscle powering into me. I wanted to know what it would be like to drown in Shep.

My head lifted as if pulled by invisible puppet strings of want and need. Shep's eyes flashed hot. Burning. I closed the distance, my mouth colliding with his. His tongue stroked in. Pure, demanding need.

Shep's thigh moved between my legs, my hips rising on instinct. That glorious friction had a moan slipping free of my mouth. At the sound, Shep jerked back.

Any hints of amusement and desire were gone from his face. "Fuck. I'm sorry, Thea. I wasn't thinking."

I blinked rapidly, my head spinning from the about-face. "What do you have to be sorry for?"

Shep scrubbed a hand over his face. "The last thing you need is me grabbing and manhandling you after everything you've been through."

Everything in me stilled as a cold chill settled in my bones. *Everything I'd been through.* A mixture of frustration and sadness swept through me as I stared at the man I was falling for. One who saw me as a victim and might never see me as more than that.

"I'm not weak," I whispered.

Shep reared back as if I'd struck him. "I know that. But that doesn't mean I shouldn't be considerate of what you've been through."

Hot tears pressed in behind my eyes. But I refused to cry. "I don't want you to treat me differently because of it."

Shep reached out, his hand taking mine. "I just think we should take things slow."

His words were a kind letdown. And that kindness only made things worse. "Okay."

"You're killing me, Thorn."

My gaze moved to Shep. The way that white tee pulled taut across his chest. How his brown hair was just a bit in disarray... He was beautiful. And that only made it harder. "Really. It's okay. I know the boundaries are a little muddy right now. I don't want to mess things up—"

My words were cut off by Shep's mouth on mine. His fingers sank into my hair, tipping my head back for better access. His tongue stroked in, strong and steady and so very *Shepard*. God, it was everything I wanted and more.

But his mouth was gone far too soon, and I was blinking into the space between us.

Shep stared back at me, his eyes blazing. "If you think for one second I don't want every part of you, you're wrong. You think I don't want to know what it feels like to sink inside you, to bury myself so deep I forget my own name? You're wrong."

My whole body tightened, nipples pebbling as if every cell was trying to move toward Shep and what his words promised. "What if I want that, too?"

My words were a dare, a challenge, and I knew it.

Shep tensed, his amber eyes turning more gold. "Thea," he growled.

My heart hammered against my ribs, chest rising and falling with each ragged breath. Each inhale begged for Shep's touch.

He sat back, shaking his head. "It's too soon. You're not ready—"

"*I'm* not ready?" I jerked to a sitting position.

"Thea—"

"Shouldn't *I* be the one to decide that?"

Shep opened his mouth to argue or soothe, I didn't know which, but neither was a good option, and I was already moving. I pushed off the couch and stalked out of the living room as the strains of the opening music to *Rocky* played.

I strode around the corner and down the hallway, slipping into my bedroom and shutting the door behind me with a shove. I wanted to slam it. But knowing my luck, I'd break the danged thing.

So much energy swirled in my body, humming just beneath my skin—anger, frustration, fear that I'd never be able to have *normal* again. But drowning out all of that was that I was turned the hell on.

That sparking attraction I'd been feeling for the past month was now an inferno, and I was about ready to come out of my skin. I might not be able to do anything about the anger, frustration, and fear, but I sure as hell could do something about the attraction.

Chapter Thirty-Five

Shep

"**F**UCK." I RAN A HAND THROUGH MY HAIR, TUGGING ON THE strands.

I'd made a mess of everything. I'd nearly lost my mind having Thea that close, her floral and coconut scent swirling around her. And the way her breasts had pressed against me with each inhale...

I wanted her more than I'd ever wanted anyone. The force of the attraction, the desperate need, scared the hell out of me, if I was honest. And that fear was only matched by the worry that I'd move too fast and screw everything up.

Only, I'd done the opposite. I'd tried to control everything. And by doing so, had taken Thea's autonomy away from her. No wonder she was pissed.

Moose sent a squawking meow my way.

"I know," I grumbled. "You don't have to say a damn thing."

I pushed to my feet and started out of the room. I may have messed everything up, but I could apologize and make it right. Give Thea back the reins.

My bare feet moved along the hardwood floors as I rounded the corner and stopped outside Thea's door. Images swirled in my head of her sitting in her room all alone, tears tracking down her cheeks. I didn't let myself wait, too worried I'd lose my nerve. My hand curled around the knob and twisted to open the door.

The moment it swung in, I froze. Thea. Beneath the blankets on her bed. Head tipped back, cheeks flushed. Back arched. Her nipples stood at attention, pressed against the thin cotton of her tank top. I could see a hint of the darker peaks beneath the pale pink fabric of the shirt. Saw her breaths coming in quick pants.

Everything in me tightened, muscles stringing tight. My already semi-hard dick stiffened to attention.

"Thea," I croaked.

Her eyes flew open and cut to me. I expected censure, Thea telling me to get the hell out. But she didn't. Her eyes stayed locked with mine. But she didn't remove her hand from beneath the covers. "What do you want, Shep?"

I missed the way she said my full name. How her mouth curved around the syllables.

My breaths came fast, sharp and stabbing as claws of need dug into me. "Tell me to go." My fingers curled around the doorknob, so tight I thought I might break a knuckle.

But my girl was too damn brave for that.

"Stay," she whispered into the dark.

I was done being an idiot, and even if I wasn't, her pull was too strong. I stepped inside and closed the door behind me before leaning against it. "Tell me what those pretty little fingers are doing, Thorn."

Her pale green eyes flashed in the moonlight. "What your fingers wouldn't."

I couldn't help the growl that left my throat.

Thea simply arched a brow in both question and challenge.

"Show me," I croaked.

Her teeth sank into her bottom lip, mulling over the request. Then, painfully slowly, she pushed down the blankets with her feet.

I sucked in a sharp breath. Thea wore nothing but that pale pink tank top. I could finally see those long, toned legs. Miles of smooth skin on display. She cupped the apex of her thighs, the place I wanted to see most.

My mouth watered. *Fuck.* She was already the most beautiful thing I'd ever seen. Seeing all of her would ruin me, but I didn't give a damn.

"What do you want, Shepard?" Thea whispered into the dark.

"I want to see all of you." My voice was pure grit. All need.

Thea shifted. There was no delay, no hesitation. Her hand moved, sliding from between her legs.

I shoved off the door, stalking toward the bed and taking in every inch of her. "So fucking beautiful."

My fingers itched to touch, feel. My tongue cried out to taste. My balls ached.

Thea's gaze locked with mine. "Shepard."

"Fucked up. Didn't give you what you needed."

Those pale green eyes flashed again. "No, you didn't." She didn't look away from me. "I'm not weak."

"No, you're fucking not. You own your body, your pleasure. You're in charge," I said, pure need coating my voice.

The hint of temper I saw in Thea's eyes melted into curiosity. But it was still full of heat. And I loved her fire, however I could get it.

"But I'd love to watch you take it," I growled.

Her breath hitched, pressing those pretty nipples against her tank. My dick twitched. I wanted to feel the tight bud against my tongue. Wanted to suck deep. To skate my teeth against it.

Thea's hand moved then, sliding between her thighs. "Tell me what you think I should do. How I should *take it.*"

Hell. She was pure fire and spice. A vision more potent than anything else I could dream up.

"Lift your tank." My voice was barely human as Thea shifted, pulling the cotton up and over those perfect swells. The skin of the buds darkened as they tightened, reacting to the cool air and her arousal. "Fuck," I muttered.

A small smile tipped Thea's lips.

My eyes narrowed on her. "Love that you're torturing me, don't you?"

"Maybe a little…" The smile grew.

"Lick your finger," I gritted out.

Thea's eyes flared, but she slid a pointer finger into her mouth, laving it with her tongue.

"Trace your nipple. Tell me what it feels like. How perfect it is."

Thea's hand dipped that pointer digit, trailing around the outside, then closer over the bud. "Hot and cold. Sensitive."

"Keep circling," I ordered, my own breaths coming faster. "Take your other hand and feel that scorching heat between your thighs."

She shifted, cupping herself, fingers starting to tease the flesh there.

"Slide those fingers through that heat. Tell me if you're wet."

Thea's back arched just as her thighs fell open. Her lips parted, and I wanted my thumb right there, to feel the swell of that bottom lip as my fingers teased that heat.

"Wet," Thea breathed. "You make me that way."

My back teeth ground together. This woman. So bold, so beautiful, so fucking perfect. "What about me?"

"Your voice." Her back arched more. "The way it skates over my skin."

God, I wanted to touch her. Wanted her to feel more than my voice. But I hadn't earned it. Not yet.

"Take those fingers, work that wetness up to your clit."

Thea's breaths came in quick pants now, her finger circling her bundle of nerves.

My dick strained against my sweats, just dying to get to her. "Slide your fingers inside. Tell me what you feel."

Her fingers moved again, and she let out a small whimper as they thrust in. "Tight, warm, wet."

She was killing me, but it was a death I'd welcome. "In and out, Thorn. Nice and slow."

She moved her hand, the sounds of her growing wetness filling the room, right along with her little whimpers. It almost brought me to my knees.

"Faster," I pleaded.

Those fingers moved in and out, her body pulling at them with each thrust.

"Not enough," Thea whimpered.

"What do you need?" I asked. Her eyes locked with mine as her hands stilled. "Remember, you make the rules."

Thea's tongue darted out, wetting her bottom lip. "Your hands. On me."

I swallowed hard, my hands fisting at my sides. "Your rules, Thorn." A grin tugged at my lips as I moved closer to the bed. "And it's a chance for me to apologize. Properly."

A devilish smile spread over her beautiful mouth. "I like the sound of that."

I moved toward the side of her bed. "So fucking beautiful." My fingers trailed up her leg, soaking in the feel of that smooth skin beneath my callused fingertips.

Then I reached for Thea's hands, pulling her up and spinning her around so she sat on the edge of the bed. I leaned over her, mouth closing around the fingers she'd had inside her, and sucked them deep.

I nearly combusted as her taste exploded on my tongue. I hummed around her fingers, letting everything about Thea soak into me. Slowly, my eyes opened, and I released my hold.

"Shepard." My name was more breath than word.

"Perfection," I rasped. I sank to my knees so Thea was above me, giving her all the control. My hands slid up the outsides of her thighs. "I'm sorry I made you doubt for even a single second how much I want you, how strong I think you are."

Thea watched me, so much emotion swirling in those gorgeous pale green eyes.

My fingers slid higher until they reached the hem of her tank top that rested above those perfect tits. "May I?"

"Yes," she breathed.

I lifted it in a flash so Thea was completely bare to me. God, she was beautiful. The kind of beauty you'd never get tired of looking at because there would always be something new to discover.

My fingers itched to explore, to tease. Her nipples tightened with the promise of what was to come. Her breasts were perfect teardrops of delicate swells. I slid a hand up, needing to feel them. I cupped her there, and Thea arched into me.

My thumb circled her nipple, making the flesh there darken even further. My dick pressed against my sweats, crying out for her.

"Everything about you is beautiful." My other hand came up to her neck, trailing down and finding her other breast. "The way your skin glows. The way your body arches."

Thea's eyes searched for me, finding me in the moonlight.

I kept my eyes on her as I leaned forward, my lips closing around her nipple. Thea moaned, arching into me again. A surge of electricity coursed through me at the sound and the movement.

One hand left her breast, sliding down lower and lower until it dipped between her thighs. I groaned around her nipple as I felt the wetness there. My fingers slid through her slit with ease.

Fucking hell. Thea really was going to kill me.

I teased that wetness, bringing it up to circle her clit.

She let out a whimper.

I released her breast, pulling back. "Tell me what you want. My fingers or my tongue."

Her eyes flashed. "Both."

I chuckled against her skin. "My greedy girl."

I sank down, resting against my heels. With one swift tug on Thea's legs, I pulled her to my face, her thighs over my shoulders, back to the mattress.

I drove in. At the first burst of her taste on my tongue, I moaned. I wanted to drown in it. It was everything that was Thea and yet completely indescribable. My tongue curled inside her, and Thea shuddered.

I felt the blankets shift and knew Thea was gripping them tightly.

"Shepard." My name was a plea.

I pulled out, my tongue trailing up as my fingers slid in. Two slipped in and out, twisting and curling. The movements followed no pattern so Thea would never know what was coming next, so her body couldn't prepare or brace.

The tip of my tongue flicked that tiny bundle of nerves, and Thea cried out, her muscles beginning to tremble.

I added a third finger, curling them in a beckoning motion that had her inner walls shaking, too.

"Oh, God. I—Shep—"

"Shepard," I growled against her clit. "When we're in this bed, you call me Shepard."

Thea's breath hitched. "Shepard."

Something about that had me nearly snapping. My fingers thrust in deeper, picking up speed. My tongue circled that bundle of nerves, exposing the most sensitive part of her. The part I knew would make her shatter.

As my hand sped up, I sucked her clit deep. Thea clamped down on my fingers. Wave after wave convulsed through her, wringing the life out of me and nearly making me come in my sweats like a damn teenager.

The sounds Thea made were better than any symphony. Real and authentic and *her*. Moans and soft cries as her body twisted, seeking more.

And then, finally, the movements slowed, and the sounds softened until Thea went completely slack against the mattress. I slid my fingers from her body and licked them clean. Her head popped up at the feel and sound, and she shook her head, amusement lining her face.

I grinned at her. "Your taste is like a drug. Gonna take all I can get."

Thea's chest rose and fell, still trying to catch her breath. "That was—I never—it's never been like that for me. Ever."

My eyes flared. "It should always be like that. Listening to your body is a goddamn gift."

She moved then, reaching for the blanket as if to cover herself.

"Don't," I whispered. Thea's gaze cut to me. "Don't steal this beauty from me. Don't be embarrassed about what we just shared. Because it was everything."

She stared at me for a long moment. "Okay." Then her gaze dropped lower. "What, um, what about you?"

I grinned up at her. "It wouldn't be a proper apology if it was tit for tat."

A laugh bubbled out of Thea. "I could get used to that kind of apology."

I chuckled, pushing to my feet and pulling back the covers. I slid in behind Thea, pulling her against me, my dick pressing against her perfect ass. "I'll be sure to piss you off on the regular, then."

Chapter Thirty-Six

Thea

THE EARLY MORNING SUN SHONE DOWN ON SHEP AND ME AS we strode toward The Mix Up, Shep's fingers laced through mine as if we'd made this walk every day for the past decade. It felt that comfortable. Something had shifted last night.

Shep was no longer holding himself back from me. And while I wasn't sure he'd ever *not* treat me as something delicate, I could see now that it was because I was precious to him and not because he didn't believe in my strength.

We slowed as we approached the door to the bakery, and I turned to face Shep. "You know you didn't have to drive me."

He brushed the hair out of my face with one hand, keeping hold of my fingers with the other. "I wanted to. I'll take whatever time I can get with you. I'm selfish that way."

I grinned up at him, knowing the smile ate up my face but not caring in the slightest. "I like you selfish."

Shep's voice pitched low. "Just like I like you greedy."

My body heated, memories of last night flooding my mind.

"That blush. Killing me, Thorn. I want to trace it with my tongue." He lowered his head, taking my mouth in a long, slow kiss. As if he had all the time in the world.

A hoot sounded from behind me, making us startle and break apart, and I whirled to see Lolli doing some sort of jig toward us, hands raised in the air, bracelets jangling.

"I *knew* it!" she cheered. "Finally got you someone to put some life back into you, Shep."

"Lolli," he warned.

"Don't you ruin my fun. Can't a grandmother be happy that her grandson's getting some of the good stuff?" She turned to me and winked. "It's always the proper gentlemen with the most surprising skills between the sheets."

"Lolli!" we both yelled at the same time.

I turned, burrowing my face in Shep's chest as I dissolved into laughter.

"Boundaries," Shep growled at his grandma.

Lolli made a *pssh* sound. "I hope you're not that uptight in the bedroom."

"I do *not* want to be having this conversation," he snapped.

"Don't be such a prude. Sex is a normal act. Nothing to be ashamed about."

"I'm not *ashamed*. I just don't want to talk about it with my grandmother, in front of my girlfriend."

I pulled back at that, my mouth curving. "Girlfriend, huh?"

A little pink hit Shep's cheeks. "I sure fucking hope so."

Lolli made a tsking noise. "You haven't even DTRed? I thought I taught you better than that, Shepard Colson. You never let a good one get away."

Shep looked confused. "DTRed?"

Lolli let out an exasperated sigh. "Defined the relationship. Get with the program."

Shep just shook his head and then looked down at me with an amused expression. "I'd apologize, but this is just going to keep happening, so I don't think it's even worth it."

One corner of my mouth kicked up. "I don't know, I kinda like your apologies."

Shep let out a growl, pitching his voice low. "If you make me hard in front of my grandmother, I'm going to make you pay later."

I pressed my lips together to keep from laughing. "Promises, promises."

Lolli let out a squeal as she clapped. "I just *love* this!"

Shep sighed. "What are you doing here so early anyway? You're never up before eight."

She grinned back at us. "I've got The Devil's Lettuce convention over in Roxbury today. I'm selling my special cookbooks."

My brows pulled together. "The Devil's Lettuce?"

"She means pot," Shep muttered. "She's going to a weed convention. Jesus."

Lolli glared at her grandson. "You sound like Trace. He thinks I'm going to get kidnapped by some drug cartel. I'm just selling cookbooks."

"Pot cookbooks," Shep argued.

She huffed, brushing invisible crumbs off her flowy dress. "I have to give the people what they want. I have the best brownie recipe in three counties."

Shep looked down at me. "When you come to dinner, and Lolli offers you any sort of baked good, just say no."

"You're no fun," Lolli complained. "You know, I've got this new strain that's really supposed to ramp up arousal. I could bring you some—"

"Lolli!"

I moved a rag over one of the many empty tables, but we'd gotten hit with the pre-holiday weekend crush earlier. If it was a sign of what was to come, we would be slammed.

The bell over the door jangled as it opened, and I looked up to see Luca running inside. "Thee Thee! Look what I made! It's so freaking cool!"

The overexcited-little-boy tone had a smile tipping my lips. "Show me."

"It's a real model of an ice rink. Just like the Seattle Sparks. Now I can memorize plays and stuff." Luca said, lifting the model for me to look at.

Sutton chuckled as she crossed the space, blond hair swishing around her. Her arms were laden with bags, a pile of mail, and multiple layers of kids' clothing Luca had clearly discarded throughout the day. "His camp counselor took pity on him and made arts and crafts hockey themed for Luca alone."

"She gets me," Luca said with a bob of his head. "She knows I'm going to be the biggest bad booty enforcer just like The Reaper. So, I gotta start now."

Sutton's nose scrunched. "I really hope you have a better nickname than that when you start playing."

"Mooooom, The Reaper is the coolest name in the league."

She sent me a wistful look. "I used to be cool, but already I've lost my shine."

"You'd be cool if you wanted to learn to skate, too. Then we could practice all the time," Luca suggested helpfully.

My lips twitched. "I've got your nickname. The Bad Booty Baker."

Sutton laughed. "It does have a ring to it."

Luca set down his model and began dancing around the bakery, shaking his little hips. "Bad Booty Baker! Bad Booty Baker!"

"You've done it now," Sutton moaned.

"We can make T-shirts," I said with a chuckle.

She set down her piles of stuff and began to go through the mail as Luca ran behind the counter, no doubt in search of cupcakes. "Oh, I forgot. There was something in the mail pile for you."

I stiffened. No one sent me mail except Nikki. And she sent all correspondence to my PO Box a few towns over.

My mouth went dry as I reached out for the envelope Sutton

held. The lettering was in a boxy shape, the kind that disguised any sort of ownership. Some part of my brain could register Sutton going on about her weekend plans with Luca, but I was too focused on the letter to truly hear her.

My fingers trembled as I tore open the envelope flap. I tugged out a piece of computer paper. On it was a picture. One of me. It looked like it was from afar, the quality was grainy, but I recognized the outfit I'd been wearing yesterday as I headed into The Mix Up. On the top of the paper read *SLUT* in angry red letters. But it got worse.

Parts of my body were circled. Next to my legs read *FAT*. My face, *UGLY*. My breasts, *WHORE*.

And it all sounded just like Brendan.

Chapter Thirty-Seven

Shep

"**D**AMN. THIS IS GOING TO BE PERFECT," ANSON SAID AS WE stood looking through the now-open space. The wall between the entryway and living room, and the one separating the living room and kitchen were completely gone. It felt like an entirely different house. Open and welcoming instead of stiff and formal.

"Just wait until we put in the massive windows on that wall."

I could see it all in my mind. The way it would bring the outdoors in and meld the structure with the nature around us. And Thea had shared some ideas for the landscaping that would take it all to the next level. She had a true gift when it came to creating art with plants.

"Won't lie, I'm getting a little bit of house envy," Anson muttered.

I chuckled. "You know the Victorian's going to be sweet when it's finished."

Anson's mouth curved the slightest bit. "It is."

And it meant something to Anson that he'd been a part of restoring it for Rhodes. It also meant something to me that Anson was willing to split his time between the two projects now. And I knew he was putting in extra hours on both.

I clapped my friend on the shoulder. "Thanks for doing this."

He glanced over at me. "It's my job."

I rolled my eyes. As much as falling in love with Rhodes had changed Anson, some grumpy-assed parts of him remained. One of those was not liking gratitude all that much. He'd just have to deal.

"Your job is eight to four, Monday through Friday. But you get to these two projects early and stay late. And I know you work weekends on the Victorian."

Anson shifted uncomfortably.

I couldn't help it, I burst out laughing.

"Fuck off," Anson muttered.

"Can't even handle a thank-you." My phone buzzed in my pocket, and I answered it without checking who was calling, too caught up in the ridiculousness that was my friend. "Hello?"

"Shep? It's Sutton."

The clear worry in Sutton's voice had the humor coursing through me vanishing in a flash. "What's wrong? Is Thea okay?"

"She's okay," Sutton said quickly. "But she, um, got a letter. Not a nice one. It came to the bakery but was addressed to her. She's freaked, Shep."

"On my way. Don't move."

"Okay. I closed up early. No one will bother her."

"Thanks, Sutton," I said, but was already moving.

Anson was on my heels. "Talk."

I moved quickly through the house, shutting the door behind us and locking it quickly. I didn't worry about the tools or gear we'd left out. All I could think about was Thea.

Fuck. Had Brendan found her?

"Shep," Anson clipped.

"Sutton said someone sent Thea a letter at the bakery. Said it wasn't *nice* and she's tweaked."

"Hell," Anson muttered. "Let's go."

I glanced over at him in question.

"I'll help if I can," Anson said quietly.

I knew that Anson's offer was more than a gift. Because it cost him to give it. He'd walked away from profiling because of everything he'd lost and everything it had stolen from him. Dipping back into that world didn't come without a price now.

"Thank you." The words were strangled, my throat tight and breathing ragged.

"Come on," Anson said. "Let's go get your girl."

We made the trip into town in record time, and I just prayed that if one of Trace's deputies caught sight of my truck ignoring the speed limit, they'd give me a pass. My tires squealed as I pulled into a spot in front of The Mix Up.

I was out of my truck in less than a second, stalking toward the front door that now had a *Closed* sign on it. Sutton saw me through the glass and crossed to the door, unlocking it. But I only had eyes for Thea. She sat at a table, staring down at the surface, but it was like she wasn't truly *seeing*.

I didn't say a word to Sutton as I passed her, going straight for Thea. I slid a chair next to her, but she didn't react to the sound or movement. The lack of awareness had my gut tightening.

Everything about this was wrong. Thea was fire and life. Prickly and combative, but only to hide the tenderness beneath. She wasn't this lifeless person in front of me now.

"Thea, baby," I whispered.

There was no answer.

I slid a hand over her jaw, turning her head gently so I could cup her face. "Thorn."

She blinked a few times as if finally *seeing* me. "Shepard?"

My full name was a gut punch, followed by an uppercut to the ribs at her confusion at my being there.

"You're okay. You're safe."

Unshed tears glistened in her eyes. "Am I?"

Hell. There was more than fear in those green eyes. There was defeat.

I glanced down at the table, and my blood ran cold. Lying there was a piece of paper. Standard-sized with a photo of Thea printed on it. She was walking toward The Mix Up but completely unaware that a photo was being taken. And around it were all sorts of ugly things. Things that had me struggling not to flip over the table.

Anson appeared then, holding a pair of what looked like food prep gloves and a fresh Ziploc bag. "Better than nothing." He donned the gloves and reached for the paper.

"Don't," Thea cried. "Don't look at it. I don't want—" Her voice broke. "I don't want anyone to see it."

Fuck. Her words sliced at my goddamn chest. I reached over and lifted Thea onto my lap, cradling her against my chest. "No one's going to see that fucking paper for anything except the lies it is."

Thea trembled against me. "No one can know. If they know, he could find me."

Anson and I shared a look as he bagged the letter, eyes scanning. What neither of us wanted to say was that Brendan might already have.

Anson pitched his voice low. "We need to call Trace."

Thea pulled back, shaking her head vehemently. "No. You can't. I can't have law enforcement involved. Everything will be on record. Please."

My heart broke at her pleas. There was so much fear and pain. I lifted a hand and cupped her cheek. "Trace will work around that. He won't expose you."

"I can't," Thea whispered. "Alone is what's safe."

I pressed my forehead to hers. "You let me in. And you stayed safe, right?"

Thea let out a shuddering breath. "Yes."

I pulled back a fraction so I could meet her eyes. "Trace can help. We need him."

Thea sank her teeth into her lower lip.

"Please?" I asked. "Trust me. Just a little more faith."

Thea's lips parted on an inhale, and those green eyes locked with mine. "I trust you."

And that slayed me. I just hoped to God I didn't fail her like I had Rhodes.

Chapter Thirty-Eight

Thea

KNEW I SHOULD MOVE, GET OFF SHEP'S LAP, AND SIT IN A CHAIR. I was fine. I was safe. So someone had sent me a cruel letter. So what?

But every time I caught a glimpse of that paper, frigid, icy claws of dread dug in and twisted. It was the kind of bitter cold that made your bones hurt. The type that should've been impossible on an eighty-five-degree day.

Shep's hand moved up and down my back in a soothing gesture. I tried to focus on that—the warm reassurance. His steady presence.

"Do you want something to drink?" he asked softly.

"Here," Sutton cut in. "I made tea."

I blinked at her a few times, just remembering that she was here and this was my place of work. I quickly slid off Shep's lap and moved back to the chair beside him. "Thank you. I'm sorry—I—Luca." I blanched, thinking about how my freakout must've scared him.

Sutton just squeezed my shoulder. "He's fine. He's upstairs playing a game on his tablet, completely oblivious to any drama." Sadness swept through her expression. "I'm so sorry I gave you that damn thing. If I'd known—"

I shook my head. "It's not your fault."

The bell over the door jingled, and my entire body stiffened. No, it braced, preparing to fight or run, like Brendan might show up wielding an ax. It was ridiculous. He'd never caused me physical harm, yet the fear was there all the same.

Instead of a crazed ax murderer, Trace walked through the door. His dark hair looked more mussed than usual, but he wore that same careful expression—the look that never gave much away.

I couldn't help but focus on the gun at his hip and the badge on his belt. I swallowed hard, the fear setting in all over again.

A hand slid into mine, squeezing. "It's okay," Shep assured me. His words from earlier echoed in my head. *"You let me in."*

And I had. One tiny crack in the fortress I'd built, and every-thing had come tumbling down. But I couldn't find it in me to regret it. I'd never be able to regret the gift that was Shep—and everything he'd brought with him. His family. His friends. They'd made me re-alize that life was about more than just running.

So, I took a deep breath and prepared to turn my fortress to ash.

"Thea," Trace greeted, his voice so gentle it almost hurt to hear. "First thing, do you need medical attention?"

Shep bristled at that. "You don't think I would've called Dr. Avery if that was the case?"

"I just need to double-check with Thea," Trace said, his voice remarkably calm in the face of his brother's anger.

I didn't blame him for asking. I was sure I was a shade of pale that looked more like death than anything. "I don't need a doctor. I just—I had a shock."

Anson handed Trace the letter now in a sealed plastic bag. I watched Trace's face change. It was brief, only for a split second, but I saw it. Gone was the careful expression, and in its place, a mask of fury. But just as quickly as that rage appeared, it retreated again.

Trace's jaw worked back and forth. "Russ?"

I hadn't even considered the possibility of Russ Wheeler sending a note like this. He definitely had the cruelty in him to do it. The tiniest bit of relief swirled inside me at the thought. It'd be far better for him to be the sender than Brendan.

Shep's grip on my hand tightened. "Could be him."

Anson's gaze narrowed on the letter.

"You don't agree." Trace's words weren't a question, but Anson still gave him an answer.

"Doesn't fit the profile I've been building. Russ likes to see the damage he inflicts. Wants to be up close and personal. He's also incredibly impulsive. Something like this took time. Taking the photo, printing it out, dropping it in The Mix Up's mailbox."

My stomach was back to churning, and my fingers dug into Shep's hand.

Trace looked between me and Shep. "There someone else I should be checking out?"

Shep glanced at me, waiting. I knew he'd give me all the time in the world. It was his way of ceding control. And I knew that cost him. Because Shep dealt with uncertainty by controlling as much as he could.

Saliva pooled in my mouth as I tried to begin. But where did you start with something like this? My eyes burned, and my stomach cramped as anxiety set in. Because there was always the worry that whoever I told wouldn't believe me. That *Trace* wouldn't believe me.

I closed my eyes for a moment, trying to calm and center myself. All I could do was speak my truth. I couldn't control what anyone did with it. But maybe just saying the words aloud would make me stronger. So, I took the first step. I began.

"I used to date Brendan Boseman."

The story tumbled out of me in fits and starts. I had to backtrack and reexplain at times. Others, I had to clarify or add something I'd forgotten. It wasn't pretty or even completely lucid at moments, but Trace stuck with me, only stopping me to ask questions if it was absolutely necessary.

Sutton had wiped away silent tears at more than one point, her knuckles bleaching white as she gripped her coffee mug. I hated that she was hurting for me. But it also felt like a gift—knowing that she cared that much.

Anson was silent. Watchful. In the way I'd grown to know meant he was putting together the pieces. Pulling at threads I couldn't see. Honestly, I didn't want to. Because that gift came with a price.

"So, I've just been here," I said finally, "living off the radar as much as possible. Going by my middle name, making sure nothing about my life can be found on the internet. No tracks or traces."

Shep leaned in, his lips ghosting across my temple. "So fucking brave."

Trace was quiet for a long moment. At some point, he'd started jotting notes on a pad of paper that Anson had handed him. There were more pages than I could count now. His dark green eyes connected with mine. "I'm so sorry this happened to you, Thea. Those words don't do it justice, but they're the best I have."

Cool relief swept through me at his words. Like the feeling of air conditioning finally hitting you after a day working in the blistering sun. Or the river skating over your skin after lying on the bank for hours.

I swallowed, trying to clear the lump in my throat as Trace went blurry in front of me. "You believe me?"

Shep's hand convulsed around mine.

"I believe you, Thea," Trace said, pain lacing his words. "And I'll do whatever I can to help."

I inhaled through my nose, trying to clear the gathering tears. "I don't think there's anything to do. Any action you take would just lead Brendan back to me."

"Well, I'm going to be googling how to hire a hitman," Sutton clipped. "Then he won't be able to get back to you at all."

The ghost of a smile appeared on Trace's face. "Gonna pretend I didn't hear that."

"Don't care," Sutton snapped. "This goes before a jury, they'll see I was doing the world a favor by ridding it of that vile scum."

"Amen," Anson muttered.

Trace sighed, pinching the bridge of his nose. "Let's see what we can do via the legal system first."

Shep's thumb skated back and forth over the back of my hand. The callused skin soothed with each pass, assuring me he was still with me. "I've thought about an order of protection, but those will just reveal Thea's location. And with Boseman's connections, we might not be able to get a permanent one approved."

That was the thing about people in power. They weren't held to the same standards as everyone else. They could bend any system to their will. And whatever legal team Brendan assembled could crush me.

A muscle fluttered in Trace's cheek. "He might be a hotshot in Hollywood, but this sure as hell isn't Los Angeles."

"It doesn't matter," I said softly. "You don't know him. Don't know how convincing he is. There's a reason he's up for every award known to man." Because Brendan used those acting skills. And he'd won gold with them. He'd just done it to destroy my life.

Trace rested his forearms against the table and leaned forward. "I'm not going to believe him. I promise. And I know that we can get a judge on our side if we need to. But for now, I want to make some delicate inquiries." Trace leaned back and glanced at Anson. "You in?"

"Already been running some searches."

Shep winced, looking at me. "I might've paid Anson so I could talk to him with shrink confidentiality protections."

Anson scoffed. "Paid me a fucking dollar."

"Hey, two dollars," Shep shot back. Then he looked at me. "I needed someone to talk to about you."

It should've made me angry, Shep sharing those details with someone without my permission. But all I could see was the lengths he'd gone to in order to make sure my secrets were protected. And the ridiculousness that was him paying his best friend a dollar to have a therapy session.

I looked at Anson. "A dollar, huh? That's a steal."

"Don't go spreading that around," he grumbled. "I am *not* open for business."

Trace's lips twitched. "Can't really see you as the warm and comforting type, so that might be for the best."

Anson flipped him off.

Sutton looked up from her tea, not joining in our amusement. "Did you find anything in your searches?"

Anson glanced at her and then at me. "Everything I've found so far doesn't show any signs of Brendan leaving the Crescent Lake area where he's filming. No hits on his credit cards outside the area—"

"I did not hear that," Trace groused.

My eyes widened. "You're in his *bank accounts*?"

Anson grinned at me, but it had a slightly disturbing quality to it. "Damn straight. Well, I'm not. I recruited help."

"Help?" I parroted.

Shep squeezed my hand. "Anson worked with some of the best hackers in the world when he was at the bureau."

"Got a white hat—an ethical hacker—on it. Dex is not down with this sort of thing. When I told him a little of what'd happened to you, the tech side, he took on the mission. He said those pictures and videos are scrubbed from everywhere other than a couple of places on the dark web. He's still doing battle there, but they should be gone within the next week or two."

The tears came then. I couldn't stop them. Hot and fast, they burned my cheeks where they fell. "They're down? People can't see them anymore?"

Shep moved in, lifting me into his lap once again and cuddling me against him. "They're down, Thorn."

A sob tore free. "I didn't think they'd ever—I thought it was impossible—"

"Fuck," Anson muttered.

"Rethinking letting Sutton google hitmen," Trace growled.

"Screw that," Sutton snapped. "I'm taking him out myself."

I tried to take them all in. Really see the people around the table who were all willing to fight. For me.

"Thank you," I managed to get out around my tears. "Thank you for helping me get my life back."

And I meant it in all the ways. More than just getting back the most intimate photos, they'd helped me remember that life was for living and not just for hiding.

Shep nuzzled my neck. "You're not alone. Not anymore."

Chapter Thirty-Nine

Shep

THE DRIVE TO THEA'S HOUSE WAS QUIET. TOO QUIET. NOT THE
easy silence we often had with one another, but a hollow one. I
couldn't help but look over at her every few seconds as though
I could keep her grounded in the here and now.

But I couldn't.

Thea was a million miles away. And I was sure she was locked
in dark and twisted places—places I'd do anything to keep her from.

As I pulled to a stop in front of her house, Thea jolted as if she
were just now truly seeing what was in front of her. I didn't wait. I
cut the engine and slid out of the truck, rounding the front to open
her door.

Thea's fingers trembled as she attempted to undo the seat belt,
each attempt stabbing at my chest. She finally succeeded, and I helped
her down. I couldn't resist the need to have her against me, to reas-
sure myself she was safe. Beeping the locks, I slid an arm around
Thea's shoulders.

The moment her body melted against mine, I felt the tremors.

My back teeth ground together as I looked down at her. "You're shivering."

"I-I'm cold."

Her voice held the same tremor as her body, and it had rage coursing through me. I guided her toward the house, doing all I could to keep from holding her too tightly. "Come on. Let's get you warm."

The bright sun on an eighty-five-degree day should've been enough. But it didn't come close after the events of the afternoon.

I hurried to unlock the front door, ushering Thea inside. Moose let out one of his mutant meows but didn't come in search of us. And the kittens were quiet, obviously still napping. All of that was good. Because if Thea thought her critters were in need, she'd go straight to them instead of letting me take care of her.

Taking Thea's hand, I guided her down the hallway and into the main bathroom. Releasing my hold on her was torture, even knowing she was right there and safe. I hurried to start the water and turned it as hot as I could with her lacking water heater. I scanned the rim of the bathtub, stopping on a bottle of bubble bath. Pouring some in, it wasn't long before a thick layer of bubbles coated the water.

I pushed to my feet and turned to Thea. My stomach dropped. There was a completely vacant look in her eyes. As if she wasn't there at all.

Swallowing hard, I stepped into her space. "Thorn."

She blinked. "Sorry, I—what are you doing?"

"Running you a bath. Need to get you warm."

"I'm okay—"

"Thorn," I pressed. "Let me do this for you."

She let out a shuddering breath. "Okay."

She slid out of one shoe and then the other.

"Do you want me to leave?" It was the hardest question for me to ask. The last thing I wanted to do was to have any sort of distance from her. But if Thea needed it, then I would give it to her.

She shook her head, tendrils of brown hair swishing around her face. "Stay."

Relief swept through me. "Okay."

I didn't let my gaze dip as she slid out of her jeans and bakery tee. It didn't matter how tempting Thea's body was, that was the last thing she needed right now.

When she was done undressing, I took her hand and helped her into the bath. The moment she sank into the foamy water, I turned off the tap. "Too hot or cold?"

"Perfect," Thea whispered as she slid deeper into the tub.

I lowered myself to the tiled floor, leaning against the porcelain. "Do you need anything? Tea? A snack?"

Thea's gaze locked with mine. "Just you."

A burn lit somewhere deep, scorching a path through my very bones. "You have me," I rasped.

Those pale green eyes flashed brighter. "Thanks for making sure I wasn't alone."

"I'm with you. Always."

I walked down the hallway of Thea's house, flipping off lights as I went. She walked ahead of me, her gait almost drunken. I would've smiled if I weren't still trying to tamp down the fury raging inside me.

Seeing her break down at the knowledge of those photos disappearing was nearly more than I could take. I knew that all of this had scarred her, but today was a wake-up call as to just how deeply. But I'd swallowed all the anger down. Because Thea didn't need it.

After I'd run Thea her bath, I'd done my best to cook her an edible dinner. It wasn't one of her gourmet creations, but there was only so much one could screw up with a grilled cheese. Then we'd curled up on the couch and finally watched *Rocky*. I'd thought that just holding Thea for two straight hours would help soothe the rage.

It didn't.

The only thing it had done was remind me just how important Thea was to me and of the tenderness she hid from the world. It reminded me how much I cared. Only it was more than that. *That* was what I'd realized while holding her.

I loved her. It didn't matter that Thea was her middle name or that she really had blond hair. I loved the woman beneath it all. A part of me knew I'd love her in any incarnation she dreamt up. Because it was *her*.

But that knowledge scared the hell out of me.

Thea nearly tripped over her feet, and I lunged forward to catch her. "Careful, Thorn."

She smiled up at me sleepily. "Sorry," she mumbled. "I'm wrecked."

I kept a hold of Thea as I guided her into her bedroom. "Adrenaline dump. It was a big day."

A little of that smile dimmed, and I wanted to kick myself.

"I can't believe Anson did that for me," she said as she took off her slippers and crawled into bed.

I slid in beside her and pulled her against my chest, still needing the contact. "People care about you."

Thea looked up at me, her pale green eyes searching. "It's been a long time since I've let them."

That knowledge sliced at me, stoking the fury burning low in my gut. I pressed a kiss to her forehead as I turned off the lamp. "Get some sleep. You need it."

"Okay," Thea mumbled. But she was already fading.

It didn't take long for her body to go completely lax against mine. Her breaths made my white tee ripple with each exhale. I watched the movement in the moonlight through the sheers and tried to take comfort in the feel of it. Of her. But it wasn't enough.

All I wanted was to take the Sutton approach and hunt Brendan down. And it wouldn't be enough to simply wipe him from the Earth. I wanted him to hurt. To feel every ounce of pain he'd inflicted on Thea and more.

The level of rage tweaked me. It wasn't something I'd ever experienced before. Not ever. Not when my dad and brother died, and not even after Rhodes had been taken.

My skin itched. Felt too tight for my body. I needed to move, run and burn off the phantom energy. But I didn't. I stayed right where I was and listened to Thea's breathing, the way it occasionally hitched with slight half snores.

I didn't move as one hour slid into two and then three. But when the clock hit one a.m., I couldn't stay there anymore. As carefully as possible, I shifted Thea off me. Stilling, I waited. Her breaths were shallower now, but within seconds, they deepened again.

Pushing to my feet, I headed for the door. As my fingers closed around the metal knob, I turned. As twitchy as I was, I couldn't help but watch Thea for a moment, see the way her exhales made the brown locks flutter around her face, how she looked so incredibly at peace.

I was thankful for that. She deserved every ounce of peace. But I wanted that in her waking hours, too. Never wanted her to fear Brendan and his twisted cruelty again.

The doorknob twisted under my palm, and I pushed as quietly as possible. Stepping into the hallway, I shut the door softly behind me and nearly cursed as Moose tore past me. Thea had warned me about her cat's *nighttime crazies*, but this was the first time I was seeing it in action.

Moose did some sort of ninja flip off the wall and took off into my room. With my luck, the damn mutant would probably piss in my shoes. I wanted to laugh, or at least smile, but I couldn't get my mouth to cooperate. Not with everything weighing on me.

Just the thought had that twitchiness returning in earnest. I moved down the hall, past the kitchen, and through the living room to the back door. Opening it, I stepped outside. The moment the cool mountain air hit me, I felt like I could breathe again.

The scent of the ponderosa pines would always bring the feeling of home. But the truth was, I had no idea if my roots were here. Had no idea if my birth parents had simply been driving through town and ditched me here. But even if they had, Sparrow Falls had become my home. My refuge. And it was for Thea, too.

I wouldn't let her lose that.

I didn't know how long I stood there, letting the night air wash over me and trying to let some of the anger pulsing inside me go. But at that point, I felt like I'd need the subzero temperatures of the Arctic for my fury to fade.

The hinges on the back door squeaked as it opened and then closed again. I didn't turn around. I knew it was Thea. Not because she was the only other person here, but because I had some sort of radar for her. It was as if my body recognized her energy signature.

She slid a hand up my spine, and the heat of her palm bled through my tee. She didn't talk at first, just took her time, reading my mood like a psychic worth millions. "You want to talk about it?"

I wrapped an arm around her and pulled her into me, inhaling that floral scent mixed with a hint of coconut. It soothed far more than the pine lacing the air had before. "I'm sorry I woke you."

Thea tipped her head back and looked up at me. "Is that a no?"

I sighed, my thumb tracing the ridges of Thea's spine through the thin cotton of her tank top and robe. "Feel like this anger is going to burn through me. Everything that asshole put you through, and he's just out there living the good life."

Thea's gaze bored into me as her hand stilled on my back. "He's not."

My focus moved to her, brows pulling together.

"There's no way he could possibly be happy with everything he did to me. Happy people don't try to break others down. They don't try to ruin them. That's what I've realized. He must be absolutely miserable, and that's the only solace I have."

I shook my head. "Not good enough." It wasn't fair that people thought Brendan Boseman was God's gift. That the world didn't know the truth. The fact that his mind was likely a miserable place didn't cut it. It didn't ease the fury coursing through me.

Thea shifted then, moving in front of me and placing her hands on my chest. "You need to let it go. If you don't, it'll eat you alive."

I didn't want to hold on to it. Didn't want it to keep burning through me.

"What helps?" she asked. "When you're angry, what helps? I

usually need to get my hands in the dirt. Plant or tend the ones I already have. Shifting that energy to something positive usually helps. When I'm sad, too."

God, she was so good. I lifted a hand, my fingers trailing over Thea's face. "Building. Or even better, tearing down to form something new."

Thea's mouth curved. "We could fully demolish the guest bath."

I wanted to laugh but still didn't quite have it in me. I wouldn't have minded doing a complete overhaul of that damn bathroom, but I didn't have the tools we needed here. "Not tonight."

Disappointment slid over Thea's face, then something flashed in those pale green eyes. Something I didn't read quickly enough.

Thea stretched up on her toes, pressing her body to mine. The moment her lips slid over mine, I was lost. Her scent, her feel, her taste. My tongue stroked in, and I took. There was nothing but Thea and me.

My hand slid down her back to her ass, pressing her tighter against me, needing more of everything that was Thea. The hoot of an owl overhead had me ripping my mouth away and breathing heavily.

"I'm sorry, I—"

Thea gripped my T-shirt, her hands fisting in it. "I'm not." Her eyes searched mine. "Let me help you burn this out."

Fucking hell.

Standing there in the moonlight and offering me the world, Thea was pure temptation.

"I don't trust myself right now." It killed to say that out loud. But my mood was dark.

Her expression softened. "But *I* trust you. And more than that, I want *all* of you." Thea's fingers ghosted over my face, tracing my features in the moonlight. "You don't have to be perfect for me, Shepard. You don't have to have everything together. I want you just as you are, even when you want to burn down the world."

My chest rose and fell in jagged pants. A scorching fire lit in my throat. "Thea."

"Trust me to handle it. All of you. I can. Because it's *you*. And there's no one I've ever trusted more."

She had no idea. Everything she'd just given me…those three words played on my tongue, but I swallowed them down. I would just have to show her instead.

Chapter Forty

Thea

I'D THOUGHT SHEP MIGHT PUSH ME AWAY AND LOCK ME OUT, AND that killed. Because each day I got to know the beautiful, broken man in front of me a little deeper, I saw that he, too, carried scars. Ones that made him feel like being anything but perfect meant being tossed aside.

I needed him to know that I wanted him in all his incarnations. To know that I *saw* him.

But just when I thought he was going to walk away, everything changed. One second, he was holding back. The next, he was on me.

Shep's mouth took mine in desperate need. But it was more. He was letting me in. Not telling me everything he was feeling but *showing* me.

His fingers tangled in my hair, tipping my head back to grant him better access. But I needed more. Craved it. The feeling of him against me. The pressure. The weight.

Before I knew it, I had my legs wrapped around his waist, and Shep was moving for the door. We nearly crashed into it before he fumbled for the knob and navigated us inside, locking the door behind him.

Then we were moving again. Down the hallway, bumping into walls, so lost in the haze of each other. When we reached my room, Shep didn't bother with the light, but he did slow his movements. He eased me down his body, the friction nearly sending me over the edge.

My breaths came quickly as my bare feet hit the floor. Shep's hair was mussed, his eyes practically glowing in the dark.

I didn't wait. My fingers went to my robe's tie, loosening it and letting it fall. Then they moved to the hem of my tank, beginning to lift.

"Don't."

Shep's single word cracked through the air like a clap of thunder.

My gaze shot to him. I waited for rejection, but it never came.

He took one step toward me and then another, his fingers covering mine. "Do you know how many times I've dreamt of peeling clothes off you? Don't steal that pleasure from me."

My breath hitched. "Oh."

"Those fucking Carhartt overalls. Nothing about them should be sexy, but all I could think about was what was underneath." His fingers traced the hem of my tank. "What would happen if I unlatched one fastener and let it all fall away."

Shep's fingers ghosted across the tender skin of my belly as he lifted my tank just a few inches higher. "How smooth this skin would feel."

My nipples tightened, pressing against the cotton of my shirt. I wanted it off. Wanted Shep's off, too. I didn't want to feel anything between us.

"Shepard," I whispered.

His eyes flashed a bright gold. "Don't rush me. Let me enjoy every second of this."

Shep's fingers moved higher, his knuckles brushing the undersides of my breasts. "So perfect." He palmed one beneath my tank.

I bit back a moan as I arched into him, seeking more.

Shep's other hand lifted my tank top up and over, sending it floating to the floor. His eyes turned hooded as his gaze dropped to my breasts. "Those pretty little nipples are just begging for attention."

He dipped his head, and his mouth closed around a bud, sucking deep.

Every nerve ending in my body woke, reaching out, searching, wanting more.

Shep's tongue circled, working my nipple, spinning it tighter. I couldn't stop myself from reaching out and gripping his tee, holding on for dear life. Shep's teeth grazed the bud, and I couldn't help the whimper that left my lips.

Shep's mouth was gone in a flash, but his hand came to my face, tracing my lips as if trying to search for where the sound had come from. "Love the noises you make. Never want them to end."

His fingers trailed down from my mouth to my jaw. He traced an invisible line to my pulse point and then down the column of my throat. He moved over my clavicle, down my sternum and belly, and then to the hem of my cotton pajama bottoms.

"Wonder what you wear," he rasped. "Still haven't gotten to see that. White cotton? Delicate lace? Silky satin?"

My tongue darted out, licking my bottom lip. I almost told him but didn't want to spoil the discovery.

Shep's hand dipped lower, and those amber eyes flashed again. "Nothing?"

My lips twitched. "Not to bed."

"And not the whole fucking time we were watching that movie, and all I could think about was sliding my hand into these damn pajama bottoms?"

The way Shep *wanted* me had power surging. And his comfort with that need emboldened me. It made me brave.

"Would've loved it if you had."

A grin spread across Shep's face. "Movie nights the rest of the week."

A laugh bubbled out of me, but the sound morphed into a moan as Shep's hand slid lower, cupping me between my thighs.

"Fuck," he murmured, pressing his face to my neck.

I rocked my hips, pressing into him. Shep's fingers parted me, sliding through the gathering wetness. He teased and toyed. My hands fisted in his shirt, pulling him closer and simply trying to stay standing.

Two fingers slid inside as Shep's hand shifted, and my pajama bottoms fell to the floor. "This heat. So smooth and wet and fucking perfect."

Another whimper left my lips.

"Give me more." Shep slid a third finger inside. They moved in and out, completely unhurried.

"Shepard," I breathed.

"Don't know what's better, those little sounds or my name on your lips as you beg."

My whole body shuddered at his words, and everything in me pulled tighter.

Shep cursed.

I gripped his T-shirt harder. "Please." My eyes met his. "All of you. I want all of you."

A muscle fluttered along Shep's jaw. "Tell me you're sure."

"I want everything, Shepard. The good and the bad. The pretty and the ugly."

His fingers were gone in a flash, and I was suddenly off my feet. Shep had me, and then my back was to the mattress. My thighs clenched with need, my body desperate for him.

Then Shep's heat was gone. He stepped back, grabbing his white tee from the back of the neck and hauling it off in one fluid movement.

I couldn't help but stare, riveted. I traced the golden planes of muscle with my eyes, memorizing each dip and ridge.

Shep's fingers hooked in the band of his sweats, and then they were down. At my first look at him, I nearly swallowed my tongue.

His dick stood at attention, thick and long. His hand closed around it, giving it one long stroke.

My core tightened as if already imagining what it would feel like to be filled by him. But at the same time, I knew my eyes had widened. Because Shep was *big*. Bigger than anyone I'd ever been with before.

As he moved toward me, his expression softened. "Tell me what's going on in that beautiful brain."

"You're big," I blurted.

One corner of Shep's mouth kicked up. "Thanks for noticing."

I scowled at him. "I just—I haven't—I—"

Shep's thumb skimmed my bottom lip. "This is you and me. If there's something you're nervous about, you tell me. We need to stop, slow down, you have the reins. There's nothing we can't talk about."

My eyes burned, and at the same time, wetness gathered between my thighs. Because everything about Shep, from his big dick to his tender heart, turned me way the hell on. "Okay."

His other hand traced designs on the inside of my thigh. "Are you on the pill?"

"I have an IUD."

"Like that, Thorn. Because that means if you're good with it, I can take you bare. We can feel *everything*. I've been checked, and I'm good."

"Me, too." I sucked in a breath. "I want that. To feel… everything."

Shep dropped his head and pressed a kiss to my collarbone as his fingers moved, teasing my opening again. One circled, stretching me. I couldn't help the moan that left my lips.

"Those noises," he gritted out. Then his fingers were gone, and his hands were on my waist.

In a blink, Shep was on the mattress and had lifted me over him so I straddled him. "Want you in control."

A rush of heat swept through me. "Shep."

"Shepard," he growled.

"I—it's been a long time for me."

His eyes gentled on me. He knew what that meant. His hand lifted to cup my face. "We find it together. This is you and me."

God, I wanted that. Wanted him.

Shep's hands slid to my waist, helping to steady me but letting me take the reins. For a man who liked control in all things, I knew this was a gift. I pressed my palms to his chest, relishing the feeling of the strength beneath them, and then slowly lowered myself.

My mouth fell open on a silent gasp as I stretched over Shep. I closed my eyes as I absorbed the bite of pain, but it quickly melted into heat. So much heat.

Shep's hand slid up between my breasts and along my sternum to the place where my jaw met my neck. "Don't hide that beauty from me. I want to see all of it. Everything."

My eyes flew open. Because I didn't want to hide from Shep. I wanted us to share it all. Nothing hidden and no being ashamed. Everything out in the open.

I moved then, my hips rocking gently at first as I adjusted to his size. Then deeper, taking more of him. I saw the strain in Shep along his jaw and in his forearms. Saw how much he was holding back. But I didn't want him to.

"All of you," I whispered.

"Thea—"

"Please."

Shep's control finally snapped, and it was beautiful. He flipped me, not losing my body for a single second. "Legs around me," he growled.

I obeyed, encircling him, my heels digging into his ass. Shep thrust into me, making me feel it all: his power and strength, the ferocity with which he wanted me, and how much every part of me yearned for him.

His body moved in powerful arcs, bending me to him as he let loose everything he'd been holding back.

My fingers gripped his shoulders, nails digging into his back. Shep thrust deeper, making tiny spots dance across my vision and my inner walls tremble. My legs shook as I tried to hold on, and I was pretty sure I was drawing blood.

"Not. Yet," Shep gritted out.

"Shepard." His name curled around us both, the promise of what he was to me.

His thrusts grew faster, impossibly deeper. Shep's face blurred in my vision, but I'd know him anywhere, even in the pitch-black. I couldn't hold back any longer.

My body clamped down around Shep, and I cried out with the force of the first wave. But it wasn't enough for him. His hand slipped between us, finding my clit as he drove into me again and again.

The pleasure was so intense it was just shy of pain. Shep's thumb pressed down on my clit, sending dark flashes across my vision. The sound he made as he came had an animalistic edge, and the ferocity of it only sent me higher. The feeling of him emptying inside me had that power surging.

But it was more. It was the knowledge that we could be what each other needed, in good times and bad.

Shep rolled us, and I collapsed on top of him, still relishing the feel of him inside me and not wanting to lose it. My chest heaved like I'd just had the workout of my life, and both of us were damp with sweat.

I tipped my head back. "We might have a problem."

Shep frowned up at me. "Problem?"

"I like when you're angry and when you're apologizing. At this rate, I could be starting fights left and right."

Shep barked out a laugh, but the action had my core tightening around him. The laugh died, and Shep cursed. "Are you trying to kill me?"

I grinned down at him. "You're the one who started it."

He knifed up, taking my mouth in a long, slow kiss. When he pulled back, I saw something I couldn't quite read in those amber eyes. "Thank you."

"For what?" I whispered.

His thumb ghosted over my bottom lip. "For making me feel worthy, even at my worst."

My heart cracked, but the pieces that splintered found their way to Shep. Right where they belonged. "Shep, your worst is only good. Because it just shows how much you care."

I wanted to give him those three little words so badly because I knew now that I felt them with every part of me.

Shep's thumb trailed over my jaw and down my neck, resting in the hollow there. "Thank you for seeing me."

"Thank you for letting me in." Because letting me see the cracks along with the perfection only made Shep more beautiful to me. And it let me give him back just a fraction of what he'd given to me.

Chapter Forty-One

Thea

I GRIPPED THE WICKER BASKET FULL OF FRUITS AND VEGGIES FROM my garden and greenhouse as Shep turned off the main road and onto a gravel one. I could see a house and outbuildings far in the distance, but they were surrounded by what felt like miles of fields dotted with cattle. And past those, forests with endless trees. And past *them*, the Monarch Mountains and Castle Rock.

I knew the view from the Colson family home had to be breathtaking, one I would kill to have day in and day out. But the idea of seeing it for the first time didn't set me at ease. My nerves were at an all-time high.

Shep dropped a hand from the steering wheel and rested it on my thigh, giving me a gentle squeeze through the sundress I now second-guessed. "You want to turn around?"

"What?" My gaze jerked away from the breathtaking landscape and toward the man next to me.

His eyes flicked to me before returning to the road in front of us. "You haven't said a word since we got in the truck. But I can feel you winding tighter and tighter." His thumb traced circles on my thigh. "My family will be here. There's no rush if you're not ready."

I let out a long breath, my throat working with the action. "What if they don't like me?"

Shep slowed the truck and pulled over to the side of the road. "First of all, you've met everyone but my mom, Arden, and Cope. Mom and Arden will love you, too. If Cope was here, he'd probably try to hit on you, and I'd have to deck him. So, it's better he's not."

My mouth curved the barest amount at that.

Shep brushed a meticulously curled strand of hair out of my face and tucked it behind my ear. "You wanna tell me what this is about?"

I worried a strand of the wicker basket with my thumbnail. "This is new for me. My family...it wasn't like this. We aren't close like you guys are. What if I say the wrong thing? Or do something that offends someone?"

He studied me for a long moment. "You don't talk about them. Your family, I mean."

Of course, Shep got to the heart of it. I stared down at the produce in my lap. It was the only gift I could think of, along with a bouquet from my garden. I wasn't even sure about that.

"I haven't talked to them since I was in college. My mom and dad had a dysfunctional relationship at best. My dad came and went, sometimes for work, and other times just to escape. When he was home, the two of them were always fighting. Screaming at each other. Half the time, they forgot I was even there."

"Thea," Shep whispered.

"It wasn't bad. I always had what I needed, but I don't think either of them really wanted a kid. I think my mom thought a baby would make things better between the two of them, but it never did."

Shep pulled me into him then, his hands cupping my face and forehead pressed to mine. "I'm so fucking sorry."

"I wanted what you have," I admitted. "Used to dream about a huge family with all these siblings. Wanted to share a room with a sister and stay up half the night talking about anything and everything."

Shep's thumb stroked my jaw. "We're not perfect, not by a long shot. Cope used to flush the toilet when he knew I was in the shower. And Fallon always stole the last brownie before I could get it."

I chuckled. "It sounds perfect."

"You're building that for yourself now. Don't you see it? Rhodes, Sutton, Luca. Hell, even Anson looks at you like a little sister now." He pulled back so he could peer into my eyes. "I know better than anyone, just because you don't share blood with someone doesn't mean your tie is any less strong. Sometimes, it's stronger. Because that tether is a choice."

A burn lit along my throat and spread to my eyes. "Shepard."

"You use my full name, and you know I'm gonna wanna fuck you. And, Thorn, then we'd be late for dinner, and you'd be even more nervous."

I burst out laughing, tugging him to me by his shirt and kissing him hard. Those three words scorched my throat, but I didn't let them free—still holding on to that flicker of fear.

"And now I'm going to have to walk into family dinner hiding a hard-on."

I grinned at him. "I promise to deal with that when we're home."

"Fuck," Shep muttered, but put the truck in drive again. My nerves flared once more as he guided the vehicle toward the massive, white farmhouse that looked like something out of a storybook. But I didn't let the feelings engulf me. I breathed through them.

Shep's family was a part of him. And that meant I'd love them. All I could hope was that they saw how much I cared about him.

He pulled in next to a black truck with intricate detailing along the sides. I knew from our night out that this one belonged to Kye. But there were countless other vehicles lined up in front of the home. Everything from a sedan to a massive SUV.

I stayed focused on my breathing as I slid out of Shep's truck. He was by my side in a flash, taking my hand in his and leading me toward the house. We hadn't even reached the porch before the front door flew open.

Then I was being engulfed in a massive hug. The sweet pea scent had me recognizing Rhodes, but I couldn't see her with how tightly she held me.

"I'm so sorry for what you've been through. Know that I'm always here for you. Whatever you need. You are the most amazingly strong person I know."

My nose stung. I'd asked Anson to fill Rhodes in on everything, knowing that telling the story for a third time would be too much for me to handle. And now I knew I'd made the right choice. I hugged Rhodes back. "Thank you. I'm sorry I didn't tell you. I—"

"Don't you dare apologize," Rhodes snapped, pulling back. "You were keeping yourself safe."

I sent her a wavering smile. "Thanks for understanding."

"Of course." She squeezed my shoulder. "Also, I had a bonfire last night and burned every Brendan Boseman DVD I owned."

A laugh burst out of me. "I like that mental image."

Shep just shook his head. "Thea's DVD obsession makes sense. *You* need to enter the twenty-first century."

Rhodes rolled her eyes. "When your internet's out, I'll be chilling, watching *Guardians of the Galaxy*."

"I tried to tell him that it's better this way. He won't listen," I said as I followed Rhodes into the house.

Shep's hand pressed into my lower back, assuring me he was right there with me.

"Shep is tech-obsessed. It's an addiction, honestly," Rhodes said.

I looked up at him. "How have you survived living at my house this long?"

He grinned down at me. "I've been busy doing other things."

"Gross!" Rhodes whined. "I do not need to know about what you two have been up to. TMI."

My cheeks flushed, but I couldn't help giggling. *Giggling?* Who was I?

Voices swirled up ahead, making my stomach flip, but the second we stepped into the open-concept living/kitchen/dining space, a tiny creature flew at me. She was a whirling dervish with gleaming dark hair, and as she skidded to a stop in front of me, I took in the deep green eyes that were just like Trace's.

"You're Thea. You're my Uncle Shep's new girlfriend. And Dad says you work at the bakery. Can you get me a cupcake from there? Dad only lets me get them for special occasions. But I want them aaaaall the time. The unicorn ones are my favorite. I—"

Trace picked up his daughter, tickling her side. "Keely, I think you're gonna talk Thea's ears off if you're not careful."

"Nuh-uh. Your ears don't fall off. Do they?"

I couldn't help but smile at the little girl's worry. "It's nice to meet you, Keely. The unicorn cupcakes are my favorite, too. And if you come visit me at work, I bet I can sneak you one."

Keely's whole face brightened. "You are AWESOME!"

Trace chuckled. "Well, you've got a forever fan in this one now."

"I'm not above a little bribery," I admitted sheepishly.

"I'm very bribable," Keely said solemnly. Then she looked between Shep and me. "Supergran says you and Uncle Shep are knocking boots. Is that a new game? Maybe I can learn it—"

"Lolli!" At least half the people in the massive space shouted her nickname, heads snapping in her direction.

The woman looked up from her cocktail, completely unfazed. "Did I lie?"

"Jesus," Trace muttered. "My kid is going to get expelled from the first grade."

"It's summer, Daddy. I can't get expelled."

"It'd be a preemptive expulsion," he said with a sigh.

But his daughter just grinned up at him like he hung the moon. Then she twisted back to look at me. "Dad's always worried about me getting kicked out, but I never do. My teachers always like me."

I struggled not to laugh. "I bet they do."

"Thea," a warm voice greeted, cutting into the conversation. "Apologies for the chaotic welcome and my *mother*."

"Don't you apologize for me, young lady," Lolli called.

"If I didn't, we would've been forced out of town long ago," Nora shot back. Then she turned back to me. "Welcome to chaos."

I did laugh then. Something about Nora's easy manner and complete acceptance of the show around her relaxed me. "Thank you for having me. I, um, brought you some things from my garden."

As I extended the wicker basket, a wave of uncertainty hit me. Was this weird? Should I have brought food instead? Would she be insulted?

But Nora's eyes brightened, the skin around them crinkling, telling me it happened often. "I won't lie. I've been biding my time before bugging Shep about bringing more of your goodies over. Those snap peas and arugula in the last batch? Incredible. And the tomatoes? I kept them all to myself."

"Hey, I like tomatoes," Kye said from an armchair in the corner, his motorcycle boots kicked up on an ottoman.

"Get your own," Nora clipped.

Kye chuckled. "You know they're good if she's hiding them from the rest of us. I'll trade you an ink session for some tomatoes if they're heirlooms."

"Is there any other kind?" I shot back.

A grin spread across Kye's face. "If Shep hadn't landed you first—"

"Do not make me punch you and get blood on Mom's chair," Shep snapped.

Kye's smile only widened. "Did you forget who has the mixed martial arts training?"

"Then I'll break your nose with a palm strike." The woman on the couch sent Kye a quelling look, her voice holding a bit of a husky air. "You know I can do it."

Kye just scowled at her. "When you're lucky."

"You mean when you let your guard down. Which is often lately."

As I took her in, I realized it must be Arden. She was stunningly beautiful with dark brown hair almost to her waist and eyes a hypnotizing gray that had an almost violet hue beneath.

She turned her focus to me. "Excuse Kye. He's a Neanderthal."

"Truer words have never been spoken," Fallon muttered into her glass of wine as she sat on a stool at the counter.

Kye didn't seem to bristle at Arden's rebuke, but he frowned the moment Fallon shared the same sentiments, sending her a searching look.

Arden pushed to her feet and crossed to me. "It's nice to finally meet you. I'm Arden."

"Nice to meet you, too," I echoed.

Nora wrapped an arm around Arden's shoulders. "Who knew all I needed to do to get you to family dinner was have Shep bring a new girlfriend?"

Arden sent Nora a sheepish smile. "It's been a hectic season."

Nora brushed the hair away from Arden's face in a gesture that was so effortless, I knew she'd done it countless times. "When isn't it, my mini van Gogh?"

Arden sent me a grin. "Let's just hope I don't cut off my own ear."

Nora's face scrunched. "No morbid talk before dinner."

I was pulled into the fold, and it only took a matter of minutes before my nerves simply melted away. The sheer number of people filling the Colsons' dining table meant the focus never stayed on me for too long. And having Keely present meant we always had an amusing distraction.

We feasted on steak and a vegetable medley that had every color of the rainbow. Potatoes au gratin that had me jonesing to get my hands on the recipe, and rolls that had the consistency of clouds. Rhodes had brought her peanut butter poke cake for dessert, and there wasn't a crumb left.

After dinner, we all helped clear the table, but Nora shooed everyone but me out of the kitchen. My stomach did a flip at being alone with her in the space, but she sent me a sheepish smile. "It's selfish. They all want to get to know you better. But Shep's my baby, and I feel like I deserve first dibs."

I scraped a few food scraps into Nora's compost bin as I tried not to let the nerves take hold once again. "He loves you so much."

That was easy to see. There was a tenderness in the way Shep was around his mom. A gentleness. But more than that, gratitude.

Nora's gaze moved to the window, watching all her children

gathered on the back deck, laughing as Keely put on some sort of show. "He's a good man."

"The best," I said, handing her the plate to rinse.

Nora moved in a way that said she'd memorized the layout of the kitchen long ago and could move through it with her eyes closed. "But he takes too much on his shoulders."

I was quiet for a moment as I scraped more plates. "I think a part of him will always feel like he needs to prove his worth." My fingers tightened on the dish I held, struggling with whether or not to say what I wanted to. But I held tightly to all the things Shep had reminded me of. Most of all that I hadn't escaped to *not* live.

"We all carry with us the weight of our experiences. The hard things change us. Sometimes, they scar us. But it's never all bad. They grow our empathy, understanding, and the way we care for others around us. Shep cares for the people in his orbit more than anyone I've ever known. He just needs a reminder now and then that he doesn't have to be perfect for us to love him."

I froze at the last words that tumbled out of my mouth. I hadn't meant to say them, but there was no denying they were true.

Nora's hands stilled, covered in soap suds, as she turned to me. "You love him?"

I swallowed hard. "I do." I let out a shaky breath. "Your son reminded me there are good men in this world when I desperately needed that reminder. He's made me brave. Made me reach for things I never thought I'd be able to have again."

Unshed tears glistened in Nora's eyes. "Thea."

"You raised an amazing son."

Nora dropped the plate into the sink and moved to me in a blur. She pulled me into her arms and hugged me tightly, not letting go. "I've seen a change in him this past month. An ease he hasn't had before. It's you. You make him brave right back. Brave to trust that he's *enough* just as he is."

My throat burned and my eyes filled. "He's more than enough. He's everything."

Nora pulled back, a few tears slipping free. "And so are you, my beautiful girl. It's so clear to see. Your kindness, your care, your *strength*. I don't know what you've been through, but I hate that it happened to you."

"It just makes me appreciate what I have now that much more."

Nora sniffed. "Want you to have it all. And if you ever need an ear or a hug or someone to cluck over you for a little while, I'm always here."

My own tears spilled then. At her kindness. At the offer to give me something I'd never really had before. "Thank you," I whispered. "It means more than you'll ever know."

"Everything okay in here?"

Shep's deep voice cut across the kitchen, making both Nora and me jump. Then we both promptly dissolved into laughter.

Nora wiped at her face and waved her son off. "We're fine. Just getting a little emotional with our girl talk."

Shep instantly moved to me, his big body curving around mine as his thumbs stroked across my cheeks, clearing my tears. "You're crying."

I shook my head. "I'm happy."

He frowned down at me as if not totally believing my words.

I wrapped my hands around his waist and squeezed. "Happy," I echoed. "And you gave that to me."

Shep's rough hands cupped my face. "You gave it to yourself. I just love being a piece of the puzzle."

Chapter Forty-Two

Shep

"**Y**OUR SMILE IS FREAKING ME OUT."

I glanced over at Anson as we headed into town in my truck, trying to lessen the grin that had been plastered on my face all weekend. But I had no luck. It couldn't be helped. "Just because you look like some sort of possessed demon when you smile doesn't mean the rest of us do."

Anson just grunted in response. "Doesn't your face hurt? You haven't stopped grinning all morning."

I rolled my eyes as I made the turn onto the main drag through town. Cascade Avenue was still extra crowded from the holiday weekend, tourists lingering to make the most of their trips. I couldn't stop my gaze from swinging to the bakery, just hoping for a glimpse of dark brown hair through the window.

"Jesus," Anson clipped. "Keep your eyes on the road."

My gaze swung back to the traffic in front of us, and I pressed down on the brake to avoid rear-ending a minivan with Idaho plates.

"You are *gone*," he muttered.

"Like you're any better," I shot back.

Anson was head over heels for Rhodes. It was like she was the center of his universe, and everything rotated around her.

One corner of his mouth kicked up. "Fair enough." The half grin dimmed. "Has everything been quiet?"

I nodded, a weight settling in my gut. "Trace is still waiting for the prints to come back on the letter. Russ's are on file, but Brendan's aren't."

"Of course, they aren't," Anson groused. "I might be able to figure out how to get a set…"

"A legal way?"

Anson winced, and I had my answer.

"If Trace can't use them, it doesn't do us any good."

Anson slumped back in his seat. "Yeah, yeah. I just want this guy to fry."

My hands tightened on the wheel. "You think I don't? He tortured her." The words felt like blades in my throat. "Thea's always battling the tricks her mind plays on her because of everything he's done. He might not have laid a hand on her, but there are still scars."

Anson was quiet as I pulled into the hardware store's parking lot and found an empty spot. "Sometimes, the mental scars are worse."

I knew that Anson understood that. Probably better than anyone. "But she's healing." I could see it in how Thea was growing bolder. How she didn't brace. How she let her guard down around my family. I looked at Anson. "And you're healing, too."

Anson stared back at me. "What about you?"

I stiffened for a moment and then let the flash of annoyance melt away. He wasn't asking to push or be nosy but because he cared. "I'll always wish that I saw Silas for who he was. And hate that I'm the reason he was able to get to you and Rho."

"But?" Anson pressed.

"But I'm starting to see just how convincing evil can be. Sometimes, it comes in a pretty or unassuming package. And I don't want to be the kind of person who searches for the bad in everyone who crosses my path. I don't want to let what happened change me."

It was the first time I'd said those realizations aloud. But the truth was, Thea had helped me see them. I saw how Brendan had charmed her, pulled her in. In feeling for her, I started having a little more empathy for myself.

"In other words, you know what happened to Rhodes wasn't your fault."

I swallowed through the tightness in my throat. "I know. Do you?"

Anson stared back at me. "She's kicked my ass into believing it."

I couldn't help but chuckle at that. "My sister is fierce when it comes to the people she loves."

Anson clapped me on the shoulder as he reached for the door handle. "So are you. And that makes us all damn lucky to have you."

As I shut off the engine and climbed out of my truck, I really let those words land. Let the feeling of them hit my chest and expand. I was so damn lucky to have the family I did. The friends. Thea. And I wouldn't underestimate the miracle that was all of that.

Anson and I walked toward the hardware store, heading for the back counter to place an order for the new windows before we went to grab lunch. But as we approached, a prickle of guilt slid over me.

Blond hair shifted as the woman at the counter looked up. The moment her blue eyes locked on me, hurt filled them.

Fuck.

"Hey, Mara," I greeted, trying to keep my expression warm.

She swallowed, forcing a smile. "Shep, hey." She glanced at the man next to me. "Anson."

He simply lifted his chin in answer.

I tugged a piece of paper from my pocket, sliding it over the counter to her. "Could you put in an order for these?"

Mara glanced down, her eyes skimming over the dimensions, brand, and product numbers. A more genuine smile tipped her lips. "Opening up the old girl?"

A little of the tension left me. This had always been where things between Mara and me were easy. Construction, rehab, restoration. "Yeah. Way too dark in there."

"I bet." She began typing away on her computer. "Those old places are beautiful but stuffy."

"Won't be for long."

Mara's gaze flicked up to me, softening. "I have no doubt." Her fingers stilled on the keyboard. "Your hand doing okay?"

I flexed my fingers on instinct. "Fine now."

She nodded, tugging the corner of her lip between her teeth. "Heard Russ was making trouble for you."

Hell.

I didn't want to get into this. "Tried to. But everything's good."

Mara started typing again, but it was slower, as if she was drawing it out. "Watch your back around that one. He's a snake. Always has been."

"I will."

After a few more minutes, she had everything ordered. "On your account?"

"Please," I said.

"You got it. Should be here in a few weeks, but I'll see if we can put a rush on it. No charge."

"You don't have to do that—"

"I *want* to," Mara assured me.

But that assurance made my gut churn. "All right. Appreciate it. Have a good week."

Mara's gaze hovered on my face for just a moment too long. "You, too."

Anson and I headed back through the store to the front door.

"She's not giving up," Anson said, pitching his voice low.

My gaze flicked to him. "She wants something that never really existed."

Because Mara and I had never had depth to our relationship. We did the normal couple things, but we never talked about the *real* stuff. She didn't make me feel seen the way Thea does. Didn't light my blood on fire.

"Maybe so, but the imagination is a powerful thing," Anson muttered. "I'd keep your distance for a while."

"I'm trying to," I gritted out as we stepped out into the sunshine.

"Don't shoot the messenger," Anson shot back.

"Well, look what the cat dragged in. If it isn't Box Baby and Murder Boy."

I looked up to see Russ striding toward us, his dad, Bob, at his side. The nickname had always gotten under my skin—the cruel reminder of a painful truth. But when it hit me this time, it didn't land like it usually did. It didn't sting or burn. It had another effect altogether. Gratitude.

And it was then that I realized something had shifted.

It wasn't like suddenly seeing the world in color, but it was a slight alteration, like the tuning of an instrument. Still, that tiny adjustment changed how you heard everything.

Because Russ's barb just reminded me of where that abandonment had brought me. To the most incredible family I could've asked for. To discovering a purpose in what I did. To finding a true home. And I could see more clearly than ever that those bonds didn't have to be earned. Not by being *good enough* or *perfect*. They were given simply because I was chosen family.

So, instead of being annoyed, I grinned. It didn't hurt that Russ was still rocking a bandage across his nose and some bruising under one eye. "Russ, see you're just as charming as ever."

Bob bristled at that. "Don't you talk to my boy. You think because the Colsons took you in that your shit don't stink. But you're nothing. Just a bastard, through and through."

I saw this clearer now, too. How Russ had come to be the cruel prick he was. He hadn't been born that way. It had been learned.

I met Bob's angry gaze. "You don't want your *boy* to run into trouble, then maybe you should've taught him not to put his hands on a woman who doesn't want them there. But I'm guessing he learned that bullshit at home."

Bob's face turned the shade of a tomato as he charged forward. "Don't you talk to me that way, you little shit. I—"

"Think that's enough," Anson cut in, shoving Bob back. "There are cameras on that building right there. And any action you take, I'll make sure a report lands on Trace's desk."

Bob blustered and fumed, but Russ didn't move an inch. His gaze stayed locked on me, furious. "Those cameras won't always be watching, Box Baby. Watch your back."

Chapter Forty-Three

Thea

THE BELL JINGLED AS THE DOOR TO THE BAKERY OPENED, AND I braced. We had been slammed for the past three days from open to close, but today around lunchtime, things had finally slowed. If the bell chiming meant a fresh wave, I wasn't sure I could handle it.

But the moment my gaze connected with the figure in the doorway, everything in me relaxed, and a laugh bubbled out of me. Lolli was standing there, her silver hair piled into two buns on either side of her head, wearing what looked like workout gear. She had tie-dyed leggings on with bright red sneakers, and her T-shirt read *Plant Manager* with a massive marijuana leaf on it.

"Lolli, you look amazing," I said, grinning at her.

She did a spin, the bracelets on her wrist clinking together. "I gave one of these shirts to Rho. Told her to show them to Duncan at the nursery. They'd make the perfect uniform."

I pressed my lips together to keep from laughing again. "What'd he say?"

Lolli frowned. "He doesn't have my vision."

I bet. Duncan was a pretty chill boss, but I didn't see him changing his family's generations-old nursery into a pot farm. "His loss."

"Is the love of my life out there?" Walter called as he walked out of the kitchen.

"Don't you start with me, you old goat," Lolli shot back.

Walter's eyes twinkled as he smiled at her. "I may be old, but you make me feel like a randy teenager."

Pink hit Lolli's cheeks. "Don't you try to sweet-talk me."

Walter clutched his chest as if he'd been wounded. "I only speak the truth when it comes to you."

"Yeah, yeah." Lolli waved him off as she headed for the bakery case. "I'm too tired to deal with your marriage proposals today. I've been pumping iron with my new trainer, and now I need my reward."

Walter was not deterred. "If you said yes to me, you wouldn't need a trainer. I'd give you plenty of workouts right at home."

"Walter!" Sutton squeaked just as she hit the bottom step of the back staircase.

He just chuckled. "Gotta tell my girl I can keep up with her."

"You could try," Lolli said with the shake of her finger in his direction.

"Everyone needs a life mission," Walter called back.

Sutton gaped at them both. "Am I going to have to separate you two?"

"You could try..." Walter said with a wink.

"Back in the kitchen," Sutton ordered.

Walter just cackled as he headed in that direction. "One day, you'll say yes, Lolli."

She just huffed. "Who does he think he is? I can't be tamed."

My lips twitched. "Might be fun to let him try, though."

Sutton threw her hands in the air, glaring at me. "You, too? Why is everyone so sex-obsessed suddenly?"

Lolli and I shared a look.

"Dry spell, honey bunches?" Lolli asked.

Sutton slumped against the back counter. "It's the Sahara over here."

A grin spread across Lolli's face, and she clapped, letting out a squeal that seemed more fitting for an excited little girl than a grandmother. "We need a girls' night. We'll get dolled up and go to that country bar up the road. There's nothing like a cowboy. I can make us some special gummies to—"

"No!" Sutton and I shouted at the same time.

Lolli frowned at us. "You both need to loosen up."

"I think a glass of wine is about as loose as I need to be these days," Sutton muttered.

"Oh, fine. But we're still going to find some cowboys," Lolli demanded. "Now, get me one of those unicorn cupcakes to go. I've got to get home for my three o'clock sun ceremony."

I didn't ask. Because in all likelihood, it involved Lolli dancing in her garden naked to worship the sun. I grabbed one of the few remaining unicorns and boxed it up for her. "On me."

Lolli took the box with a grin. "You spoil me, sweet girl. I'll repay you with brownies next week."

With a wave, she headed for the door.

"You know you can't eat those brownies, right?" Sutton asked.

"Oh, I know. Rhodes said she accidentally ate one in college and hallucinated for hours."

Sutton just shook her head. "All the shenanigans must keep her young."

"They must," I agreed, turning to face my friend. She'd just gone to pick up Luca from camp and had settled him upstairs with a snack and some activity to keep him entertained while we finished up our day. Sutton always looked beautiful, even when she was covered in flour, but I could see the hints of dark smudges beneath the cover-up under her eyes. "You okay?"

"Huh?" Her gaze snapped to me. "Oh, yeah. I'm good."

I could hear the lie in her voice. "Sutton."

"It's nothing. My ex just found my new number. Called a bunch last night."

I stiffened. I had no idea the history there, but it was clear she didn't want to hear from him.

Sutton's face paled. "Shit. I'm sorry, Thea. It's nothing like that. He was looking for money, that's all. He's a nuisance but not a threat."

But as I took Sutton in, I wasn't sure she was giving me the whole truth. "You know I'm always here if you need to talk."

She smiled at me, but it was strained around the edges. "Thank you. But what I think I really need is that girls' night. A little dancing, a cocktail or two, maybe I'll even remember what it's like to flirt."

Maybe that was a piece of what Sutton needed. She put so much into the bakery and taking care of Luca, she rarely had time for herself. "Okay, we're going to make it happen. But if Lolli offers you a gummy…"

Sutton chuckled. "Just say no."

"Gold star," I said with a grin.

The soft strains of country music shifted suddenly, turning to blaring hard rock.

Sutton winced and jogged over to the stereo system controls. She quickly turned down the volume and switched it back to country. "So sorry about that," she called to our one remaining customer.

The middle-aged woman waved her off as she stood, gathering her purse. "No problem. That techy stuff is always so twitchy."

Sutton laughed. "I swear, if there's a way to set it up wrong, I'll find it."

"You and me both," the woman said.

The bell over the door jingled, and I grimaced as I checked my watch. Who came into a place of business two minutes before they closed? As I turned, pasting on a smile, I froze. Everything in me turned to ice as I took in the tanned face and blue eyes. Eyes that I knew disguised a coldness crueler than anything you could imagine.

"Hey, Selly. Miss me?"

Chapter Forty-Four

Thea

I STARED SO HARD AT BRENDAN THAT MY EYES BURNED. THE stinging bite made me realize I wasn't blinking. Too scared that if I shut my eyes for even a millisecond, he would lash out and turn my world to ash all over again. And I had so much more to lose now.

Saliva pooled in my mouth as the panic set in. The idea that he could poison all the people in Sparrow Falls against me. That he could pull countless photos and videos I never consented to and post them anywhere he damn well pleased. It wouldn't matter if Shep, Sutton, and the Colsons stuck with me. Even if Dex eventually got them pulled down again, I'd still get leveled with the stares and whispers.

It would turn my safe escape into a prison.

"Oh. My. *Goooood!*" the woman who'd been on her way out shouted. "You're Brendan Boseman!"

I saw the briefest flash of annoyance in Brendan's eyes before he turned to her, all charm and bright smiles. "I am. And what's your name?"

"I'm Nelly Parker. I am your *biggest* fan. I must've seen *Kisses for*

Christmas a million times. I know every line. And your *Mask Crusader* movies? I'm obsessed."

Brendan's expression transformed, getting serious now as his eyes glistened. "Nelly, you have no idea what that means to me. Fans like you make my world so much brighter."

Nelly waved a hand in front of her face. "You're going to make me cry."

Brendan grabbed a napkin from one of the dispensers on a table. "Now, don't do that."

She dabbed at her eyes. "Could we do a selfie? My whole quilt group loves you. How generous you are with your fame and fortune. I have to get proof."

My stomach soured. This was how it always was. Everyone seeing exactly what he wanted them to.

"Of course." Brendan wrapped an arm around the woman as she took several shots.

"Thank you so much. I just knew you'd be just as kind in person. You've made my year!"

He winked at her. "Anything for a *true* fan."

Nelly squealed and ran for the door, surely off to call every one of her friends.

Brendan turned then, the weight of his stare coming directly to me. My breaths came quicker and quicker as he started toward the counter, that easy smile stretched across his face. Even now, it was hard for me to see the falseness there. To read beneath the plaster to the evil that lay below.

"The lighting gaffer on my newest movie has a thing for bakeries. Can't get enough. Wherever we film, she just has to try all the best ones around. Came here after she saw a writeup on some blog and swore the woman behind the counter looked just like you, only with darker hair."

A bead of sweat slid down my spine, like ice melting against my burning flesh.

Brendan's smile just widened. "You're not even going to say

hello? It's been so long." He shifted then, turning that charming smile to Sutton. "Hi, I'm Brendan. An old friend of Selena's."

A fresh bolt of panic jolted through me. How many times had he charmed friends of mine? Colleagues? So charming that they all started looking at me differently after we broke up. Started believing his lies.

The idea that he might succeed with Sutton was too much to bear. Losing her, one of the first friends I'd had in years? I wouldn't be able to take it.

"I know who you are." There was a frigidity to Sutton's tone that had my head snapping in her direction. Cold fury blasted across her expression. And if it was possible to murder someone with your eyes, then Brendan would be dead. "And you're not welcome in my bakery."

A look of hurt flashed across Brendan's face, so real I would've believed it if I hadn't fallen for his tricks before. "Selena's always taking things to the extreme. I see that hasn't changed."

"I've never known her to do that," Sutton ground out.

Brendan flashed her another of those smiles. "Maybe you haven't known her long enough. But that sort of thing happens with heartbreak. I know I was a mess after she left." His gaze moved to me, the contact of it feeling like claws digging into my skin. "I'd like to talk. Make things right."

"No." My voice was stronger than I thought it would be. Because my insides were shaking, and I hadn't moved an inch.

"Selly—"

"I said *no.* Go back to your set and sycophants and whatever makes you happy these days. Leave me the hell alone."

There was the briefest flash of something in those blue eyes. The kind that used to make me feel crazy because I wasn't sure if it had been real or imagined. "Selena, that's not very kind—"

"I think it's incredibly kind. I'm leaving you to live the rest of your miserable life in peace even though you *ruined* mine."

He chuckled, but tension radiated through it. "I think that's a little extreme, don't you? We broke up. It was messy. That happens to people every day. I don't think that makes me a monster."

My fingernails dug into my palms so hard, I felt the flesh give way. "You know what you did. If this world was just, you'd feel every ounce of pain you inflicted."

"Careful," Brendan snapped. "You wouldn't want to say something you can't take back. Something you'd be liable for."

"Leave now, or I call the cops," Sutton barked.

Walter moved out from the kitchen. "I got a phone right here."

"Funny," Brendan began, "every other establishment I've been into around here has bent over backward to be hospitable to me." His expression morphed in a flash, going dangerously cold. "It would be a shame if word got around about how bad the service is here."

Bile surged in my throat as nausea swept through me, the urge to empty the contents of my stomach so strong.

Brendan turned back to me. "Selly, I'll be seeing you."

His words were a threat, pure and simple—to me and anyone who stood beside me. My eyes burned, tears just trying to break free. Free the way I never would be. Because Brendan would always find me. Would destroy any glimmer of happiness.

My vision blurred as I watched him walk out of the bakery and disappear across the street. It didn't matter that he was retreating now, he'd never truly be gone.

"Thea." Sutton's hand curled around my arm. "Want me to call Trace?"

I jerked at the touch, at her words. I shook my head vehemently. "I need to go."

I was already moving, grabbing my purse and heading for the door.

"Wait! Thea!" she shouted as I stepped outside, searching for my bike.

Suddenly, all the things that had happened over the past six weeks made more sense. The slashed bike tires. The person watching me outside the diner. The note. It had nothing to do with Russ. It had been Brendan all along.

My stomach roiled as I remembered the music blaring to life in the bakery just before Brendan came inside. It was his way of telling me he could get to me anywhere. And he could get to those I cared about, too.

I unlocked my bike and climbed on. Shoving my purse into the basket, I took off. I'd never ridden faster. My muscles strained, and my lungs burned. But it wasn't until I felt the sting of the wind on my cheeks that I realized I was crying.

He'd won. Again.

I couldn't stay in Sparrow Falls. Not with Brendan hovering, the long reach of his cruel fingers looming around me. Not knowing he could do the worst at any moment. I wouldn't put Sutton through that. Not when she'd worked so hard to start over. And I wouldn't put Shep through it either. Because if Brendan found out there was a man in my life, he would rain down hellfire on him.

I had to leave. There was no choice.

The moment I reached my house, I jumped off my bike and ran toward the front door. My hand shook as I tried to undo the lock. It took me a good six tries to get my key into the deadbolt.

As I stepped inside and locked the door behind me, Moose let out a warbled meow, and the kittens echoed him from the living room. I'd have to get the burner out of my nightstand and text Rhodes, ask her to come get them. But for now, I needed to move.

I hurried into my bedroom, moving to the closet and feeling for the loose floorboard. Popping it up, I pulled out the lockbox and input the combination. The moment it was open, I started shoving all the contents inside my purse. Passport, cash, legal documents.

I straightened from my crouch and reached up for the duffel bag on a shelf high above my clothes. As my fingers closed around the strap of the bag, the tears came faster. I hadn't wanted to use this bag. Not ever again.

The duffel had been my only companion other than Moose on my trip from LA all around the Pacific Northwest. Until I found Sparrow Falls. The calming pull of the mountains here. The way the air soothed. I'd worked so hard to make it my home.

And Brendan had stolen that, too.

I yanked the bag down and dumped it on my bed. I moved

quickly to my dresser, pulling out only what I'd need to get me to where I was going next. I needed to go farther this time. Maybe the East Coast? Canada?

My heart gave a vicious squeeze as if rebelling against the idea. Because all of that meant being far away from the last person I wanted distance from. Tears spilled over, sliding off my chin and landing on my comforter.

My fingers fisted in my clothes as I shoved them into the bag. Shep didn't deserve the nightmare headed my way. He didn't deserve people whispering about him because his girlfriend's naked body had been up on porn sites. He didn't deserve to have his finances hacked, or his business ruined by rumors of shoddy work or whatever else Brendan could dream up.

He deserved so much better. He deserved *everything*.

I was so caught up in shoving clothes in the bag, I didn't hear the footsteps. I didn't hear anything at all. Not until the deep voice boomed across the space.

"What the hell are you doing?"

Chapter Forty-Five

Shep

THEA WHIRLED AROUND AT MY WORDS, HER HAIR FLYING IN ALL directions. The look on her face cut me to the quick. Eyes red. Tear tracks staining her cheeks. Skin pale. And more than that was panic. Terror.

She shook her head, faster and faster, hands gripping a T-shirt. "I have to go."

Pain, hot and brutal like a scalding poker, pierced my chest. "No."

Thea's gaze jumped around the room, looking for a way out. Like she was a wide receiver looking for a hole to run through. "I have to, Shep. He's going to ruin everything." The tears came faster then. "He'll ruin Sutton's business. Yours. He'll destroy every single person who stands with me just because he can. He'll put the pictures up again. He'll make sure the whole town sees them."

Fuck.

If I'd thought I wanted to kill Brendan before, it was nothing compared to what I felt now. When Sutton called, panicked that Thea was about to do something reckless, I'd dropped everything and bolted for home. I'd thought it hurt to find Thea packing, but that had nothing on seeing her brokenness now.

I crossed the room in three long strides.

"Don't." Thea's voice cracked like a whip. "It'll be so much harder if you touch me. I won't be able to do it, what I need to, what's right. I have to do what's right, Shepard."

"Thea." My voice cracked on her name.

"If you wrap your arms around me and make me feel safe, leaving will be that much harder, and it's already going to rip my heart out."

"If you leave, I'm going with you." The words were out before I could stop them. But the moment they were, I knew they were true.

"You can't," she whispered. "This is your home."

"*You're* my home." It was the simple truth. Thea had become the place I felt most myself, the place I felt seen and understood, where I could simply *be* without needing to prove myself.

A fresh wave of tears spilled down Thea's cheeks. "I'm a mess. You don't want your home to be with me."

"Thea." Her name was more rasp than word. "Then we'll fix it. Together. Because whatever we build, it's always better when both our hands are in it."

She scrubbed at her face, brushing the tears away.

"I love you, Thorn. And there's nothing anyone can ever do to change that. There are no lies that could be told to taint it. I don't care what that bastard throws at us. I *love* you."

Thea's chest rose and fell in ragged pants as she struggled for composure.

"I'll never see you as anything but perfect. Not because you don't make mistakes but because of *this*." I stepped into her space and placed my palm over the left side of her chest.

"Your heart is the most beautiful thing I've ever experienced. Beautiful because it's been broken. Those cracks let it become something else entirely. Stronger. Wiser. The fiercest defender of anyone who needs it. And the gentlest confidante for anyone who needs understanding. You see it all. And you don't look away. You come alongside without judgment, and you simply *love*. You can't ask me to walk away from that after I've experienced it. It would be like living in the sun, only to exist entirely in darkness."

"Shepard." Her voice cracked on my name.

"So, if you need to go, then I go, too. Wherever you need to be, that's where I am."

She didn't move or speak for a long moment. We just stood there, my hand against her heart, feeling each rapid beat. Thea stared into my eyes, those pale green orbs searching. Then she moved.

So fast I didn't have a chance to brace. She threw herself at me, her legs hooked around my waist, her arms linked around my neck as she shoved her face into it. And she let the tears flow. The sobs shook her body, and I took them all. Every ounce of pain and fear that she had to release.

I knew this was the last wall. The final barrier Thea had constructed to keep people out. She was letting me see it all. And there was no greater honor. So, I simply held on.

Slowly, the tears subsided, and the trembling lessened. When Thea pulled back, her eyes were swollen, but that terror was no longer there.

"I love you, too," she whispered, her voice hoarse.

I brushed the hair away from her face. "I know."

Her mouth fell open in adorable shock. "You know?"

"I know."

Thea scowled at me, her legs still locked around my waist. "That's cocky."

My thumb stroked across her cheek, clearing the remnants of her tears. "Not cocky. You just show me every day."

Her expression softened at that. "You show me, too. I've never really known what it's like to feel completely safe. Not until I met you. It's more than the physical safety. It's feeling safe to be who I truly am. No pretenses. No fear of judgment."

I pressed my forehead to hers, soaking in that floral scent with hints of coconut. "You give me the exact same feeling."

"I'm glad."

We stood there for a long time, and then I finally asked the question I needed to. "Are we staying or going?"

Because from now on, it would always be a *we*. Thea and I were a team. Stronger together for so many reasons.

Thea pulled back, studying my face. "I don't want to leave. I don't want to lose the things I've fought so hard to have."

Cool relief washed through me. Both at not having to leave behind all I loved, but also that Thea was ready to fight. My thumb ghosted over her lower lip. "That's my girl."

Chapter Forty-Six

Thea

FATIGUE HIT ME LIKE A MACK TRUCK AS SHEP CARRIED ME INTO the kitchen. "I can walk."

"Nope," he muttered.

"Shep…"

"Just give me this, Thorn. Need to know you're okay."

A sigh left my lips, but I burrowed my face into his neck. It was more than just knowing I was okay. Shep wanted to make sure I wasn't bailing on him. A stab of guilt hit me straight in the solar plexus.

"I'm not going anywhere," I whispered against his neck. "I promise."

Shep slowly lowered me into a chair at the kitchen table. As he released me, his hands came to my face, and his thumbs ghosted under my eyes as if searching for any remnants of tears. Then they trailed lower, over the curve of my cheeks, one to my bottom lip and the other down my neck. It was as if he was memorizing the feel of me.

"I know."

His gaze flicked down to my lap, and he frowned. He grabbed

one of my hands, lifting it for his inspection. There were smears of blood on my palms, along with crescent moon-shaped wounds. "What happened?" His finger ghosted—featherlight—over the injuries.

I winced. "I think I did it when Brendan came into the bakery. I didn't realize I'd broken the skin."

A muscle along Shep's jaw fluttered wildly. "Stay here."

His voice had gone gruff, all Mr. Control. But I didn't argue. I was too exhausted to move anyway.

A few seconds later, Shep reappeared with countless items in his arms. He set them on the table and then moved to the sink to wash his hands.

I studied the array of goods. Hydrogen peroxide, ointment, Band-Aids, gauze, tape. "It's not that bad. I can just wash my hands—"

Shep turned to me as he dried his hands, cutting off my words with a look. "We don't want them to get infected. And if I remember correctly, you did the same thing for me."

I snapped my mouth closed as he strode across the small kitchen and pulled out a second chair. The scent of cedar and sawdust swirled around me, soothing more than any ointment ever would. Because it was Shep.

Sitting, he picked up a piece of gauze and coated it in hydrogen peroxide. Then he took one of my hands in his, palm up, and studied the wounds. "I'm so sorry this happened."

"Shep—"

He swept the gauze across my palm. "I'm sorry I wasn't there."

"You can't be with me every moment of every day," I said softly.

"I want to be."

"Shepard…"

The use of his full name had Shep looking up.

"That's not the answer. Being together twenty-four-seven isn't healthy for either of us."

His mouth turned down in a frown. "I don't want him to blind-side you again. Don't want him to get you alone."

"I wasn't alone. And I never will be. Because I carry you here." I pressed my free hand to my heart, not caring if I got blood on my shirt. "You've made me realize my own strength, my bravery. You've made me a fighter."

"Thorn," he whispered.

"It's true. And I know Brendan. He won't risk doing something publicly. He'll do it behind the scenes."

"That's not going to happen," Shep gritted out.

"You can't control what he does or doesn't do. We just have to deal with whatever happens."

Shep's amber eyes lifted to mine. "And we'll do it together."

Warmth spread through me at that. "I love you."

His mouth curved. "Love hearing those words on your lips."

"Better get used to it."

Shep returned his focus to my hands, cleaning each wound and coating them in the thick ointment before covering both my palms with massive Band-Aids.

"Don't you think this is a little much?" I asked.

He glowered at me. "We're not taking any chances."

I knew he meant it as much more than a possible infection on my palms. I opened my mouth to assure him that I was okay when a knock on my door cut me off.

My body reacted on instinct, pushing from my chair, muscles tensing.

Shep curved around me in an instant. "It's Trace. I called him on my way over here."

The tension left me on a single exhale. Trace. Not Brendan. Everything was okay.

Shep's lips ghosted over my temple. "You're safe."

"I know."

Shep didn't release me right away, and I knew it was a battle when he finally did. I could feel the tension thrumming through him. But when the second knock sounded, he moved for my front door.

"Thanks for coming," Shep said as he ushered his brother inside.

Trace moved down the hallway toward the kitchen, his gaze missing nothing as it did a quick sweep of me and my surroundings. "I'm so sorry this happened, Thea."

"Me, too," I said. "Do you want a drink or—?"

"I'll get them. You sit," Shep ordered.

I stuck out my tongue at him. "Bossy, much?"

Trace chuckled. "He always has been. Tried to boss me all the time when we were teenagers. Even though I was older."

"You narced on me the one time I skipped class in high school," Shep shot back.

Trace grinned as he pulled out a chair at the kitchen table. "Payback's a bitch."

I looked back and forth between the brothers. They had the kind of closeness I'd always craved growing up. And now, with time, I knew I'd be a part of it, too. I'd have funny stories with the Colsons, inside jokes. All of that was worth fighting for.

Shep slid the pitcher of lemonade I'd made yesterday onto the table along with three glasses and a platter with cheese and crackers. He took the chair next to mine and pushed the snack plate toward me. "You need to eat something."

I grabbed a cracker to appease him, but when I looked up, it was to find Trace studying me and Shep. His expression was a mixture of happiness and longing. I didn't know much about his previous marriage or why it had come to an end, but it was plain to see that he missed the sort of closeness that Shep and I shared.

That longing had my heart aching for the man who was so incredibly kind. It had to be hard to be so focused on taking care of your daughter and the town, but not to have someone giving that care back.

Trace cleared his throat. "I have to ask, did Brendan make any threats against you when he came into the bakery?"

The little bit of cracker I'd eaten soured in my stomach. "He just said that it would be a shame if people found out about The Mix Up's poor service and that he'd be seeing me. That's his version of a threat."

Shep's knuckles bleached white as he gripped his glass tighter. "There has to be something you can do. He's stalking her."

Trace scrubbed a hand over his jaw. "For an order of protection, we need to prove threats were made."

"He's torturing her," Shep growled.

"I know," Trace assured him. Then he turned back to me. "Anson was able to get me the LAPD's records on the case. They won't know who pulled them or why, but at least this way I can see what evidence was gathered."

My stomach twisted as I remembered all the fruitless conversations with officers in LA, all the times I'd been made to feel that everything that had happened was *my* fault.

"They did a crap job of thoroughly looking into things," he went on.

"Tell me something I don't know," I muttered.

"Anson has Dex on it now. He's going to see if he can find any proof that links Brendan to the cyber-attacks against you."

I straightened in my chair. "Do you think that's possible?"

My heart hammered against my ribs. I'd given up on Brendan ever being brought to justice. I just wanted him to go away. But having him live with the repercussions of his actions? Having the world know the truth? That was more than I'd ever dared hope for.

"If anyone can do it, Dex can," Trace said. "Anson's told me about what he does for the FBI. The guy has serious skills. And I definitely wouldn't want to cross him. He's got a finely honed need for justice."

Shep's eyes narrowed on his brother. "You mean he's a vigilante."

"That would be the word. But he's a vigilante on our side."

Shep jerked his head in a nod. "You tell him we'll get him whatever he needs."

"Shep—"

He turned back to me, his hand going to my face and cupping my cheek. "Brendan is done tormenting you. And he's going to get what he deserves. I'll make sure of it."

My stomach bottomed out. As much as I wanted Brendan to be served a healthy dose of justice, I knew what he did to people who crossed him. He ruined them.

Chapter Forty-Seven

Thea

I HOISTED A BAG OF POTTING SOIL FROM THE BACK OF A GATOR onto the display pile Rhodes and I were currently erecting at the side of the potting flowers.

"I'm thinking we could've hit it big in Ancient Egypt. Our pyramid-building skills are next level," Rhodes said as she dropped another bag of soil on the pile.

I chuckled, putting the next one in place. "How's your arm feeling?"

Rhodes rolled up her T-shirt sleeve and flexed her cast-free biceps. "Good as new." She let her arm fall to her side. "How are you holding up with everything?"

Her gaze moved to the parking lot where a Mercer County Sheriff's Department vehicle was parked. They'd been my frequent companions over the past week. Not twenty-four-seven but fairly constant. Trace must've been in contact with Shep because on the days when he picked me up from work, they peeled off quickly. But when I drove myself, they followed me home or were waiting for me at work when I got there.

But everything had been quiet. Too quiet. There'd been no word from Brendan. And that almost unsettled me more.

"I'm doing all right." It wasn't a lie, but it wasn't the whole truth either. My nerves were eating away at me. But there was good, too. Every time I got too wound up to sit still, Shep found *other* things to keep me occupied.

And more than that, there were no more walls between us. Everything was out in the open. We'd spend time in the greenhouse or at Shep's restoration project, planning out the landscaping for all around the house. Despite everything swirling around us, we were building a life.

Rhodes' lips pursed, her eyes squinting. "I'm sensing a lie."

I couldn't help but laugh. She looked like she was trying to see through my skull. "Practicing that X-ray vision?"

"You know, I've always wished I was psychic. It would come in so handy."

I grinned at her. "Have one of Lolli's brownies and you might get there."

"Oh, hell no. Been there, done that. I still haven't recovered."

I laughed again as I lifted the final bag of soil onto our perfect pyramid. "She probably did change your brain chemistry."

Rhodes shook her head. "That woman needs someone to watch her every move. It's a miracle she hasn't ended up in jail yet."

"Comes in handy having a grandson who's the sheriff."

Rhodes raised her arms over her head, stretching out her back. "Trace would be the first one to lock her up in an attempt to get her on the straight and narrow."

"I can see her mugshot now."

One side of Rhodes' mouth kicked up. "It would make for a great Christmas card."

I brushed the dirt off my hands. "Kind of want to report her for something now."

Rhodes was quiet for a moment.

I glanced at her. "You okay?"

She blinked a few times as if coming out of a haze. "I love having you as a part of our family."

The words were like a surprise attack, sneaking in with a sucker punch to my diaphragm. "Rho."

"Love it for me because you're awesome, funny, kind, and you'll talk plants with me until we're blue in the face."

My lips wanted to twitch, but I was still trying to stay standing in the face of her words.

Rhodes' eyes misted. "But I love it for Shep more. He's different since you two started spending time together. I can't totally explain it, but he's more at ease. At peace. And I know he's happy."

My eyes began to burn. "He gives me the same. More."

Rhodes reached out and took my hand, squeezing, "You deserve all the more." She released me, wiping at her eyes. "Now that I've turned us both into puddles, I'm going to take the Gator back. You good here?" She did a quick survey of our surroundings as if to check for the bogeyman.

"I'm good," I assured her. There were plenty of patrons around. Duncan was helping a couple pick out trees, and other staff members milled about, working on various tasks. "Shep should be here in a few to pick me up."

"Okay." Then Rhodes shot me a grin. "Can't wait for our girls' night."

"Not you, too," I groaned.

She laughed as she climbed into the Gator. "Not going to miss Lolli hitting on cowboys."

I barked out a laugh as I gave her a wave and headed toward the parking lot to wait for Shep. On my way, I caught sight of a woman loading up a cart with various potted plants from our sale section. She struggled with an especially heavy one, and I hurried to help her.

"Here, let me help you with that." I bent to help her lift it.

As she straightened, the light brown hair shifted out of her face. Panic slid through Raina Wheeler's hazel eyes. I saw it then. The yellowing green of a fading bruise beneath her makeup. She'd done a good job of concealing it, but helping her with the plant, I was close enough to see beneath the mask.

"Th-thank you," she mumbled.

"Of course." My stomach twisted as I struggled for words. I wished Fallon was with me. She'd know what to say. What to do. "What are you working on?"

Raina kept moving, grabbing more flowers as quickly as possible. "I'm putting the finishing touches on the yard at one of our houses."

I shifted from foot to foot. "With all of these, it'll look amazing. Do you need any help? I've got a day off coming up—"

"No." The single word snapped out, but Raina flushed, quickly ducking her head. "I'm sorry. I just…Russ wouldn't like you being there."

The pain in my stomach intensified, a vicious cramping that wouldn't let go. "You shouldn't have to fear your partner, Raina. There's a way out. I promise. I've been there—"

"I'm fine. I don't need your help or anyone else's. Please, just stop."

There was a desperation in Raina's voice that had me taking a step away. It hurtled me back in time, to a season where I'd done the exact same thing. I'd lied to Nikki's face and told her everything was fine. That I was happy. Because admitting how bad things had gotten was more than I could bear.

"Okay. But if you change your mind, I'm always here. Anytime, day or night."

Raina ignored me, going back to loading up her cart.

I stayed for a moment longer, hoping she'd change her mind and tell me she wanted to leave the bastard. But she didn't.

Shoulders slumping, I turned toward the parking lot. The second I looked up, my eyes locked with amber ones that flashed gold in the afternoon sunlight. Shep leaned against the back of his truck. It was a sight that had my mouth going dry.

That damn white T-shirt and dark-wash jeans, his Colson Construction ballcap shielding his eyes. But the way the sun was positioned, I could still see them beneath the bill. As I started toward him, Shep pushed off the truck. His muscles bunched and flexed as he moved—broad shoulders, defined chest, powerful thighs.

The moment I was within reach, he hauled me into him. "You okay?"

I didn't hold back, simply burrowed into Shep. Because he'd come to mean comfort, safety, and reassurance when the world went haywire around me. "Raina has a bruise on her cheek. It's old, but I saw it."

Shep tensed, and I felt his focus flick to Raina and then back to me. "She say anything?"

I pulled back just enough that I could see his face and shook my head. "Nothing except she didn't need my help."

Shep's expression softened, but I didn't miss the fury beneath it. He reached up and brushed my hair away from my face, fingers lingering in the strands. "You tried. But you can't force her to take your help. She has to reach out."

"I know," I whispered. "I just…I hate him for doing this to her. He's broken her."

"Thorn."

"I know what that's like. To be too scared to even reach for help."

Shep's hold on me tightened. "But you did. You got out. And we have to hope Raina will, too. We've given her all the paths we can."

My hands fisted in Shep's tee, the soft cotton soothing. Sometimes, it felt like my getting out of the relationship with Brendan had been nothing less than a miracle. I'd been so exhausted, I was ready to give up altogether. It had been one tiny flicker of strength when everything else had been pure darkness.

The blast of rage I'd received in return had been a weird balm. Because Brendan had been thousands of miles away filming a movie, I'd felt safe, even relieved. But I hadn't realized he could reach me even then.

Shep's thumb ghosted over my bottom lip. "I'm in awe of you."

I blinked up at him.

"So fucking strong."

"I don't always feel like that. Didn't feel that back then. I felt so weak."

His thumb stayed there, right at the swell of my lip. "You got out when you felt weakest. That just shows the depth of your strength. You clawed your way out, even if you had to crawl. Strength doesn't matter when we're at our best; it matters when we're at our worst. And I don't know anyone who's stronger than you."

My breath hiccuped, a hitch at the power of his words. Shep was always one who could shift my view of an experience just enough that my whole world changed. "I like the way you see me."

He stared down at me, his gaze locked on mine. "I just see the truth."

My throat burned, but I refused to get teary for a second time today. "You gonna take me home so I can show you how I feel about that, Shepard?"

Shep's eyes flashed gold. "Fuck."

I couldn't help it, I laughed.

Shep bent then, throwing me over his shoulder and stalking toward his truck.

"Shep!" I squealed as I tried to twist out of his hold.

His arm locked across my thighs.

"This is my place of work," I hissed, but I couldn't help the hint of laughter that bled into my tone.

"Then you probably shouldn't have made me hard in the damn parking lot. You're a goddamn temptress, Thorn."

Warmth surged through me at his words, a sensation that was nothing less than empowering. Even if I was being carted off over the man's shoulder.

Shep opened the passenger door of his truck and deposited me inside. He pulled the seat belt across me, clicking it into place but not moving. My chest brushed against him with each inhale, that scent of sawdust and cedar swirling around me.

"Gonna be the death of me." He took my mouth, tongue stroking in. Each languid lash had my insides twisting tighter at the promise of what was to come.

When he pulled back, we were both out of breath. Shep shook his head. "Like a drug. One of these days, I'm gonna end up fucking you somewhere we definitely shouldn't, and I'm gonna get arrested for indecent exposure."

A giggle bubbled out of me, my hand flying to my mouth.

"And she's fucking cute on top of it," he muttered. "I'm absolutely screwed."

Shep shut my door, continuing to mutter to himself as he rounded the truck and climbed inside. Once we were on the main road toward my house, his hand slid up my thigh, thumb tracing absent-minded circles on my jeans.

"Did you make good progress today?" I asked as he drove.

Shep's work had been interrupted since he played chauffeur to me half the time. He mixed up which days he took me and picked me up so Brendan wouldn't be able to plan to get me alone if he was watching. Between him and my sheriff's department detail, there was no way Brendan would try anything.

"We're humming along. I'm hoping when one of my crews finishes up on another project, I can steal them for this for a few weeks. It would make a big difference."

I toyed with a loose thread on my jeans. "I'm sorry I'm slowing things down."

Shep's gaze flicked to me. "You aren't."

I sent him a look. "If you weren't picking me up, you'd still be working."

"No, I'd be leaving to get a few hours in on your bathroom. I gotta pay my rent, unless you accept sexual favors."

My lips twitched. "I don't think I could afford that tongue of yours."

Shep grinned. "Damn straight." He moved his hand from my thigh, weaving his fingers through mine. "The house will get done. There's no rush. And you'll always be more important to me than any project."

My fingers tightened around his. "Love you."

"Love you, too."

Shep turned onto my long drive, his truck bumping along the gravel road. As we got closer, I caught sight of an SUV parked in front of my tiny house.

"You know who that is?" Shep asked.

I shook my head. "I don't recognize it."

The SUV was black, or maybe a dark blue with tinted windows. It had Oregon plates, but they weren't ones I'd seen before, and that was the sort of thing I paid attention to.

Shep pulled up to my house but put some distance between us and the other vehicle. "Stay here."

"Shep, wait."

But he was already out of the truck. The moment he rounded the vehicle, someone stepped out of the SUV. My stomach sank the moment I saw the blond hair and blue eyes.

I shoved the door open as Shep stalked across the gravel toward Brendan, panic racing through me.

"You need to leave," Shep barked.

Brendan's face was a polite mask, but I saw the anger in his eyes, the way the blue went so cold you knew it would burn. "And you are?"

"No concern of yours, but you're on private property. You've got to the count of five before I get the sheriff's department out here."

"But it's not your property, is it?" Brendan's gaze moved to me. "Come on, Selly. We need to talk."

"I don't have anything to say to you." My voice was calmer than I felt. Just having him anywhere near my house was almost more than I could take.

Brendan sent me one of those smiles that used to reel me back in. The kind full of disarming charm that promised the world, only to pull the rug out minutes later. "Don't be like that. I've missed you—"

"Don't talk to her. Don't even fucking look at her," Shep ground out.

Rage flashed across Brendan's face for the briefest of moments before cocky arrogance replaced it. "But I've more than *talked* to her, Shepard. I know every inch of her body. I know what it sounds like when she—"

Shep lunged. He was fast, but I had sheer panic on my side. I grabbed hold of Shep's T-shirt, trying to hold him back from decking Brendan. "Don't," I begged. "That's exactly what he wants. He'd have you in jail before you could blink."

Shep struggled for control, knowing I was right but not wanting to listen to reason.

Brendan started to laugh. "She's got you on a short leash."

A muscle ticked wildly in Shep's jaw as he pulled his phone out of his pocket. "Calling the sheriff's department."

Anger flashed again in Brendan's expression. He knew that a public police report was the last thing he needed, but his gaze cut to me. "It's good that you remember who's in charge, Selena. Who always will be."

Shep made a move for Brendan again, but he slid into his SUV, gunning the engine and peeling out of my drive. Shep jumped back, narrowly avoiding a spray of gravel. He didn't turn back to me until he was sure the SUV was gone for good. When he did, fury blasted across his face.

"Are you okay?" he gritted out.

No. I wasn't okay. Not because Brendan knew where I lived or because he wasn't leaving me the hell alone, it was for another reason entirely. One that brought all my fears roaring back to life.

"Shep, he knows who you are."

Chapter Forty-Eight

Shep

I SLAMMED THE DOOR OF MY TRUCK SO HARD IT SENT THE ENTIRE vehicle rocking. My back molars ground together as I stalked up the walkway to Trace's Craftsman. It wasn't one of my builds, but I had redone the kitchen and bathrooms, along with putting in a window seat for Keely in her bedroom.

But I couldn't take in the family charm of the place now, or how hard my brother had worked to give Keely everything he hadn't had growing up. I was too furious.

I'd taken my time to make sure Thea was okay and wasn't triggered or frightened. But all she seemed to be concerned about was me. That Brendan knew who I was. That he would hurt me. My business, my reputation. But I didn't give a damn about that. All I cared about was her.

I'd waited until Anson and Rhodes could get to my place before taking off for Trace's. I hadn't wanted to leave her alone, not when Brendan thought he could show up at her house whenever he pleased. But I needed to talk to my brother. And I had to do it alone.

Taking the steps two at a time, I reached the front porch in record time. I knocked twice but didn't hear an answer. I knew he had to be home. His shift had ended an hour ago, and Keely was with her mom this week.

I knocked again, louder this time.

Footsteps sounded from inside, and the door swung open. "Jesus, Shep. Give me a second to get to the door—" His words cut off as he took in my face. "What happened?"

My jaw worked back and forth. "Brendan was waiting for Thea when we got home."

Trace was on alert in a split second. "Inside or outside?"

"Out."

"Damn it. I wanted to get him on breaking and entering at least."

"Trespassing?" I suggested.

Trace shook his head, motioning me inside and shutting the door behind me. "I've been to Thea's place. There are no signs that state it's private property. It'd never stand up in court."

I cursed.

"Come on, walk me through it," Trace said, leading me to the kitchen.

So, I did. I gave my brother every detail I could think of. But just recounting it had my fury blazing brighter. Remembering how he'd taunted her, goaded me. Knowing that he was free to continue tormenting Thea.

Trace was quiet for a long moment when I finished. That was his MO, though. His mind had a similar quality to Anson's, always taking its time to look at all the puzzle pieces. Trace just saw them through a different lens.

"Thea's right. Brendan was hoping you'd hit him. That maybe he could get you out of the way long enough to break down her defenses again. Get her to come back to him, most likely."

A growl tore from my throat at the mere thought of it.

Trace's gaze snapped to me. "It's not going to happen, so just breathe. Jesus."

But I couldn't. Each breath felt like it was made of razor blades.

"How would you feel if the tables were turned? If someone who'd tortured the person you love could just walk right up to her and throw all that shit in your face?"

Trace's eyes flared in surprise before he quickly covered it. "Someone you love?"

"Yes. I fucking love her. I'd do anything for her. So, *help* me."

Trace leaned against the kitchen counter. "I'm doing everything I can. But it's not easy. And Dex said Brendan must have a hacker working for him or have those skills himself. His computers are locked down tight."

Hell. Thea had said Brendan was an expert at tech.

I scrubbed a hand over my stubbled cheek. "So, he can just show up? Mess with her?"

Trace shook his head. "I'll mark on the official record that you and Thea asked him to leave her property. Sutton has refused him service at the bakery. If he shows up at either of those places again, we'll have grounds for a restraining order. I'm going to put that in writing to his attorneys so they can't plead *misunderstanding* to a judge."

"It's not enough." I wasn't sure anything would be until Brendan Boseman was no longer breathing.

Trace's gaze locked with mine. "You need to watch yourself. This asshole isn't going to like that you're with Thea. He could mess with you in a multitude of ways."

"Let him try," I gritted out.

Worry filled Trace's expression. "Don't be an idiot. You need to play this smart."

The sound of the front door opening had Trace's focus shifting away from me.

"Yo, dipshit. Where are you?"

Cope's voice rang out through the entryway and had Trace and me looking at each other with a mix of concern and confusion.

"In the kitchen, jockstrap," Trace called back.

Heavy footfalls sounded, and Cope's massive frame filled the space. He grinned at us. "Two idiots for the price of one. How the hell are you?" He pulled Trace into a back-slapping hug and then me.

Trace studied Cope carefully. "What are you doing here? I thought you decided to stay in Seattle."

Something swept across Cope's face so quickly I almost missed it. Something dark. But he covered it with that patented easy grin of his. "Can't I just miss my fam bam?"

Trace and I shared another look.

"Oh, piss off," Cope said, giving me a shove. "I needed to get out of the city for a while. Actually get a little R&R."

"Fair enough," Trace acquiesced. But I knew my older brother better than that. Trace would quietly dig until he figured out what was going on with Cope. "You want a beer or a soda?"

"Beer," Cope said, then looked at me. "What's got your face looking like you sucked on a lemon?"

Right to the point as always. I hadn't talked to Cope in weeks, other than the occasional group siblings' text, so he had no clue what was going on. And I didn't have the first idea where to start.

But Trace did it for me. "Shep's in love."

Cope winced as he took the beer and raised it to me. "I'd be looking like that, too."

I glared at him. "Don't be an asshole."

"That's his natural state," Trace muttered.

Cope flipped him off. "Tell me what's really going on."

So, I did. And by the time I finished, Cope was nearly as furious as I was. "How the hell do we nail this guy? Kye might still know some guys from—"

"No." Trace's single word rang with finality. And I didn't blame him. When Kye had gotten mixed up with underground fighting in his teens, it had almost cost him everything.

Trace sighed. "We play this smart, and we work together. We'll make sure Thea stays safe."

I wanted to believe my brother. And I knew he was right when it came to Thea's physical safety. But I'd seen the devastation Brendan could inflict with a few simple keyboard strokes. How the hell did I protect Thea from that?

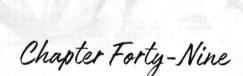

Chapter Forty-Nine

Thea

I WATCHED SHEP CHECK THE LOCKS ON EVERY WINDOW IN THE living room as I fed the kittens their last meal before bed. They were officially up on the Wags & Whiskers website, ready for adoption. I had no doubt they'd be snatched up in a matter of days. They were too cute not to be.

That should've made me happy, but I couldn't seem to let the emotion land. Not when worry and concern crowded it out.

Shep had been quiet all night. When he returned from Trace's house, he'd barely shared about their conversation, only saying, *"We're working on it."* Since then, he'd been trapped in his thoughts, and it left me feeling strangely alone, even though Shep was physically present.

When the kittens were done with their meal, I lifted the bowls, taking them to the sink to wash. I could feel Shep continuing his movements through the house, checking every possible point of entry. But I knew that wasn't how Brendan would lash out. When he did, it would be in a way no one could trace.

After washing my hands, I headed for the bathroom to get ready for bed. Even after taking my time to do every single step of skincare, Shep still wasn't done with his assessment of my home. So, I moved to my bedroom, changed into my nightie, and slid beneath the covers, grabbing my book from the nightstand.

I'd moved on to a new romance with a tortured hero who had a thing for control. I wouldn't lie and say that I hadn't wondered if Shep's need for control could express itself in rough ropes or soft, silken cords. But tonight, I couldn't focus. I read the same sentence over and over until Shep moved into the bedroom.

My gaze instantly went to him. He wore navy sweats that hung low on his hips, and a heather-gray tee worn in all the right places. "Everything good?"

He nodded. "You tired?"

I shook my head. "Not really." The truth was, I wanted Shep. Wanted to feel the connection between us bloom brightly. Wanted to feel *him*.

Shep pulled his T-shirt over his head, exposing all those planes of muscle. "Read as long as you want. The light won't keep me up."

He shucked his sweats and climbed into bed beside me. He leaned over to kiss my shoulder and then rolled away to find sleep.

I stared at his broad back. The view had my nose stinging as I felt the disconnect from him. I forced my gaze back to my book and breathed through the sensation. I knew that Shep had to feel powerless at the moment, something he absolutely hated. He didn't need my disappointment. He needed my understanding.

Holding on to that, I disappeared into the pages of my book again, finding the escape I needed this time. I lost myself in the push and pull between the two characters as they struggled to give each other what they both needed.

As I reached a scene where the heroine gave in to the hero's darker desires, I shifted beneath the sheets, restless. My breaths picked up speed as he bound her feet to the end of the bed, her hands above her.

When a hand slid across my belly, I jumped, gaze snapping to Shep.

He stared back at me, eyes hooded. "Good book?"

My lips parted, but I couldn't get the words out. So, I nodded.

"I can tell."

My brows pulled together. "How?"

One corner of Shep's mouth kicked up. He ghosted a finger over my face. "Cheeks flushed." Down the column of my neck to my collarbone. "Breaths quick." He moved lower, tracing his finger down my sternum and belly to my thigh. "Clenching those pretty thighs."

Shep's eyes flashed gold. "So, tell me. What's happening in those pages?"

There was a brief flicker of fear and worry that Shep's playful curiosity would turn to the darkness Brendan had been consumed by, but that concern quickly disappeared when I focused on Shep's face. There was no judgment there. There was only heat.

The fact that I was turned on by what I was reading only turned Shep on in return. Something about that made me fall a little more in love with the man pinning me to the mattress with his golden gaze. And that love made me bold.

"He, um, likes to tie her up."

That heat in Shep's expression intensified. "You like that."

It wasn't a question, but I still nodded.

"You want to try that?"

I bit my bottom lip but nodded again.

"Fuck," he murmured. "What else?"

"He, uh, blindfolds her."

Shep studied me for another moment. "You like the sound of that?"

I swallowed, my mouth going suddenly dry. "Yes."

Shep's fingertips grazed over my thigh. "Cutting off one sense heightens the others. Makes you more aware."

My pulse pounded in my neck. It was somehow already like he'd removed a sense, my hearing maybe? Blood roared in my ears, and I could feel the barest touch of Shep's fingers on my thigh more than when I'd tried to bring myself to orgasm countless times before.

Those fingers traced a figure eight that nearly drove me over the edge. Shep watched my face, fascinated, almost reverent. "Didn't give you what you needed tonight, did I?"

I pressed my lips together and shook my head.

"I need to apologize, then."

My mouth parted again, and I sucked in a breath. "I like your apologies."

Shep chuckled, throwing off the covers and sliding out of bed. He stalked across the room toward my closet, muscular ass visible through the black of his boxer briefs. He opened my closet and rummaged around for a few minutes before reemerging laden with what I could just make out were scarves.

Lots and lots of scarves.

My breaths came quicker as he strode back across the room. To the bed. To me.

Shep let the array of fabrics and colors flutter to the mattress, like the sweep of hummingbird wings. He stared down at me, heat and need and tenderness all mixed together in his gaze. "You sure about this? We've had a day."

"I'm sure," I whispered.

"You say the word, wherever we're at, and this stops. Okay?"

I nodded. "Okay."

I waited for Shep to argue, maybe suggest that he knew better, but he didn't. Something about that made me fall even more in love with him. That we could learn, grow, and change...together.

Shep's eyes stayed on me as he reached for the pile of scarves. Heat swirled in those amber depths. Then his gaze dropped to the array of fabrics. I missed the feel of his attention on me. The way it made energy crackle between us, to the point where I could almost feel the contact.

Shep pulled a pale green scarf out of the pile and ran his long, thick fingers over the fabric, assessing the feel. Then his hands gripped it, pulling it taut in two quick snaps.

I felt the bite of that movement across my skin. A flush of warmth swept through me, and I pressed my thighs together in an attempt to relieve the ache there. It did no good.

Shep pulled out more scarves, one after the other until he finally reached a silk one. I didn't know why I'd even bought the damn thing. It wasn't like I needed a silk scarf in Sparrow Falls, but I'd seen it at the secondhand shop in town, and it was so beautiful. It looked like a delicate painting you could wear.

As Shep studied it, running those long fingers over the water-color detailing, I was beyond grateful that I'd made the rare impulse purchase. He took the remaining scarves and placed them on top of the dresser. As he stalked back to the bed, my heart rate ratcheted up.

Shep came to a stop at the end of the bed, between the two short posts at the footboard. Those amber eyes were on me again.

He bent, his hand fisting in the blankets and slowly tugging them down. The glide of the sheets against my overheated skin felt like a cool caress. They inched down lower and lower until they were gone completely.

Shep's gaze cascaded over me, landing in different spots. He traced my collarbone, then dipped lower over my breasts and belly, down to my thighs where my nightgown had ridden up.

"Have I ever told you how much I love these fuckin' nighties?" Shep growled.

My tongue darted out, wetting my bottom lip. "I don't like pajama bottoms. They ride up and get all twisted when you sleep."

Shep's eyes swept back up my legs to the apex of my thighs, as if he could see through the material to what was beneath. "So damn pretty. All soft satin and lace. And what do you wear under it, Thorn?"

My lips parted on an inhale. "You know it's nothing."

Shep let out a sound that was almost a growl. Not exactly that, but it definitely had an animalistic edge. And something about it had wetness gathering between my thighs and my nipples pebbling.

His hands latched around my ankles, and he tugged me farther down the bed. That, too, had me sucking in breath. Shep's grip wasn't harsh in any way, but there was power behind it. Something I wanted to feel.

Shep grabbed one of the scarves and tied one end to the bedpost and the other to my ankle. The moment the soft fabric locked around my limb, heat surged through me.

"Too tight?" Shep asked, his voice going gritty as he traced the tie with his finger.

I shook my head.

"Words, Thorn. I need your words." There was a command in Shep's voice that had my nipples tightening to a point just shy of pain.

"Not too tight," I breathed.

He gave the scarf a testing tug. "Good."

Then Shep moved to my other ankle, repeating the steps. As he rounded the bed, he kept his hand on me, a point of contact. Fingers ghosted up my leg and over my belly, then along my sternum to my chin. Shep's thumb skated over my bottom lip as if memorizing the swell.

"Arms up. Grab the headboard."

My arms obeyed before I even made the conscious choice. My fingers latched on to the wooden slats in the furniture, and Shep moved with deft grace, weaving a pale pink scarf around them and tying it off.

"Good?" he rasped.

"Good," I echoed.

But it was more than good. My breaths came quickly, pressing against the satin of my nightgown. I shifted, trying to alleviate some of the building pressure but couldn't, not with my feet tied in place.

One corner of Shep's mouth kicked up. "Can't press those pretty little thighs together, can you?"

"Shepard." I didn't know what the single word even meant. It was searching and reprimanding all at once.

But it only made Shep grin. "At my mercy," he whispered, his fingers trailing lightly over the lace at my breasts. Then they moved lower, circling a nipple. "Do you know what a gift that is? That trust?"

"Shepard." It was as if all I could say was his name. But this time, I was begging.

"Don't worry, Thorn. I'll take care of you." His fingers moved in a flash, clamping down on that bud. There was a bite of pain that lasted a millisecond and then spread into the heat of pleasure. Wetness pooled at my core.

Shep's hand was gone and reaching for the final silk scarf. He placed it gently over my eyes, carefully wrapping it around my head and tying it off.

Darkness descended and engulfed me completely. I had a moment of panic when there was nothing, and then Shep's hands were on me again. They trailed down my sides to where the hem of my nightgown rested.

"Need to see all of you," he ground out. "Tell me I can."

"Yes," I breathed. I wanted him to look. Such a foreign feeling, but one that I felt the sweet relief of.

Shep's roughened fingertips felt like sandpaper kisses across my skin, lifting my nightgown higher and higher. The cool air swept over my bare flesh, the nightie scrunched up over my breasts. The feel of it had my back arching, searching for more.

"So fucking gorgeous. I've never seen anything more beautiful in my life."

Shep's words were another caress. The feel of them landing, digging in, had a different kind of heat spreading.

He moved again, and I heard the soft footfalls in the nothingness of the darkness around me, but I couldn't tell where he stopped. All I could do was wait.

That waiting turned everything up. That tension inside me pulsed, and my core cried out for him. My lips parted as I sucked in air.

It wasn't Shep's fingers that found me this time. It was his mouth. His lips closed around my nipple, sucking it deep. His tongue circled the bud, and it twisted, tightening to the point of pain. His hand found my other breast, his thumb mimicking the movements of his tongue.

Tension swept through me again, weaving my muscles impossibly tighter. My back arched, leaned into all of it, my body wanting more. A cry left my lips, an audible plea.

Shep hummed around my nipple, and then his mouth was gone. The flash of cold after the heat was almost too much to bear.

"Those sounds," he growled. "Best thing I've ever heard. They're like a drug. Just need more and more."

I sucked in a breath, my body moving in the direction of Shep's voice, searching for him even though I couldn't see him.

Then his hands were on me again, sliding up my thighs. "Thorn, so fucking wet. Glistening for me."

Shep's thumb swept through the wetness, spreading it up and over my clit. I couldn't help the moan that left my lips.

"Yes," he ground out. "Tell me how it feels. What you want. What you need."

"Feels like tiny little fireworks exploding across my skin."

Two fingers slid inside me, and my body bucked against them, pure relief at the feel of some part of Shep entering me.

He slid them in and out in a smooth glide. "This?" he practically purred. "Or this?" His fingers curled as they as slid out, creating a delicious friction. "One?" The smooth glide. "Two?" The friction.

"Two," I panted.

"That's my girl. So fucking good at telling me what she wants. What she needs."

Shep's thumb made another pass around my clit, getting closer and closer to that bundle of nerves. My hips arched up to meet him, wanting more, wanting everything.

My muscles strained, legs tugging at the scarves, fingers digging into the fabric in a search for purchase.

"Love it when you're greedy. Love watching you writhe against my fingers. Tell me what you need, Thorn."

"More. I need more."

"Be *specific*," he pressed.

That was Shep, always challenging me, helping me come into my own. To be comfortable in that sexual side of myself.

"Want your cock," I breathed. "Want to feel all of you."

"That's my girl."

His fingers were gone, and I almost cried out at the absence. I heard rustling, movement above me, then Shep lifted my hips, sliding a pillow beneath them.

"This image," he ground out. "Burned into my mind for eternity."

"Shepard." His name was a plea.

His thumb traced my opening. "So beautiful. So ready."

Then I felt him hovering over me, tip bumping against my entrance. "Perfect," he breathed.

Shep slid inside.

His girth had me sucking in a breath, trying to adjust, but that flicker of pain only drove the pleasure higher.

Shep thrust in deeper, and thanks to the pillow, the angle of my hips had him hitting that perfect spot each time. My eyes watered beneath the scarf as my hands gripped the wooden slats harder.

My hips rose to meet Shep with as much movement as the bindings would allow. The fact that any motion was limited, and everything was so out of my control when that was something I'd held so tightly to, drove everything higher.

I lost myself in the buzz and heat. The sounds our bodies made. The feel of Shep's power coursing through me. He thrust deeper, his speed picking up. My walls began to flutter around him, and he cursed.

His thumb found my clit, circling and finding the spot where I needed him the most. He pressed down, and I shattered with a force I'd never felt before. Weight pressing down, all around, as Shep powered into me, releasing on a shout. Wave after wave hit me as he rode out his orgasm.

Even as he slowed, my body shook with aftershocks. Tremors twitched through me as Shep's mouth found mine, featherlight. The kiss was a soothing promise as his hands reached above, freeing mine.

He slid out of me, the absence of him sending a small whimper from my lips. The ties on my legs were gone in a flash, and then Shep's body was curved around mine as he pulled the blindfold free.

The low lamplight felt bright after all the dark, and Shep pulled me against him, curling around me. He inhaled against my neck, breathing me in. "Was it more?"

My body melted against his. "It was everything."

Chapter Fifty

Shep

"YOU'RE WHISTLING AGAIN."

I stilled my finger on the nail gun, easing off. *Hell.* I *had* been whistling along to the tune of *Wild Horses*.

Anson chuckled. "I really thought after everything that happened yesterday, you'd be all snarls and demo. Nice to see I was wrong."

I shot a nail into the two-by-four we were using to frame out the transition from the entryway to the living space. "Fuck off."

That only made Anson laugh harder. "I gotta find out what drug Thea is injecting you with. We should bottle that shit. We'd be billionaires."

I just shook my head and shot another nail. It wasn't like either of us was hurting for cash. Anson had written a few books on the criminal mind that kept him flush, and business was booming for Colson Construction. So much so that I had a waiting list out almost a year.

Anson released the plank the moment I shot the final nail we needed. "How are you really?"

"Trying to keep my cool." It wasn't easy, though. Just knowing

Brendan was walking around free as a bird ate at me. "Trace sent the official letter to Brendan's lawyers this morning."

Anson straightened, mulling that over. "How he reacts to that will tell us a lot. It's possible he moves on in search of another target."

As much as I wanted Brendan far away from Thea, I hated the idea of him doing this to another woman. "Dex making any progress at all?"

It was a dumb question. If Anson's hacker had found anything monumental, he would've shared.

"He thinks he's making progress on finding a way in. He's got Brendan's email, and if he can get him to click on a link, he'll be able to gain access. I'm trying to come up with something that will make him bite."

I studied Anson for a long moment. "You're profiling him so you can hack him."

One corner of his mouth kicked up. "I am."

"Thank you." My words had a rasp to them, carrying an emotion I didn't have the ability to express. Because *thank you* wasn't nearly enough.

Anson clapped me on the shoulder. "I'll always have your back."

A honk sounded from the front of the house, making both Anson and me look in that direction.

Anson turned back to me. "Expecting someone?"

I shook my head.

We both braced. There'd been too much bad shit these past few months. It wasn't like an assassin was going to honk before they shot us dead, but we were prepared for anything.

As we headed outside, I caught sight of the approaching flatbed truck. Not an assassin, after all. My windows.

"Damn, those look pretty," Anson muttered.

"I was right to go with the black frames."

He nodded. "I wasn't sure if that would look too modern, but it's going to be perfect."

"Especially with the worn gray tones we're going with for the exterior," I agreed. A familiar twitchiness spread through me, but the good kind. The kind that meant I couldn't wait to dive into work.

The truck pulled to a stop, the engine shutting off. The driver's door opened, and Mara slid out, a smile across her face. "Delivery, boys."

I hated the way my gut soured at her arrival. Mara hadn't done a damn thing wrong. I just didn't have the energy to deal with tiptoeing around feelings this afternoon.

"Thanks," I said, forcing a smile out of politeness.

She crossed to me, blond hair pulled up into a ponytail of loose waves. She handed me a clipboard. "They came in this morning. Hal wasn't going to deliver for another three days, so I offered to bring them out. The only payment I require is a tour. This place is awesome."

I could feel Anson's eyes on me, part assessment, part warning. I took the clipboard and quickly scrawled my name. "We're pretty slammed today. Maybe when we're farther along."

Mara's smile stayed in place as she gave me a playful smack with the board. "Aw, come on. Five minutes. I just want to see her guts and how you opened her up."

Hell.

"Sure," I gritted out. "A, why don't you come with us?" I didn't want to be rude, but I didn't want to give Mara the wrong idea either.

Anson coughed in an attempt to hide his laugh at my discomfort. "Sure thing, boss."

I flipped him off behind Mara's back as she headed into the house.

"This is incredible," she called from inside.

I kept the tour as brief as possible, not even venturing to the second story. Anson moved through the house with us but kept his distance. As we reached the entryway, Mara grinned at me. "You are going to make a mint when you sell this place. And it's going to make some family ridiculously happy."

Her words were kind, but they still grated. I didn't care about making millions. I wanted to do good work. And usually, I loved the idea of a family making a home in a space I'd created, but this was different somehow. This place felt like mine more than any other. And maybe that was because Thea had been a part of it, too.

From the walls she'd helped me knock down to listening to me incessantly talk about my plans and ideas, she was woven into the fibers of the farmhouse. And I couldn't imagine giving that up.

"Thanks," I muttered, my tone a bit crisper.

Mara's brows drew together in confusion, and I didn't blame her.

At the sound of tires crunching gravel, we all moved outside. At the sight of Thea's ancient sedan, a grin spread across my face. But it quickly died when I remembered who was here. *Shit.*

Anson clapped me on the back. "Good luck with this one."

I would've flipped him off again, but we were in plain view of everyone.

Thea pulled into a makeshift spot in the front of the house and climbed out, her gaze sweeping over her surroundings.

I scowled. "Did you come out here alone?"

She sent me a droll smile. "My deputy detail followed me to the drive to make sure I got here safe and sound."

A little of my anxiety eased at that, but it was still risky. What if I hadn't been here? What if Brendan had been watching, waiting? I struggled to let those fears go. She could see my vehicle and Anson's from the road. She was being careful.

I crossed to Thea, dropping my head to give her a quick kiss. "Work go okay?"

She knew what I was asking. "Everything was good. Other than the fact that Luca was hanging with us today and ate his body weight in icing. He was bouncing off the walls when I left."

I chuckled at the mental imagery of the seven-year-old pinballing around the bakery. "Sutton deserves a medal and a crown."

"And a day at the spa," Thea agreed, then turned her focus to the others present. "Hey, Mara. How are you?"

The woman's answering smile was strained. "Good. Just got a tour of Shep's new baby." Her gaze came to me, going soft in a way that made me want to wince. "He's doing such an amazing job, don't you think?"

Thea stiffened slightly but kept an easy smile in place. "It's pretty incredible."

Mara's eyes flicked back to me. "He's always dreamed of fixing up one of these old, historic farmhouses. Love that it's finally happening."

Annoyance surged. Mara spoke as if she knew all my innermost dreams, but we'd never had that kind of connection.

Thea stayed quiet, not taking the bait, and her play worked. The silence had Mara shifting in place. "Well, I guess we'd better get the windows off the truck."

Anson and I moved then, unfastening the tethers holding everything in place and setting the windows against the house.

Mara hovered for a moment, not getting into the truck. "Call me if you need anything else, Shep. I've got some days off if you need extra hands for anything."

I ignored the offer. "Thanks for driving them out here."

"Anything for you." With that, she hopped into the rig, made a wide turn, and headed for the road.

Jaw tight, I shifted to look at Thea. "On a scale of one to ten, how pissed are you right now?"

Chapter Fifty-One

Thea

THE MOMENT I'D SEEN MARA STEP OUT OF SHEP'S HOUSE, annoyance had settled in. But I'd swallowed the feeling down because Shep hadn't done anything to suggest I couldn't trust him.

But everything she'd said only had the annoyance digging deeper and shifting to anger. And now, her words echoed in my head on repeat. *"Anything for you."*

I took a deep breath, struggling to keep my anger reined in as I focused on Shep.

"I'll just be inside," Anson muttered, making a quick escape.

As I really took Shep in, reading the uncertainty and concern in his expression, my anger melted a fraction. "I'm a three. I was a five, but seeing your face brought it back down."

Shep pulled me into him. "I'm sorry. I didn't ask her to make the delivery. She just did."

"I know." I burrowed into his hold, breathing in sawdust and cedar. That brought the three down to a one. "I don't want to be like Brendan."

Shep reared back, brow furrowing. "What are you talking about?"

My fingers fisted in Shep's tee. "He used to hate me talking to *any* guys. Even ones I worked with. I don't want to be that person."

"You're not," Shep assured me, brushing the hair away from my face. "You never could be."

"I was jealous," I admitted. "She's known you for so much longer than I have." I knew from Mara coming into the bakery that she'd been born and raised here. She and Shep had gone to school together from kindergarten on up. That was a history I wouldn't ever share with him.

"Thorn," Shep whispered, pulling me closer. "Doesn't matter if I spent every waking second with her since birth. There would still only be one person who knows me best. You."

His words soothed a little more of my raw edges. Shep's thumb ghosted over my bottom lip. "You saw parts of me I didn't think I'd ever let anyone into. You saw all of me. Healed things I didn't even know were still broken. And there's only one woman I've ever loved. You."

My breath hitched. "Do not make me cry, Shepard Colson."

His lips twitched. "Baby, you full-name me like that, and you know I have to fuck you."

I squealed as he hauled me up and over his shoulder. "Shep! Anson is here," I hissed.

"Good thing there's a barn."

"I can't believe how much they change the space. It's incredible. Like we're hovering over the fields out there." My words were quiet, reverent as I stepped back, taking in the two massive windows I'd helped Shep and Anson install—after Shep's and my detour to the barn.

Shep's arm slid around my shoulder. "Can't you just imagine sitting here and taking in all your amazing landscaping ideas?"

Warmth spread through me at how excited he was about my vision for the backyard. "Curling up with a book and a cup of tea," I said, picturing it now. "God, it's going to be breathtaking when it snows."

"That house envy is rearing its ugly head, so I'm going to get back to the Victorian," Anson muttered, heading for the door.

I glanced over my shoulder. "Tell Rho hi for me."

"Will do." Anson gave Shep a salute. "See you tomorrow, boss."

"Later," Shep called back.

I turned back to the view in front of me. You could see *everything* through the massive windows. From Castle Rock to the Monarch Mountains. "I don't think I'd ever leave this spot."

Shep grinned out at the view. "Not even for the massive tub I ordered for the primary bedroom?"

"Okay, maybe for that."

Shep's grip on my shoulder tightened a fraction. "I don't think I want to give this one up."

I looked up at him in question.

"I'm keeping it."

A smile tugged at my lips. Shep had been moving from flip to flip, never settling anywhere longer than a year at most. The moment things were done, he started getting twitchy to get on to the next one. "Are you sure?"

Shep kept staring out the windows. "There's something special about this one. I felt it the moment I pulled up. And it's the place where you first let me in. I can't let it go, not to someone who won't understand what it all means. Not to anyone. I can see myself building a life here." His head dipped, gaze coming to me. "A family."

My heart hammered against my ribs. "Love that idea."

And I wanted to be a part of it. Wanted to paint myself into the picture. To tend the gardens and watch amber-eyed little ones chasing each other around the yard.

"I'm glad." Shep lowered his lips to mine, kissing me softly and slowly. When he pulled back, there was a warmth in his eyes that spoke of love, and more than that, hope. "Let's go home."

"Sounds good to me." My back muscles demanded a bath but

not before I tackled chores at home. "I need to water the plants in the greenhouse and the garden."

"I'll help," Shep offered, leading me outside.

"Not going to argue with you there."

That was another thing about falling in love with Shep. He was a true partner. I tackled nothing alone unless I wanted to. While he wasn't the best cook, he always offered to help. He always cleaned up after. He threw my clothes in with his when he did laundry, and he always helped with the yardwork.

"Leave your car here. I'll drive you to and from work tomorrow," Shep suggested.

I sent a look his way. "You don't have to—"

"I *want* to."

I wasn't going to argue with that. Just like I didn't argue as Shep's hands gripped my hips as he helped me into his vehicle. Or when he lingered after he'd fastened my seat belt.

As Shep pointed his truck in the direction of home, I studied his scruff-covered jaw and the slope of his nose. "You're a catch, you know that?"

His gaze flicked to me, amusement threaded through it. "That so?"

"It is," I told him. "I like doing life with you."

More than was safe, but I didn't care. For once, I would be reckless and let the chips fall where they may.

Shep's fingers threaded through mine. "You make that life a hell of a lot more fun."

I grinned at him. "You're not too bad at that yourself. Even if I do still have hay stuck in my hair."

Shep barked out a laugh. But he didn't let go of my hand the whole way home. It felt like a promise, a vow. And I held on to the feeling of that even as Shep let go of me to get out of the truck.

He opened my door and helped me out. "Inside for dinner first or out to the greenhouse?"

"Greenhouse. If I sit, I'm not getting back up."

Shep chuckled. "Fair enough. I'll run you a bath after dinner."

That simple, tender offer swirled through me in the best way as we headed for the gardens. But the warmth died, only to be replaced by icy dread as my steps faltered. What I was seeing didn't compute right away.

The image came together in pieces. Smashed-out panes on the greenhouse. Gardens torn to bits. And on the one intact side of the structure, there was spray paint. A single word.

WHORE.

Chapter Fifty-Two

Shep

I pulled Thea tighter against me as we watched law enforcement personnel crawl all over her backyard. She shivered against me, even though it was in the mid-eighties. Those tiny tremors had me wanting to burn the whole damn world down.

Instead, I tapped the side of Thea's mug with my finger. "More tea?"

She shook her head, watching as a camera flashed in the fading light. The crime scene techs had been taking photos of everything. Each flash made Thea wince and killed another part of me.

"It was my favorite place," she whispered.

The words sliced at my chest, like razor blades coated in acid.

Thea's grip on the mug tightened, her knuckles leached of all color. "It was where I started to find myself again. Hear my own voice. Remember who I was after all his lies beat me down."

Fuck.

I was going to kill Brendan Boseman. And I wanted to take my time doing it.

I swallowed all the anger swirling inside me and forced my hold on Thea to remain as gentle as possible. "We'll fix it. We'll rebuild. Even better than before."

Thea simply stared at the greenhouse and the ruined garden. At the way the techs were only ruining it more with all their stomping around. "It'll never be the same."

My hand slid along her jaw, carefully turning her head so she was looking at me. "No, it won't. But it only proves how strong you are. Everything you've made it through."

Unshed tears glistened in her eyes. "Sometimes, I don't want to be strong. I'm tired, Shep."

My throat worked as I tried to swallow, the burn there so intense. "Then let me take the load for a while."

Thea blinked up at me, trying to clear the tears away. "Okay."

"Okay."

She dropped her head to my chest and let my arms engulf her. It was too much. Getting Thea to let me help her was a battle on a good day. To have her give in so easily now…it ground into me. I missed that stubborn streak. The fire.

But I held on to Thea. As if I could somehow bleed reassurance, strength, and safety into her.

A familiar black truck pulled up amidst all the law enforcement vehicles. I knew what it took for Anson to come here with all of them present. It took him back to a time he hated remembering, but still, he'd come. A true friend. A brother.

Rhodes got out of the truck first, her dark brown hair flying around her as she charged toward the back deck. Even in the low evening light, I saw the concern and fear in my sister's hazel eyes.

But I didn't take it on as mine this time. Because it wasn't. I didn't instantly try to fix it either. Because I knew that worry was a gift for a friend she loved.

Thea straightened at Rhodes' approach, and I took the mug from her hands, setting it on the small table next to the chaise. It was a good thing I did because the second Rhodes was within reach, she pulled Thea up and into a tight hug.

Rhodes held on to her for a long time without saying anything. Then a few curses left her lips. "I'm going to *kill* him. But I'm thinking I'll torture him first. Gonna remove a few fingers. Or maybe I should start with his balls."

"Jesus," Anson muttered, making his way onto the deck. "Do I need to build you a murder shed, Reckless?"

Rhodes turned angry eyes toward him. "Whatever it takes to make that douchebag, dipshit, puke stain suffer."

A laugh bubbled out of Thea, and it was the sweetest sound I'd ever heard. I waited for relief to come at hearing it, but it didn't. I was still too keyed up.

"Puke stain?" Thea asked, pulling back from Rhodes' hold.

She shrugged. "It fits. Not even his own stomach wants him."

Thea shook her head, but a faint smile stayed on her lips. "Thanks for being such a good friend."

"I'm okay, but when I turn ole Bren-Bren into a ballless wonder, I'm really going to deserve a gold star."

Thea turned to Anson. "Are you watching your back when you sleep?"

He chuckled. "Definitely careful not to step a toe out of line."

Rhodes rolled her eyes. "You spanked my ass in front of the entire crew this morning."

Anson simply shrugged. "You were getting sassy. And you know what those shorts do to me."

"Please, God, make it stop," I muttered as I stood.

Thea laughed again, moving to me and wrapping an arm around my waist. "Earmuffs?"

"Even the world's best noise-canceling headphones wouldn't be good enough."

"Sorry, Shep," Rhodes singsonged.

"You are not."

She just grinned back at me. But that smile died as she took in the greenhouse. "I didn't know it was this bad."

Thea stiffened next to me, and I wanted to curse. But I bit it back and forced calm to my tone. "We're going to rebuild it. Even better than before."

Rhodes turned back to us, worry in her eyes. "I'll help. And you know Duncan will give you an extra discount for plants."

Thea shook her head. "He doesn't have to do—"

"He'll want to." Rhodes met Thea's eyes. "It's what family does."

Thea's hand fisted in my tee as those words hit. "Thank you," she whispered.

Heavy footsteps sounded on the back deck, and we all turned to see Trace headed our way. His expression was careful, but I could see the tension humming beneath it. "We're almost done, and then I'll get everyone out of your hair."

"Find anything promising?" Anson asked.

"Too soon to tell. Plenty of prints, but I'm guessing most of them are Thea's and Shep's. Hoping we'll get lucky and find another set." Trace's gaze moved to me and Thea. "Put a call in to Brendan's lawyers asking for an interview. Getting the runaround there."

"Of course," Rhodes spat. "I'll give him the runaround with my garden shears."

Trace's eyes widened. "I did not hear that." Rhodes just scowled at him. He turned to me. "Got a call on my way over here from the county inspector."

Confusion swept through me, but Trace kept right on going. "Some anonymous calls came in suggesting you cut corners on recent projects. They have to reinspect."

"Shep," Thea whispered, anxiety clear in her voice.

My back molars ground together. "Nothing to stress about. I do good work. There's nothing for him to find."

A muscle fluttered along Trace's jaw. "I'm sorry, Shep. You know none of this will stick." He brought his focus back to Thea. "I'm going to take a trip up to where he's filming tomorrow and ask some questions."

Thea's body went solid against mine. I felt the fear radiating through her. And it had that murderous rage flaring to life inside me again. I pressed a kiss to Thea's temple, breathing in her calming scent. "It'll be okay," I promised her.

Thea's throat worked as she swallowed. "It'll make him even more furious—you making this public," she told Trace.

"That might not be a bad thing," Anson said.

We all turned to him.

He went on. "If Trace can evoke a rage response, Brendan might do something reckless. He may not hide his tracks as well as he normally does. I'll have Dex at the ready. Trace, can you keep a tail on him?"

Trace jerked his head in a nod. "I can try. I heard he has a security detail that makes following close tough, though."

"He won't bring security if he's up to anything shady," Anson pointed out.

"True," Trace agreed and then turned to Thea. "Are you okay with this?"

She let out a shuddering breath. "Whatever it takes. I want this to be over."

My gut roiled, acid churning. Because none of them were saying the one thing we were all thinking. What if Brendan slipped through all those precautions? What if he got to Thea?

Chapter Fifty-Three

Thea

"YOU KNOW, YOUR BODYGUARD IS PRETTY DAMN CUTE," Sutton said as she wiped up around the coffee station.

I looked toward the windows at the front of the bakery, searching for the man in question. Deputy Allen was in his early thirties with light brown hair and a muscular form. He strolled past just as he'd done every forty-five minutes to an hour for the past three days, his gaze clocking the surroundings as he patrolled the block.

The first day after the greenhouse incident, Shep had come to work with me. He'd parked himself at a table in the corner that gave him a view of the entire bakery and hadn't moved. I'd tried to get him to go to work, but he'd refused. He wasn't taking any chances with Trace making a visit to Brendan that morning. Even with my sheriff's department detail.

I couldn't lie to myself and say that I hadn't been worried. I'd jumped at every sound and movement, just waiting for Brendan to lash out. Only, it hadn't come. While Trace had said that he could see Brendan's underlying rage at being questioned, he had kept his public mask in place and denied any involvement. He also hadn't made any outward moves since then. And Dex hadn't found anything computer-wise either.

So, we waited.

Shep had tried to come with me to work on the second day, too, but I'd told him that I'd have Sutton ban him from the bakery. He'd glared and grumbled but finally went off to work on the farmhouse.

It wasn't as if I wasn't protected. Deputy Allen had been my shadow from morning through late afternoon. And another deputy sat outside of my cabin through the night, just in case. Their presence brought comfort in one breath and anxiety the next.

"Thea?" Sutton asked, her fingers lightly grazing my shoulder.

I jolted out of my spiraling thoughts. "Sorry." I shook my head and forced a smile. "Maybe you should bring the deputy there a cup of coffee and one of your *famous* cupcakes."

Sutton choked on a laugh. "How did you just make a *cupcake* sound dirty?"

I grinned back at her, shrugging. "It's a gift."

"I don't have time for *cupcakes,* if you know what I mean. I barely have time for sleep."

I glanced at my friend as I rounded the bakery case with my rag and a bottle of glass cleaner. We were almost done for the day, and while two customers still lingered, we were starting our cleanup routine. "Want me and Shep to babysit this week?"

Sutton's eyes danced with warmth. "Practicing?"

A little flicker of something fluttered in my belly. Hope, maybe? "No. But a distraction wouldn't hurt, and I love that kiddo of yours."

She was quiet for a moment before speaking. "You and Shep would make pretty babies. And he would be such a good dad."

There was longing in Sutton's voice when she said the word *dad.* Something I didn't miss. But my mind kept pulling back to *pretty babies.* God, I wanted that.

That flicker of hope turned to an inferno, a need to see what Shep and I could come together to make. Would the child's eyes be green? Amber? Or something else altogether? Would their hair be blond or light brown? Regardless, some part of me knew they'd have his kindness.

"Holy cannoli, you are a *goner*," Sutton teased.

I tossed my rag at her. "You're the one who told me I should go for it."

She threw the towel back at me. "And I'm glad to see I was right. Just like I always am."

I laughed as I sprayed the bakery case and swiped my rag across the surface. But a flicker of movement caught my attention out the window.

A familiar hulking figure stood there glaring at me. There was such hatred in Russ Wheeler's eyes. A healthy dose of disgust, too.

A few months ago, I would've let that send me tumbling into a fear spiral. But I wasn't the same person now. Shep had helped me grab hold of the strength I'd always had and own it.

So, I didn't look away from Russ. I met his hateful stare and did something that was very un-Thea. I flipped him off.

The surprise that flashed in his dark brown eyes almost had me laughing, but the look was quickly replaced by an intensifying fury.

"What in the world?" Sutton looked at me and then followed my line of sight toward Russ. "That piece of work—"

But her words cut off as Deputy Allen stalked down the sidewalk toward Russ. We couldn't hear what the officer said, but I could make out just enough by reading his lips to get the gist. *"You need to move along."*

Russ said something colorful back but stalked off down the block.

"You okay?" Sutton asked.

I straightened, continuing my work on the case. "Better than. That felt damn good."

"Flipping off a douchebag always does."

We dissolved into laughter as we continued our cleaning duties. As the next hour passed, we swept and packed up day-old bakery goodies. Sutton always passed them along to a shelter in the next town over. As the two remaining patrons left, she flipped the sign to *Closed*.

"You can go. All I have left is the mopping."

I shook my head. "It'll go faster if we do it together."

I started lifting chairs on top of the tables as Sutton grabbed a bucket of soapy water. We worked in tandem, the country music bleeding out through the speakers. It only took us another hour to finish everything.

"Time to get Luca?" I asked.

Sutton glanced at her watch. "Not for another hour. He went to the ice rink with a friend after camp."

I grabbed my purse from the cabinet behind the counter. "He still determined to be the next hockey star?"

Sutton sighed as she wrung out the mop. "He brought home forms for their kids' league. Did you know they let kids as young as *five* play? *Five.*"

I winced. "It does seem a little dangerous. But they're wearing all those pads."

"I guess. But they're trying to pull together a camp before the season starts. Of course, Luca has his heart set on it."

I sent her a gentle smile. "And his mom, who loves him, will of course say yes."

"Because I'm a sucker," she muttered.

I pulled Sutton into a hug. "Not a sucker. An *amazing* mom."

"Thanks, Thee Thee. Love you."

"Love you, too." I released her. "See you tomorrow."

"Get home safe," she ordered.

"I've got your future boyfriend making sure of it."

Sutton grinned and waved me off.

As I stepped outside, warmth swirled around me, and I took a deep inhale of the pine air. The scent even made its way downtown.

Deputy Allen waved as he approached. "How was your day?"

"Good," I said. "Yours? Other than boring as all get out."

He chuckled. "I don't mind it. It means a lot that the boss trusted me with this job."

That was a sweet way to look at it. "Well, I appreciate it."

"Anytime. I'll follow you home. Just don't go blowing any red lights on me."

I grinned. "I'll try to restrain myself."

We headed down the block and around the corner to where we'd parked just a few spots apart. Deputy Allen waited as I got into my car and started it up, locking the doors behind me. Then I waited for him to get into his vehicle.

Once he was in, I put my car in reverse and navigated out of the parking spot. Downtown had plenty of people milling around, and I couldn't help looking for any signs of Brendan's blond hair.

I bit the inside of my cheek, forcing my gaze back to the road. I wouldn't let him continue haunting me, not anymore.

It only took a few minutes to get out of the town's tourist traffic and on to the road that would lead me home. *Home* to Shep and Moose. Even if some of the structures had been destroyed, the people and creatures were what mattered. I just had to hold on to that.

Cold metal pressed into my side from the back seat, making me jerk.

"Eyes forward. Keep driving. I'd hate to put a bullet in your spleen."

It was more snarl than voice. But it wasn't male.

I tried to turn to see who it belonged to, because there was something slightly familiar about it. But the metal object jabbed into my ribs. "I said eyes on the road, slut. Or maybe I'll go for your heart right here and now."

Chapter Fifty-Four

Shep

THE AFTERNOON SUN BAKED THE EARTH BEHIND THE OLD farmhouse. It was the kind of summer sun that cast everything in a golden hue. And the tone had me seeing nothing but possibilities.

I counted off footsteps as I walked away from the house, trying to give myself a rough idea of distance. Living with Thea these past few weeks, I'd seen just how much her outdoor space meant to her. She spent far more time outdoors than in. And it had me seeing my own space through new eyes.

Reaching a slight dip in the ground, I stopped. This really would be the perfect spot for a pool. But not just any pool, one that felt like it was a part of the nature surrounding it. Hell, I might even put in a lazy river. The thought was ridiculous, but I didn't give a damn. Not when I could picture Thea out here in a bikini, floating in an inner tube.

My gaze lifted as I envisioned it. Thea laughing as I chased her through the water, lush gardens springing up all around us and melting into the natural landscape she'd envisioned. Gardens that Thea could make her own.

And a greenhouse. Thea needed a greenhouse. The most epic one I could build her.

As I stared off at the property to the east, I began drawing up plans in my mind. I tried different styles and colors but none of them were exactly right. I turned back to the house, taking in the worn siding Thea had liked so much. It hit me then.

The greenhouse needed history. To feel like it fit with the house. The framing needed that worn, weathered look I was keeping on the main structure. But every single surface would be paned.

I'd have to go with a specialty glass that would be unbreakable in the face of snow and hail. It would cost a pretty penny, but it would be worth it. Because it would have the same kind of strength Thea had.

"What the hell are you staring at so hard?" Anson asked, coming up behind me.

"Going to build Thea a greenhouse right there." I pointed to the spot.

Anson was quiet for a long moment. "This your place?"

"It's my place."

"Finally," he muttered.

I turned to face him, one corner of my mouth kicking up. "Says the guy who only had an ancient bed and one overstuffed chair until he moved in with my sister."

Anson grinned. "I'm starting to see the value in settling."

"Me, too," I said, turning back to that perfect spot.

"You love her?"

"She's it." The knowledge of that settled something deep in my bones. A sense of grounding I'd been searching for, for as long as I could remember.

"Love that you've found that," Anson said, his voice going rough.

"Love it for you, too."

Because Rhodes had soothed something in Anson in a similar fashion. He'd just had different wounds to heal.

"Just got a call from Dex."

I turned back to Anson so fast my vision blurred. "And?"

Another sort of smile spread across Anson's face. But this one had a feral edge to it. "He's in."

I gaped at Anson. "Brendan's computer?"

He nodded. "Dex found enough to bury him for a long fucking time. And it's not just Thea. That asshole has done this sort of thing to at least six other women."

A mixture of rage and relief coursed through me. "How do we get him? All of this was obtained illegally—"

Anson cut me off with a wave of his hand. "Been down this road before. All Dex has to do is send the evidence to Trace and the cybercrimes unit at the FBI anonymously. There's no proof it was obtained illegally."

"You're sure?" We couldn't risk Brendan sneaking out of this. He'd just be more careful next time.

"One hundred percent. I'll have Trace interface with the FBI. They can make a plan to seize all his electronics at once, both from his rental here and his place in LA. Dex will freeze his computers from the inside so nothing can get wiped. We got the bastard."

Relief swept through me, almost sending me to my knees. It wasn't the torture that Brendan deserved, but it was something. And he'd lose the adoration of the public when everything came to light, which might be the worst sort of death blow for a man like him.

Anson clapped a hand on my shoulder and squeezed hard. "This is over. We got him."

My throat burned. "Thank you. I know...I know it's not easy for you to delve back into that world."

Anson shook his head. "Worth it. And the truth is, it's getting easier. Having Rho to talk things through with if I get triggered makes it easier. I like helping. It heals somehow."

God, I was happy to hear that for my friend.

He gave me a shove. "Now, get out of here and tell your girl the good news."

Finally giving Thea that news would be a sweet moment.

I started toward the front of the house, but my phone rang. I slid it out of my pocket, seeing Trace's name flash on the screen. I grinned, hitting accept. "You hear the good—?"

"Shep," he cut me off, his voice tense.

I froze, every ounce of relief disappearing in an instant. "What's wrong?"

"Thea missed the turnoff for her house. Allen got worried and sped up. She's not pulling over."

Ice-cold dread slid through me as I turned. I knew Anson was there, but I couldn't see him. All I could see was the spot where I wanted to build Thea's greenhouse.

Trace's voice crackled over the line. "Allen tried to get a look in her car. Someone was in the back seat, but he can't see who."

I should've known. Just when I'd grabbed hold of the happy and good—it all got ripped out from under me.

Chapter Fifty-Five

Thea

THE GUN WAS SHOVED INTO MY SIDE WITH A VICIOUS PUNCH, making my ribs flare in pain.

"I said *keep driving*," the woman snarled. "Faster!" She jabbed me with the metal barrel again as if to make her point.

The voice was so familiar yet different. Changed enough that I couldn't quite grab hold. And the way the figure was tucked behind the passenger seat, right on the floorboards, meant I couldn't get a look at her through the rearview mirror.

"If I go any faster, Deputy Allen will know something's wrong." My voice didn't sound like mine. It was calm, collected, like it wasn't even a part of me. As if the words hadn't come from my mouth.

A curse sounded from behind me. "Those pigs. Always sticking their noses in business that isn't theirs. Always making things so much worse. Why can't they just leave us alone?"

"He's trying to help. To keep me safe." I didn't know why I tried explaining that to a woman holding me at gunpoint. She obviously didn't give a damn about my safety. But somehow, I feared silence would make her angrier.

"You don't need to be safe! You have to be gone. Everything will be fine if you're just GONE." She pulled the gun back, then jabbed it into my ribs again.

The force of it sent me doubling over against the wheel, wheezing as the car drifted to the side, sending us over the rumble strips.

"Get back on the road! Can't you do anything right?" she snarled, pushing up so she was sitting in the center of the back seat, right in line with the rearview mirror.

Everything swirled, twisting in my mind until I could put the pieces into place. It took precious seconds for my brain to compute the image I was seeing as I righted the car.

"Why anyone likes you is beyond me. You can't even drive a car," she snapped.

"Raina?" I croaked.

Her name was a question on my lips as my gaze snapped back and forth between the road and the rearview mirror, still trying to make sense of what was happening. It felt like some sort of fever dream.

She ignored my pseudo-question, her gaze tracking over me. "You're ugly. Shaped like a skinny boy. You dress awful most of the time, and then you slut yourself out the rest of the time. Shep will thank his lucky stars when you're out of his life. I'm doing him a favor."

Raina's words hit me like ammunition from a machine gun. Blow after blow. The cadence of them was so familiar. So similar to Brendan's. The breaking-me-down that didn't even make sense. Dowdy one second, a whore the next.

That push-pull, along with the manic feeling of the words themselves, had my heart beating faster. My palms dampened as I tried to grip the wheel tighter and attempted to stay in the here and now. "You want to help Shep?"

"I'm helping everyone. We'll all be better off with you gone. You ruin good men. You ruin *everything*."

My mouth went dry as memories slammed into me. *"You ruin*

everything. You tear people's lives apart, and you don't even care." The words echoed in my mind, the image of Brendan, bleary-eyed as he started to slur, right before he shattered a glass against the wall. The memory of how I'd curled into a ball on the bathroom floor and wished for it all to be over. The pain. The anxiety. Everything.

"Watch it!" Raina yelled, jabbing me with the gun again and hitting the tender spot she'd already abused.

I'd let the car drift into the lane for oncoming traffic on the road leading up to the Monarch Mountains. Thankfully, no one was opposite us, and I quickly righted my vehicle. I blinked, trying to clear my stinging eyes, along with the memories.

I adjusted my hold on the wheel, my gaze flicking up to the rearview mirror. Raina's face filled it, but beyond that, I saw Deputy Allen's squad car. He was close. I just had to find a way to give him a chance to help. Maybe I could crash my car?

The feeling of the gun's barrel against my side told me that was a very bad idea. Raina's finger was on the trigger. If we made any sort of impact, she'd likely shoot me for sure.

"What do you want?" I rasped.

Raina's hazel eyes flashed a molten gold. It wasn't the kind I found in Shep's amber gaze; it was pure anger. Rage. Her grip on the gun tightened. "I told you. I want you gone." She let out a shuddering breath. "I tried to warn you to leave, to *stop*, but you just wouldn't listen. I slashed your tires, sent that photo, destroyed your stupid little greenhouse. But you're too dumb to hear me!"

"Why?" It was the most simplistic of questions, but I didn't understand Raina's motives. I'd always been kind to her.

Those eyes flashed again. "You think I don't know you're trying to steal my husband? That you're trying to break up our marriage? That you're making him hurt me?"

Each sentence was a blow that had me spinning one way and then the other. They didn't entirely make sense either.

"Raina, I don't want Russ to hurt you. I want you to get away from him."

She moved so fast I didn't have a prayer of blocking the blow.

She reared back the hand with the gun and clocked me in the side of my head. Spots danced in front of my vision as the car veered to the side, making Raina grip the seat to stay upright.

"You bitch!" she snarled. "All you want is for me to hurt. You tempt Russ. Tempt him to stray. He told me what happened at the bar. That you came on to him, touched him. And then played the victim. He was so mad when he came home."

My stomach roiled. I didn't want to hear what'd happened next because I knew it would be bad.

"He threw me into a wall so hard it knocked me out. Could barely move the next day. All because of you."

My breaths came in quick pants, each inhale making my lungs burn where Raina had hit me with the gun. "I'm so sorry," I whispered.

She grabbed the back of my hair so hard I saw stars. "You're not. You're a whore. Just like the rest of them. You try to fool everyone into thinking you're so innocent and perfect. But you're not. They're going to see. Going to see it all now."

Panic flared brighter.

"Turn right. The road up the mountain," Raina ordered.

"No," I whispered.

I couldn't. Following her orders would only bring bad things. The worst of them.

Raina gripped my hair harder, shaking me. "You will listen to me. You will obey."

"No." It was all I could do. Quiet resistance.

Her other hand moved, and a deafening crack sounded next to my ear. The driver's side window shattered, sending glass everywhere. I jerked the wheel to the side, nearly sending us down an embankment.

"The next one goes into your kneecap if you don't listen."

The lights on Allen's squad car lit up as the siren pierced the air.

Raina swung around to look at it and then back to me. "Look what you did. You're going to pay for that, too. All your failings." She shook my head. "Turn the car, or I will kill you here and now."

Tears leaked out of the corners of my eyes—ones of frustration and fear. Because I didn't know what to do. Listen or resist?

I glanced at the turn she wanted me to make. We'd been slowly gaining altitude as we wound around the road that led to the mountains. But this one would take us directly up. It was also flanked by plenty of tall trees. Ones I could possibly send the car into. It was my only hope. I'd just have to pray that if her gun went off, the bullet wouldn't hit me, or that it wouldn't be a lethal shot at least.

"Turn!" Raina yelled.

I jerked the wheel, making the turnoff and sending gravel flying. Raina's hold on my hair tightened as she used me to steady herself, making a fresh wave of pain dance across my scalp.

I managed to keep the car on the road, straightening and heading up the side of the mountain. The incline would make it hard to get enough speed to crash like I wanted and needed to. I pressed my foot to the gas, praying I wasn't making a mistake and sending us careening over one of the steep drop-offs to my left.

Raina kept a hold of my hair, gripping it tightly as she turned around. "Fucking pigs," she snarled and leveled her gun at the back windshield.

Fear spiked, and I prayed she wasn't a good shot. That she wouldn't hit Deputy Allen.

Another crack sounded, and glass spiderwebbed. Then another shot and another. *How many bullets does a gun hold?* I had no idea. She could be out for all I knew, or she could have a dozen left.

A laugh pierced the air, but it had a sickening quality to it. "We'll see how he does getting up the mountain missing a front tire."

My gaze flicked to the rearview mirror for a split second, just long enough to see through the smashed-out window that Allen's vehicle had slid to a stop. My gut soured. If I crashed now, there'd be no backup. I just had to hope that I could hit with enough force that it would cause Raina some injuries.

That thought had nausea swirling. Even with all she was doing, I didn't want to hurt her. She'd had enough pain in her life. Agony that had clearly twisted her mind in unbearable ways.

I knew what it was like to not trust your own brain or memories. They became a gnarled knot you couldn't see the beginning or end of.

Like a cord you couldn't identify. You didn't know what it had once been because it was something entirely different now. Something you couldn't see your way out of.

But I did see now. I knew. The truth had finally found me. And falling in love with Shep had helped me—as if he'd pulled away a veil that had been left over my eyes. I could see the world through new eyes now, all the shades and colors as they truly were.

It was a gift I'd never be able to repay.

But I would be brave enough to fight for what we had.

My gaze locked on the road ahead. Through the trees to my left, I knew there were sharp, cliff-like drop-offs. I wasn't about to risk going through those trees to a rocky death. But only forest was to the right.

Those trees had been one of the things that had soothed me when I moved to Sparrow Falls. Their endless beauty and calming scent. I just hoped they could rescue me one more time.

I turned the wheel toward them and pressed the gas pedal to the floorboard just as Raina screamed.

Chapter Fifty-Six

Shep

"**G**ET IN," ANSON ORDERED, YANKING OPEN THE DOOR TO HIS truck.

I didn't wait for another barked command, just hauled myself into the cab and slammed the door as he climbed in opposite me.

Anson started up his truck and threw it in reverse. "Open the glove box. I've got a police scanner in there. We can figure out where they are."

Trace hadn't shared that piece of information, telling me to wait for his call. Like hell would I sit at home twiddling my thumbs while Thea was out there fighting for her life.

Her life.

Just thinking the words had an invisible fist slamming into my gut and forcing all the air from my lungs. Everything burned as if my entire body had been engulfed in flames.

Which was exactly what it would be like if anything happened to Thea. I couldn't do life without her now that I knew what it was like to be loved by her. She made everything…more. As if just having her in my presence made the world around me crisper and more beautiful.

"Hit the orange power button. It should already be tuned to the Mercer County channel," Anson said as his foot pressed harder on the gas, making gravel fly.

I fumbled with the device that looked like a walkie-talkie. The moment I hit the orange button, static crackled.

"Unit four in pursuit of Thea Stewart and unknown subject on Terrace Road just past mile marker thirty. Allen's vehicle is out of commission. Shots fired. Unknown subject is armed."

I gripped the police scanner so hard the plastic began to crack. I instantly loosened my grip, forcing my body to release so I wouldn't lose the one connection I had to Thea.

Shots fired.

My eyes burned like they'd been dunked in hydrochloric acid. Was Thea hurt? Bleeding? Worse?

"Hold it together, brother. We're going to get to her," Anson assured me as he floored it down the two-lane highway.

We weren't far from the turnoff the officer had described. But not nearly close enough. Not when it only took a split second for everything to change.

Anson made a hairpin turn onto Terrace Road. It had been named for the many overlooks terraced into the mountain that looked out on the valley below. It was a beautiful, scenic stretch of road, but one that could be treacherous at night or in the snow.

My gut twisted as we passed Deputy Allen, who stood examining his squad car with a smashed-out windshield and a blown tire, but Anson didn't stop. He kept his speed until we saw gathered law enforcement vehicles up ahead. He eased off the gas, slowing to a stop.

But my door was already open. I was out of the truck in a millisecond, charging ahead until I saw it.

Thea's car. The navy sedan looked more like a pile of scrap metal. It had crashed head-on into a massive ponderosa pine. The front end was completely smashed in. The glass on every window shattered. Airbags deployed.

I stopped breathing. Was that blood on the driver's side airbag? Where the hell was Thea?

A hand clamped down on my shoulder. "I told you to wait for my call."

My gaze snapped up to Trace. "It's Thea."

That was the only answer he needed. The only reason. Because Thea was everything.

A shadow passed over his face. Pain streaking there because he *knew*. Knew that Thea had helped me find the peace within myself that I desperately needed. And he had seen how special she was. This world was a better place because she was in it.

Trace's throat worked as he swallowed. "They're on foot. We're about to start combing the woods."

There was a flush of relief that Thea was still alive, but it was followed by fury laced with terror. "Where the hell is he taking her?" I snarled. Brendan didn't know these parts. He shouldn't have even known this mountain pass was here.

"He?" Trace asked, brow furrowing.

"Brendan," I growled.

"It's not Brendan who has her. It's Raina Wheeler."

The name hit me like a physical blow. The slight woman who always had a nervous smile for me was the last person I would've expected to hold Thea at gunpoint. "What—why?"

The one-word questions tumbled over each other. None of this made any sense.

Trace shook his head, worry carving lines into his face. "I have no clue. I thought they were friends."

Anson moved into our huddle, looking at the car and then up the mountainside. "If she's been a victim of ongoing abuse, that kind of thing can lead to episodes of psychosis."

A sick feeling spread through me, quickly followed by fear that stole all the oxygen from my lungs. I moved then, couldn't stop myself. I had to find Thea. Now.

"Shep, wait," Trace barked. But I kept right on moving. He cursed. "Fletcher, you're with me. Hansen, you run the search."

Anson jogged to catch up with me. "Stop."

I ignored him.

He grabbed my arm, and I shoved him off me. "Like you stopped when Silas had Rho? Fuck, Anson, you should know that I'm not going to stop. I have to find her. I can't let anything—" My voice broke, pierced by shards of invisible glass. "I can't let anything happen to her."

Anson didn't take offense to the shove. He moved right back into my space. "I *know*. I'm not telling you not to look for her. I'm telling you to stop and *think*. Where would Raina take her up here?"

I stilled. There was nothing but the pounding of my heart against the faint chatter of law enforcement in the background. My gaze swept the forests on either side. "There's a forest service cabin at the summit, but that's at least a couple hours' hike from here." I swallowed against the lump in my throat. "If they're injured, they wouldn't make it that far."

"So, where would she go that's close? If Raina just wanted to kill her, she would've done it already."

Anson's words were harsh but comforting at the same time. And they got my mind spinning, twisting in a way his normally did. Raina obviously wanted to cause Thea harm, but she hadn't gone with bloody violence. Why?

Because some part of her couldn't handle it. Likely hated it because she'd been subjected to it herself. So, how would she hurt Thea?

My spine snapped straight. "The bluffs."

Anson's brows pulled together, but I was already moving.

Trace jogged ahead of me, Deputy Fletcher at his side. "You let us take point. You can be with her as soon as we've contained the situation."

Fuck.

I knew he was right. I didn't have a gun or body armor. Trace and Fletcher had both. So, I let them lead, even though it killed me.

Anson was at my side then. "What are the bluffs?"

"There are these terraces in the mountainside that the road is named for. Natural overlooks." I swallowed hard. "Raina didn't want to shoot her." I couldn't say the rest, but Anson already knew. It was just the way his genius mind worked.

"She'll force Thea over one of them."

I jerked my head in a nod, pain spearing through me. I couldn't think about it, couldn't let the image grab hold or I'd break right then. Instead, I focused on Trace's back, the Kevlar that read *Mercer Co.*

I focused on those letters as we quietly picked our way through the woods. Until we heard voices in the distance.

"Keep walking, whore," Raina snarled. Her voice didn't sound like the one I was familiar with. That one was softer, sweeter. This voice was full of rage.

"My side—I can't—" Thea begged.

I could hear the wheeze in her words, even at a distance. Thea was in pain, injured.

Trace made a motion for me and Anson to stay back and another for Fletcher to go around. He switched something on his radio, making it go silent, and then whispered commands into it.

Blood roared in my ears as Anson and I followed my brother. The trees thinned, spreading wider and wider apart. And then I saw them.

Thea's body was turned to the side. Her bakery tee was torn, and blood trickled down the side of her face. She tried to limp forward but stumbled.

"Stop faking," Raina snarled. "I told you that innocent act won't work on me. I'm going to free everyone of your manipulations, your ruin."

"I didn't want him to hurt you," Thea pleaded.

"The hell you didn't. It just kept getting worse and worse. You talked back at the office; you tried to seduce him at the bar. Who do you think he took that out on?" Raina screamed. "Then you try to get me to leave him. Do you know what he'd do if I tried to leave? He'd kill me."

Her breaths came in ragged pants now. "So, there's only one choice. *You* have to die." She shoved Thea, making her stumble again.

I tried to surge forward, but Anson grabbed me by my shirt, hauling me back.

Trace moved then, his gun raised. "Mercer County Sheriff's Department. Lower your weapon and get down on the ground."

Raina whirled, her eyes wild and full of panic, but her gun remained trained on Thea. "You can't be here. It's not how it's supposed to be. If I end her, it'll be okay. She just has to be ended."

"Raina," Trace soothed. "Let me help you. If you lower your gun, I can make sure everything is okay. That's my job."

Something flashed in Raina's eyes. "You only make it worse! Every time you come, he hits me harder!"

Blood drained from Trace's face. "I'm so sorry. He's wrong. But we can stop him. Together. I just need you to help me."

"I am," Raina growled, her jaw hardening. "If I erase her, then Russ will be okay, and you won't have to come to my house. And Shep will be okay because this lying whore won't be in his life anymore."

I surged forward then. "Don't." The word was a desperate plea. "I won't be okay if Thea's gone. I need her."

Raina's gaze jumped to me. "No. No. No. You don't. She lies. She tricks. She ruins. You're better off without her. We all are."

"Please," I begged, my eyes burning.

My gaze collided with Thea's pale green depths. They glistened in the fading light, full of tears. Her mouth formed silent words. *I love you.*

"Raina." Trace took a step forward. "Put the gun down. We'll make sure you're safe. That no one can hurt you again."

"She hurts me! It's because of her that everything hurts!" Raina charged forward then, shoving Thea with all her might.

Thea's slight frame went flying, stumbling backward. Her name tore from my throat as I ran forward.

But it was too late.

Thea tripped. For one horrifying second, she was suspended in air, over the edge.

And then, she was simply...gone.

Chapter Fifty-Seven

Shep

THE MOMENTS CAME IN SNAPSHOTS. IMAGES CAPTURED WITH each beat of my heart against the walls of my chest.

The horror of everyone around me.

The shouts.

The flurry of movement.

My legs were moving, pushing me toward the cliff before I could even tell them to do so. My body knew that it had to get to Thea. That it was the only thing that mattered.

Trace was three steps ahead of me, tackling Raina to the ground as she screamed and wailed. But I didn't have time to even look. All I could think about was Thea.

I skidded to a stop at the edge, dirt and rocks flying as I almost went over myself. I braced, a million cruel possibilities for what I might see dancing in my head. My gaze went first to the rocks below, jagged and angry. But there was no broken body there.

I trailed my focus up the mountainside until I saw her. Thea. Everything in me froze as those pale green eyes locked with mine.

She was several feet down, gripping onto a sharp, pointed rock as her feet scrambled for purchase.

Relief and terror swept through me, each one tripping over the other in a battle for dominance. "Thea." Her name was barely audible, but I knew she heard it when those green eyes flashed.

Bits of rock crumbled away as Thea tried to find a foothold for her shoes in the side of the mountain.

"Fuck." I instantly lowered myself to the ground, trying to reach her as Raina wailed in the background.

Anson crouched next to me, letting out a curse of his own. Thea wasn't that far down. The sharp outcropping had stopped her fall, likely injuring her in the process, but she was still battling to save herself. Just like the fighter she was.

"Hold on, Thorn," I called. "We're going to get you. Just hold on."

Anson looked at me. "If you grab her, you're going over, too."

"If I don't, she'll fall." I'd risk losing my life to save Thea because, without her, I knew I wouldn't truly be living anyway.

Thea let out a cry as another piece of rock slipped away.

"Hold my legs," I ordered Anson.

He didn't wait, just dropped to the ground and put all his body weight across my lower half. He called out to Trace for help, but I could hear my brother trying to cuff Raina with Fletcher's help. We might be on our own.

"Shep."

The fear in Thea's voice dug into me with angry, vicious claws, but I didn't let it show. "I've got you. I'll always have you."

She nodded slowly, tears tracking down her cheeks and mixing with the blood dripping from the side of her head. "You have me," she whispered.

My fingers reached out, covering hers. The feel of her skin had strength surging within me. But I wasn't close enough. I couldn't grip her wrists.

"You gotta lower me another five inches, A."

"Shep—"

"Do it."

"Don't," Thea whispered. "I can hold on. I'll wait for help."

But I could see her fingers trembling as she held fast to the rock. She wouldn't make it.

"Anson," I growled.

Then there was more weight on my legs.

"We lower him together. On three," Trace ordered. "One, two, three."

They shifted me down just slightly. But it was enough. My hands wrapped tightly around Thea's slender wrists. They seemed so fragile now, like I might snap one on the way up.

My eyes locked with Thea's. "On the count of three, I want you to let go of the rock and grab my arms."

"I-I can't. I'll fall. I'll take you with me."

"Thea." I let everything I felt for her bleed into my voice and gaze. "I need you. I need our *more*. Please, trust me."

Those were the magic words, because she nodded.

"Okay, boys. On three, you haul me back, too. Ready?"

"Ready," Anson and Trace said in unison.

I stared down at Thea, memorizing the way those pale green eyes shone. Remembering every moment she'd given me. Her grounding peace, her humor, her fierce spirit. I remembered every single thing we had to fight for.

"One."

Thea's eyes flared.

"Two."

She closed them, shutting me off from the green.

"Three."

She released her hold on the rock just as Anson and Trace pulled me back. I held on to Thea with everything I had. My chest and abs scraped against the rocky ground as we slid along it, and I pulled Thea with all my might.

The moment she crested the edge, I hauled her against me, cradling her as she burst into tears. "You're okay. I've got you. I'll always have you."

Chapter Fifty-Eight

Thea

THREE DAYS LATER

MY HOUSE WAS CROWDED. PACKED TO THE GILLS WITH people. Moose sat atop his cat tower, taking everybody in with curious fascination because it had never been this way before. Not once in the two years that I'd lived in Sparrow Falls had my home been full of voices, laughter, and the sounds of cooking. Not to mention flowers. So many bouquets. I could've opened a florist shop.

One of the most beautiful arrangements had come from the most surprising sender. Mara. With a note that read: *I'm so sorry for what you've been through. Get well soon.*

Rumblings of my ordeal had made the rounds in town, and Rhodes had assured me that it had given Mara a wake-up call. As had hearing about Shep putting his life on the line for me.

Shep shifted me on the couch as he checked his phone. The timer app had a minute to go, but Shep didn't need it. He had radar that bypassed the damn thing. "It's time for your next dose of pain meds."

I moved so I was sitting up fully, the quilt still over my lap. "I think maybe we could wait a little longer."

Shep frowned at me. "I don't want to chance you being in pain."

My body was stiff and more than a little sore, but given everything I'd been through, I'd gotten off lucky. I had stitches in my head and in several places on my torso, bruised ribs, and a mild concussion. But not a single broken bone or serious injury.

"Shep is right," Nora said, bringing over a tray that held a bowl of soup, some rolls, and a glass of lemonade. "You need to stay ahead of the pain right now. In a few days, we can talk about tapering you off."

Lolli held up a wand that had feathers at the end for Moose to bat at. "Or you could let me make you some of my poppy tea. That's all natural, and it'll cure what ails you."

"Lolli," Trace growled as he strode into the living room. "It's an opiate."

She just smirked at her grandson. "Not selling it, Mr. Po-Po. You can't lock me up."

"Jesus," Kye muttered from his spot on the chair in the corner. "Just remember, your bail is too expensive for my blood."

Lolli huffed. "You and your fancy tattoo studio could cover it."

"Not at the rate you're going," Fallon argued with a shake of her head.

"You're all just a bunch of prudes. No fun at all," Lolli complained.

"I'm with you," Cope agreed. "They need to live a little."

Trace's gaze moved to his brother. "You mean breaking every speed limit known to man in their two-hundred-grand SUV?"

Cope slowly turned on his stool, a devilish grin on his face. "I'd never."

Trace's eyes narrowed on him. "According to three deputies in the past twenty-four hours, you've been doing exactly that. I told them to arrest your ass next time. You and Lolli can share a cell."

Lolli held up her hand for a high five, letting out a hoot. "We're living now!"

Cope slapped her palm. "Damn straight."

I watched as lines carved into Trace's face. His words had held humor, but there was more than a hint of frustration behind them, too.

A phone rang, and Cope stood, sliding off his stool. The moment he pulled the cell out of his pocket, his expression changed. Gone was the devilish amusement, leaving nothing but storm clouds in its place. "Gotta take this," he muttered, heading for the back door.

Trace's worried gaze followed him until the door slammed shut.

Rhodes pushed the tray that Nora had left me across the coffee table. "You need to eat so you can take your meds."

The warmth of her concern, that of all the Colsons, was like a balm. They were all up in my business because they cared.

Anson cleared his throat, glancing at Trace from his spot next to Rho on the floor. "You have any updates?"

I stiffened, my hands tightening around the bowl. Trace had been scarce these past few days, working around the clock on both the Raina and Brendan fronts.

Raina wasn't saying much of anything, but Trace had worked his magic, getting her placed in the locked ward of a psychiatric facility several towns over instead of the jail. Fallon had jumped in to help, making sure that we found a lawyer who'd take the case pro-bono. I loved them both for that. They could see through Raina's actions to the pain beneath. She didn't need punishment, she needed help.

It had been harder for Shep to be at peace with that. Because he'd had to watch me go over that cliff. Had to pull me up, bloodied and broken, worried he'd lost me for good.

I set the bowl down again and burrowed into Shep's hold. His arm gently went around me, but I could feel the tense muscles beneath his shirt.

Trace looked at me, waiting for a moment as everyone around us went quiet. "The FBI arrested Brendan Boseman on set today, and the paparazzi trolling the place got more than a few shots. He was charged with seven counts of nonconsensual pornography, twenty-two counts of fraud, and ten counts of stalking. At the same time he was arrested, teams served search warrants on multiple properties and vehicles. They seized all his electronics."

I froze, tears welling in my eyes. I swallowed hard, trying to keep control. "You got him."

Trace's expression gentled. "We got him. He is going to jail for a very long time."

"I'm free," I whispered.

Shep's lips ghosted over my temple. "You're free."

A phone dinged, and I saw Anson shift in my periphery, pulling out a device. He stared down at the screen, a massive smile spreading across his face.

"It still weirds me out when he smiles," Kye muttered.

Fallon smacked his chest. "Don't say that."

Kye caught her wrist, giving it a little tug as he grinned. "What? It's true."

Rhodes turned toward Anson. "What is it?"

Anson's head lifted, but he didn't look at Rhodes, he turned to me. "Just heard from Dex. Apparently, all Brendan's money vanished from his accounts overnight. He's going to have a hard time paying for that fancy legal defense team."

My jaw went slack. "What?"

Anson just grinned wider. "And somehow, the exact amount that went missing was donated to women's shelters and domestic abuse nonprofits across the country."

The tears returned, and I didn't even try to stop them.

Shep pulled back the covers on my bed and helped me get settled. He didn't move his gaze from my face as he slid in behind me. "How's the pain level?"

I rolled carefully into him. "Not that bad."

He sent me a pointed stare.

"I swear," I argued. "But it'll be a miracle if I can sleep with all the food your mom and Lolli fed me today."

Shep chuckled at that. "It's how they show their love. Well, that and poppy tea for Lolli, apparently."

I grinned up at him. "I love what a troublemaker she is."

Shep trailed light fingers over my back in a soothing gesture. He'd already memorized where each injury was and deftly avoided them all. "How do you feel about everything else?"

"I'm not sure it feels real." Pressure built behind my eyes. "The most I'd ever hoped for was for Brendan to leave me alone. The fact that he'll actually be brought to justice? It's more like a miracle."

And it wouldn't just be a miracle for me. Dex had eventually found nine other women that Brendan had done similar things to. They would all get the gift of closure like I did. Knowing the peace that would bring was sweeter than anything I could imagine.

"You're the miracle," Shep whispered. "You never stopped fighting. Never gave up."

Wetness gathered in my eyes. "I didn't stand up to him. Because there were still tiny, dark places in my mind that believed his lies. But you showed me the truth."

"Thorn," Shep rasped.

"You gave me back my life. I'm different than I was before. But it's a better different. I know where my value lies. I know I don't take anything for granted."

His lips pressed to my forehead as he breathed me in.

I just kept going. "Like today. Such a gift. Shep, you gave me the family I never had. And you're right, the fact that it's something we all chose makes it that much sweeter. Stronger."

He pulled back, unshed tears glistening in his eyes. "Love you, Thea. That word doesn't do the feeling justice, but it's the best I've got."

My mouth curved. "I'll take it."

Shep's thumb traced the swell of my bottom lip. "I don't want to move into that rental."

I stilled. I'd known that his lease had already started. I just hadn't wanted to think about him possibly leaving my little cabin in the woods. "You don't?"

"Can't imagine sleeping without you. Or not having Moose scare the crap out of me with his nighttime crazies. Don't want to wake up and not have the first thing I see be your face."

"Shepard," I whispered.

"That full-name biz had better be a fuckin' yes," he growled.

"Yes," I breathed. "Stay."

Epilogue

Thea

"**F**INALLY," NIKKI SAID AS SHE PICKED UP MY CALL. "I'VE ONLY called you half a dozen times today."

I couldn't help but chuckle as her voice rang out over my SUV's speakers. An SUV that Shep had begged and pleaded to get me after the ordeal with Raina.

I'd given him the win. That, along with getting a cell phone and hooking up high-speed internet at the house. But I'd let Shep lay the cable for the latter. He was my roommate, after all.

A roommate I never wanted to be without. We'd made it through the worst and come out of it stronger and more bonded than ever. It didn't hurt that we'd gotten to witness the fall of Brendan.

The press loved a golden superhero, but the only thing they loved more was tearing that superhero down. People had come out of the woodwork with stories of Brendan's true nature. And those stories had set me free. Along with the fact that Brendan would be in jail for years to come.

Sadly, Raina wouldn't be walking free for some time either. Thankfully, a judge had sentenced her to the psychiatric facility instead of jail. She was getting help, and through her healing, had finally opened up about her abuse.

Between her firsthand account, X-rays, and corroborating witnesses, Russ was serving five years in a state penitentiary and had to pay a fine that would wipe him out. In some ways, he was serving Raina's sentence just as it always should've been. Because he was the one who'd warped her mind in the first place. And Russ's father, Bob, had closed the doors to Castle Rock Construction and moved out of state in shame.

"Earth to Thea," Nikki singsonged. She'd gotten used to calling me by my middle name over the past year. I liked going by Thea. Because, in so many ways, it marked my new beginning.

"Sorry, brain swirls. What did you say?"

She sighed. "I asked how your last day was."

I smiled through the window at the gathering twilight. I loved this time of day, the way it cast the beautiful land in a magical purple hue. "It was good. Bittersweet. But Duncan brought cake, and Rho brought champagne."

"Sounds perfect to me. And now you get to watch that hunk of a man up close and personal every single day."

I laughed again. Nikki had been to visit three times, so she'd seen all the glory that was Shep. I'd started helping him out with landscape designs about nine months ago, and now he had enough jobs to bring me on full time.

The gig was a dream. Not only did I get to play in the dirt for a living, I got to create magic with the person I loved most in the world. And it didn't hurt that I got to see him shirtless in the summer months. It was icing on the cake that I'd also begun volunteering with the local library's literacy program.

"New job perks for sure," I said, smiling through the words as I turned onto the long drive that led to the old farmhouse.

"You heading to the new place now?" Nikki asked.

"Almost there. Shep said they finished today."

Shep and his crew had been working overtime on all the finish work for the past few weeks as I'd been hard at work in all the garden beds. The spaces around the farmhouse were a riot of color and texture. And the ridiculously over-the-top pool that Shep had gotten installed, complete with lazy river, had been the final jewel.

But he'd asked that I not come by this past week so he could get everything cleaned up for the final unveiling. He wanted that gasp moment from me. *"You know I love the sounds you make, Thorn. Don't rob me of that."*

Nikki let out a squeal. "Tell me everything tomorrow! I demand pictures."

I grinned as I keyed in the gate code. "Deal."

"Love you, Thea."

My throat constricted. "Love you, too. More than words."

She clicked off, which was a good thing because I cried at the drop of a hat these days. Something about letting my walls down put me more in touch with my emotions. I guided my SUV down the gravel road, frowning as I saw that there were no lights on in the massive farmhouse. But Shep's truck was sitting outside.

I slowed my SUV as I caught sight of small lanterns lining the stone path around the side of the house. My heart picked up speed, and I shut off the engine, climbing out of my vehicle and shutting the door.

The lanterns guided my way alongside the beautiful home Shep and I had built together with our blood, sweat, tears, and love. As I reached the backyard, I gasped. In the distance was a glass house completely illuminated with lanterns and fairy lights. A greenhouse. And it was glowing.

Tears gathered in my eyes as I picked up my pace, my sundress ruffling in the warm evening breeze. I had to stop myself from all-out running, my pale pink cowboy boots clacking against the stone path.

The closer I got, the more the tears built. There were lights on every available surface, curling around the framing with tiny, illuminated hummingbirds amidst the lights. And there were so many plants I lost track—vegetables and fruits that I knew Rho had to have a hand in helping Shep pick because not only were they my favorites, but they were also in perfect condition.

And through it all, my eyes came to rest on one thing, my *more*. Shepard. He stood in the center of the greenhouse, amber eyes locked on me as I walked toward the door. All the lights made him glow, too, but it was more than that. That light came from within him, too. His love for me, radiating out.

My hand closed around the antique glass knob and twisted, my eyes burning as I stepped inside. A smile tugged at Shep's lips, only intensifying his light. "You needed a greenhouse to make our home perfect."

"Greenhouse?" I choked out, tears slipping from my eyes and sliding down my cheeks. "This is a plant mansion."

He chuckled, that warm, sandpaper tone skating over my skin. "Do you like it?"

"Like it?" I croaked. "It's incredible. You're incredible." I couldn't wait any longer, I moved into him, my arms going around his waist.

"I'm glad you think so," Shep whispered, shifting to tug something out of his back pocket. "Will you build *more* with me? A life. A family. This home?"

He tugged my left hand from around his waist and slid a gorgeous oval diamond onto my ring finger. The stone was just like him and his white tees, shiny silver truck, and innate goodness. It was pristine, sparkling *light*. It was just another reminder of how loving Shep had brought me back to life and made me believe in the goodness that was out there again.

The tears came harder, falling down my cheeks. "You didn't wait for me to answer."

Shep chuckled again, more of that sandpaper warmth. "You're going to say yes."

"Cocky."

"Sure," he argued. "Sure of what you give me each and every day. Sure of what we share, what we're building. Sure that I love you to the depths of my soul."

"Yes," I whispered. He didn't need the word, but I gave it to him anyway.

Shep tugged me to him, taking my mouth in a kiss that put all his words into action and lit everything inside me. When he pulled back, his eyes glowed gold. "We're going to make a beautiful life."

"I know."

He grinned, wrapping an arm around me and guiding me toward the door.

"Wait," I protested. "I need to see all the plants."

"That can wait," he said, his grin turning into a smile.

The moment we stepped outside, more lights came on—lanterns and café lights all around the massive back deck. A strangled sound left my throat as I took in all the people filling the space. Nikki, my little liar of a best friend, grinned and waved. Anson and Rhodes, arms around each other as they took us in. Duncan and Walter stood watching, Mara and her fiancé, Deputy Allen, beside them. Sutton held on to Luca's hands as he jumped up and down. Cope stood next to them and popped a bottle of champagne as Lolli hooted. Trace twirled Keely, and Arden lifted a glass in cheers. Fallon wiped at her eyes as Kye handed her a napkin. But Nora was already running down the garden path.

She caught me and Shep in a hug far stronger than her small stature suggested she was capable of and held us to her. "Love you both." She pressed a kiss to my cheek and hovered there. "You're already family, but I'm so happy to make it official."

The tears came harder as I pulled back. "Thank you. I can't imagine a family I'd be luckier to have."

Shep's lips ghosted across my temple. "One we'll choose each and every day."

I looked up at him. "Easiest choice I've ever made, choosing you, Shepard Colson."

"Baby, you know what that full name does to me. Do I need to take you back to the greenhouse?"

I burst out laughing as I felt the last shreds of weight from my nightmare lift and I finally, fully stepped into the light.

Acknowledgments

I always find it incredibly interesting to know what the writing process of a specific book was like for an author. Did it flow out of them like water? Was it like pulling teeth? Who helped them along the way?

Delicate Escape had some flowing water and some teeth pulling, and *so* many people helped me along the way. There were some deeply personal aspects to this story. And whenever I write one like that, the journey is never entirely smooth. But they are always the books that end up meaning the most to me.

A huge thank you to Sam, who gave me some desperately needed perspective and assurances when I finished my first draft and wasn't sure that it would be a book that would touch anyone other than me. To Elsie, who not only sprinted day in and day out to make sure I finished but also got a panicked phone call when I wasn't sure the spice was working quite right and talked me through it. To Paige B, who encouraged me to write it, even though I was scared. To Melanie, who helped troubleshoot this couple's meet-cute when it was tripping me up left and right. To Rebecca, who sat on the couch with me months earlier and listened to what I had planned, talking through all the pitfalls with me. To Amy, Laura, and Willow, who made sure the edits got done with epic sprint sessions and texts that made me cackle-laugh. Here's to being punch-drunk as we got it all done! And, as always, to the *Rocky* theme song and memes! To Jess, who listened to me ramble about plot issues via voice memos so long they could qualify as podcasts. I am so lucky to have you all as a part of my community and hype squad. And, most of all, to have your friendship.

To all my incredible friends who have cheered and supported me through all the ups and downs of the past few months, you know who you are. This business can be hard at times, but you lighten tough loads and make the mountaintop moments all the sweeter. I am so lucky to have you all in my life. Thank you for being on this journey with me.

And to the most amazing hype squad ever, my STS soul sisters: Hollis, Jael, and Paige, thank you for the gift of true friendship and sisterhood. I always feel the most supported and celebrated thanks to you.

To my fearless beta readers: Crystal, Jess, Kelly, Kristie, and Trisha, thank you for reading this book in its roughest form and helping me to make it the best it could possibly be! And to my sensitivity reader, Tiara, there are no words to thank you for your feedback on this story. I am so grateful. And beyond thankful for all your support!

The crew that helps bring my words to life and gets them out into the world is pretty darn epic. Thank you to Devyn, Jess, Tori, Margo, Chelle, Jaime, Julie, Hang, Stacey, Katie, and my team at Lyric, Kimberly, Joy, and my team at Brower Literary. Your hard work is so appreciated!

To all the reviewers and content creators who have taken a chance on my words…THANK YOU! Your championing of my stories means more than I can say. And to my launch team and the influencer crew, thank you for your kindness, support, and for sharing my books with the world. And a massive thank you to Tori, Jess, and Devyn, for keeping all those ships afloat so that I can write as much as humanly possible!

Ladies of Catherine Cowles Reader Group, you're my favorite place to hang out on the internet! Thank you for your support, encouragement, and willingness to always dish about your latest book boyfriends. You're the freaking best!

Lastly, thank YOU! Yes, YOU. I'm so grateful you're reading this book and making my author dreams come true. I love you for that. A whole lot!

Also Available from
CATHERINE COWLES

Sparrow Falls
Fragile Sanctuary
Delicate Escape
Broken Harbor
Beautiful Exile
Chasing Shelter
Secret Haven

The Lost & Found Series
Whispers of You
Echoes of You
Glimmers of You
Shadows of You
Ashes of You

The Tattered & Torn Series
Tattered Stars
Falling Embers
Hidden Waters
Shattered Sea
Fractured Sky

The Wrecked Series
Reckless Memories
Perfect Wreckage
Wrecked Palace
Reckless Refuge
Beneath the Wreckage

The Sutter Lake Series

Beautifully Broken Pieces
Beautifully Broken Life
Beautifully Broken Spirit
Beautifully Broken Control
Beautifully Broken Redemption

*For a full list of up-to-date Catherine Cowles titles,
please visit www.catherinecowles.com.*

About

CATHERINE COWLES

Writer of words. Drinker of Diet Cokes. Lover of all things cute and furry. *USA Today* bestselling author, Catherine Cowles, has had her nose in a book since the time she could read and finally decided to write down some of her own stories. When she's not writing, she can be found exploring her home state of Oregon, listening to true crime podcasts, or searching for her next book boyfriend.

Stay Connected

You can find Catherine in all the usual bookish places…

Website
catherinecowles.com

Facebook
facebook.com/catherinecowlesauthor

Catherine Cowles Facebook Reader Group
www.facebook.com/groups/CatherineCowlesReaderGroup

Instagram
instagram.com/catherinecowlesauthor

Goodreads
goodreads.com/catherinecowlesauthor

BookBub
bookbub.com/profile/catherine-cowles

Amazon
www.amazon.com/author/catherinecowles

Twitter
twitter.com/catherinecowles

Pinterest
pinterest.com/catherinecowlesauthor

Made in the USA
Middletown, DE
05 September 2024

60436773R00224